### SERGIO
Son of the powerful and vindictive Gaetano Adamo, he fails his only mission in life, until tragedy gives him one last chance at redemption.

### LIANA
She rises from the poverty she knows as Sergio's daughter to find sudden success on the silver screen.

### MARCO
Determined to change his people's fate, he takes a law degree—and a corrupt politician's daughter—and challenges a system some say cannot be beaten.

### NATALIA ANDREANI
Gaetano's former lover, she tries to relive the past in a new and unforgiving country.

### MARIO ANDREANI
Natalia's son, he comes with his mother to America and falls madly in love with a woman who just may be his sister.

### WILLIAM "BIG BILL" DEVLIN
An old-style politician with ties to both the underworld and Tammany Hall, he stops at nothing to achieve his political and personal goals.

### CATHERINE DEVLIN
Big Bill's beautiful daughter, she tastes the forbidden fruit of love with an Italian immigrant, only to find she must choose between the man who raised her and the man she loves.

Also by Robert DeMaria
*Published by Ballantine Books:*

SONS

A PASSION FOR POWER

# BROTHERS

## Robert DeMaria

BALLANTINE BOOKS • NEW YORK

Library of Congress Catalog Card Number: 84-91036

ISBN 0-345-31936-2

Manufactured in the United States of America

First Edition: November 1984

TO
THEODORE BUZZEO

# Note

*Brothers* continues the chronicle of the Adamo family that was started in *Sons*.

The first members of the Adamo family to come to America were Luigi and Lorenzo. At the end of his first winter here, in March, 1888, Lorenzo died while shoveling snow in the Great Blizzard. He had left behind in Naples his wife and five children. He had hoped to earn enough money to send for them. His children were Gaetano, Angela, Pietro, Vincenzo, and Maria. By 1900 Gaetano, the oldest, was married and had children of his own. He had been in the first Ethiopian war, in 1896. After a run-in with the Mafia he decided to come to America. His friends Renato and Silvio followed him to the new world. Gaetano and Silvio became involved for a few years with underworld figures in Little Italy. Renato was a crusading radical who fell in love with a Jewish activist named Fanny Marks. She had left her husband, but remained undivorced.

# I

# Massachusetts 1912

"I seek only freedom, not anarchy."

—Carlo Tresca

# 1

Six years after Fanny Marks first came to Renato's apartment she was still with him. She had not even gone back for her things. She had faced only her mother and father to tell them that she never wanted to see Aaron again. He was remarkably docile about the whole thing, having realized that the marriage was as much a mistake for him as it was for her. There was some talk of divorce, but since Renato did not believe in marriage, it did not seem to matter. It was only when Aaron decided to marry again that something had to be done. Fanny allowed herself to be accused. And Renato allowed himself to be named as her lover. It was a brief but distasteful business, and when it was over Fanny said: "Now I feel truly free." Renato looked at her and wondered about their own relationship. In spite of his beliefs, an old possessiveness made him uncomfortable. He had grown up in a certain way, with a certain attitude toward women. And though he was a revolutionary, it was not easy for him to change his feelings.

They had long conversations in the night. Sometimes they began by making love in silence. Sometimes they talked themselves into a dreamy drowsiness before making love. And sometimes they did not make love at all, but only talked, circling like hounds in the woods of their confusion.

Often they talked about marriage. "I believe in the family," said Renato on more than one occasion, "but I don't believe in marriage."

"How can you have a family without marriage?" said Fanny.

"By an agreement between a man and a woman to have children and to raise them together."

"If you have an agreement, you have marriage," she said.

"Not necessarily, because marriage is surrounded with mysticism. It is a holy sacrament of the church. If you are a Catholic you cannot get a divorce."

3

She smiled. "I was lucky to be a Jew."

He did not miss her irony. He had said once that she carried on her back the suffering of her race, just as Christ carried the cross. "He, too, was Jewish. They have the gift of suffering."

Their conversations were always inconclusive. And they seemed to run together, as if it were all one long exchange of feelings and ideas struggling toward a resolution. They had reached a kind of impasse, and the days and months went whirling by like so many dry leaves in December.

Suddenly it was January, 1912. In the six years they had been together it seemed as though a million things had happened, and yet nothing had happened. Renato was forty-two and Fanny was thirty-one. The world was changing very rapidly. There was a machine that could fly and a machine that could talk and pictures that could move. There was a machine for almost everything. And there were predictions of a great technological revolution. In Italy a devastating earthquake had claimed the lives of thousands of people. There was an uprising in Turkey and another in Spain. King Carlos of Portugal was assassinated, and so was the crown prince. In Persia the Shah Muhammad Ali was deposed. And in the year that had just ended, there had been a revolution in Mexico, the Russian prime minister had been assassinated, as had the Spanish prime minister. Italy and Turkey went to war over Tripoli. And in England there were dockers' strikes and suffragette riots. In spite of these upheavals, life went on, and the world's greatest ship, the *Titanic*, was preparing for its maiden voyage.

The printing shop made a reasonable living for Renato and Fanny, but they were both more interested in changing the world than they were in making money. They went to endless meetings, they walked in picket lines, and they continued to publish their weekly newspaper at a loss.

January 11 was a Thursday. They had been to a fund-raising dinner for Eugene Debs, the perennial presidential candidate of the Socialist party of America. They went not as contributors but as members of the press. Renato wanted to do a story on the gathering for the next issue of *La Cronaca Proletario*. It proved to be a dreary affair. The hall was cold, the food was bad, and the speeches were uninspired.

It was almost midnight by the time they got back to the apartment behind the shop. Fanny looked tired and discouraged.

She took off her coat and stood by the iron stove to get warm. Her gray woolen sweater was drawn tightly around her and her arms were folded across her chest. Renato looked at her from the alcove. He sat on the edge of the bed and removed his shoes slowly. It occurred to him that she looked worn, and that her clothes also looked worn. She was still a very beautiful woman, but she made no effort to enhance her beauty. Her hair was parted simply in the middle and drawn back into a bun. Renato was suddenly annoyed at her appearance. It was as if she were trying to deny something in herself, that part of herself that was feminine and frivolous. To be plain and even drab was for her a political statement. He agreed with the principle, but he did not like the result. Or was he just irritated by the whole evening, which struck him as another exercise in futility?

He placed his shoes neatly together on the floor by the bed. "Why don't we buy you a new dress?" he said. "That one is falling apart."

She looked down at herself, a hint of martyrdom in her smile. " 'A thing of rags and patches . . .' " she said, half singing the line. "There are people in this world who would feel rich if they had this dress."

"That's not the point," he said.

"Oh? Well, then, tell me. What *is* the point? Are you trying to tell me that you don't like the way I look?"

"I'm trying to tell you that your dress is worn-out and that you should do something about it."

"Perhaps I should mend it again. But I'm not going to, because I am sick of mending things. It reminds me of my mother. Do you know that next Friday she will be fifty-six years old, poor, miserable woman, and that she is still working in a sweatshop as a sewing-machine operator?"

"Yes, I know," said Renato patiently. He had felt the oddness of her mood all evening, but now he was sure that she was slipping into one of those spells of theatrical self-pity that came upon her from time to time. He was never sure what brought it on. Perhaps it was cyclical, he thought, something to do with her period. All women had irrational moments. Sometimes they cried for no reason at all. He looked at her. She looked tired. "Why don't you come to bed?" he said.

"What you mean is, why don't I be quiet. Am I saying things that annoy you?"

"No," he said, "I'm not annoyed. I think that we are both tired and that we should go to bed."

She sighed. "You're right. I *am* tired. I'm tired in my bones and in my heart." She hugged herself and shivered, as if a sudden chill went through her.

He got up and went to her where she was standing by the stove. His woolen shirt was open, revealing his yellow-white winter underwear. He tried to put his arms around her. She drew away just enough to discourage him. It made him feel helpless, and suddenly everything about him seemed dreary and pointless. He tried to sound ordinary. "I guess it wasn't a very pleasant evening, was it?"

She shrugged. "It was all right, but we've heard it all before. Another voice crying in the wilderness. Sometimes I think that what we are all trying to do is futile. We really don't have any power, do we? And there are so many factions. Syndicalists and socialists, anarchists and Bolsheviks, the IWW and the AFL. Is it all worth it? Look at us, Renato. Our lives are half over—more than half over. And what have we got to show for it? This miserable room and a half. This ugly dress. And all you can say is that we are tired and we should go to bed. I know what you are thinking. You are thinking that this woman of yours is slovenly and ugly."

"No, no, that's not what I'm thinking. You—"

"Please, Renato, don't try to be nice. It's true. Look at me. What am I? A drudge for the shop and the cause and for you. No better than the factory girl I once was. No better than my mother."

"But what is it that you want? A child, a family? Isn't that what all women want? To feel fruitful and beautiful. We have considered it. You have rejected it."

"What do you mean *I* have rejected it? It is you who have rejected it. It is you who do not believe in marriage."

"You think I don't want a family and a normal life? Of course I do. But not in these circumstances. When you are poor, marriage is bondage. And when you have children, you must give up everything for them. It is only natural. They are the new life. They are the future. How many of our friends have been swallowed up by their families, devoured by their children? Are we prepared for that? Are you?"

Rubbing her hands together in an agitated way, she walked across the room. She sat down on the bed and for a moment said nothing. Then she took off her sweater and started to undress. "I don't know," she said. "I don't know what I want. My body wants a child. My mind wants a revolution. And my heart—I don't know what my heart wants. I get so restless. I feel so . . . so lonely sometimes."

"But we are together all the time. How can you feel lonely?"

She shook her head. "You don't understand."

She sat there on the bed. Her unpinned hair fell over her shoulders. In her hands was an unlaced shoe. Overhead, dangling from a black wire, was a single electric light bulb. It cast its naked yellow light on the scene and made of the alcove a kind of little stage. "I feel trapped," she said. "All my life I have lived in a kind of dungeon of duty. I have never been free. I was born a Jewess. And my very Jewishness demanded things of me. My mother demanded things of me. She tried to rob me of my independence. I know it wasn't her fault. It was the only way she knew. She, too, had been robbed. She had been indoctrinated, enslaved by her heritage, by her poverty. So I put aside that little secret part of me that was myself, but I did not let it die. I lived the way I had to live, but I had my private dreams. As a girl I was very romantic. I dreamed of lovers. I dreamed of traveling around the world. I dreamed of somehow becoming a great woman someday. It was all ridiculous, of course. At fourteen I went to work in a flower factory. I made artificial roses, leaf by leaf, with a hot iron. I scorched my hands. And you should have seen the hands of the women who had done it for years. Scarred and leathery. Hands no man would touch. My mother was afraid I wouldn't find a husband. She found me a job in a shirtwaist factory, but I was never very good at sewing. It was piecework, and my mother scolded me because I was so slow. She called me a dreamer. She was right. In my mind I had escaped. In my real life I was nothing. I was a little Jewish factory girl, living in a two-room apartment on Hester Street with a mother and a father and a sister and a brother. It was bad enough to be poor, but to be poor and a woman was impossible. For me there would only be one possibility—marriage. For me there was to be no education. It was out of the question. It was my brother who had to finish high school. It was my brother who had to go to college. And the rest of us were expected to sacrifice for him. The terrible irony was that my brother, David, was not very intelligent. I had ten times as much talent as he did. After two

years of college he could not continue. He found it too
difficult. And do you know what he is today? He is a clerk.
That's all. Just an ordinary clerk in an ordinary insurance
office. And there he will stay and rot for the rest of his life.
He has a fat wife and three fat children and nothing at all in
his head. He is thirty-five years old and looks fifty. He is
near-sighted and bald and stingy. I once, only once, made the
mistake of asking him for money. All I got was a sermon and
a sneer. 'You have a husband,' he said. And that was that. I
had a husband. I was a woman. I belonged to my husband. I
was a piece of furniture. I didn't exist. Now do you
understand?''

"But you left all that behind," said Renato. "You're here
now. Things are different."

"Are they? I'm still a woman. It is like a prison from
which I can't escape. I have not been taken seriously. In our
meetings they listen to you differently from how they listen to
me. You're a man. It's all right for you to do things in the
world. But I am only a woman. They look at me as though
there is something wrong with me. They wonder why we are
not married. They wonder why I don't have children. They
make me feel unnatural. And who knows? Maybe I am.
Sometimes I even feel unnatural. Sometimes I just want to
give it all up and just marry the first man who will have me
and raise children and have a house with lamps and rugs and
pretty curtains."

"Is that what you really want?" said Renato.

She threw the shoe down angrily. "Damn it," she said,
"you weren't listening. You're just as bad as the rest of
them. Even now you are probably saying to yourself that I am
acting just like a woman. And all you want is for me to take
off my clothes and get into bed so that you can relieve
yourself on my body."

"That's not so. That's not how I think of you."

"But that's how you think of women. It's not your fault. I
shouldn't accuse you. I'm sorry. Your way is Italian. Your
attitude was shaped for you, long before you had a chance to
think about it for yourself. That is the prison of history. For
us there is no utopia. There is only this life and, God, how
short it is. I feel time running out. It runs through my fingers
like water, and soon my womb will be as dry as my hands,
and that part of me that is a woman will have died. I will
have failed at everything. I will have given up a family to do

something serious, only to find that I have not been taken seriously."

She suddenly covered her face with her hands to hide the tears. But her body shook with sobs.

Renato stood there, feeling helpless. He made a gesture with his hands, turning them outward as if to show that they were empty. Then he frowned, as though some insidious thought were forming itself in his confusion. He went to her. He sat down beside her and put his arm around her shoulders. She stiffened and drew away but could not stop crying. He persisted. She weakened and allowed herself to be drawn to him. "It's all right," he said. "It will be all right."

Behind the mask of her hands she shook her head.

His voice was low and comforting. "Is there something more you want to tell me?"

In a moment or two her sobbing began to subside and she lowered her hands, to reveal a tear-stained face and red eyes. She tried to use the back of her hand and the sleeve of her dress to wipe away the tears. He dug into his pocket and offered her his handkerchief. In the silence he saw in her eyes that there was, indeed, more to tell.

"What is it, Fanny?" he said. "Has something happened? Are you—are you pregnant or something?"

She looked away from him and said in a distant voice: "I don't know yet."

He could feel himself swallow, because his mouth was suddenly dry. "If you are, we'll manage. Somehow, we'll manage."

"But I don't want just to manage. And I don't want to force you to do anything you don't really want to do. I want to have a choice. I want us both to have a choice. You don't want to be married. You don't want to have children. If necessary, I could find someone—"

"What do you mean?"

"I mean, not to have it. To—"

He stood up abruptly, as though he had been attacked. "No," he shouted. "No!"

"But you have said yourself that you believe in such things—in birth control, in abortion."

"Yes, but . . . I could not . . . I—" He was suddenly tongue-tied. He walked back and forth, rubbing his hands together and shaking his head.

"You see," she said. "You see! It is the old indoctrination. The long arm of your childhood and your church. The guilt!''

He sat down again and took both her hands in his. "No," he said, "it is not the guilt. It is something else. Something that we don't talk about very much." He was embarrassed. "It is love." His voice trailed away. And then he said it again more firmly. "Yes, dear woman, it is love. And if there is to be a child, then I want us to have it." He kissed her forehead and her cheek. She was flushed as if with a fever.

"But how?" she said. "I mean, to live like this?"

"We live as man and wife."

"But if we are to have a family, this is no way to live. There are papers. There are legal matters."

"Who will know the difference?"

She looked at him with a whole catalogue of feelings in her eyes. "I will," she said

He sighed. "We can talk about it another time. You're not even sure yet. Come, we'll go to bed. It's been a long day." He put his arms around her and kissed her tenderly on the mouth. She softened and responded. The storm of her outburst left her.

In bed they held each other close. The barriers that had been building between them disappeared. He smelled the fragrance of her flesh and sex. She wanted him. She opened herself to him. In this new excitement he was very hard and very strong. They made love as they had never made love before in all those six years.

The next morning they overslept. Renato did not wake up until he heard Sergio in the shop. Then he leapt out of bed like a delinquent schoolboy and threw on his clothes. Fanny stirred. She drew the covers up to her chin, and with half-open eyes looked at him and smiled. He bent over to kiss her. "Stay there," he whispered. "There's no need for you to get up. But Sergio is here. . . . ."

Renato washed his face with cold water but did not shave. He combed his dark hair, now touched with gray, and glanced in the mirror over the sink. He went into the shop and tried not to give the impression that he had just gotten up. Sergio looked up from the press, a big old platten jobber geared for an electric motor. His shirt sleeves were rolled up and he wore a long, gray, ink-stained apron. He was a tall young man turning twenty-one on his next birthday. With his long hair and his newly cultivated mustache he looked even older. Some of his adolescent gauntness was gone, though in his large eyes there was still a vaguely haunted look. He had a shy smile and a gentle voice and seemed happiest when he was alone. His brothers were not at all like him. They were sturdier and more outgoing. Antonio worked with his father, and Stefano, who was seventeen, worked in the Cafe Savarese.

"What's the matter?" said Renato.

"It's those rollers again. They really should be replaced."

"All right. I'll talk to Marelli when I go downtown. Maybe tomorrow. Don't worry about Gino's invitations. Pull a proof on the hand press of that IWP pamphlet. I'm going out for the papers." He glanced around the shop as if to see that everything else was in order. The place was a clutter of paper and fonts of type, of plates and blocks and overflowing wastebaskets. The floor had not been swept, and the cat played in the paper trimmings.

Renato went out, and Sergio went to work on the old Albion press. He preferred it to the larger machine. Sometimes, without telling Renato, he used it to print up a few of his poems. He did not make many copies and he did not show them to anyone. He was in love with words, with the way they sounded and with the way they looked on paper. He was learning, too, to love the very paper on which the words were printed. His fingers were becoming sensitive to it. He studied the weave, the weight, and the shades of white and other colors.

When Renato came back into the shop he was carrying half-a-dozen newspapers and had an excited look on his face. He went straight through the shop and into the back apartment without stopping to see what Sergio was doing.

Fanny had gotten up and, wrapped in a blue robe, was filling the coffeepot at the sink. "Look at this," he said, holding up one of the newspapers. The headline read: "TEXTILE WORKERS WALK OUT. *Mills in Lawrence, Massachusetts, Scene of Angry Demonstrations.*" Renato read aloud from the text: " 'An estimated two thousand workers stopped work suddenly at the Everett Cotton Mill in one of New England's busiest textile centers. The industrial city of Lawrence, with a population of eighty-six thousand, employs almost thirty-two thousand operatives, most of them immigrants or the offspring of foreign-born parents. The work stoppage seems to have been precipitated by a cut in pay, which in turn was a response to a new law that reduced the hours for women and children to a maximum of fifty-four from fifty-six.'

" 'The average wage cut was thirty-two cents from an average weekly pay of eight dollars and seventy-six cents. One company official was quick to point out that there had not, in fact, been a wage cut at all, and that the decision to reduce the work week to fifty-four hours was out of their hands. The company has asked that the local police, and if necessary the militia, be called in to protect their property from rampaging strikers and vandals. . . .' "

"Do you think it will spread?" said Fanny.

"Who knows. Without leadership it may come to nothing."

"But the IWW has been organizing in Lawrence."

"Yes, but I don't think they have more than five hundred or a thousand members."

"Is there anything we can do?"

"We can give them support in our paper. And maybe the IWP can do something. We should ask Arnaboldi to call a meeting right away. . . ."

On the morning of January 12 in Lawrence, Massachusetts, it was cold and gray. This mill town that straddled the Merrimack River was never very beautiful, but under such a sky as this it was grim and ugly. Smokestacks from the red-brick factories and a thousand smaller chimneys on the wooden row-houses of the workers helped darken the sky. The water in the Merrimack River, running under several bridges, was as foul as the air.

Arturo Bassano went to his job as usual at the Washington Mill, one of several mills in Lawrence owned by the immense, Morgan-controlled American Woolens Company. Arturo was a stocky man in his mid-forties. He was square-jawed and bald and strong as an ox, in spite of the chronic bronchitis that stayed with him all winter. He was much respected among his neighbors, because he knew how to work hard and because he suffered in silence and with dignity. He and his wife, Concetta, had lost two young children to pneumonia one year. Their last child, a girl of sixteen, had been disfigured by acid but still worked in the mill. Concetta also worked, as did most of the mothers.

Arturo had heard, of course, about the walkout at the

Everett Mill. The lights in Lawrence had burned late into the night as workers met to talk about what would happen next. There was no plan. In the morning some went to work, some did not. Families were divided. There was fear and anger. If they did not work they would not be paid. Without pay they might starve. But even with their jobs they only barely survived. Despair made some of them reckless.

"What the hell," someone was shouting when Arturo came in. "Better to starve fighting than to starve working." The machines were idle. The aisles were crowded. The foreman came in but was shouted down. He marched out again, his face flushed with anger. The speaker went on. "I say we strike. Full pay or no work." The phrase was picked up by others. "Full pay or no work!"

Then Arturo, the quiet man, heard himself shouting: "He's right. We cannot go on like this. We are not animals. We are not slaves. We have had enough. Enough!" And he suddenly picked up a stool and hurled it against one of the machines. His gesture was greeted with cheers. And the rampage began.

Down the aisles they swept, led by Arturo Bassano and the speaker, Pietro Pedrini. "Stop work! Stop work!" they shouted, turning every other phrase into a chant. "More money! More money!" They dragged men and women away from their machines. They slashed the leather belts. They jammed the gears. They broke windows. And every violent act was met with cheers as they gave vent to the rage inside of them that had been festering for so many years. Their eyes came alive and color came back to their corpselike faces. To break something was to regain one's self-respect. And oh, how good it felt.

By the time the police arrived, work in the Washington Mill had been brought to a standstill. But the police were a hundred and ten strong and well armed. They brought the riot under control and drove the workers out into the streets. Once outside they continued the demonstration and marched on to the Wood Mill nearby. The drama was repeated there and at three more mills. By the afternoon there were ten thousand workers on strike, almost a third of the whole work force in Lawrence.

The leadership vacuum was filled by an IWW organization, Local 20 of the National Industrial Union of Textile Workers. A handful of men came forward and took charge. They called for a mass meeting at the Franco-Belgian Hall.

The scene was all chaos and noise at first, like a town meeting in the ancient city of Babel just after God confounded the language of Noah's descendants. And for a while it seemed as though the strike would suffer the same fate as the tower that those ancients tried to build. But out of the confusion emerged one clear decision. They must send a telegram immediately to Joseph Ettor and ask him to come to Lawrence to organize the strike. ''Smiling Joe'' Ettor was a member of the executive board of the IWW. At the age of twenty-seven he was already nationally known as one of the best labor organizers in the country. On the West Coast he had helped organize construction workers, miners, and lumberjacks. He was tough and he was smart. He was fluent in English, Italian, and Polish, and he could get by in several other languages. He had moved back East, and there was no reason to believe that he would not come.

And he did. The very next day. By Saturday afternoon he was addressing a mass meeting in Lawrence. And the workers listened. With his blue suit and windsor tie he did not look like a man who had come up the hard way. But as soon as he spoke, it was clear that he knew exactly what had to be done. He was short and broad-shouldered. He wore his hat jauntily pushed back on his head, revealing wavy black hair. He complimented the workers on their determination, but he warned them to avoid violence. ''Make this strike as peaceful as possible,'' he said. ''In the last analysis, all the blood spilled will be your blood.'' He asked for a strike committee of fifty-six members, four from each of fourteen different ethnic groups. And another fifty-six as backup members. He lectured them on the basic strategies of a strike, especially mass picketing. The idea was to close down the mills, to choke off production and, therefore, profits.

Arturo went back to his rowhouse apartment flushed with excitement and the feeling that he was involved in something important for the first time in his humble life. Instead of sitting in silence in the small kitchen as he usually did, he talked at length and gestured with his thick hands. ''We are many and they are few. Without our work there is no wool, no cotton, nothing. We are their profits, and we will refuse to be taken advantage of. There has been too much suffering. Too much!''

He had been made a member of the Italian committee, and he was very proud. His daughter, Lucia, sat at the table but said nothing. Her hair was carefully braided under a kerchief. There had been several accidents at the mill in which young women had had their hair caught in the machinery. In one case a girl's scalp was literally torn off. Lucia was shy and subdued and always conscious of the scars on the left side of her face. They made her left eye seem to droop and they spoiled her otherwise good looks.

"And the women will walk too?" said Concetta.

"Yes. Everybody. The children too."

Lucia looked up at him. "What will we do?" she said. She looked frightened.

"We will carry signs and march. We will stop the others from going in at all the gates. At Everett and Washington, at Arlington and Atlantic, at Wood and Ayer, at all the mills."

Concetta had the olive skin and hard, bony look of a peasant. She put a steaming bowl of pasta and beans in front of her husband and listened to him talk. He reached down for the wine, which he kept in a gallon jug on the floor near his leg. "And what will the owners do?" she said.

"They will try to frighten us, because they know that fear is their best weapon. They will tell us that we have broken the law. They will tell us that we have lost our jobs. They will bring in scabs and armed guards and maybe the militia. But with the unity we will win, because it is money to them. And that is all they understand."

"Good," said Concetta. "I am ready to do whatever has to be done. And if they kill us, what does it matter? We are dead already, the way we live. Look at us. Look at her!"

Lucia leaned her head to one side, as though she were trying to hide her scars. And then she lifted her eyes to her father, and he could see in them, beyond her fear, her love and admiration.

Within two days of Ettor's arrival there were twenty-four-hour picket lines at the gates of a half-dozen textile factories in Lawrence, Massachusetts. Signs blossomed like flowers in winter, slashes of red against the gray sky. They grew from the shuffling pickets, who were bundled more in rags than clothes. "Don't Be a Scab," said the signs. "In Unity Is Strength." And the simplest of all: "Solidarity!"

It was Monday, and those workers who tried to go to work were booed and taunted as they crossed the line. Arguments broke out, shouting discussions about what was right and what was wrong. The police intervened. The pickets were

warned by their own leaders to stay calm, to keep moving.
They cheered when new converts came over to their side.
And then they sang. Nobody knew where it began or how
they knew the words. They sang "Solidarity Forever," to the
tune of "John Brown's Body":

> When the union's inspiration through a worker's blood
>        shall run,
> There can be no power greater anywhere beneath
>        the sun.
> Yet what force on earth is weaker than the feeble
>        strength of one?
> It's the union makes us strong.
>
>     Solidarity forever, solidarity forever.
>     Solidarity forever, for the union makes us strong.

Some of the plants across the canal were still operating,
and in the afternoon a cry went up to shut them down.
Thousands of pickets surged toward the bridges that crossed
the canal. The police and militia were waiting for them and
drove them back with firehoses under high pressure. The
pickets retaliated with chunks of ice from the canal. The
skirmish was brief, but it resulted in the arrest of thirty-six
strikers. The workers learned that afternoon that the enemy
was formidable. He seemed to have everything on his side:
money and weapons and the law. Even the fire department.
The whole monolith of society. "It is like a great rock," said
Arturo Bassano to his wife that night. "And we are like ten
thousand ants. But we shall find a way to lift it, because we
are no longer afraid."

By the end of the week there were 22,000 workers on
strike and the "worsted center of the world" was virtually
shut down.

In New York, Renato and Fanny and all their friends of the
Immigrant Workers party followed the headlines in the
newspapers and talked about what they could do to help.
After the incident at the canal the *New York Times* reported:
"Bayonet Charge on Lawrence Strikers." It was an exag-
geration, perhaps designed to sell newspapers, perhaps to
create a sense of urgency and danger. One editorial pointed
out that it was more a revolution than a strike. And the New

York *Sun* said: "Never before has a strike of such magnitude succeeded in uniting in one unflinching, unyielding, determined, and united army so large and diverse a number of human beings."

Renato read this aloud in the shop to Fanny and Sergio as they drank coffee. Their own weekly paper would be off the press that afternoon with a bold headline and a passionate editorial. Renato had stayed up most of one night to write it. And when Sergio read it the next day he said: "It is very beautiful, very strong. I wish the whole world could read it."

Renato was pleased, and as he put his arm around Sergio he was surprised by a sudden wave of emotion that almost brought tears to his eyes. He realized, more sharply than ever before, that he had been like a father to Sergio, and that all these years he had wanted a son. Secretly, somewhere inside of him he had wanted a child, a family. And he thought of the woman who was almost his wife and of how in her womb there might have been conceived a new life. Since she had told him a week earlier, he had pushed the thought to the back of his mind. Now it came forward, and it was another kind of excitement to mingle with the excitement of the battle in Lawrence, Massachusetts. It filled him with protective affection.

When the IWP decided they would send volunteers to Lawrence he said: "Are you sure you want to go? I mean, if you are not feeling well . . ."

She laughed at him. "I insist on going," she said. "Even if I am pregnant, it will be a long time before it matters."

"Would you like to see a doctor first?"

"I don't need a doctor," she said. "I know what's going on in my body."

"And you think—"

She nodded slowly. "Yes, Renato. Yes, I think . . ."

He looked confused. And then he took her in his arms and said: "Good! I'm very happy. I did not think I would be, but I am. And—"

"And what?"

"And I love you."

She blushed. "You're turning into a romantic fool. Come on, we have work to do."

Two days later they closed the shop and all three of them boarded a train for Boston together with fifty other volunteers. They were off to the war with banners and songs.

* * *

At the railroad station in Lawrence they were greeted by a large crowd of demonstrators carrying special signs to welcome the groups of sympathizers who came to march and help. Arturo Bassano fought his way through the confusion, calling out the name *Arnaboldi*. He had been asked by the Italian committee to work out arrangements for the volunteers from the IWP. The two men finally met and shook hands vigorously. They spoke in Italian, raising their voices to be heard over the noise of the crowd.

Winter clouds moved across the sky, obscuring the sun, which came out here and there like a momentary blessing. Colors flared, then faded once again.

Directions were shouted. The volunteers picked up their belongings and marched. It was not exactly a parade, just a mob of people ambling down the main street with signs and banners. Renato carried a canvas bag with a drawstring, and Fanny carried a large leather handbag. "So this is Lawrence, Massachusetts," he said.

"It doesn't look bad," she said.

"It's not the factory district," he said. "It's not where the workers live."

They were walking down a wide street lined with stores, most of them with lofts or apartments above them. There were telephone lines and lampposts. And there were cars and trucks parked along the curbs. In the middle of the street were tracks for a trolley, and after a few minutes one of them came along, clanging its bell at the marchers. There was an air of excitement in the town. There were policemen on horseback and many pedestrians on the sidewalks. One could not tell offhand whether it was a festival or a disaster. The big banner strung across the street, however, was a fair indication of what was going on:

> For God and Country!
> The stars and stripes forever!
> The Red flag never!

One of the workers who walked beside them said: "It is the battle of the banners. Yesterday the Bostons come with a big sign." He paused and pointed back at another group in the march. Across two poles they carried a banner that read:

Arise! Slaves of the World!
No God! No Master!
One for all and all for one!

There was hooting and whistling from the sidewalks on both sides as the banner passed by. "It makes the bosses mad. It is a revolution, they say. No strike. Today they put up this big rag for 'God and Country.' To me it says, 'For Blood and Money.' My blood. Their money."

As they moved from the business district to the factory district and the rowhouses and tenements of the workers, the sun that had been so indecisive disappeared for good, as if it were ashamed to illuminate this dismal part of town. And under the now overcast sky, the place looked sadder than ever. The houses were jammed together and dilapidated. Instead of lawns and gardens there was garbage and the debris of broken lives. Confused children in rags watched the marchers go by. Even the dogs looked half starved and too weak to bark. They retreated from the commotion, their tails between their legs.

Renato took Fanny by the hand as they walked. It was not necessary to say anything. This is what it was all about. This is what they had been fighting all their lives. Poverty and hunger and injustice. When he glanced at her, Renato could see that Fanny's face was damp with tears. And he remembered that she was carrying a child in her body. How difficult it must be for her, he thought, to see these children of Lawrence living like this.

Over the whole scene brooded the textile mills. Dirty red brick and tall smokestacks. Windows like blind eyes. Wire fences and mud. Railroad sidings and freight cars. They looked sinister, almost like prisons. In his mind Renato rehearsed a dozen editorials for his newspaper. He was moved. He was angry. Had he been a worker here he would have blown these factories off the face of the earth.

"How terrible," said someone beside him. It was Sergio, who had fallen behind and now rejoined them. His face was pale with disbelief. "I never imagined it was as bad as this."

Renato merely shook his head. He could not speak.

The new arrivals soon gathered into an open square, where several speakers addressed them. The crowd cheered wildly. Joe Ettor held up his hands to quiet them down. "Now, provisions have been made for you. You have been assigned to certain committees, who will tell you where to go and where to put your belongings."

Two hours later Renato and Fanny and Sergio found themselves in the house of Arturo Bassano. "It is not much, but we will manage," said Arturo. "We only have one child left, and she will move into our room. There is a bedroom for you and the signora. And the young man can sleep here on the daybed."

He introduced his wife and his daughter. "They also work in the Washington Mill."

Lucia glanced up shyly and smiled, but then looked away again. As she did so, Sergio could see the scars on her face. Concetta nodded. "Come," she said, "I will make you something to eat. You must be hungry after such a long trip."

They all went into the kitchen and sat at the round table with its wine-stained white tablecloth. Concetta busied herself at the stove. Without turning around she said: "I don't know why you people come here. It is a grief for us, but you must have troubles of your own in New York. I don't understand."

"We come to help," said Renato. "It is a brave thing you are doing, and we all fight for the same cause."

She shrugged. "I don't understand the politics, but you must have the very good heart." She turned and gave them a warm smile.

"And how does it go?" Renato said to Arturo.

He poured them a glass of wine. "It goes well, but very hard, because the owners in Boston have decided that they will break us. They know that if they give in here there will be strikes in all the mills along the river. They own the courts and the police. They have made many arrests, but then they have to feed us in the jails, so they let us go. It is only a harassment."

"Are there negotiations?" said Renato.

"Some meetings, yes, but not with the big bosses. The governor wants to make an arbitration, but Ettor says no. He wants to go to Boston with a committee to see Mr. Wood, the president of American Woolens. This is the way, I think, that we must go."

They talked and ate and learned about each other. Even Lucia was seduced out of her shyness by the congenial atmosphere. After dinner they went to another meeting. There, Fanny learned that she had been assigned to one of the soup kitchens. And Renato and Sergio had been assigned to the committee that prepared signs and leaflets and other propaganda. The committee included a local printer who was sympathetic. He and Renato liked each other instantly.

When they came back it was clear that Fanny was very tired. They all were. They went to bed. In the bedroom there was a crucifix on the wall and a statue of the Virgin Mary on the bureau. "You must feel at home," said Fanny. "Do these things remind you of home?"

Renato said nothing for a moment. The word *home* sent him suddenly back over the years to a small room in Naples where he had shared a bed with his brother when he was a boy. For many hours in the hot nights he would stare at the pathetic body of Christ as it hung from the cross on the wall.

"Yes," he said at last, "it does."

She was subsiding into sleep. "One never forgets," she mumbled. And then she sighed and was asleep beside him.

The next morning Lucia Bassano and her mother were up before dawn. Sergio heard them moving about and also got up. He had slept in his clothes and only had to put on his shoes and sweater to be ready. It was cold in the apartment, and even colder in the bathroom, which had been built as an appendage on the back wall of the frame building. When he came into the kitchen, Lucia offered him a metal basin of warm water. "To wash, if you want," she said. Her mother was stoking the iron stove, on which a pot of coffee had already come to a boil. The others, apparently, were still asleep.

"Lucia goes to the line this morning," said Concetta. "I go later, at noon."

Sergio offered to walk her to the gates in the predawn darkness. "You don't have to," she said.

"I don't mind," he said. "I'm eager to see what's going on."

With quick fingers Concetta braided her daughter's hair and pinned it snugly behind her head. Sergio could now see the full extent of Lucia's scars. She knew that he was looking at her, and it made her uneasy. He didn't know what to say, so he said nothing. He could see that she was sensitive and had once been attractive. It occurred to him that her life, which had barely begun, was virtually over. What could she dare to hope for in this gray town and cruel world?

By the time they got to the gates of the Washington Mill,

there were about a hundred people there, mostly women. They were bundled in clothes of every description against the cold. There was a hint of light in the sky. In the midst of a group of women a banner was unfurled. When it was raised above their heads, a shout of joy and laughter rose. The banner said: "We Want Bread and Roses Too." It was given to a group of young girls to carry. There were other signs and armbands, but this one stuck in Sergio's mind. He wished Lucia luck, and she went off to join the others.

He watched for a while from a distance. Stationed in front of the gates were half-a-dozen security guards with holstered guns and billy clubs. Two policemen on horseback came down the road. Sergio saw Lucia march away with the young women who held the banner. A confusion of feelings stirred in his young heart. Raw hate and naked love. But not merely for the men who guarded the gate or for the girls who carried the banner. His hatred was for all things brutal and ugly, and his love was for all that was beautiful and tender in the world. He was feeling the blossoming of his own manhood, the willingness to fight, and the desire for love. He straightened his shoulders and walked back up the street. And as he did so he thought, for some reason, of his father and of the stories of the war he told him when he was young.

In the days that followed, Fanny helped organize a soup kitchen for the Polish families in Lawrence. She worked long hours with the other women over steaming cast-iron cauldrons discovered in a junk shop on a side street. The half-open shack was subject to the wind and cold, but the fires that blazed in the oil-drum stoves kept them warm, and they sang as they worked.

In the evening she would return exhausted, her clothes smelling of soot and grease. "You are trying to do too much," said Renato. "I mean, in your condition—"

"There are plenty of pregnant women out there, walking on the picket line," she said.

But one morning she was sick, and Renato had to help her to the cold bathroom, where she threw up in the sink as he supported her and comforted her. An hour later she insisted on going to work. He knew it was useless to try to stop her.

He and Sergio helped do the layout for the leaflets, set their type, bundled them, and delivered them to the line and throughout the city. The two men stood on streetcorners until they were chased by the police. There were state troopers in town, and about fourteen hundred militiamen under Colonel E. Leroy Sweetser. Sergio was especially bold. Once he was knocked down by a trooper, and Renato had to keep him from fighting back. He was impressed by Sergio's courage. "He's no longer a shy and timid lad," he told Fanny. "But he is the stuff that martyrs are made of, and we have to keep an eye on him."

There were speeches and parades all week. When Big Bill Haywood arrived to give moral support to the strikers, he was met at the railroad station by fifteen thousand cheering people and marched to the commons, where he gave a great speech. This hulking, one-eyed legendary leader of the IWW was a man of immense energy. He had been through the horrors of Cripple Creek and other labor wars in the West. He held up his big hand with his fingers spread apart. "This," he said, "is how the AFL organizes. Weavers, loom fixers, dyers, spinners. All separate, all selfish." And then he closed his hand and made an enormous fist. "And this is how the IWW organizes. One for all and all for one. One big union."

Other IWW leaders came, among them Elizabeth Gurley Flynn, who at twenty-one was already a veteran speaker and organizer. Even at sixteen she had attracted large crowds with her fiery oratory. She was a New Englander, descended from Irish immigrants. She was also beautiful and passionate and well informed. "Why," she said, "did you leave your native land to come to this country, where the language and the way of life is so different? It was because you dreamed of a new life, free of tyranny and oppression. But what freedom have you found in these prisonlike mills, in these slums and tenements? You thought you would be rich, but you are poor. You thought you would see your children educated, but they are dying in the mills. You thought you would be respected, but you are called 'Greenhorns' and 'Hunkies' and treated as inferiors and intruders. . . ."

Fanny was deeply moved by the power and dedication of this young woman. She forced her way in to see her one night and spent hours talking with her and with some other women who had come from New York and Boston.

Half that night she lay awake talking feverishly to Renato about Elizabeth Gurley Flynn and the rights of women and the coming revolution.

Carlo Tresca, the famous anarchist with his dashing appearance and aristocratic background, also spoke. But perhaps the most brilliant speaker of all was Arturo Giovannitti, coleader of the strike with Joe Ettor. He was only twenty-seven, a poet and journalist, and his speeches were masterpieces that could move the crowd to tears.

It was an exciting and exhausting week. Hope was building that there would soon be a settlement. When Joe Ettor and five others of the committee went to Boston to meet with President Wood, the strikers could smell victory in the air. Rumors spread prematurely that the strike had been settled. But then came the crushing news that all the demands of the workers had been flatly rejected by Mr. Wood and his colleagues.

On Monday, January 29, the committee called for a massive demonstration and parade. Everybody put aside ordinary work to join in, including Fanny and Renato and Sergio. The march was led by Joe Ettor himself.

As they marched from factory to factory with their banners and signs, singing and shouting, they could see that the enemy was out in force. At one mill the militia barred their way. Joe Ettor called his army of strikers to halt and conferred with the authorities. "There will be trouble now," said Bassano.

"We should go through," said Sergio.

The soldiers were lined up with fixed bayonets. The horses of the police were urged into the crowd, but they snorted and reared to avoid stepping on people. "The horses are on our side," shouted someone from the crowd. "The horses are IWW. They have more sense than their riders." There were shouts of laughter as one policeman toppled from his mount.

But they did not go forward. It would have been suicidal to go against the troops, who had orders to shoot to kill if necessary. Joe Ettor led the demonstrators another way. Up one street and down another they paraded. More barricades appeared. Some rocks were thrown and there was much noise, but the word went again through the mob: "No violence! No violence!" And they backed off and found still another route.

They were jammed so tightly together that at times they could not move. Sometimes they were forced to reverse their direction, and there was much confusion. The police and soldiers closed one street after another. Anger grew. There were many who wanted to fight. "They will kill us if we fight," said Renato. He held Fanny around the waist as the crowd surged this way and that, as though it had lost control of itself. They felt as though they were being rounded up like cattle. A woman fainted, and room had to be cleared for her to lie down while several other women attended to her.

"It is getting ugly," said Renato. "Perhaps we should go."

"No," said Fanny. "I want to stay. Whatever happens, happens."

Behind them Sergio had taken hold of Lucia Bassano, who was wide-eyed and near hysteria.

They were crowded into the main street. A trolley car could not get through. Suddenly, rocks were hurled at the trolley. There were screams. At the edges of the crowd the police were using their clubs.

The soldiers advanced with fixed bayonets, and the strikers were driven up still another street, an even narrower one this time. Workers lived in the houses that lined the street. From their windows they threw down water and pieces of coal at the police and militia. There were curses in a dozen languages. Joe Ettor tried to control the mob, but no one seemed to know what was happening any longer or which way to go. There was soot-covered snow and ice on the streets. Some of the wilder young men threw snowballs and chunks of ice at the police.

A police sergeant was hit. In fear and rage he ordered his men to draw their guns. There was a moment of terrible tension. Then there was an outburst of shoving and flying fists. One could feel the difference between the ordinary surge of the crowd and the quicker animal movements that meant real violence. Even with their guns drawn the police were being forced back. Then someone fired a shot. There were screams and more shots. Some people fell to the ground to protect themselves. Some tried to run.

When the firing stopped, a woman was dead on the street. A young woman named Anna LoPezzi. Blood had been drawn. The sacrifice had been made, and it put an end to the battle. The crowd dispersed. The militia moved in to take command of the streets.

Once they had broken the back of the demonstration they became even more aggressive. They swung their clubs at the retreating strikers and they used their rifle butts. A group of Italian boys held their ground and hurled insults at the police:

*"Testa di cazzo,"* they shouted. *"Figlio di una mignotta!"*
And they gestured indecently with their hands and arms.

As the crowd thinned out Renato could see that Sergio was
among the Italian boys, and that he, too, was taunting the
police. "The idiot! He'll get himself killed." He wanted to
run to him and drag him away, but he had his arm around
Fanny, who was pale and unsteady on her feet.

"Go to him!" she said.

His indecision was an agony. He looked from her to Sergio
with a pained expression on his face. A bottle fell from
somewhere and broke on the cobbled street. Renato forced
Fanny to the sidewalk and up against a red-brick building.
They came to a shop. There were already several people
taking shelter in the doorway. It was a butcher shop, and in
the window, hanging upside-down from a hook, was the leg
of a slaughtered animal. "Wait here!" he said. "Don't try to
run. Stay off the street." And then he was gone.

He was only fifty yards from where the skirmish with the
police was taking place. The Italian boys were hurling chunks
of ice. He saw the police form rapidly into a line and charge.
Before he could reach the scene he saw the uniformed men
overwhelm the small group. They knocked them down, kicked
them, beat them with their clubs, and dragged them toward a
police van. He stopped. There was nothing he could do. He
saw Sergio lying facedown on the street, his hands protecting
his head. Then he saw him lifted roughly to his feet and
shoved along with the others. He looked to his left and saw
the militia emerging from a side street. They ran between him
and the fighting and drove him back. He did not retreat until
the last minute. He saw their faces. They were mostly young
men and some of them looked scared. Their bayonets flashed
in the cold sunlight. A sergeant ran among them, shouting
orders. They formed their ranks from sidewalk to sidewalk
and started up the street to clear it.

Renato ran back to the shop where he had left Fanny.
When he found her she was alone. All the others who had
taken cover there had fled. She was sitting in the doorway,
leaning against the locked door, her head forward against her
knees. When he tried to lift her up she looked at him and he
almost didn't recognize her. There was a bloody bruise across
her nose and cheek, and one eye was swollen closed. "My
God!" he said. "What have they done?"

She couldn't answer. There was blood in her mouth. He

got her to her feet. He could feel her hand clinging to the back of his coat. The troops were advancing methodically. He led her up the street, half carrying her along. At the corner he turned onto a narrow street. She began to sag. He could feel her dead weight. He lifted her in his arms and carried her the rest of the way home, almost half a mile. His heart was pounding as if it might burst, and his arms were numb.

Concetta got her into bed and told Renato to leave the room. "Get some hot water," she said to Lucia, who had found her way home safely. There was a strength and sureness in Concetta's whole bearing and the way she moved. It was as if there were certain things in this world that were reserved for women to do and about which women knew best. Renato thought of his mother, and of the women of his youth. They were like an ancient cult, all in black, bringing life into the world and washing the bodies of those who had died. Life and death! Life and death! He was staring out the kitchen window. A few people wandered by as if it were an ordinary day.

"Where is Sergio?" said Lucia. He heard her fragile voice behind him. He turned to look at her. For a moment his mind had gone blank. "Is he all right?" she said.

"I don't know," he said. "They took him away with some of the others. There was a fight."

"There were so many people. Suddenly he was gone. I didn't know what to do. I just ran."

"You did the right thing. It was very bad. And it could have been even worse."

"Is it true about Anna LoPezzi? Somebody said she was killed."

"Yes. I saw her lying on the street. It was not far from us."

"Oh," she said, and then just sat there for a while at the kitchen table, her hands folded in her lap, her eyes fixed on the wine-stained tablecloth, as if she would find in those vague designs the explanation for all this violence.

"Is there anything to drink?" said Renato.

"Yes," she said, and went to the cupboard where her father kept the wine.

In the bedroom Concetta washed Fanny's wounds and took off her clothes to make her comfortable and to examine the rest of her body. The bruises on her face were not as bad as they looked. Her cheekbone and lip were cut. She folded a wet rag and pressed it against her swollen eye. On her body there were other marks—on her arm and breast. "The filthy brutes," she mumbled in Italian.

Fanny was awake but too puzzled to speak. She seemed feverish. Concetta leaned forward and put her lips to her forehead. It was not a kiss, but the old way of taking the temperature. "*Dio santo!*" she said. "You are burning." She got her into a woolen nightgown and put another blanket on the bed.

She sat with her for a long time, until Fanny was able to talk. "Be still," said Concetta. "It is all right. You will be all right."

"Renato!" she whispered. "Where is Renato?"

"He's here. He's all right. He brought you back."

"I don't remember. There was fighting. I was knocked down."

"Yes, yes. Don't try to talk now."

"A man was standing over me. I thought he was going to help me up. I saw his eyes, his beard. He was not a policeman, but he had a club. He hit me. And then again—"

"You must rest, signora. You must not think." She held her hand and stroked her hair. After a while Fanny closed her eyes. Her breathing was heavy and quick, but she seemed to be sleeping.

When Concetta came out of the bedroom she saw that her husband was home. He had just come in and was talking quietly at the kitchen table with Renato. Lucia was standing by the stove as if waiting for the pot of water to boil. It was the learned habit of removing herself from the conversation of men.

Concetta, too, did not interfere. She said nothing to her husband. The glance they exchanged was enough. Then Renato looked at her. "The signora is asleep," she said. "She will be all right after a while." She did not go on, almost as if it were none of his business. She went to the counter by the sink and began to prepare some food, as though nothing unusual had happened.

"The men are very angry," said Arturo Bassano to Renato. "We are afraid of what they might do tonight. There is talk of an eye for an eye. We must do everything we can to control them. If we don't, more will die. And then the martial law will come and the strike will be crushed."

"What will happen to those who were arrested?"

He shrugged. "We don't know. If they make an example, then it will go hard. Otherwise, they will be released tomorrow or the next day." He hesitated. "Your young friend is very brave, but foolish. It is the impatience of youth. But you cannot fight guns with rocks and sticks."

Renato nodded.

After a simple supper of soup and pasta, Arturo got up to leave. Renato also got up. "You don't have to come," said Arturo.

"I want to."

"All right, then, we go."

It was very late when they came back. The house was quiet and there was only a kerosene lamp burning on the table, its flame turned down low. Renato went to the bedroom door, but before he went in Concetta emerged. She put her finger to her lips, then shook her head. "No," she whispered. "You sleep there tonight. I will look after the signora."

Renato frowned. "What is it? Is she bad?"

"No, no. She's resting. A little fever, that's all. I will watch."

"Should we get a doctor?"

"There is no doctor. Go! Go to bed."

He hesitated and then obeyed. He went into the sitting room and without taking off his clothes went to sleep in the narrow bed that Sergio had used. He was exhausted but restless, and his dreams kept waking him up. Again he saw the violence of the afternoon, and then the narrow, crowded streets of La Fontana. Across a bay red with blood he saw the brooding presence of Vesuvius.

He woke up at dawn and heard Concetta in the kitchen. She was putting coal on the fire with a little shovel. He saw her bending over the scuttle. She put the lid in place and then filled the coffeepot with water.

He got up quietly and came to the kitchen doorway. She was lost in her work and did not see him at first. She poured hot water into a bucket in the sink. And then from the bucket she lifted some rags that seemed to be dripping with blood. At that moment she heard him and turned suddenly to glare at him. "What is it? What do you want?" she said, letting the rags fall into the bucket.

He was startled by her tone. "What's going on?" he said.

"Nothing! You stay there. You wait."

"What is it?"

"I said it is nothing. She will be all right now."

"What do you mean *now*? I want to see her." He started toward the bedroom door.

Concetta had to move only a few steps to block his way. She reached out and touched his arm. "Please, I must wash her. Then you can go in. She has had much blood. She was with child."

Renato stepped back away from her. His eyes fluttered. He felt suddenly weak. He went to the table and sat down. She watched him for a moment as the realization sank in.

"She's lost it," he said.

"Yes," said Concetta. "But she will be all right, and there will be others."

He swallowed to hold back the tears. Concetta watched him, reading him as she had learned all her life to read men. There was sadness in her eyes, but acceptance too. She waited another moment, and then said: "You stay here. You have some coffee. I will tell you when to come." And then she rung out the rags in the bucket, filled it again with water, and went back into the bedroom.

It was several hours before Renato went in to see her. She was weak from the loss of blood, but she smiled at him, and he could see that she was going to be all right. There was a strange odor in the room, a combination of brown soap and something else. He sat on the bed and took her hand. It was limp and her face was pale. "Thank you," she said.

"For what?"

"For carrying me. I remember that."

"I didn't know you were so heavy," he said, trying to laugh.

"Small but tough," she said.

"How do you feel?" he said more seriously.

"Like one big bruise."

"You know what happened?"

"Yes," she said, "I know. I could feel it happening in the night, even with the fever. I'm sorry—"

He touched her cheek and hair. Then he bent forward to kiss her gently. "It's all right," he said. "As long as I have you—"

"You wanted it very much, didn't you?"

"Yes, I did."

"Me too. I should have been stronger."

"It wasn't your fault. Someday we'll have another."

"Yes."

"But first you must promise me something."

She fixed her eyes on his. "What?"

"That you will marry me as soon as we get back to New York."

Her smile was restrained by the cut on her lip. "All right," she said, "if you insist."

"I insist!"

"Good," she said. "I'm glad. We have been foolish long enough."

"Too long," he said, and kissed her again.

# 2

The next day the militia took over. Picketing, parades, and demonstrations were forbidden. It was illegal for three or more people to congregate. Lawrence was like a city under siege from within. Still, there were disturbances. Sometimes half-a-dozen or more workers would link arms and walk down a sidewalk, sweeping aside everyone in front of them. It was a game, a kind of guerrilla warfare. A favorite tactic was to send scores of "shoppers" into the stores, just to jam them up. The shopkeepers were terrified, but technically the law had not been broken.

The frustrated police and the furious judges struck back with beatings and penalties that were brutally excessive. Sergio was not released the day after the death of Anna LoPezzi. Nor was he released the following day. He was held for a hasty trial without a jury and found guilty of assaulting an officer, inciting a riot, and resisting arrest. He was given a fine of five hundred dollars or a year in prison. In a way he got off easy, considering the hostile climate. The authorities blamed the death of Anna LoPezzi on a certain Salvatore Scuito. He was assisted, they said, by a man named Joseph Caruso. Scuito disappeared, but Caruso was arrested. They also arrested Joe Ettor and Arturo Giovannitti on the grounds that their inflammatory speeches had inspired the crime.

There was no way Sergio could get out of jail without asking his father for help. He was determined not to do that, but Renato insisted that it was absolutely necessary. He felt very sorry for the lad. "If I knew how, I would steal the money to help him," Renato said to Fanny. "Anything not to see him crawl to his father. His new manhood is so fragile."

"But why is Gaetano so hard on him?" she said.

"I don't know. He was forced to marry Francesca because of him."

"She was pregnant?"

"Yes. And her family forced him to do the honorable thing. It was not unusual where we came from. But there is more to it than that. Sergio is different. He doesn't even look like the other boys. He's more serious, more independent. He's a dreamer and an idealist."

Fanny smiled. "Like you."

They went to see Sergio in jail. The place was crowded and they were only allowed a few minutes. They talked through a wire screen. When they told Sergio that they had sent a telegram to Gaetano, he looked down, his shoulders hunched forward. "But there was nothing else we could do," said Renato. "You don't want to stay here, do you?"

He shook his head. "No," he said, "I don't want to stay here." Then he looked up. "Did you say that I would repay him?"

"No," said Renato. "That is for you to say."

Gaetano did not come himself with the money. He sent a little man named Caminetti, who worked for Maresca, the accountant. Caminetti was a disbarred lawyer from Salerno who had small eyes and thick glasses. In a black leather briefcase he carried cash and some papers, and he gave everyone the impression that someone important was behind him. Within a few days Sergio was free. And the very next day he and Renato and Fanny returned to New York.

Gaetano was very angry. They all knew he would be. He came to the shop even before they had a chance to unpack. "So," he said, "you have all had a nice adventure." He was wearing a new hat and a new overcoat. He paced back and forth like a military officer.

Fanny's face was still swollen. Sergio's head was bandaged. A patch of hair was shaven off around the wound above his ear. They all looked exhausted and disheveled. Their clothes were wrinkled and dirty.

"It was no holiday," said Renato.

They were in the apartment. Fanny was lighting the stove. Sergio retreated to the opposite end of the room, as if to be as far as possible from his father.

"But why did you go? That's what I don't understand. What business is it of yours what happens in Massachusetts? Look at you. All beaten up. And for what? Somebody else's politics."

"It is something we believe in," said Renato.

Gaetano raised his voice. "And I say it is idiotic. You are making a religion of socialism. You are all becoming fanatics. Just as bad as those religious fanatics who crawl on their hands and knees up the steps of the church or drag their tongues over the stones of the street until they bleed. Who do you think you are? Jesus Christ? Are you going to save the whole world? Are you going to get yourselves killed so that some factory worker can make two cents an hour more? You think they care about you? You think they would give you a dime if you were starving in the street? They don't give a damn. Workers, bosses, they're all the same. Everybody thinks of number one. Everybody looks after himself. The bosses, they squeeze the workers for every cent they can get. And the workers push back and ask for more. Let them fight it out. It's their business, not yours, not mine. The world is a marketplace: buyers and sellers."

"But that's not right," said Fanny. "It shouldn't be that way."

"Who are you to say it shouldn't be that way? You are a dreamer. To make the socialism you talk about you have to change human nature. It is like telling the fox that he must not kill the chicken. There are the hunters and the hunted, and some must die."

"The weak die," said Renato.

"Yes, that's right. The weak die. The strong live. What the hell is the difference?"

Renato frowned as though he were in pain. "But Gaetano, what are you saying? That is monstrous and cruel. We are human beings. We protect the young and the old and the weak. We have rights. We have a morality. We believe in humanism, freedom, democracy.''

Gaetano laughed loudly and bitterly. "You want to know what we believe in? War. It is as natural to us as air is to birds. I had a friend in Abyssinia who taught me that sixteen years ago.'' He paused for a moment and then shook away the thought of his old comrade Roberto.

Sergio stepped forward, as if to stand up to his father. "You have a right to your views. I have a right to mine.''

Gaetano's face grew red. "Then sacrifice your own money and not mine.''

"You didn't have to pay.''

"What do you mean I didn't have to pay? I'm your father. It is a family obligation. I paid to get you off my conscience, not because I give a damn what happens to you.''

Renato shook his head in disbelief. "Gaetano, don't say that. It is the anger talking, not you.''

"No,'' said Sergio. "He means it. He has always resented me. If it was Antonio—''

Gaetano made a wild gesture with his hand. "I treat you all the same. But I want you to respect me, not take advantage of me.''

"You mean you want us to obey you,'' said Sergio.

"*Dio Santo!* You don't understand. I want you to act like a man, not like a sniveling boy who runs to his papa. When you do something, think of the consequences.''

"I was prepared to take the consequences.''

"Were you? Then why aren't you still in jail, where you belong, instead of here, where we can all look after you?''

"You are being unfair,'' said Renato.

"No, my friend, it is not I who am being unfair—it is you. Yes, you! Because you have put all these ideas into his head. He was young and impressionable. You filled him with your stupid propaganda. You took him away from my influence. You tried to be his father. Well, damn it, you are not his father. You had no right to corrupt him like this. Look at him. He doesn't even know what he is talking about. He has a broken head. He could have been killed. And if he was, it would have been your fault. Yours and hers. I am sick and tired of both of you—you and that Jew mistress of yours. I'm finished with you. Do you understand? I want you out of here. Out of the shop. Out of the apartment. I don't care how you live, but stay away from me and my family."

They were all too stunned to say anything. Renato looked at Fanny. He could feel her pain, but he knew she would not cry.

Gaetano's hands were shaking. He looked like someone who knew that he had gone too far but could not return. Suddenly, he walked out. They heard him go through the shop and slam the front door behind him.

Sergio's face quivered as though he might cry. "I'm sorry," he said. "It's my fault."

"No, no," said Renato, putting a comforting arm around him. "It's not your fault. He's angry for many reasons. Even he doesn't understand. Talk to him tomorrow or the next day."

"But what will you and Fanny do?"

"Don't worry about us. We'll find another place."

"And will you want me to work for you?"

"Of course, you fool! We may even give you a raise—just to keep you from going on strike." He smiled, and Sergio responded with a weak smile of his own.

The storm came and went. Even Gaetano was surprised at his own outburst. He described the incident to Silvio that night, and they drank a great deal of wine at the Cafe Savarese. In the morning he was a bit contrite, but too proud to admit it.

He could tell that Francesca had heard all about the argument, because she was silent and abrupt at breakfast. They now lived in a brownstone, which they owned. They had taken two floors of the small building for themselves and turned them into a spacious apartment, with the bedrooms upstairs and the other rooms down, including a large kitchen made from two smaller rooms. Three of their children still lived with them. Laura, the youngest, was only fourteen and still in school.

Even before he came into the kitchen Gaetano could smell the *prosciutto* and eggs and coffee. His head throbbed and he had a small scab on his chin where he had cut himself shaving. The children were almost finished and about to leave. Francesca was at the stove. She had the old habit of feeding her family before she herself ate.

Laura was the first to leave. She came to Gaetano where he

sat and kissed him on the cheek. He grumbled, but affectionately. She was already a young woman and very beautiful. She had the full figure of her mother, which made her seem older than fourteen, and she had very dark hair, which actually reflected sunlight. Her face was still clearly the face of a girl. With her small mouth and wide eyes she looked like innocence itself. And her cheeks, in spite of the winter, were full of color, as if the very fact of being alive made her blush. Her beauty and maturity made Gaetano uneasy. He never complimented her, and he was troubled by the fact that men were beginning to notice her.

"She's getting ripe," said Silvio one day. "You'd better keep an eye on her."

"Keep an eye on your own. You got three. Thank God I have only one."

"Don't remind me. Julia is already twelve. I can't believe it. She has the little apples already. *Madonna!* What am I going to do when they are all a little older? Such a curse! Three daughters and no sons. It is a punishment, *compare*, for the sins of my youth."

"Eh, for your sins you would need a hundred daughters."

Gaetano was distracted by this fragment of a memory. When he looked up again, Laura was gone and the boys were getting ready to leave. "I have to go to the market," said Stefano. He was lean and clean-shaven, with precise features. Antonio was even taller and sturdier than his father. He had the broad shoulders of his grandfather after whom he was named. His face was square and handsome and he was already cultivating a fashionable mustache.

When they were all gone, Gaetano ate in silence. Francesca did not join him; she merely served him. She put his food on the table in a deliberate way, as if to say: "I am angry, but I am only your wife and have no right to speak."

After a while he grew uneasy. "And what's the matter with you?" he said.

"You know what's the matter. I don't have to tell you."

"So you think I was wrong?"

"He was wrong, and you were wrong."

"Ah, so everybody was wrong, except you! How do you know what's wrong and what's right? You don't know nothing about it."

"I know my son. He—"

"*Your* son! I like the way you say that."

"All right, *our* son."

"Sometimes I wonder."

"You wonder about everything. You don't trust anybody. Not me. Not your own children. I see now the way you look at Laura."

"She's a girl. She's growing up."

"Sure! We all grew up. So what?"

"What do you mean *so what*? You know what can happen. It happened to you."

"Only because of you."

He shook his head and went on eating. He drank some coffee and put his cup down. "I had to tell him what I thought. It was a stupid thing to do. It cost us over five hundred dollars. And what's more, he could have been killed or sent to jail. And for what?"

Twenty-two years of marriage and a certain amount of prosperity had made Francesca bolder and more sure of herself. She had come to understand this man who was her husband. In a thousand little ways they had become intertwined. Perhaps it was not love, but whatever it was it was binding, and she knew it. She knew that he had been unfaithful to her from time to time, but it didn't matter, because she knew he wouldn't leave her, that he had invested himself in his family and his success in America. What's more, though she was a bit heavier she was still attractive and only thirty-eight years old. Other men noticed her, and she was sure that Gaetano was aware of this and that it increased her value in his eyes, especially since she did nothing to encourage admiration and was in every way a good wife. And so her position grew stronger over the years. And the stronger it became the more it annoyed Gaetano, because now he could not prevent her from saying what she thought.

"He is a good boy," she said. "He has always been good. Maybe too good. He thinks of others, which is more than I can say for you."

"What are you talking about? I have given everything for my family. All I want is respect. He knows I don't like what he is doing, and still he does it. Sometimes I think he has become a socialist just to annoy me."

"You are too hard on him. Always you have been too hard. With the other boys there is an acceptance. If they do something wrong, you laugh. But not with Sergio. Always there is resentment. By now he is afraid of you, and who can blame him? He doesn't understand, and I don't understand. But when you hurt him, you hurt me. I am his mother. He is from my body, and he was the first.''

"You favor him. You always have. And you protect him. Even from me. Whenever I tried to discipline him, you came between.''

"Because you have always been unfair.''

He pounded the table with his fist. "No, damn it, I have not been unfair. He is quiet, but he has the spirit of rebellion. He does not treat me as a father.''

"Because you don't treat him as a son. He has turned to Renato because you have never given him the love of a father.''

"A father doesn't give love. He gives strength and guidance and judgment. I tried to keep him on the right track, but you wouldn't let me.''

"*Dio santo!* Gaetano, he's not a criminal. What has he done? It is the politics, that's all. In your time you were worse.''

"What I have done is beside the point. He is—I don't know—peculiar in some way. He is so dedicated—like a priest. Like my brother Pietro. Maybe he should have been a priest, instead of a socialist. He would have had more respect.''

"Respect, respect! Is that all you can think of? When you were younger you used to say that you didn't care what other people thought. Now it's all you can talk about.''

"But he *is* peculiar. Can't you see it? He broods. He writes poetry. He . . . he isn't even interested in girls. He's twenty-one years old, and he doesn't look at women.''

"How do you know he doesn't look?''

"I know. I can tell he's afraid.''

"In time he will meet someone. He doesn't have to run around. He doesn't have to be like you and your brother-in-law. He's a quiet boy. He's shy, that's all.''

Gaetano made a gesture of disgust, but he looked more subdued. When his plate was clean he pushed it away and leaned back to light a cigarette. Francesca brought the pot to the table and poured him a second cup of coffee. Then she sat down and she, too, seemed to be willing to put her anger aside. "Please, Gaetano, talk to him. Tell him you did not mean all those things you said to him. Don't push him out of the family.''

He looked from side to side, as if for some way out of a

difficult situation. Finally, he nodded his head. "All right, all right. I'll talk to him. Now, leave me alone. I don't want to hear any more about it. I have more important things to think about."

She knew when to stop. Without another word he got up, put on his coat and hat, and went out. She began to clear the table. Order had been restored.

Antonio Adamo followed in what he imagined were his father's footsteps. He not only looked like him, but he moved like him and talked like him. Tenants and customers often commented on this resemblance, intending a compliment to both of them. The tenants lived in the half-dozen houses in East Harlem that Gaetano now owned, and the customers bought the olive oil and other products he imported through Raimondo Campo. The new business was called Adamo Imports, and the name was painted, with an appropriate flourish, on the side panels of a small truck. It had all started with a proposition from Campo that also involved Johnny DeMarco. Raimondo had suggested that with the "cooperation" of DeMarco it would be an easy matter to line up customers. What he meant was that the store owners and restaurant owners in DeMarco's territory could be persuaded to deal with certain distributors. It was not an uncommon practice in Italy, and it was becoming more common in America. Fortunately the olive oil, their chief product, was good, and the customers did not complain, except sometimes about the price. But that was to be expected because of the way the competition was controlled.

For this new business Gaetano bought an old brick stable on First Avenue. He had it converted into a garage and storage area. There was also an office and room for expansion, including space for a second truck when that should become necessary. And across the facade, once again, was the sign: ADAMO IMPORTS.

Antonio was very proud of this business, which, he was assured by his father, would one day be his. And most of all he was proud of the truck. He played with it as if it were a large toy. He had a quick understanding of mechanics, and he soon knew all the parts of this snub-nosed van intimately. It was painted olive green, and the lettering on the panels was in gold.

When Gaetano made his peace with Sergio, as he promised Francesca he would, he offered him a job in the family business. Sergio thanked him but refused. "It has taken me years to learn the printing trade," he said, "and one day I will open a shop of my own."

Gaetano was angry. "And how much do you make now with Renato?"

"Ten dollars a week," he said.

Gaetano laughed scornfully. "All right, I'll pay you double."

Sergio's refusal almost precipitated another serious falling-out, but Gaetano was growing accustomed to his son's independence. "All right, have it your own way, but you are throwing away a good opportunity, because I will not ask you again."

Sergio went away feeling that perhaps he had made a mistake, and occasionally he envied his brother because of his handsome air of importance when he made his rounds in the new truck.

Antonio thought of himself as a salesman, though he also had to carry cases of oil and crates of cheese. He wore a green denim worksuit, but also a tie and a cap that had a sort of military look. He wore the cap pushed back at a cocky angle so that his shiny black hair showed. He had a quick and winning smile and was liked by both the men and the women he met.

On a typical spring day in early June he visited his customers. He had rolled back the sideflaps of the driver's seat and he sang as he drove. He went down over cobbled streets along the river and was exhilarated by the sun and the air and the machine that he commanded. He was in love with life and with himself. He saw the docks, the water, a red tugboat hauling barges. And in the distance he saw the several bridges that spanned the river. He went by several horse-drawn wagons, one piled high with boxes of vegetables. He honked at a little Ford and cursed amiably at another truck driver. He cut back to First Avenue and, in the heavier traffic, went more slowly. There were pushcarts along the curb, and the sidewalk was crowded with women of all ages, carrying shopping bags and children. Some were old and wore black kerchiefs. Some were young and had loose-flowing hair and cheeks like summer fruit. And some were big-bellied and proud and walked with awkward, careful steps.

He parked his truck beyond the row of pushcarts. From it

he took two cases of olive oil and carried them through the crowd to a grocery store that was hung with cheeses and dried meats. He went to the rear and put the cases down. Mr. Selvaggio, the owner, came up to him, one hand on the white mound of his apron. "What's this?" he said. "I ordered only one case this week."

"My father said you will need two," said Antonio.

"But I have no room. It don't move that fast."

"What do you mean it don't move? Everybody uses olive oil. Unless you're buying from somebody else—"

"No, I don't buy from nobody else. I'm just overstocked, that's all."

"You want to talk to my father? I'll send him around. Maybe he made a mistake."

"No, no, never mind. Forget it. Maybe I ordered two. I don't remember."

Antonio smiled. The old man grumbled and walked away. On his way out Antonio helped himself to a handful of olives from an open barrel. A young woman watched. He gave her a playful look as he went by. She blushed.

He made deliveries to two restaurants and another store. Then he stopped to see a young widow who kept house for her father. The widow was, theoretically, in mourning. She had shown some interest on the street one day, and he had promised to bring her a bottle of some very special olive oil. It was all understood. She was no more than twenty-five, plain but passionate. He made love to her in the cool bedroom of the small apartment. The yellow shade was drawn against the brilliant sun. Her appetite astonished him, and he was too full of energy to control himself.

He drove away delighted with the simplicity of the conquest. How much easier an older woman was, he thought, than the guarded girls of the neighborhood.

When his rounds were done he stopped at the Cafe Savarese for a cold beer. There he found his brothers sitting at a table, having a cup of coffee. Sergio greeted him with the air of an older brother. "Finished for the day?" he said.

"Yes, and what a day. I have to tell you what happened."

"You want a beer?" said Stefano.

"Sure!"

Stefano, wearing his apron, went back to the bar. "What happened?" said Sergio.

"Do you remember I told you about that widow on 104th Street?"

Sergio shrugged, as if it were too trivial a thing to remember.

"Well, she asked me to bring her a few things. And today I did." He made a gesture with his hand. "What an animal!" He pushed his cap back and laughed.

When Stefano came back with the beer, he told them both the story in detail, lowering his voice and then bursting into laughter. Sergio pretended to be amused, but actually he was angry. He didn't know why. He, too, had such desires, but they seemed to be dissipated by other passions. He had never had a woman, and the fact was beginning to embarrass him. When his brothers asked him about his private life he was evasive. Antonio teased him good-naturedly. "What about all those girls in Massachusetts? Those factory girls. You could have had a good time up there."

"How do you know I didn't?" said Sergio.

"Well, did you?"

"What I did up there is none of your business."

"Well, I hope you got something out of it for all your trouble."

Silvio came over and joined them. He was the same age as Gaetano, but there was more gray in his hair. And he was beginning to show signs of a happy expansion around the middle. When his wife made fun of him he said: "Eh, what am I going to do? I'm surrounded by food all day long."

He had a glass of wine with his nephews and they talked about politics. The Italian papers were full of news about the war between Italy and Turkey, and about the strikes and riots in the northern cities. "It's the agitators, the radicals, who make the trouble. I used to be a socialist. Now I have my own business. How can I be a socialist? And it is the anarchists, like you and Renato," he said to Sergio. He was not passionate about politics, and he believed that Sergio would outgrow his idealism.

"I am not an anarchist," said Sergio, "but I do not believe in the tyranny of the state."

"Then what do you believe in?"

"I believe the workers should own the factories and share the profits of their labors."

"And I believe in this." Silvio made an indecent gesture with his fingers, putting one into a hole made by the others.

Antonio and Stefano laughed. "Why are you always so serious?" said Antonio.

"Because millions of people suffer."

"People have always suffered," said Silvio. "It is the nature of things. What can you do?"

"I can do whatever I can do," said Sergio.

"You should look after yourself. Everybody should look after himself and everybody will be better off."

"You should have come to work with me," said Antonio. "You still can. You want me to talk to Papa?"

"No, he already offered and I already turned him down. He won't change his mind."

"He will. I can make him change his mind. We can make a big thing of this business. We can make a lot of money."

"I'm not interested in making a lot of money."

Antonio looked away in disgust. "What's the matter with you? I don't understand."

"You could have a place here too," said Silvio. "I have to hire another waiter. Why should I give it to a stranger?"

"I don't want to be a waiter."

"Eh, you don't want this. You don't want that. What the hell do you want?"

"I want to help make the world better for the masses. I want to be a printer and a journalist."

"Like Renato!"

"Yes."

"But he doesn't make the world better for anybody. He only makes it worse for himself. He's forty-two years old. He has no family. He has nothing."

"He has his principles."

"Big deal! Can he eat his principles? And when he is old, will his principles look after him? Will they gather around him on his deathbed and make a family for him?"

"He has Fanny."

"Sure, but what is she? A live-in whore, that's all."

"Don't say that. She's a good woman. They are going to be married."

"Married? How? She's a Jew."

"Not in the church."

"Where, then? In a synagogue?"

"No, in the City Hall."

"I'm sorry. I shouldn't make fun of him. He's an old

friend, even if he is crazy. But you're my nephew. And your father and I, we worry about you.''

"Don't worry about me. Worry about this." He unfolded his copy of *La Cronaca Proletaria*. The headline read: *"WAR IN EUROPE?"*

Silvio grabbed the paper. "What are you talking about? There ain't going to be no war.''

"Renato says there will be a war for sure. Germany is very aggressive. They are building their army and navy. They want a colonial empire. They are a challenge to the French and the British. The Ottoman Empire is falling apart. Everybody wants a share. And then there is the Slavic movement, and Russia—''

"No, no, there can't be a war. Don't you understand? It's too expensive. Nobody wants it. They can't afford it. And now it is too terrible a thing, with all the modern weapons. They make noises, that's all, like barking dogs.''

"And if there is a war in Europe, who cares, anyhow?'' said Antonio. "We are in America now. It's three thousand miles away. Let them kill each other if they are stupid enough to go to war.''

Silvio stood up. "Enough of this stupid talk,'' he said. "I got work to do.'' He put a hand on Sergio's shoulder. "Take my advice. Forget about all this nonsense. Enjoy yourself once in a while. A little wine, a little music, and a good piece of ass. If you want, I will take you someplace where—''

Sergio shook his head and looked awkward. His brothers smiled.

A few days later Gaetano came into the Cafe Savarese with a serious look on his face. The place was filled with lunchtime customers. Silvio and Maria were both very busy in the kitchen. Gaetano took his brother-in-law aside and told him the bad news. "It's Johnny DeMarco. He's dying. He had a heart attack this morning, and they say he's very bad. We should go to the house to see if there is anything we can do, and out of respect.''

They did not go until the afternoon. Many others had also come. Some of them stood outside the building, talking and smoking quietly in little groups. In the downstairs parlor Eddie DeMarco said that only members of the immediate family were allowed to see his father, but he thanked them for coming. Doctors and friends and relatives milled about the brownstone residence. Johnny DeMarco had refused to go to a hospital. If he was going to die, he said, he wanted to die in his own bed. There was an air of importance and ceremony about the whole event, and it was almost as noisy as a baptism or a wedding.

The next day he was dead. There was general mourning throughout the neighborhood. A few days later there was an enormous funeral. The hearse was drawn by white horses. There were masses of flowers, and the procession through the streets was three blocks long. On the sidewalks people wept and made the sign of the cross as the coffin went by. The band shuffled slowly behind the hearse and played its mournful funeral march.

Gaetano walked in the procession wearing a black armband. It was a beautiful early summer day, a day for life, not death. On such a day he did not want to think of mortality, especially his own. Against death what could one do? Nothing! There was the church, of course, but it was not for him, because it was not true. And so his thoughts drifted away. Later he was lost in all the eating and drinking and talking, which was even better than the earth itself for burying the dead.

When he came home he found letters on the table, one of them from Italy. It was a thick blue envelope that at first he did not recognize. But as soon as he touched it, as soon as he saw the handwriting, he knew it was from Natalia.

He stuffed it into his pocket and went into the kitchen. His heart was pounding. He felt a moment of confusion.

"It's all over now," said Francesca. "Don't look so sad."

He frowned, as if her remark had something to do with the letter. "What do you mean?" he said.

"He had a good life, a nice family, and a beautiful funeral. What more can a man want? If God forgives him for his sins, he will go to heaven. And if he does, Silvio says everybody else will have to move over to make room."

He looked distracted. The letter seemed to be generating a mysterious heat in his pocket. He imagined it might burst into flames and set his suit on fire. "I'm going to lie down for a while," he said. "If anyone asks for me, tell them I'm out."

She looked at him carefully. "Are you all right?" she said.

"Yes, yes, I'm fine," he said. "Just tired, that's all. The procession, the funeral—"

She let him go without another word, but she registered the expression on his face in the back of her mind. It did not quite correspond to the hundreds of little things she knew about her husband, the way he looked, the way he talked. She thought about it for another moment, then shrugged and went about her business. Surely it was the funeral that made him look that way, but she was not entirely convinced.

Gaetano went upstairs to their bedroom. He stretched his legs out on the bed and leaned back against two pillows. He lit a cigarette and put on his reading glasses. He opened the letter slowly and with great attention. And then he read it, savoring every word, pausing to catch all the meanings: "My Dear Gaetano." Was there something odd in that salutation? He read it again: "My Dear Gaetano." In the old days she would have been more affectionate and more imaginative. Once she had begun a letter with: "My Darling Hero." He had accused her of being a bit sarcastic. She denied it.

He was suddenly besieged by so many memories that he could hardly concentrate on the letter he now held in his hands. He adjusted his glasses and began:

"How surprised you must be to hear from me after all these years. How long has it been? I hate to think. Sixteen? Seventeen years? Since before the birth of my daughter, Mariana. Did you know about that? Perhaps you heard from someone. Nicolo loved her very much. There is so much to tell that I hardly know where to begin. . . ."

Gaetano could hear her voice, feminine, evasive, and he could see her delicate, exotic face, her gray-green, almond-shaped eyes, her Mona Lisa smile. Her presence filled the room, and suddenly he was reminded of all those other rooms in which, years ago, they had made love. The memories, surging up like that, made him shiver and close his eyes for a moment. He put out his cigarette and continued to read:

"After the war we left L'Oliveto, that dreary place with all those stables and horses and peasants. I hated it. For me it has only one worthwhile memory: It is where we first met. Do you remember? I was the unhappy young bride, and you were the handsome young soldier. How romantic and foolish we were! What Nicolo saw in that place I will never know. In any case, we went north to Milan. He was given a decoration for his bravery in the war, and a new post closer to home. You probably know better than I do what the 'bravery' was all about, because he has never talked about anything that

happened in the war. It must have been terrible for him—for
all of you. Such a disaster! There were many inquiries. I
suppose there always are in such cases, but nothing much
came of them.

"We moved into the family house in Milan, an ancient and
beautiful place. A bit heavy. Too much marble. But really
quite comfortable and, of course, elegant. Not far from the
Cathedral or the Corso Venezia. Right in the center of things.
I found in Milan many of the things about which I had
dreamed as a young girl. I blame those dreams on my
grandmother, who insisted that we had 'unofficial' royal
connections. The truth, of course, has died with her and all
those other women before her who wanted to be loved by
important men. I, too, I suppose, was one of them. My life
with Nicolo taught me many things.

"The house was grand and we had many lavish times, but
the people proved to be small-minded and often cruel. I
cannot say now that I did the right thing, but I am not sorry. I
had many advantages and learned a great deal. Mariana, too,
had advantages, and became a beautiful young lady. She talks
like an angel, not only in Italian but in French.

"There was a darker side to all this, about which I prefer
not to write. I will say only that Nicolo was much older, and,
therefore, his friends were older. I felt like a child among
them. And, also, he was sad, haunted by the war, I think.
And, finally, he became rather morbid and weak and very
religious. His sisters and his cousins took advantage of him.

"They never fully accepted me and Mariana. They were
afraid that I had married him for his fortune, and they were
determined to keep it for themselves. The relatives of Nicolo's
first wife also felt that they had a claim on the estate. A few
months ago poor Nicolo died, after a long illness. His mind
and spirit declined more quickly than his body. And they took
advantage of him. Through legal maneuvers that I still do not
understand, they were able to exclude me and Mariana from
the will. An incredible conspiracy! They made all sorts of
accusations. I was unable to defend myself. I am afraid that it
was all a bit of a scandal. It gave everybody a great deal to
talk about. And oh, how they love gossip!

"So, we were left with nothing. The property was all
entailed. His income was from holdings that reverted to other
members of the family. We were given the impression that he
really did not own anything outright. I know it was not true,

but the lies became legal, and we even had to move out of the house. Fortunately, I had inherited my aunt Theresa's house. You will remember it, of course. We went there for a while, but I could see that it was going to be impossible. In Naples one day I saw an old friend of ours. Do you remember Aldo Pedrini? He told me what he knew of you, and said that I could get your address from your sister Angela. I went to see her. We had a very nice lunch together. She is a formidable woman. And so here I am, writing to you after all these years. But it is not merely because of our old 'friendship' that I write; it is because I have come to an important decision. I have decided to come to America. I see nothing here but a dead end. And the whole country is in despair. There is a war and much confusion. In Milan there were riots recently, and there were troubles in other cities. My own family, what there was of it, is gone. So what do I have? A small annuity, some jewelry. That's all. But enough to get us there and to keep us until an opportunity comes along.

"Would it be asking too much for you to find us a place to live? Anything will do for now. And perhaps to meet us at the boat, so that we will not be entirely lost. Mariana knows a good deal of English. I know a little. Write to me at the following address. I will do nothing further until I hear from you. I have had some offers of help here, but you can imagine what kind of offers *they* are. . . ."

He was stung by that last remark. It was as if it didn't belong there but was appended at the last minute. A hasty warning, perhaps. A hint of desperation. What he felt he did not immediately recognize as jealousy. After all, it had been a long time.

He folded up the letter and put it back into his pocket. He did not have to read it a second time. He had absorbed every word. He lit another cigarette and stayed there on the bed in the growing darkness of the room. He thought about what he should and should not do. He knew that he should not encourage her to come. It would only complicate his life. There were scars where once there had been wounds. And yet he wanted to see her. And the child. Before the room was entirely dark, he had made his decision.

The next day Francesca was sitting by the window, sewing. She looked serene in the sunlight that came through the parted curtains. From time to time she glanced down into the street.

Her hands were quick and calm and seemed, somehow, to echo her thoughts. When Gaetano came in she said: "There was a letter yesterday from the other side. Did you see it?"

"Yes," he said. He sat down and opened his paper.

She waited a moment. "Who was it from?" she said.

He tried to sound matter-of-fact. "It was from the widow of my old commanding officer, General Andreani. The poor man has died, and she is thinking of coming to America. My sister Angela suggested she write to me, because I might be able to help her find a place."

Francesca went on sewing. In a few moments she paused and looked up. "Doesn't she have any relatives here?"

"No," said Gaetano.

"Is she alone?"

"She has a daughter."

"A daughter? How old?"

"About sixteen, I think. What difference does it make?"

"Why would a widow with a sixteen-year-old girl want to come to America?"

"I don't know, and I don't care. Her husband and I were in the war together, and it's not too much to ask."

She shrugged and said nothing further, either then or in the weeks that followed. But Gaetano had the feeling that she had not put the matter entirely out of her mind.

Everything happened with surprising speed. It was just like Natalia, he thought, to act upon a decision as soon as it was made. Perhaps she did so to prevent herself from changing her mind. He remembered her moodiness, her sudden decision to take him as her lover, and her equally sudden decision to end the affair. Yes, that was Natalia. She had apparently not changed very much. Before long he would find out. A hasty note named the date and the ship on which she and Mariana would arrive. It was the *Concordia*, and it would come into New York on the twelfth of August.

It was only after this second letter from Natalia that Gaetano said anything to Silvio, who listened and shook his head.

"*Compare*," he said, "you're asking for trouble."

"What trouble?" said Gaetano. "It was all over a long time ago. Anyway, how could I refuse?"

"What do you mean *how*? You just refuse, that's all. You say 'I'm sorry, Natalia, I'm a married man and there's nothing I can do for you.' "

"I was married before too. Besides, it's not like that."

He laughed. "That's what you think. Why did she get in touch with you? Why not somebody else? And why come to America in the first place? If she needs a man, she can find one over there. She must have heard that you were doing well."

"I *am* doing well. So why shouldn't I help her?"

Silvio shook his head again. "How stupid can you be? She will expect you to look after her. She will use her daughter. *Your* daughter. You will have two families to look after. It won't be like last time, just a girl friend or a mistress. I don't know what you have in the back of your mind, but believe me, it won't be like last time."

"I don't expect it to be."

"Yes, you do. You think you're still in love with her. Is that it?"

"No, no, it's nothing like that." He was unconvincing. "But I . . . I have feeling for her. And I would like to see the girl."

"It would be better if you never saw her."

"Well, it's too late. They're coming."

"And what are you going to tell your wife?"

"That they are the family of my former commanding officer. That's all she has to know. You won't say anything—"

"Of course not. You think I'm crazy? But she will know anyway. Women always know."

"How will she know?"

"She will look at your stupid face and she will know."

Gaetano laughed. He took Silvio's arm as they walked along. "Come on," he said, "I'll buy you a drink at somebody else's cafe."

"Sure! Why not?" said Silvio.

During the next few weeks Gaetano worked frantically to get an apartment ready for Natalia. The only vacancy he had was in a tenement house on First Avenue. Three rooms in the front on the third floor. He was worried that it was not good enough for her, but what could he do? He was afraid that it was too noisy, because there were pushcarts along First Avenue. And he was afraid that it was too crowded and that the people of the neighborhood were too common. It was almost like moving her into La Fontana—a real lady, an aristocrat. What's more, the other tenants would notice that she was different, and they would wonder what it was all about. And what about the girl? Educated by the Andreanis. Fluent in French, for God's sake! He ran his hands through his hair and felt the rage of frustration. How could he put her in a place like that? He considered asking Eddie DeMarco for something, but he was pretty sure there was nothing in the two elegant buildings on 116th Street. He even considered buying a whole building and having it renovated, but that would take too long. Besides, it was ridiculous. What he was doing was enough. But no, it was not enough. He called in the painter and had the apartment completely repainted. The hefty woman across the hall, Signora Buscemi, watched with her hands on her hips. She asked who was moving in. He said, without thinking, that it was a cousin of his. What a stupid thing to say!

When the place was painted it still looked drab. He decided to have one room wallpapered. Signora Buscemi shook her head. She thought he was crazy. When the carpeting arrived she didn't quite know what to think. She gossiped with the other women in the building. All they could agree on was that their new neighbors were going to be *special* in some way.

Gaetano picked out furniture. He haggled with Rossini, the dealer. The furniture was second-hand but "good stuff." He ordered bedding and curtains—everything. "His cousin must be a grand signore," said one of the neighbors. "Then why is he moving into a building like this?" said another.

Two days before the boat was due to arrive it was all done. He walked through the rooms and nodded his head. It would do, he thought, in spite of the neighbors. Let them talk. To hell with them. He sat in one of the soft chairs and smoked a cigarette. The sun came through the curtains and the leaves of the plants on the windowsill. He sat for a long time and thought about what he was doing, about the expense, about what Silvio had said, about his wife's silence on the subject. Then he shook his head and muttered aloud: "I must be crazy. I must really be out of my mind."

On August 12 Gaetano woke up before dawn and could not go back to sleep again. He lay there beside his wife, staring at the ceiling and at the shade until he saw the first hints of gray light around its edges. Francesca breathed evenly and heavily. She slept on her side, facing away from him. It had been a hot night, and though the windows in the bedroom were open the air was still heavy. There was only a white sheet over them, and it had worked its way down to Francesca's hips. Her nightgown was black and had slipped off one shoulder. The sight of her like that might ordinarily have aroused him. He liked to make love in the morning and then fall asleep again for a while. Francesca was always obliging, though not always interested. She had never refused him, even when she was pregnant. Now, however, he was not aroused. He was merely aware of her being there, and aware of her flesh and the heat. He could smell her body and the bedclothes. It was not unpleasant, just familiar. He lay very still, to avoid waking her, as if he needed his privacy to mull over what he was about to do. It was all very simple, he told himself for the tenth time. He would take the truck. Antonio would work on the inventory. He would wait for her at the Ellis Island ferry. It was all arranged. She had a letter from him to show to the authorities, and undoubtedly she had other letters and documents. A person of her class would not be detained long. He would take her and her daughter to the apartment, and that would be that. If he needed help with the luggage he would get one of his boys. Later, if Natalia was not too tired, he would offer her dinner at the Cafe Saverese. He went over it again, rehearsing nervously how he would greet her, what he might say.

By the time he got up, his sons were gone and Francesca was in the kitchen, her hands white with flour as she worked a mound of dough.

"I don't know when I will be back," he said when he was ready to leave. "There will be the inspection and the luggage. I am taking the truck."

"Will they come here for supper?"

"I don't know what their plans are."

"What plans can they have? They have no family. You'd better bring them here. I will make enough."

"All right," he said, but only out of an unwillingness to argue.

Outside it was already warm. There were some clouds in the sky, but no wind. And there was a dampness in the air, as if before the day was out it would rain. He wore a tie and a collar and was uncomfortable in the humidity and heat.

He drove all the way down First Avenue until, below Houston, it became Allen Street. He went along East Broadway to Park Row, and then down Broadway to the Battery. He arrived too early.

He parked the truck near the ferry landing and went for a walk. He was impatient and nervous and a little frightened. He remembered something that Silvio had once said about how men are afraid of women, of their displeasure. He realized that he had been worried for some days now, not only about pleasing Natalia but about appeasing Francesca. She, too, had that feminine way of making him feel like a failure when things were not as she wanted them. They were all like that, he thought. The revelation made him smile. "Ah, women!" he muttered philosophically.

Two hours later they had still not arrived. He was beginning to sweat in the increasing heat. The crowd that waited at the ferry grew larger. There were carts and wagons and automobiles. Several ferries came and went. He stood on the runningboard of the truck and scanned the passengers as they came ashore. It was a familiar sight. They were mostly poor immigrants. They carried bundles and dragged children. They wore kerchiefs and ill-fitting dark clothes. He remembered his own arrival. How long ago it seemed.

At noon another ferry came in. As soon as they stepped from the shadows of the ferry building into the sunlight he recognized them. That is, he recognized Natalia. From where he stood she looked exactly the same as she had seventeen years earlier. It was incredible. It was as if all that time in between had never existed. He wanted to look at himself to see if, possibly, he too had not changed. Perhaps his whole life since Natalia had been a dream.

She looked slim and elegant in her blue dress and hat. She carried a small leather bag. Beside her walked her daughter, who was as tall as she was but without her mother's bold way of moving. Of the two she was clearly the girl, and Natalia was clearly the woman. Behind them came a porter with a large handcart. It contained a steamer trunk and several suitcases.

He waved from the truck but they did not see him. He leapt from the runningboard and made his way through the crowd. He almost knocked over a man in a derby hat and turned briefly to apologize. When he turned back Natalia was waving at him. She took Mariana by the hand and hurried forward. He had not foreseen it that way, but he opened his arms and in a moment she had left her daughter standing there to come into his embrace. They both suddenly seemed breathless, as though they had run a long way. The familiar slightness of her body sent a sensation through his arms and chest that took him completely by surprise. For a moment he couldn't speak and was even afraid he might cry. "Gaetano," she whispered against him. "I thought you might not be here. I thought for sure there would be a mistake. But here you are." She drew herself away a bit and looked at him. "How good you look."

"You too," he said. "You look . . . the same."

"Do I?"

"Yes, exactly. I can't believe it."

"Ah, what lies you tell! But here is my daughter, Mariana. Isn't she beautiful?"

"Yes, yes, very beautiful. Hello, Mariana." He hesitated, as if he didn't quite know how to greet her. He extended his hand and then, suddenly, both hands. He held her gently by the arms and kissed her on the cheek. She smiled shyly. In her large brown eyes there was a hint of confusion. She looked like her mother, but with a softer, more vulnerable quality.

"How do you do!" she said with such formality that both he and Natalia laughed.

For a moment he could not take his eyes off her. Her black hair was like his under the brim of her yellow bonnet. And in spite of her smile there was a touch of sadness in her face. He glanced at the porter and motioned for him to follow. "The green van," he said. "Over there."

He walked between them and took each by the arm. "How tired you must be, and it's so warm. But we'll be there before you know it. Was it a hard trip?"

"Oh, no, not at all," said Natalia. "It was an unforgivable luxury, but we came first class. And Captain Todd was so nice, so English. He had us for dinner at his table almost every night. And since he could not speak Italian I was forced to speak English. It was very good practice. Our cabin was absolutely spacious, and everyone was very good to us. It was like a holiday at sea. I felt very sorry for the passengers in steerage, but I saw no reason to share their misery."

She went on that way, talking quickly and nervously while he and the porter put the luggage in the rear of the van. It was an old habit of hers, he remembered, perhaps exaggerated now by time and life in the circles of the Andreanis.

He locked the van and paid off the porter. Then he helped them both up and into the truck. "Ah, a new experience," she said. "I've never been in one of these before. In Milan we had a big motorcar with a German name. It was like a coach without horses.''

Gaetano drove. Natalia talked. And Mariana looked out the window at America with a mildly frightened expression on her face.

Natalia's arrival at the apartment house on First Avenue was something of an event. The women in the building who had gossiped and speculated for so long were eager to see this mysterious ''cousin'' who required such fancy wallpaper and such fine furniture. They stood aside on the stoop as the luggage was brought in, their heavy arms folded across their heavy breasts, their harsh peasant eyes passing judgment on the pretty lady and her pretty daughter. They smiled and nodded. Some were intimidated by the obvious signs of class, recalling their lives in the old country, where the aristocracy expected from them visible signs of humility. Afterward they had a good deal to talk about.

''And where is the husband?''

''There is no husband. She is a widow.''

''Then why doesn't she wear black?''

''The daughter is beautiful. Like an angel.''

''The mother is beautiful too, but she has an eye like a fox.''

''The men will come like flies to molasses.''

''Unless she is, you know, the *amante* of Adamo.''

''But she is his cousin.''

''Listen, if she is his cousin, then the pope is my father.''

''But why does he put her here, right around the corner, right under his wife's nose? He might as well move her into his own house.''

Though they all disapproved of what seemed to them the obvious, some of them were secretly pleased to have such a classy neighbor and such a juicy bit of scandal to chew on.

In the apartment Natalia took off her hat and sat down in one of the chairs in the living room. Mariana sat on the daybed that was heaped with cushions to make a sofa.

''Is the place all right?'' said Gaetano

''Oh, yes,'' said Natalia, ''it's fine. It will do very nicely for now.'' She suddenly seemed a bit fatigued and distracted. ''I hope it wasn't too much trouble for you.''

''It was nothing, really.''

''You've been too kind, Gaetano. You had every right to

refuse to help me. . . ." She hesitated and glanced at Mariana, whose eyes were fixed on Gaetano.

There was an awkward moment. He cleared his throat and said: "Well, I suppose you will want to unpack and settle down. I will come back later and show you around a bit. The neighborhood is not as bad as it looks."

"It's very colorful. It reminds me of Naples. Pushcarts on the streets. Wash hanging from the balconies."

He smiled. "Here they are not balconies. They are called fire escapes."

"Is the whole building for us?" said Mariana.

Natalia laughed. "No, no, my darling, just these rooms." And then to Gaetano she said: "Mariana has never lived in an apartment before. Always in a house."

"I'm sorry. I realize that both of you are used to much better, but—"

"Nonsense! You have done more than enough. Besides, beggars can't be choosers."

She was so perfectly ambiguous that he could not tell whether she was disappointed or delighted with the place. He gave her the keys and explained about the electricity and gas. He showed her the icebox. It was brand new. Inside there was already a block of ice. "You will have to remember to empty the pan." He slid it out and then pushed it back again.

On his way out he paused at the open door. "Oh, yes," he said, "I almost forgot. Francesca insists that you come to our house for dinner tonight."

"How generous of her. At last we get to meet. I have always been curious—" Again she hesitated and looked at her daughter.

"Good! I will see you later, then."

On his way down he nodded to the people he knew. As he walked down the street he could feel the eyes of the women on him, and he knew that putting Natalia in such a place was a terrible mistake.


Sergio came for dinner, as he often did since his reconciliation with his father. He lived alone in a furnished room and did no cooking at all. He either ate with Renato and Fanny or at the cafe or at home. He did not know it was a special occasion until he saw the table opened up and set for eight people. When his mother explained who was coming, his curiosity was aroused.

It was not until they were all gathered around the table that Gaetano, seated at the head, realized he had brought together, in effect, two families—*his* two families. He was amused by the idea. All his wives. All his children. It was a kind of triumph in a way, and he drank too much wine. He was proud of his accomplishments in America and talked about them in detail. And to the newcomers he described each of his children, and was humorously critical, especially of Sergio. "And this one," he said, "makes a big crusade for the revolution. He reads books and marches with the socialists and anarchists. Someday he will get himself killed, but he is very clever."

Francesca, as usual, spent more time at the stove than at the table. Natalia made a polite offer of help, but it was clear that she would not have known what to do. She seemed at ease at the gathering and talked in a sociable and superficial way about her past, her dead husband, and her journey to America on the *Concordia*. In the movement of her eyes Gaetano could see that she was taking in everything. Once her gaze lingered a bit too long on Francesca, as though she were studying her. And once she reached across Gaetano to touch her arm and say: "What a handsome family you have. You are so lucky."

Francesca did not know how to respond. She looked embarrassed. Gaetano rescued her. "Eh, be careful what you say. These boys have big enough heads already. They think they are God's gift to the ladies."

Everyone laughed. The talk became easy. Even Mariana was drawn out when Laura asked her where she went to school and when Antonio asked how she liked America. "I don't know," she said. "The buildings are so tall. The trains run up in the air. It is all so different. So busy. So many automobiles."

Sergio's eyes kept drifting back to her. Her speech was so formal and precise, and her voice so soft and feminine that he was fairly hypnotized by whatever she said. He was fascinated by her beauty and several times caught himself staring at her.

At first they were all conscious of the difference in speech. And something Laura said in her Neapolitan accent made Mariana laugh. But before long the difference did not seem to matter, except perhaps to Francesca, who said very little. She seemed, in fact, quite subdued in the presence of this "lady." On the streets she could hold her own with the other women, in a full voice with a harsh edge and all the usual gestures of her class. But now she suddenly seemed aware of her crudeness and embarrassed by it. Gaetano noticed. He tried to bridge the gap between them by encouraging Francesca. "Tell Natalia how you made the *spaghetatta*," he said. And then to Natalia: "My wife is a very good cook. She has all kinds of secrets from her mother and her grandmother."

"It was nothing special. Very ordinary," said Francesca.

"It was excellent. I would love to know your secret."

"Another time," she said abruptly and went back to the stove.

Natalia understood instantly Gaetano's desire to keep everybody happy, and she conspired with him to make the dinner a happy occasion. She talked, a bit flirtatiously, with Antonio and Stefano, but with Sergio she was more cautious, sensing from the beginning that he was different and probably the most interesting of the sons. He spoke in a more educated and serious way, and there was a certain depth in his eyes. His appreciation of her daughter's beauty did not escape her notice.

Later, when their guests had gone and everyone was in bed, Francesca lay beside Gaetano, and he could feel that she was upset. He did not have to ask her what it was about. "This woman," she said, looking not at him but straight ahead, "what is she to you?"

"Nothing," he said. "It is only for her husband—"

"Yes, yes, I know, he was your commanding officer in the war. But why does she turn to you now? Was there something between you before?"

"I hardly knew her."

"But you are like . . . like old friends."

"I often went to their house when I was stationed at San Sebastian. They helped me to get my commission. I owe them—"

"I wish I could believe you."

He turned to her persuasively and stroked her arm. "Believe me!" he said.

His attentions became more affectionate. She softened. "Well, who could blame you? She's very beautiful. But you keep your hands off her. I don't want people talking about us."

"Eh, what do I need her for, anyway, when I have you?"

"If you talk like that, then for sure I will think that something is wrong." There was just a trace of a smile on her face, but it was enough to tell him that they would make love—and that the question of Natalia would be postponed.

Gaetano visited Natalia frequently in the weeks that followed, but Mariana was always there. "When can I see you alone?" he said one day.

She was evasive. "Perhaps it is better this way," she said. And he was unable to argue with her, because Mariana was in the next room.

He persuaded her to have lunch with him downtown, so that they could escape the annoying eyes of the neighbors. They met at a restaurant called Alberto's and talked intimately for the first time since her arrival.

"I haven't had a chance to tell you how happy I am that you came," he said. He reached across the table and covered her hand with his.

She allowed him to show his affection. "I am happy too," she said, "but I will be a lot happier when I have made some plans. I must do something with my life and with Mariana. We just can't go on like this from day to day."

"Perhaps you can put her in a good boarding school, a convent school. I have a friend whose daughter is at the Sacred Heart Academy upstate. He says it's very good."

"No, I don't want to send her away. I want her with me. She is all I have now."

"You have me."

She laughed and withdrew her hand. "Gaetano, you are very sweet," she said, "but you have a wife and four children. You can't go on looking after me forever. In any case, it's not right. Already people suspect there is something between us."

"I wish they were right," he said.

"My dear, it was a long time ago. We were young. Now—well, now it's different."

"Not for me. I thought it would be, but it isn't. From the moment I saw you at the ferry I knew nothing had changed."

"You mustn't talk that way. Of course things have changed. I am forty-two years old. My life is in ruins. And I have a daughter, for whom I must find a good husband, preferably one who is educated and wealthy. I mustn't complicate things any further by falling in love all over again with you."

He frowned. "But then why did you come here? Why did you come to me?"

"I came for help. I came because I was closer to you than to anyone before or since. I thought you would understand."

"I do. But you also must have come because of her, because I am her father."

"Please, Gaetano, she must never know. She loved Nicolo very much. He was good to her. I think he honestly believed she was his."

"Surely, he knew—"

"He never talked about it. He never accused me."

"But in the war . . . I told him."

She looked stunned. "You told him?"

"Yes. He had done something very stupid and we were almost killed. I wanted to shoot him. We were alone in the ruins of a church. I wanted to hurt him. He had been a coward, and many of the men had died. And now you tell me he was decorated for heroism."

"Stop. I don't want to hear any more. He may have been a weak man, but he was not malicious. He was good to me. Better than I deserved."

"Why do you say that? Because of me? Or were there others?"

"That's a cruel question, Gaetano. If I answer it, you may be sorry."

"Well, were there?"

"What difference does it make to you? You were not my husband. Not even my lover anymore."

"So there *were* others."

She looked at him defiantly. "Yes. Several, as a matter of fact. Life was not uninteresting in Milan. I was involved in a wonderful scandal shortly before Nicolo died. It was used against me by his relatives, as you can imagine. But you might as well know the whole story. From the time he came back from the war he was—how shall I put it? Impotent."

Gaetano shook his head. He didn't know what to think about this woman, whom once he had loved so profoundly. He stared at her. Was she the same woman? He felt, suddenly, that he didn't know her at all. And yet hadn't she always been that way? He wound up by apologizing. "I'm sorry," he said. "I'm acting like an idiot."

"Or a jealous lover," she said.

"It's the same thing, no?"

They smiled. He took her hand again.

"You were always like that," she said.

"Like what?"

"Jealous. Possessive."

"Only with you."

"Oh, no, with your wife too. I can tell. She's been good for you, hasn't she? In spite of the bitterness at the beginning."

"Yes, she's a good mother and a good wife. I must say that for her. But between us there has always been something missing. We were not in love—"

"Ah, love, love, love." She sighed sarcastically. "When we are young we make so much of love. Sometimes I don't think we even know what it is, especially when we are young."

"I knew."

"Did you? And did I break your heart?"

"You're making fun of me. Yes, I was miserable. Are you glad?"

"Of course. It was a great sacrifice for me. Why shouldn't you suffer too? Ah, but what times we had. We were very good lovers."

"And can be again."

"No, for now we will just be good friends. And let's not talk about it anymore. You're getting me all *interested*. Perhaps someday—when things are clearer and I know what I am doing."

"I've been thinking about that."

"About what?"

"About what you might do."

"I would get a job, but what can I do?"

"No, no, you must never work for anyone else in America. The only way to get rich here is to have other people work for you. Open a business. A shop maybe. Dressmaking. Millinery."

"But I don't know anything about it."

"Don't worry. We find somebody who does. I have friends. I will ask them. Do you have any money?"

"Some. Perhaps enough. But I don't want to risk everything."

"I can help. Maybe we can be partners."

"Sure, and what will your wife say about that?"

"Don't worry so much about my wife. She believes everything I tell her. Besides, business is business."

"Francesca may be a simple woman, but she's no fool. I can tell."

He held up his hands in a gesture of innocence. "But we're just friends."

She laughed. "Of course. I almost forgot."

One day Gaetano came to the apartment and found Sergio there. "What's this all about?" he said to Natalia.

Sergio and Mariana were sitting at the kitchen table. There were some books in front of them. "Oh, your son has offered to tutor Mariana in English and American history."

"But she already knows English."

"She knows school English. She needs practice in conversation, and everyone in this neighborhood speaks Italian. Besides, she needs some company."

"Perhaps I should send Laura to see her."

"Laura comes once in a while too, but she is in school all day. I think it's very nice of Sergio to do this, don't you?"

"Yes, yes, very nice," he said, but she could tell that he did not approve.

The next time they were alone he said: "We must be careful with those two. If they spend too much time together, God knows what will happen."

"I think it will be all right," she said. "If you make a fuss, you will only arouse their curiosity. Mariana is still a child. And Sergio does not seem to be very aggressive."

"Perhaps you're right. He has never shown much interest in women before. If it was Antonio—well, that would be another matter." He smiled rather proudly. "He's a devil with the girls."

"Like his father, I suppose."

"Yes, only worse."

Toward the end of September Silvio's wife, Maria, took a day off from the restaurant and came to see her sister-in-law. She came early, but only after she was sure that everyone else would be gone. She was in her mid-thirties and looked strikingly like her older brother. Her once girlish beauty had broadened into sturdy womanhood. She was handsome and hardworking and not afraid to say exactly what she thought. They had tea in the kitchen. Maria took off her red kerchief and adjusted one of the combs in her dark hair. Then she leaned forward with a serious look on her face. "So," she said, "what is this nonsense all about, this business with Natalia Andreani?"

"Don't ask me," said Francesca. "If anything was going on I would be the last to know."

"That's not true. The wife always knows. In bed, I mean. Has he been different?"

"No, nothing is different."

"Then it is probably what it seems and the talk is not true."

"What talk?"

"What do you mean what talk? Are you stupid? Your husband visits a beautiful widow almost every day. What do you expect people to think? Whether he sleeps with her or not, he gives her too much attention—and maybe money. It's not right, Francesca."

"But what can I do about it? And now they have business together."

"What business?"

"They are opening a millinery shop for her and her daughter. The other side of Second Avenue on 116th Street."

"Nothing but the best, eh?"

"He says it will make money, and that it is a good investment."

Maria drank her tea meditatively and seemed to be reconsidering the matter. "If she was just a businesswoman, it would be all right. Do you know what I mean? There are women like that. They use their looks, but in the end it's only money they want. But this one—I don't know. She looks as if she wants something else. And a woman like that can make a fool of a man."

"So what can I do? I can only wait to see what happens."

"You could make him miserable."

"If I fight him, he will only get angry. And then what? He will have a good excuse to turn to her. If I keep quiet and give him no cause—"

"There is another way." Maria lowered her voice and a conspiratorial look came over her face.

Francesca was drawn forward, as if to listen to a secret.

"You could make her your friend. Do you understand? You could go often to see her. Then it would be more difficult for them. There would be a feeling of guilt and betrayal. What's more, if you were her friend, there would be less talk. He would not be seen so often alone with her."

"But how can we be friends? We have nothing in common."

"If you don't do something, Francesca, you *will* have something in common—your husband."

Francesca made a brave attempt to follow her sister-in-law's advice, but she knew from the beginning that it wouldn't work. Natalia looked annoyed, as though perhaps "the wife" had hoped to surprise the lovers in bed; she felt falsely accused by the visit, and later was even angry with Gaetano, as if, somehow, he could have prevented the awkwardness. But Natalia was persuaded to come to dinner, and the evening was a mild success despite certain subterranean currents that stirred Sergio's imagination. That night, alone in his room, he wondered whether or not his father was Natalia's lover.

Gaetano was not until the middle of November. Then something happened. It was all rather sudden—even accidental. Late in the afternoon they had gone to the shop to see what the carpenter had done with the shelves. The sky was cloudy, and after a while it began to rain. Gaetano stood in front of the empty display window and gazed into the street. A naked arrangement of mannequins seemed to be waiting for hats and clothes in the deepening shadows behind him. "We will have to wait," he said. "It won't last long."

There was a fitting room in the back with a sofa and chair and two tall mirrors. He found a bottle of wine and two glasses. With an amusing flourish he said: "Shall we retire to the parlor, madam?"

"I really must get home," said Natalia. "Mariana is alone."

"Mariana is almost seventeen years old," he said. "She can look after herself for a while. Besides, it's pouring. You'll get soaking wet and sick if you go out now."

They went into the back room and had a glass of wine. The rain did not let up and the dim light deepened. The electricity had not been turned on yet, and so they sat there in the growing darkness. Natalia was on the couch. She wore a fall dress that had a jacket with many buttons down the front. It showed the fullness of her bosom and the slenderness of her waist. A white ruffled collar outlined her face, and in the dying light she suddenly seemed much younger to Gaetano. The wine relaxed her, and she smiled in the old way.

He moved from the chair to the sofa and sat close to her. She did not retreat. The sound of the rain was hypnotic.

"We really must go," she said, but made no effort to move.

"Do you remember our room in Naples," he said, "in that horrible little hotel?"

"It was not horrible," she said. "Only small. I was very fond of it."

"Do you remember how sometimes we were there in the rain, and it ran off the roof through the broken gutter, like a waterfall outside our window?"

She smiled. "I remember."

"It was like a dream. We never talked about the future."

"We had no future."

"It was the happiest time of my life," he said.

She stared straight ahead, her eyes a bit limp, as though she were seeing it all again. He put his arm around her shoulders. For a moment she leaned against him and then tried to draw away. "Gaetano," she whispered, "it's getting late."

He leaned over and kissed her gently on the lips. She started to protest but failed. Her lips were very warm and he could feel them tremble and part. They gave in to the darkness and the wine and the memory and fell into a long embrace and kisses that grew more passionate. "Oh, Natalia," he said, "how I've missed you."

She responded with hungry arms that held him against her. He kissed her cheeks, her eyes, her lips. And he felt her breasts and the curve of her hip as she leaned toward him. "What if someone comes?" She sighed.

"The door is locked. The lights are out."

He undid the buttons of her dress and searched through her clothes for her naked flesh. "Ah," she said, "how long it's been. I thought I had died inside."

They helped each other out of their clothes with impatient hands. She was in a kind of trance of passion, in which she could not wait to have him. He could hear her breathing and sighing and urging him onto her, into her. And then she let out a cry of pleasure and dug her fingers into his back and ran them along his muscles and over his naked hips.

The couch was narrow, but it did not seem to matter. Their bodies found a way to become one. Her legs were lifted—almost around him—and her head moved from side to side until her hair came lose. He buried himself in her with long, definite motions, as if each were a loving stab or a kiss. And she rose to take him with all the passion of a woman who had been denied. . . .

*     *     *

As Maria had suggested, it was in bed that Francesca would discover the truth. For a while, after Natalia's appearance on the scene, Gaetano had become more attentive, more physical, as if the mere presence of an attractive woman stirred him and drove him more often to the simple satisfaction of his needs. It was his use of Francesca in this way that led her to believe that perhaps her husband was not sleeping with Natalia, after all. In fact, she had become quite convinced. There were no signs of betrayal, no rejection, no weariness or irritation. He made love to her with vigor, not with romance— but he had never been very romantic.

Once Gaetano made love to Natalia, it was easy to continue. He had awakened in her the old desires, and she had reached an age at which those desires were even more intense. Sometimes she seemed uncontrollable, even a little savage, in her lovemaking. They went regularly to a small hotel near Madison Avenue, where they soon became known to the discreet manager. They were too newly reunited in their old passion to talk about where it would all lead.

The change in Gaetano was dramatically clear to Francesca. He went for two weeks without touching her. She dared to mention the subject, and he said he had not been feeling very well. When occasionally he did make love to her it was quick and without enthusiasm, a kind of required domestic act to pacify his wife. She could almost feel him thinking of something else. Her despair and anger increased, but for a while she said nothing, hoping that the obvious would prove to be untrue.

Then one day, when he turned away from her in bed, she could no longer contain her feelings.

"Go to sleep," he said. "Can't you see I'm tired?"

She burst into tears and an angry tirade. "Sure, you're tired. You were with her today. She makes you tired, and she makes me sick. I can smell her on you, you pig, you bastard!"

Startled, he sat up and watched her pace back and forth beside the bed.

"Be quiet. You'll wake up the whole house."

"Ah, so now, all of a sudden, you care what people think? When they laugh behind my back you don't care. What's the matter, are you ashamed of what you are doing? You should be proud. You have two women. You are a big man. A hero!

You should stick your head out the window and boast to the whole neighborhood: 'I am Gaetano Adamo, the famous *stalone* of La Fontana.' The women will all come running and lay themselves down naked at your feet.''

He got out of bed and tried to approach her. "What's the matter with you? Are you crazy?''

"Yes, I am crazy, because you make me that way. I give and give—everything for you. Everything for the family. And what do I get? Some fancy lady comes along—not even young—and you become an idiot. She has you on a string like a monkey. She says *jump* and you jump. *Dio santo!* I could kill you. I could kill the two of you.''

He grabbed her by the arms and shook her, as if to bring her to her senses. "Stop it! That's enough!'' he ordered.

"No, *you* stop it, because *I* have had enough—''

He cursed and hit her with the back of his hand. She was stunned and stumbled backward into a sitting position on the bed. She held her face and glared at him. He said: "We'll talk about it tomorrow. I'll sleep outside.''

"What is there to talk about? If you want her, have her, but don't touch me.''

"You would refuse me?''

She went silent. When she spoke again, she was calmer. "What am I supposed to do? I am your wife.''

"You are my wife because your family forced me to marry you," he said.

She suddenly looked wounded and deeply hurt. "You will never forget, will you? And you will never forgive. You promised from the beginning that you would make me miserable, and now you have succeeded. I hope you are happy.''

He shook his head in exasperation and left the room. Sometime during the night he came back and apologized. She did not accept. There was no point. They knew where they stood, without knowing what to do about it.

Christmas came and went. The situation settled into a stalemate in which everyone held his ground and no one offered a resolution. The family was aware of the trouble and stayed away from the Andreanis and the new shop they had opened. Everyone, that is, except Sergio, who refused to take sides. He still visited Mariana, read with her, and took her for walks. Natalia described it as a "brotherly friendship" and saw in it no signs of romance.

Her own situation was another matter. She had allowed something to happen that she had hoped to avoid. And she told Gaetano that she had been put into a very compromising position, an impossible position. "What can come of it? Nothing but trouble. I feel sorry for your wife. I really do. And for all of us. You can't leave her. Even if you wanted to, I wouldn't allow you to. And so we will never have a life together, except for what we already have."

His response was another confession of love and need. "I lost you once before; I don't want to lose you again." It was only an expression of his helpless anxiety.

During the long, dreary winter they were all enmeshed in the "problem," and it became familiar like a chronic disease to which one could adjust but from which one was never free. What they felt or said seemed almost to depend on the weather or some incidental mood. A phrase could evoke tears. A kiss could evoke memories. Natalia threatened several times to break it off, but was never resolute. One day Francesca told Maria that she was afraid Gaetano might actually leave her. The very next day she said that she was sure he never would. Gaetano considered a separation, rejected it, considered it again, lost heart, got drunk, did nothing. He offered hypothetical situations, as though he were playing a very serious game. "If I went back to Italy on my own," he said once, "would you come and join me there? I could provide for my family and still have enough left over to establish myself in some kind of business." She said she herself had thought of going back to the house in Caserta. The picture she painted of herself, living out her life in widow's weeds, was nothing more, he said, than a kind of self-pity. She got angry. He said he was sorry for being cruel. From time to time they fell into each other's arms, as if it were for the last time. The feeling of hopelessness heightened their excitement, and they made passionate love.

In the spring, with the good weather, came renewed resolutions. It was Natalia who seemed most determined. The shop was going well, and she and Mariana were kept busy. They worked up front while three women sewed in the back. The mannequins were decently dressed and made an inviting display in the window. Her success made her confident. Over lunch one day she said: "Gaetano, I'm not going to see you for a month."

He looked puzzled. "What do you mean? Why?"

"Because as long as you are seeing me, I don't think you are able to discover how you feel about your wife."

"My wife and I barely speak."

"That's the whole point. I've said a hundred times that I do not intend to steal you away from her. On the other hand, if your marriage is hopeless and you leave it, that's another matter. If you were a free man our choices would be different, even if she refused to give you a divorce. But it is ridiculous to talk about what we would do if this or that. And I am not suggesting for a moment that you leave her because I have promised you anything. I have not."

"But Natalia, for a whole month?"

She patted him on the hand in a motherly way. "You'll manage, Gaetano. One way or another."

He didn't argue with her, but later he was angry, because he suspected she might be growing tired of him, or that she might be using this as an excuse to find another admirer. He was ready to believe almost anything but the truth. Her proposition was a serious one, almost a business proposition. She meant it, and it took him a while to realize it. When it finally sank in he was terrified. What she was doing was putting him to the test, perhaps even calling his bluff. He had talked too much about how unhappy he was with Francesca, but he had never actually said he would leave her. Now he had to decide.

That month was an agony for him, worse than the siege at Fort Macalle. In this more subtle battle it was not clear who or what the enemy was. Perhaps he himself was the enemy. He was thrown into doubt and confusion. He got angry and tried to deny that his love was real. "Love is an illusion," he said one night to Silvio, "that makes a man imagine he can live forever."

"Love is the invention of women to have a man by the balls," said Silvio.

"I must be crazy to be thinking about running off with her. I have a wife. I have a family."

"Leaving your wife was her idea, not yours."

"No, it was I who first suggested it."

"But *compare*, she's a very clever woman. She knows

how to put ideas in your head. She's a widow. She has your child. And now she wants you.''

''She doesn't know what she wants.''

Silvio laughed and refilled their glasses. ''She knows *exactly* what she wants. She wants to destroy your marriage and make a slave of you. She is the kind of woman who can break a man, who can bring him to his knees and make him beg. They are irresistible and dangerous, like the fire to the moth. And if she is ever yours, which she will never be, she will lose interest in you—because you will no longer be her romantic dream, her lover, but only her husband. Forget it, *compare*.''

Gaetano was persuaded. But no sooner had he made up his mind to give her up than he felt a yawning abyss inside of himself. He looked at himself in the mirror. There was a touch of gray in his hair. Pretty soon he would be getting old. He owed it to himself to take from life what he really wanted. But what was it that he really wanted? Was it love, money, success? Was it all these things? Was it none of them? He considered his assets and his family and weighed them against the intensity of those moments he had had with Natalia, moments in which he felt truly alive and happy. What did it matter that she was selfish and scheming? He could condemn her and love her all at once. It was a kind of madness.

He stayed away as he had promised, and in time he made love again to his wife in the old silence. She had been patient and now was forgiving. He admired her for that, and it made him more affectionate and understanding. Still, there was no love, no great love as with Natalia, and he had to decide how much that love was worth.

The days of the month went by, and he almost failed to notice how glorious the weather was, and how the trees in the park by the river blossomed and the old men took off their coats and rolled up their sleeves to play at *bocce* and smoke their hard black cigars. But one day he sat on a bench in the sun to watch and think, or maybe to forget, and a great warmth and calm came over him. He saw the women go by, pushing their baby carriages with a certain arrogant pride, or flaunting their fertile bellies, or carrying baskets of fruit and vegetables from the market. And he saw a group of boys playing in the distance along the river, their joy revealed in the energy of every movement. And he watched the old men lean forward with caution to roll the ball over the cinders of the *bocce* court, and then follow it with contortions of their bodies and exhortations or curses until it came to rest in victory or defeat.

By the time he was ready to get up and leave, he knew that his decision had been made—that this was his reality and Natalia was his dream.

# 3

Natalia was surprisingly understanding, but there was more in the expression on her face—a mixture of fatalistic acceptance and disappointment. It was this unresolved struggle in her that gave Natalia her special intensity and made her, at least for Gaetano, so difficult to resist. But he did. And he told her that he could not leave his wife. She smiled and said she understood. "Of course you can't," she said. "Why should you?"

The changes that followed were not very dramatic. In fact, from a distance they were hardly noticeable. Gaetano still saw her. Sometimes they even made love. But the dream—the romance—was over. And Francesca, sensing that the danger had passed, became herself again. She was, if anything, a little sorry for Gaetano—for what he had lost. She offered him affection, and she was pleased when he accepted, though she knew that he would never call it love.

The spring was viciously beautiful that year, as if designed by nature to distract the world from the grim weeds of war and chaos that were everywhere more apparent. The summer of 1913 was a strange season, lovely and ghostly all at once, a sad dream. It was as if the whole world were sailing away from the familiarities of the nineteenth century into the vast and unchartered sea of the modern world. Some people looked longingly backward, their hearts already sick with nostalgia; others looked forward with fear and trepidation.

Renato's heaviness of mind was due not only to the world situation but to things closer to home. He had never quite

recovered from his break with Gaetano. And they had moved
into a small and unpleasant shop on Second Avenue over
which the elevated train rumbled. He and Fanny had had their
dismal little marriage in City Hall, and then agreed to have a
child as soon as possible. But the child did not come, and
they were afraid it never would.

The problem was always with them, but they talked less
and less about it and tried to lose themselves in work and
politics. There were important upheavals on the labor front.
They found themselves deeply involved. In Westchester County
there was a rash of construction strikes. The IWP sent
volunteers. Sergio traveled frequently to the scene as a reporter.
There was an attempt to form a national union of Italian
workers. Behind it was Felix D'Alessandro, whose headquarters was in Mount Vernon. They gave him their full support
in *La Cronaca Proletaria*. Its circulation increased, and for
the first time they began to show a little profit. But their
bread and butter was their printing business, and they went on
turning out invitations, business cards, and leaflets.

Without asking, Sergio was given a raise. He now made
twelve dollars a week, which finally put him in a class with
ordinary laborers. He was shy about money, and even shyer
about women. A few months earlier he had celebrated his
twenty-second birthday and had asked himself the age-old
question: What was he going to do with his life? He could not
just do what he was doing year after year. He would wind up
like Renato, living in a small, sunless apartment and marching on endless picket lines to help some workers get a ten-
cent raise. He had to make plans. But what could he do?
Sometimes he walked to the West Side and looked longingly
at the buildings of Columbia University. One day, he promised himself, he would make inquiries there—and at the City
University farther uptown. He also thought about other jobs
he might find, but he was afraid of offending Renato, who had
done so much for him. He thought, too, about his personal
life, about women, about the possibility of getting married
someday. His "innocence," as he called it, was an embarrassment about which he never talked. On a list of resolutions he
made that summer he included: "Experience the act of love."
It was always best, he had heard, to approach an older
woman for this baptism of the flesh. He had had some minor
encounters, some flirtations, even an occasional kiss, but
most of what he knew came from his brothers and friends,

and from books. At a union excursion up the Hudson he had walked with an Irish girl, who said he was very handsome and that if he dared to kiss her she might find it difficult to resist. He misconstrued her feminine advances as maiden terrors and did everything he could to assure her that he had no such thing in mind. It was only later that he realized what it really had been all about and scolded himself for not taking advantage of the opportunity. In his daydreams he still saw the wooded path, the sun and shade, the mossy clearing by the stream, and he imagined how he might have taken that brazen young woman with the red-blond hair and creamy skin. He had only to assert himself and he might have had his way. His vision was novelistic. He could imagine the kisses and the fondling and the passionate embrace. He wasn't quite sure about how one got out of all those clothes, and about the act itself. He forced himself to think about it. The naked thighs. The little forest of hair. The soft belly, slightly rounded like a fruit. And then the thing itself. The woman's secret place. The gates of heaven, the gates of hell. The vision blurred. His heart pounded. The very opening itself remained a mystery. As schoolboys they had drawn pictures of it—a slit buried in hair. But he knew it wasn't quite that way. It was also a place of blood. The seed went in and babies came out. Other things, too, came out. His desire was spoiled by disgust and fear. Had he been religious, there were times when he might have chosen the priesthood and celibacy.

It was all very confusing. His body urged him on. It demanded this act of love, as he called it. He had wet dreams. And he indulged in that private erotic pleasure that did not require the presence of a woman. It was a crisis from which he could no longer escape. His father seemed to be aware of what was going on, and there were times when Sergio wished they were closer. Their conversations were brief and awkward. One day Gaetano said: "Perhaps you ought to think about getting married. You are not the type to fool around with the women, like your brothers. You will need a wife, somebody to look after you. My friend Primo Gentile has a very nice daughter, Felice. She's about eighteen or nineteen now. She is modest and hardworking and very healthy. She will make a good mother. If you want, I will talk to him and—"

Sergio wanted to appreciate this paternal interest, but he blushed and felt his anger rise. "No," he said, interrupting his father, "don't talk to him. I am not ready to get married, and when I am I will find my own woman."

"Suit yourself," said Gaetano, "but don't wait too long. It's not right for a man to be too long without a woman. And this girl won't last. She has a nice dowry. Gentile has a big meat market. He does very well. He just bought a new car. What's more, there are no sons. So, eventually—"

"Eventually, I can be a butcher. Is that what you're saying?"

"No, no, but he has to leave his money and his business to somebody. He will treat you like a son. He will be generous. I will too. You and Felice can have a good life. She is not a great beauty, but she has a nice way about her."

Sergio relented. He reluctantly agreed to meet the girl and give the matter some thought. But once he was out of the house and striding down the street, with his hands thrust into his pockets, his anger returned. His father made him feel like a boy, unmanly and weak. Gaetano's instinct for authority was oppressive. Sergio felt like an unfinished piece of business that his father had to take care of. It was not that way with Antonio and Stefano. No, he thought, he would keep his distance. He would do things his own way in his own time.

There were prostitutes in the neighborhood. He knew who they were, but he could not bring himself to use them. They filled him with disgust and contempt. He imagined the parade of men pushing themselves into their stinking bodies. Dirty sheets. Perfume. Semen. Sweat. The humiliation of buying it like a piece of meat in the marketplace. It was not for him. He needed a woman who cared. Not a young woman who might be ruined, but one who was already mature and compassionate. But who? He tried to think of the women he knew. None of them suited that romantic ideal he had in his mind, that wonderful courtesan of the novels.

Spring ripened into summer. July was hot and humid. The three-room apartment over the printshop was directly opposite the elevated subway. The trains went by and rattled the windows. They were so noisy that one had to stop talking for a few moments. One could see the passengers, rows of anonymous faces. Straw hats and newspapers. Women with bandannas or bonnets. Sometimes the trains were very crowded and the passengers sat and stood like animals in a trance.

One rainy Sunday Fanny insisted that Sergio come for dinner. Renato was in Mount Vernon conferring with Felix D'Alessandro. "I don't want to eat alone," she said. Sergio often had dinner at the apartment, but Renato was always there. Still, he gave very little thought to the invitation until he actually found himself alone with Fanny. The gloomy afternoon, the rain against the windows, and the fragrance of food cooking all conspired to make him sharply aware of her presence. What's more, she had done something to her hair that made her look younger and more attractive. She was only thirty-two, but she had developed the habit of frowning, as though she could not conceal her deep disappointment with life. That dismal Sunday, however, the frown was gone. "I refuse to be miserable," she said. "Let him go off to Mount Vernon. Let him walk the line with D'Alessandro. We will have a marvelous meal and a bottle of good wine. I am sick and tired of worrying about other people's hardships and unhappiness. I have a few problems of my own. And today is for me. I even bought myself a dress. We can't afford it, but I don't care. Do you like it?" She held out her arms and turned to show him. It was a soft green, like a meadow, and revealed her full figure.

"It's very nice," he said. "You look very . . . beautiful." He stumbled over the compliment, afraid it might not sound quite right.

She smiled. "Thank you, Sergio. You're very gallant. Some woman is going to be very lucky to have you." Then she kissed him quickly on the cheek and went off to the kitchen, leaving him there in the living room, flushed with embarrassment.

He stayed there for a few moments, struggling with indecision and desire. Was this more than an invitation to dinner? he wondered. A train rumbled by. He glanced out the rain-streaked window. But no—he scolded himself—it was unthinkable. Not Fanny. Not Renato's wife. And yet weren't they all free thinkers? Didn't they all deny that anyone could own anyone else? It was not even a question of morality—

He was interrupted in his speculations by Fanny, who came back with two glasses and a bottle of wine. She handed the bottle and a corkscrew to him. "Here," she said, "you open it. It is a thing that men like to do."

She watched him as he carefully turned the wooden handle until it went in almost to the hilt. Then he put the bottle between his legs and began to pull. It was something he had learned from his father many years ago. At first the cork would not yield, but then slowly, gently, he drew it out. It made a whisper of a *pop* that made Fanny smile. "Ah," she said, "well done. Your father would be proud of you."

"I only wish—" said Sergio, pouring the wine into the glasses. He paused to pick out a piece of cork.

"What's the matter? Have you two been fighting again?" she said.

He reached across the coffee table to hand her a glass of wine. She was sitting on the sagging couch. He sat down on an old oak chair that looked as though it had been rescued from Massafero, the local junkman. "No, not exactly," he said. "But he's not proud of me. He never was. I really don't understand why."

"Are you sure? Maybe it's just your imagination. Maybe it's just a misunderstanding. You should have a talk with him. You should say what you feel—straight out."

"I can't talk to him. He doesn't want to hear what I have to say. He shuts me out. But still he wants to run my life. Now he wants to arrange a marriage for me—with the butcher's daughter." He said this with a little smile that Fanny's eyes returned.

"He's just old-fashioned," she said. "And a man."

"And what am I? A boy? I'm twenty-two years old."

"Yes, but without much experience in these things."

"How do you know?"

Her smile was playful. "I can tell," she said.

He blushed and reached for his wine. "Well, I don't care. He has no right to interfere in my private life. This is America, not Italy."

She looked toward the kitchen suddenly. "Ah, the water is boiling. I have to put in the pasta. Are you hungry?"

"Starved," he said.

The meal was simple but in its own way rather elegant: clear soup, spaghetti with oil and garlic, and a breast of chicken in an egg-and-lemon sauce.

"Ah," said Sergio. "Wonderful. Delicious. Too bad Renato is not here."

Fanny shrugged. "It was his choice to go."

They ate at a small table in the living room. It was covered with a linen cloth that had grown yellow with age. In a glass vase there were two roses. "Remember the signs that the shopgirls carried in Lawrence?" she said.

"Of course."

"We want bread and roses too." She tilted her head and

looked for a moment toward the rain-streaked window. Then she picked up her glass and emptied it. "Well, that's what I want too. I think of those girls often. How sad. And how quickly that bloom of youth fades. A few years—and then it's gone." Her eyes blinked. Her lips quivered.

Sergio frowned. He didn't know what to do. Then he reached across the table and touched her hand.

"I'm sorry," she said. "I'm acting just like a woman. Perhaps we *are* all the same after all." She forced herself to smile, as if to hold off the tears. "Come, we'll open another bottle of wine. To hell with the rain and the revolution and everything."

She took the wine to the sofa and said: "Come, sit here by me and tell me all your secrets. We never get a chance to talk about anything but politics. Tell me what's going on in that funny head of yours. Tell me about all the women you've made love to."

He laughed. "That would be the world's shortest conversation."

She looked at him in disbelief. "You mean you have *never even once*—"

He shook his head. "Never. There, now you know it all. Isn't it boring? I wish I had adventures to describe, but I don't. Perhaps I could make up a few."

"But surely there have been opportunities."

"I suppose there have been, but I think I was too stupid to take advantage of them."

"Why? Are you afraid?"

He shrugged. "I don't know. Shy. Afraid. Naive. Something."

"But not without desire."

"Oh, no, I have plenty of that. Sometimes it's hard to think about anything else."

She smiled. "You poor boy. But you must remember, Sergio, that women, too, have desires. They, too, want to make love, whether they are married or not. If you approach them properly—"

"But how is *properly*? Am I supposed to marry them before I kiss them? Girls are so guarded. It's as bad as the old country. They are afraid of their fathers. They are afraid of being ruined."

"Yes, but they still have desires. It is unnatural to deny

them. The fear of being ruined is beaten into them. But there are ways—"

"What do you mean?"

"Ways of avoiding—" She took a deep breath. "Sergio, dear boy, it is not as easy as you think for a woman to become pregnant. It can only happen during a few days. Do you know these things?"

"I guess so. But what exactly am I supposed to do? I can't just walk up to a girl and—"

"Of course not, you silly thing. A woman must be *approached*. You have to talk to her. You have to arouse her interest."

"I can talk. But I can't seem to touch, for some reason."

"You can't just grab them. You have to be gradual. You have to reassure them. Come here. Come closer. I will give you a lesson."

"But I—but we—"

She laughed. The wine showed in the color of her cheeks. "No, no, you naughty boy. Don't imagine that I am trying to seduce you. I am only going to give you a little advice. But first you must give us a little wine. It is a nice way to relax. It lifts the spirits."

He came closer, until they were sitting shoulder to shoulder on the sofa. He could feel her warmth and smell her fragrance and the room was still alive with the perfume of food. The rain was falling harder and made a soft sound against the window.

"Now," she said, "put down your glass. Turn a little toward me. Pretend to take a serious interest in what I am saying. Look sympathetic and loving. Then put your arm across the back of the sofa, and after a few minutes let it slip to my shoulders. There. You see? It is possible to touch a woman after all. If she allows you a little liberty, then after a while she will allow you more."

"Like what?"

"Well, you could touch her hand or her arm. Eventually, her cheek. You could compliment her on the softness of her skin. You could say something about her eyes or her lips. Women like to be complimented. Men are vain, but we are worse."

"Fanny," he said in a lowered voice, "you are very beautiful."

"That's very good. Very convincing."

"No, I mean it. You *are*. And you understand."

"I'm older than you are."

"Yes, but it's more than that."

"Now, don't get carried away."

"I'm sorry. I—I would like to kiss you. Do you mind?"

"No, I don't mind. But just a little. Remember, it's just a game. Don't get too serious."

His lips were trembling when they touched hers. He lingered for a moment without parting them, and then withdrew. "Not like that," she whispered, and then urged him toward her again. "Like this." Her lips were moist and open. He felt her tongue instructing him. And in another moment he understood what the kiss was all about. His own tongue responded. Their mouths conversed. The revelation made him more passionate. He pressed himself against her and could feel her breasts and how quickly she was breathing. She pulled away.

He looked puzzled. "And what now?"

She reached for her wine. "This is the crucial point. If we were serious—well, we would get serious."

"And what would I do?"

She took a long sip of wine and looked at him for a moment. Then she put her glass down and said: "You would do this." She took his hand and placed it on her breast. She held it there until he overcame his shyness and began to fondle her. They kissed again. His voice became a low whisper. "And then?"

He felt her doing something to her dress. She had opened herself to him and he felt the nakedness of her breast. She stiffened and softened and sighed. She stroked his back and his hair and then urged his head down until his lips were touching her nipple. She held her breast to him as though he were a child. "Yes," she sighed, "yes, do that."

He was aroused, but at each step seemed to need her permission to go on. He could no longer speak. The sound he made was a kind of incoherent moan, a plea for help, for some relief from the mystery that drove him, almost against his will.

"It's all right," she said, stroking him. "It's all right." He devoured her breast like a baby. Her head tilted back against the sofa. Her eyes were closed. Her body lifted toward him. And then, suddenly, she pulled herself away and stood up. He looked at her with a dazed expression on his face. His mouth was red and moist. There was a moment of indecision.

Then she reached out her hand to him. "Come with me," she said. He took her hand and she led him into the shaded semidarkness of the small bedroom.

He stood there like a schoolboy, still not sure what his teacher had in mind. "Take off your clothes and come to bed," she said. "And don't say anything. Don't think about anything."

He obeyed as though he were moving in a dream. But he paused at the final garment. She, too, had taken off her clothes and she was sitting on the edge of the bed watching him. "Come here," she whispered. He stood before her, his excitement impossible to conceal. She pulled down the cotton shorts and could almost feel him blush. He was stiff and throbbing, as though at any moment he might lose control. She caressed him gently and kissed him there. Then she took him in her mouth, and he came with a cry of agony and joy. She did not wince but took him hungrily, as if she, too, desired this.

After a moment or two she got onto the bed, which was made up with only a sheet. She made room beside her. He lay down and stared at the ceiling as though it were the sky— from which he expected some terrible judgment to descend upon him. They were quiet for a while. She lay on her side and watched him, her head propped up on one elbow. She touched him as if to calm him, running her hand over his chest and limbs. Before long she saw his manhood rise again, stirring like a creature that had a life of its own. She touched the creature. It hardened in her hand. He sighed.

He turned toward her. She eased back against the pillow and opened her legs. "Now you must make love to me," she said. And she urged him onto her, touching him and kissing him as though to say it was all right. Her voice faded into excitement. Nature now guided him. He held his weight from her with his arms and looked down into her face. Her mouth was open. Her eyes were closed. He felt himself at the dampness between her thighs. And then he felt himself pressing into her, slowly, with small strokes, until he was all the way in. He paused for a moment, as though he were recording that first union in the deepest part of his mind. And then the animal in him took over and he lost control. His body plunged and heaved. He felt his muscles tighten. He felt himself sweating. She was moaning and whispering, but he could not make out anything. There was the rush of the sea in his ears, and the pounding of surf. It happened suddenly. The wave rose, gathered itself, and broke. His arms trembled. His weight descended upon her. And she received it with accepting arms and warm white thighs.

They slept for several hours and then, in the middle of the night, made love again, this time more calmly and with a different kind of satisfaction.

In the morning, when Sergio woke up, he found the place beside him empty. He heard Fanny in the kitchen. He had to shake his head to make sure that he had not been dreaming. Then he got up and quickly put on his clothes.

Fanny was making coffee. She was dressed for work and looked businesslike, but there was a softness in her expression. Sergio paused in the doorway, his shirt half buttoned, his hair disheveled. "Come and have some coffee," she said. "And for God's sake don't say anything foolish. And don't imagine that anything like this is going to happen again. It was good for you and it was good for me. But that's all—"

"Are you going to tell Renato?"

"No. And neither are you. In a way, I wish I could. But for all of his idealism I don't think he would understand."

"No, I don't suppose he would."

"And don't feel bad. You did nothing wrong. You're young and passionate. Now, sit down and have some coffee. We have to open the shop. . . ."

# 4

Dr. Carlo Martello's office was in a brownstone on 116th Street. The narrow three-story building was also his residence. There he lived with his meticulous wife, Theresa, and his twenty-four-year-old son, Alfredo. He also had a daughter, Isabella, who was married to a lawyer in White Plains—"a very influential lawyer," he was always quick to point out.

One late afternoon in August he and his family entertained Natalia and Mariana. It was understood by everyone that the purpose of the get-together was to introduce Mariana and Alfredo. The whole occasion was painfully formal and awkward.

They sat in the parlor. The drapes were drawn against the hot sun. Everything was shaded and subdued. The Martellos even talked in a soft, controlled way that gave one the impression someone had just died. It was Theresa who established the tone of the house. She came from a good family in Rome and was very contemptuous of all these Neapolitans and Sicilians in the neighborhood. Her face was tight and her lips were drawn together in such a way as to make her mouth look abnormally small. She wore a summery gray dress and a double strand of pearls, which she handled constantly. "Would you like some more tea?" she said to Natalia. "Tea is very refreshing in such weather."

"Yes, it is," said Natalia. "I have always preferred it to coffee."

She hesitated, as though she were uncertain of how she should proceed with these people. The Signora Martello was not easy to talk to. She had distant and disapproving eyes. And she was, if anything, more calculating than Natalia herself. Natalia felt, instinctively, that it would have been a mistake to ramble on in her usual light and talkative way. It would have betrayed her nervousness and her eagerness for the match. And she *was* eager—for several reasons. There was Sergio's increasing interest, which, of course, had to be discouraged. And then there was always the possibility that Mariana might be attracted to one of the cruder young men in the neighborhood. That, in her mind, would be an even greater disaster than incest. But there was still another development that filled Natalia with concern. Her daughter, under the influence of a certain mother superior, was becoming too interested in the religious life, and there was some danger that she might be seduced into becoming a nun. Mariana was her only child, and Natalia was determined to see her marry well and provide her with the grandchildren she always imagined she would have when she was old.

Signora Martello's smile was like a wince. She held a silver tray covered with a small pyramid of cakes. Corseted and perched, she turned to Mariana. "Another cake, my dear?"

"No, thank you," said Mariana, barely managing a sickly

smile. Behind her shy facade she was hacking Signora Martello to pieces with an ax.

Dr. Martello was talking about his illustrious family. He stood by a wall of portraits and photographs in carved and gilded frames. He was a portly man with a large mustache that was parted in the middle. In his hand the coffee cup seemed ridiculously small.

"And this," he said, "is my beloved father, a doctor of veterinary medicine at Latina." An oval face stared from an oval frame. It was a proud sad face from a sepia past, but now firmly in the grip of death. One knew it without asking. "It was my home, until I moved as a student to Rome. Ah, yes, the eternal city . . ."

In Mariana's mind his voice faded into noise, into a kind of punctuated hum. Her eyes drifted about the room. She was uncomfortably warm. Her cotton dress was buttoned to a white collar. Prim and schoolgirlish. She sat with her hands folded in her lap. She glanced at her mother, who was pretending to be interested in the Martello genealogy. She looked surreptitiously at Alfredo. He was inoffensive enough, but dreary-looking, as though his parents had drained out all his blood and embalmed him to look like the perfect son. She knew instantly that she could never allow such a creature to touch her, and she promised herself that she would resist to the death whatever arrangements were made.

Mariana was not a simple girl. There was something deceptive about her appearance. Her smooth white skin and absolutely symmetrical face gave her a saintly look. In severe convent schools she had learned composure and poise. She wore no makeup, of course, and her black hair was parted in the middle and neatly drawn back. In her deep brown eyes there sometimes shone a sensitivity that bordered on violent intelligence. She had loved her father but had never really trusted her mother. There were only two people in the world to whom she could talk with any degree of honesty. One was Mother Margaret Mary of the Sisters of Mercy, a convent devoted mainly to the running of an orphanage near Lexington Avenue. The other Sergio Adamo.

Dr. Martello moved from the wall of portraits to his son. Alfredo sat as though he, too, were already prepared to take his place in the gallery of the dead. He was a clean-shaven lad with the gaunt look and blank eyes of a mediocre scholar.

Dr. Martello put his hand on his son's shoulder. "By next

summer Alfredo will be graduated from the School of Optometry at Columbia University.'' He squared his shoulders with pride. ''We plan to establish him in a practice right here in the area, where there is a great need. It is a wonderful field, full of opportunities. Of course, I tried to persuade him to follow in my footsteps, but he has a certain aversion to some of the—how shall I put it? Some of the more unpleasant aspects of my profession.'' He was addressing himself mainly to Natalia, acknowledging her as the negotiator for her daughter's hand. And Natalia had a way of looking receptive and understanding. Signora Martello eyed her with cold suspicion.

When the visit was over and they were on their way home in the hazy heat, Natalia said: ''Well, my darling, what did you think of them?''

''What do you want me to think?'' said Mariana, containing her fury.

''Whatever you want.''

They walked on, arm in arm. Mariana said nothing. Natalia became impatient.

''Well?'' she said.

''Well what?''

''Don't you have anything at all to say?''

''What I have to say you won't like, so why should I say it?''

''Mariana, don't be difficult. I grant you they are a bit stuffy, but you must consider our future—your future.''

Mariana stopped on the sidewalk and drew away from her mother's grasp. ''All right, then, I will tell you what I think. I think the Martellos are dreadful people. And I will have nothing to do with that horrible son of theirs. I would rather join the Sisters of Mercy and do something useful with my life.''

''Useful? You call that useful, surrendering your womanhood and personal happiness?''

The perfect symmetry of Mariana's face gave way and she burst into tears. ''There is only one person who can make me happy,'' she said, ''and he doesn't even know it.'' She turned and ran the remaining block to their house, leaving her mother standing there dumbfounded.

The meaning of Mariana's outburst descended suddenly on

Natalia like a summer storm. Oh, my God, she said to herself, she's in love with Sergio Adamo.

The following Sunday Sergio took Mariana to a band concert in Central Park. Natalia would like to have prevented it, but it had already been arranged. That would be the last time they'd be alone together, she promised herself, and she would have a serious talk with Gaetano right away.

The day was beautiful. The haze and heat had gone, and the air was crystal clear. There were horse-drawn carriages in the park, and bicycles and parasols and people in their Sunday clothes. Children ran across the meadows and sailed their boats in the lake. Life seemed to be bursting from every bush and tree, from the very air itself.

For both of them everything seemed different. For him because he had been initiated into the mysteries of man and woman by Fanny; for her because she had been forced to see herself as a prospective wife and, therefore, a woman. The children's game of tutor and student was over. He offered her his arm, and she took it. She smiled at him, but there was a sadness in her smile. "Is anything wrong?" he said. Without hesitation she told him about the visit to the Martellos'. "How awful," he said.

"It was very humiliating. They kept looking at me, as though I were something in a store window that they were thinking of buying. Like one of those mannequins in our shop."

"You know, it never occurred to me, Mariana, but I guess you are getting to that age—I mean, where marriage is a possibility. Somehow I've always thought of you as—as younger."

"As a child, you mean."

"Well, as a matter of fact—"

"On my next birthday, in a few months, I will be eighteen. I can assure you, Sergio, that I am not a child in any way."

Sergio had to pause in their walk and look at her more closely. "For a moment you sounded just like your mother."

"Don't say that. I'm not like my mother. Not at all."

"I'm sorry. I meant it as a compliment."

"Well, if you want to compliment me, think of something better to say than that."

"I had no idea you had such a temper."

"There's a great deal you don't know about me, Sergio.

You've been treating me like a child, and so, naturally, I've been acting like a child. But I know more than you think I do.''

"About what?"

"About everything."

"That's a big boast."

"You'd be surprised."

He looked at her and smiled, delighted by her fiery manner. He had known her for a year—yet perhaps he had not known her at all. All during the concert he was preoccupied with her. A certain excitement made his heart beat as fast as the martial music on the bandstand.

Afterward they walked around the lake and lingered against some large gray rocks. Not far from them a couple picnicked amorously on the grass, half hidden by a striped umbrella. The man was in shirt sleeves and suspenders, and the girl's hair was loose and long. They basked in the sun, the man on one elbow, the girl reclining. Then they saw him lean over and kiss her. She did not resist. They heard her laughter across the lush green lawn.

Mariana stared with obvious curiosity. "Have you ever done that?" she said.

"What?"

"That!" She nodded toward the couple.

"Oh! Well—a bit. But it's not the sort of thing one talks about."

"Why not? You're supposed to be my tutor, but you never teach me anything really interesting."

"I thought you already knew everything. A little while ago you said—"

"I was lying. I don't know anything. Sometimes I feel so stupid." She stooped down and picked up a stone and threw it petulantly into the lake.

"You really *are* upset, aren't you? What is it? The Martellos?"

"Oh, I don't know. It's everything. It's all so confusing. Sometimes I just want to run away from it all—from my mother, the shop." She hesitated. "From you."

"From me? But what have I done?"

"Nothing!" she said, and walked away from him along the edge of the water.

He followed, confused and apologetic but on the brink of

the revelation that there had, for some time, been something between them that he could not allow himself to realize.

She stopped in a sheltered clearing. Ducks swam away from the shore, leaving trails in the water behind them. He stood close to her. Suddenly she turned and was in his arms. He wasn't sure how it had happened. Then he was kissing her. Or was she kissing him? Her face was flushed. Her breathing was heavy. It was as if a secret door to passion had been opened for both of them, and they no longer needed words. They spoke in kisses. They sighed. They smiled. And, after a while, he whispered: "Little Mariana, I love you. I should have known. How could I have been so stupid?"

"Sometimes you *are* stupid," she said, and they laughed and then lost themselves in another embrace.

They wandered back, wrapped in the joy of young love. The world dissolved. Nothing else mattered. Horses trotted by. The sky was very blue, and the white clouds were the cotton hills of a magical universe.


Natalia arranged to have lunch downtown with Gaetano on Wednesday. It was Mariana's afternoon at the orphange of the Sisters of Mercy. They went to Alberto's, where they had not been for some time. A familiar old waiter greeted them with an understanding look and brought them a carafe of chilled white wine.

"Ah, you remembered," said Gaetano.

"Of course," said the waiter. "And you are in luck today. The cannelloni is very special."

"Good! Then we'll have the cannelloni and a nice salad. Whatever you think."

Gaetano poured the wine. Natalia looked around nervously. "So what are we going to do?"

"Is there any chance at all of engaging her to Alfredo Martello?"

"No, none whatsoever. She doesn't like him, or his family."

"I can't say that I blame her. That Martello is such a pompous old fool. And his wife—*Dio santo!* The kiss of death. She must be like a corpse in bed. Is there anybody else? Anybody more congenial—more manly?"

"No. What do you expect to find in a neighborhood like this? Laborers and shopkeepers. Besides, she won't even look at anyone these days. I can see by the way she acts that she's hopelessly in love. I never imagined it would happen. They seemed to be so much like brother and sister. I was beginning to think it was some recognition in the blood.''

"I warned you, Natalia. I warned you at the very beginning."

"But you said he was not interested in women. And he wasn't. Now, all of a sudden—"

"Yes, all of a sudden he's come to his senses. And all of a sudden Mariana is a grown woman. However we do it, we must keep them apart. We must forbid them from seeing one another.''

"But what can we tell them? What reason can we give?"

He looked at her with a wrinkled forehead and raised eyebrows. "I can think of one possibility."

"What?" Her eyes narrowed, as though she already knew what he was going to say.

"We could tell them the truth."

"No! I don't want to do that. Mariana would never forgive me. It would break her heart. She loved her father too much."

"You forget, my dear, that *I* am her father."

"Please, Gaetano, I can't. Don't ask me to. She is too fragile. And besides, it would not be fair to him. Nicolo so desperately wanted a child. He accepted the circumstances. To take her from him now would be like robbing the dead. No, let it be. Let it be as it is. We must find some other way. Perhaps Sergio can be persuaded to marry this Gentile girl. This Felice, or whatever her name is. You said he liked her well enough.''

"He does, but he doesn't love her."

"If it weren't for the business I would take Mariana back to Italy. But really, Gaetano, there's nothing for us there anymore. I couldn't go into business. I couldn't even work. Here I have an opportunity to make some money, to become independent. Perhaps in a few years—"

"In a few years it will be too late. Maybe even in a few months or a few weeks. What if they should be alone? What if something should happen?''

"Don't even say it. Oh, God, what a horrible retribution for such an ordinary sin. I never thought—"

"Who could have imagined such a thing?" said Gaetano. "It's my own fault. I should have discouraged you from coming. I should never have answered your letter."

"And I was a fool to write to you. But I thought—I thought there was still something possible between us.''

"If it had happened that way, what then? What would you have told Mariana?"

"I don't know. But it never came to that, did it? You could not leave the woman you never wanted to marry in the first place."

"Don't be bitter. You know how these things are."

"I'm sorry. Sometimes I think I must be insane."

He reached over and touched her hand. "Sometimes we are all that way. We don't know what we want."

The food came. They ate and talked about other things, but then, afterward, drifted back again to Sergio and Mariana. "Is it true," said Gaetano, "that she has talked about joining the nuns?"

"Yes, but I don't want her to do that. It's not right for her. Anyhow, I don't think she's serious. Not now."

"Well, then, there's nothing left for us but to forbid them to see each other again. And it will be mainly up to you, because your daughter is not of age. God knows what I will tell Sergio. Forgive me if I lie to him. It is all a lie anyway. . . ."

On Sunday Sergio came for dinner. Francesca, who was always delighted to have the whole family together, made a special meal, from the *zuppa di zucchini* to the stuffed leg of lamb. But the edge of their joy was blunted by a vague uneasiness in the air. She could not tell exactly what it was, but she sensed that something was wrong. When Gaetano insisted that Sergio come out for a walk after dinner, she was sure of it.

They walked toward the river in the late August heat. It was about four o'clock, and there was a Sunday lull over the city. "I mustn't be too long," said Sergio. "I was planning to stop at the Andreanis."

"You still go there, then?"

"Oh, yes, but not very often. Mama doesn't know. I guess she would rather I didn't. I mean, after all that—"

"Yes, yes, I understand, but perhaps she's right. Perhaps you should not go. It's an awkwardness for all of us."

"I only go to give lessons to Mariana."

"Well, she doesn't need your lessons anymore. And her mother would prefer that you stayed away now."

"If she wants me to stay away, why doesn't she tell me herself?"

"Because she's embarrassed. She asked me to talk to you." He lowered his voice and tried to sound confidential and man-to-man. "You see, son, it's like this. She has a hope of making a good match for her daughter, and she doesn't want her affections distracted. Do you understand?"

Sergio's voice hardened. "No, I don't understand. If you mean Alfredo Martello, forget it. She's not interested."

"How do you know?"

"She told me."

"Well, it's none of your business. And if Mariana's mother no longer wants you there—well, that's it. The girl is only seventeen. She has no choice in the matter. So give me your word that you'll stay away."

"I can't do that."

"Why not?"

He hesitated. They crossed the street quickly against the traffic of cars and carriages. When they were on the other side Sergio stopped and looked at his father. "Because I am in love with her, and I hope to marry her someday."

"Impossible!" shouted Gaetano.

"But why? I'm as good as Alfredo Martello. And what's more, Mariana is in love with me too."

"Don't ask me why. Believe me when I tell you that it can never be. I will not permit it. Nor will Natalia."

"And you expect me to obey you—just like that?"

Gaetano was shaking and he was almost panting for breath. "Yes," he said. "Yes. I am your father. Don't ever forget that. If you don't do what I tell you, you will pay for it one way or another. Is that clear?"

They fell into a silence and came to the river. Gaetano took out his handkerchief and wiped his forehead and the back of his neck.

"And what is *her* reason?" said Sergio in a quiet voice that was suddenly tense with suspicion.

Gaetano shook his head as though he were lost in a private quarrel with himself. "It's no use," he muttered. "No use!"

"What do you mean?"

Gaetano looked at his son with sad eyes, in which almost all was revealed. "What I mean, Sergio, is that her reason and my reason are the same. Now do you understand?"

Sergio turned pale. "You're her father," he said in a heavy whisper.

"Please, Sergio, she must never know. Never!"

He backed away, as if from something monstrous. ''Oh, no! Oh, Christ!'' he said. And then he turned and broke into a run along the river and out of sight into the park. Gaetano sat down on a stone bench and buried his face in his hands. A flight of gulls circled and landed on the pilings of the wooden pier.

Sergio walked aimlessly for hours, on into the darkness and the gathering storm. The sun went down on a bed of embers under a curtain of clouds. He had come clear across Manhattan Island and looked into the swirling waters of the Hudson River from an abandoned pier. The curtain descended. The sunlight faded, and another kind of light flashed in the turbulent sky, followed by thunder. The world was a vast drum, across which some rough beast galloped. The Palisades disappeared into darkness. Lightning cracked the sky. The rain came down. He hardly noticed it at first. Then he welcomed it as a blessing that dowsed the fever in his brain and washed away his rage. Still he went on, his clothes wet through, his body feeling naked against the elements. He was left now only with the open wound of this latest revelation. His own self-pity was like salt in that wound. He thought of killing himself. He thought of killing his father. He thought of running away. But each successive thought washed over the previous one and wiped it away.

By midnight he was exhausted, emotionally and physically. He made his way back to his furnished room and fell asleep instantly in his damp clothes, as if sleep were an easier kind of death. He woke up at dawn, feeling as though he had been beaten up in the night. His body ached. His mouth was dry. He had almost forgotten what it was all about until he took off his wet clothes and found himself standing naked in the middle of the room. He went to the mirror, as if to see who this wounded creature really was. He barely recognized himself. And then it all came back again—the impossible situation and the only possible solution. He would go away for a while, far away, and hope that time and distance would conspire to set things right.

Within less than a week everything was accomplished, including a letter for Mariana, which Gaetano had promised to deliver in person in exchange for Sergio's promise that he would say nothing in it about her real father.

Mariana read the letter over and over in the weeks and months that followed, hoping to find in it hidden meanings that would contradict the obvious message. At last a dull fatalism settled over her, and she accepted as truth what she read:

Dearest Mariana,

My sudden departure for Naples may come to you as a surprise, but I had come to a crucial time in my life, and my decision had to be made swiftly. I would have seen you in person before leaving, but seeing you was probably the only thing that could have kept me from going, and that would have been a mistake. We were on the verge of something that could never be. You are too young for such commitments, and I am too devoted to other things. Love is a luxury that I cannot afford. And I have nothing else to offer. I have given my life to mankind, as surely as a priest gives his to God. I have been thinking for a long time about continuing my education. My father's brother Pietro is now a monsignor and the dean of a very good college in Rome. The opportunity came suddenly, and it would have been foolish of me to turn it down. The term will begin almost as soon as I arrive, and I will have a hundred preparations to make. Forgive me if I have disappointed you in any way. My thoughts will be with you always, but I must find my way alone.

                    With Deepest Affection,
                    Sergio

Winter came like a stranger, and Mariana felt alone in the cold gray days. She spent less time at the shop and more time at the convent, in spite of her mother's objections. Natalia was shrewd enough to know that the best way to drive her into the hands of the church would be an open conflict. Therefore, she did not absolutely prevent her from going; she merely tried to point out to her that she had certain obligations at the shop. When this appeal to her sense of duty failed, she turned to a more personal approach. "Mariana," she said one day, "I realize that you have had a terrible disappointment, but it would be so childish of you to assume that your life is over at seventeen. If every girl who ever had a broken heart joined a convent, we would all be nuns.''

Mariana responded with mild curiosity. ''Did you ever have a broken heart?''

Natalia's eyes fluttered for a moment. ''Of course. When I was young. Your age, perhaps.''

''Tell me about it. Who was he?''

''Well, really, it was so long ago. . . . In fact, I can barely remember him. You see how time takes care of these things, like the broken skin that heals and leaves no scar.''

''Yes, but who was he?''

Natalia grew impatient. She had the feeling that her daughter was probing maliciously, that in a way she was taunting, as if to say that perhaps Natalia had never really been in love.

''Believe me, my dear, you are not the first girl who has ever fallen in love.''

''And did you have a love affair when you were young? A *real* love affair?''

''At that age it is hard to tell what is real.''

''But when you married my father, were you—''

''Mariana! What are you thinking? Of course I was.'' Her face had blossomed into a blush of embarrassment and anger.

''And did he leave you?''

''Who?''

''The boy you loved.''

''Oh, this is getting ridiculous. It wasn't like that at all. He was just a young soldier. We talked. We laughed. I imagined I was in love with him, but in a schoolgirlish way. And when he left I cried. You see, that's all I meant. Young girls are very susceptible to this sort of thing. They try their little wings of love. It takes time to learn to fly.'' She was pleased with her metaphor and gave her daughter a bosomy smile and a reassuring kiss on the cheek.

It didn't work. Mariana's sadness deepened with the gloom of winter. She grew more silent and more serious. She brought home religious literature to read, given to her by Mother Margaret Mary. Natalia began to think of the Mother Superior as a kind of rival. She was convinced that her daughter was being seduced into the convent by this woman, and perhaps even seduced in another way. She had heard stories about such women and the strange things that went on in convents. She was worldly enough to believe that no woman's passions could be entirely contained. And she could even understand how one woman might love another, even as men and women do, though the thought was repulsive to her. She knew that her daughter was vulnerable, spiritually and otherwise. And that she might easily find comfort in the arms of the church and affection in the arms of a strong personality like Mother Margaret Mary. But she did not know how to say these things to Mariana, and as the winter wore on, she had the awful feeling that she was failing and that she would lose her only child.

Mariana attended mass at St. Joseph's, a local church in the old Neapolitan style with plaster saints and a bleeding Christ. And she went there often just to pray. It was a poor church, but it had a certain warmth and mystery. The stained glass was so dim that hardly any light came in. Incense lingered in the musty air. In the winter the stone floor was often damp with melted snow, and there were strange drafts that made the candles flicker as though there were ghosts or spirits in the place.

In a shallow niche to the left of the altar was a tall statue of the Virgin Mary in a typical pose—her hands held out, her pale face tilted, her eyes soft with compassion, her blue robes descending in convincing folds. This statue was Mariana's favorite, and she often knelt before it. She preferred to come at odd hours, when there were not many people in the church, and she spoke her prayers in a private whisper.

One day she stopped on her way home from the Sisters of Mercy. Mother Margaret Mary had asked her to think seriously about joining the order, and to pray for guidance. "It is a calling that must come from within, from your very soul. It is the courtship of Christ, to whom one day you might make your vows, much as the bride at the altar gives herself in holy promises to the man she loves." She had talked many times before about the inner workings of the order, and about the long hard road from novitiate to final vows, but this time she seemed more intense, and before she released Mariana into the dark evening she took her firmly by the arms and kissed her gently on the lips. "Remember," she said, "that here you will be loved."

Mariana knelt before the statue of the Virgin. Outside it was snowing quietly, the flakes drifting down like pieces of heavenly air.

"Dear Mother of God," she whispered. "What shall I do with this little life of mine? I have such doubts, such hesitations.

Give me a sign. Be a guide to me. I have seen so little of the world, and yet I have seen enough of it to know that there's more agony in it than joy. I am afraid of the anger and cruelty of strangers, and even, sometimes, of those I love. It seems such a heartless place, such a getting-and-spending place, that I am not sure I can endure it for long. I long for silence and warmth and love. Inside of me a woman is weeping, and I want to comfort her, as though we were not one and the same. Oh, what shall I do? What shall I do?'' She closed her eyes very tightly and repeated over and over that ancient prayer: ''Hail Mary, full of grace, blessed art Thou amongst women. . . .''

When she opened her eyes again, she imagined that the expression on the statue's face had changed and that the air stirred in its blue robes. Her heart leapt. She made the sign of the cross. She knew that it could not be—that it was only an effect of the light, the flickering candles, perhaps—but still, it frightened and excited her. She remained there on her knees in the cold church for a long time before her heart stopped pounding and she was able to rise and leave the presence of the Mother of God.

Halfway home in the whispering snow she realized that her decision had been made. She would ask to be accepted as a novice by the Sisters of Mercy.

# 5

Sergio's letters to his parents were infrequent and brief. They revealed little about his personal thoughts and feelings but reported faithfully his visits to relatives and familiar places. He came down on the train from Rome, he said in one letter, and found Naples bigger than he remembered it, but La Fontana smaller and dirtier. Most people remembered him, but few really recognized him. He had been, after all, only nine when he left. The church was the same, but the old priest was dead. Nonna Theodora was very happy to see him, and she looked well, though she would soon be seventy years old.

In his letters to Renato and Fanny he could speak more freely, because he felt they were his equals and more likely to understand what he had to say about the dramatic political scene, of which he was rapidly becoming a part. His first visit to Naples, for instance, was quite different from what he reported to his parents:

> Naples is an absolute sink of poverty and crime. I had no idea that the moral and social disintegration of this city had gone so far. It is a living (or dying) illustration of the failure of capitalism and the need for radical change. La Fontana is a dreary and unwholesome place, from which I feel lucky to have escaped. The people seem to me diseased and dwarfed by malnutrition. The men are mostly unemployed and demoralized. The women are brutalized and miserable. They grow old before their time and sit about like a flock of wretched vultures picking on the bones of the latest scandal. How could I ever have longed to return to this place, as if it were a paradise? How innocent we are when we are children!

Sometimes he touched on things more personal, but usually obliquely, as if he were determined never to discuss the problem again with anyone:

> I should be glad, in a way, that things have turned out the way they have. I might otherwise have never had this opportunity to come here and to the college. It was guilt, I think, that made my father so generous. His money arrives with regularity. I do not have to work. I am reading like a madman and learning things that fill me with hope and despair. What an incredible creature this *Homo sapiens* is, half angel, half beast, unreconciled, the best and worst of all the species that inhabit this globe. . . .

About the college his feelings were mixed. He found the students arrogant and conservative, except for two young men, Giovanni and Enrico, who shared his political views:

Most of them come from families that are financially comfortable, and almost all of them will go on to more advanced studies at the university. I am a little older than the average, but not as well prepared, though I have had time to think, whereas at least half of them do not know the meaning of the word. I do not see my uncle Pietro very often. He is a bit distant with me, but not unkind. I find him supremely intelligent and a little detached and distracted, as though he is preoccupied with a problem for which there is no solution. He is lean and ascetic (I suspect he is fond of fasting), and though he is younger than my father his hair has all turned white. There are rumors that he will soon be offered a much more important appointment.

By the spring of 1914 it was politics that dominated his letters, and it was clear that the situation in Italy, as in all of Europe, was growing perilous:

Premier Giolitti, who barely carried the elections last fall, has now resigned, as we all knew he would. He has been succeeded by Antonio Salandra, a rightwing Liberal. It is not likely that he will find a solution to either our political or our economic problems. The only promising note now is the increasing number of Socialist deputies. However, they do not have control, though their influence is growing. There are general strikes and riots. There are demonstrations against the military buildup. The army is to be reorganized under General Cadorna. I marched and we were scattered by the police. . . .

I have joined a syndicalist organization, and we hope now for a national disturbance that will bring the government down. But I must be careful what I say. Enrico was arrested and severely beaten. He is being held on a charge that he was in the possession of explosives. I can assure you that the charge is not true, and that he is being harassed by the police because of his political views. . . .

There were riots in Ancona at the beginning of June. Some of us went to contribute our support to the anarchist Malatesta. He is a very impressive man, as is the editor of *Avanti*, one Benito Mussolini. Such oratory is the stuff that revolutions are made of. . . .

Things now grow very difficult and this may very well be the last letter you receive from me. Everybody talks of war, and conscriptions for the army have been increased. We are not immune. I was visited by my aunt Angela, who insists that I get out of the country right away. She is a wonderful woman, sturdy and sensible and worldly. She treats me like a son. What a pity that she never had children. She has been the longtime mistress of an aging *camòrrista*. She says that all the bosses now think it is only a matter of months or maybe even weeks. But how ironic that we should find ourselves in an alliance with Austria when we are so at odds with them. Nobody believes for a moment that we will ever fight on their side against the French and the English. If there is a war most people here would prefer to remain neutral. But I am an interventionist, along with Malatesta, Mussolini, and D'Annunzio. . . .

His last letter was very brief and had a sense of urgency about it that made them worry:

I must leave immediately for America by whatever means I can find or I will be taken into the army. I have left the college, and I am on my way to Naples, where my aunt and some other people may be able to help. Everything is now happening so quickly that I may even arrive before my letter does. . . .

The letter arrived before Sergio, but only by a matter of days. Then, suddenly, he was there, walking into the shop, looking older, thinner, more serious, with his new mustache and short haircut. Renato and Fanny embraced him and then stepped back to have a better look. "My God!" said Fanny. "Where did you get those awful shoes?"

He stayed with his family, but between him and his father there was a coldness that made it difficult for them to speak. But gradually, over the days that followed, all the news came out. His brothers pumped him for information, a little jealous of his adventure. His mother complained that he had lost too much weight. And one day his sister, Laura, said, in all innocence: "Mariana has gone to the convent of the Sisters of Mercy."

His heart sank at the mere mention of her name. Laura was sixteen now, and full of curiosities of her own. When she revealed this news she had a strange expression on her face, as if she did not understand the full significance of it but assumed her brother would. "Oh," he said, "and when did she go?"

"In March. They sent her to some place upstate and they say that she cannot be visited for a while."

She went on talking in her lively, girlish way, but he was no longer listening to what she was saying. He was remembering that day in Central Park by the lake. . . .

Two months later he was married in St. Joseph's to Felice Gentile. They were given a grand wedding, and everyone said they were a handsome couple and wished them great happiness. That was in September. In Europe, war had already broken out.

# 6

It had been triggered at Sarajevo on the twenty-eighth of June.

On that day, a Sunday, the archduke of Austria, Franz Ferdinand von Este, and his wife, Sophie, arrived at the railroad station of the capital of Bosnia, with all its mosques and minarets and its Turkish market. In the summer heat they were greeted by bemedaled dignitaries and taken by motorcade along the Appel Quay. The archduke was a heavy man with a double chin. He was uncomfortable in his tight military uniform, and not in perfect health. He would have preferred not to have made the trip, but ever since the annexation of Bosnia and Herzegovina by Austria-Hungary a certain amount of ceremonial encouragement was necessary for the troops stationed there and for the mixed population (many of

them Serbs) that talked more and more militantly about a
union with Serbia. Extremists from that fierce little Balkan
country agitated for such a union, which angered the Austrians.
Serbia alone could not take on Austria, but she had as allies
certain other Slavic nations, among them Russia, that great
shaggy bear that had to be respected.

The archduke was fifty years old and beginning to feel that
his eighty-four-year-old uncle, the Emperor Franz Josef, would
never die, that he would stubbornly deprive his nephew of the
throne.

He stared in silence from the lavish limousine. He saw
banners and uniforms and pictures of himself, but he was
bored and irritable. He would have preferred to be out hunt-
ing or at home with his children, whom he loved. He was
not, all in all, an attractive man, but he did his duty in spite
of the danger.

That danger was symbolized by an occasional arrogant
Serbian flag in the crowd. To give the impression that all was
well, the military governor, who rode in the car with Franz
Ferdinand, did not order out any special guards, only the
ordinary police, who lined the sidewalks. It was a fatal
mistake.

Nedjelko Chabrinovitch was a young Serbian fanatic who
had come to Sarajevo specifically because of the royal visit.
He had sworn to assassinate the archduke. He was a nervous,
wayward lad who had drifted from trade to trade and eventually joined the secret society known as *Union or Death*. Two
other members of the society came with him from Belgrade: a
slender, intense young man named Gavrilo Princip, and another youth named Trifko Grabezh. They were all trained in
the use of weapons and the making of bombs. And they were
all prepared to take their own lives when the deed was done,
in order to keep the secrets of their deadly society. Their
fanaticism bordered on madness, but as terrorists they had
little experience.

The top was down on the limousine as it made its way
along the Appel Quay. It was the second car in the motorcade.
Chabrinovitch waited near the Cumurja Bridge. When the
procession arrived he stepped forward in the crowd and hurled
his bomb. In those few seconds of confusion the driver saw
what was happening and sent the big car surging forward.
The bomb hit the folded top and fell under the next car in the
motorcade. It caused only minor injuries and the royal car

went on to the ceremony at the city hall. The archduke dismissed the whole thing as an isolated incident, the bungled attempt of a political fanatic.

Chabrinovitch swallowed his poison just before he was captured, but he did not die. He vomited up enough of the potassium cyanide to survive. The police questioned him brutally, but he refused to talk.

Assuming that the plot had failed and that Chabrinovitch might talk, Gavrilo Princip wandered off in a state of shock. He considered killing himself, but he was, for the moment, incapable of any action at all. At a cafe he gulped coffee to pull himself together. When he emerged, there before him, by some miracle, was the royal motorcade, stalled in the process of changing directions to avoid another incident. The limousine was no more than ten feet from him. All he had to do was draw his gun and fire. One bullet hit the archduke in the neck. Another hit his wife in the abdomen.

And so it began. . . .

# 7

By the spring of 1917 America was in the grip of a patriotic passion and national outrage that was sweeping it headlong into the European conflict. "It is inevitable," cried the hawks of war. "It is madness," cried the doves of peace. Vigilante defense leagues sprang up and accused the pacifists of being spies, traitors, and cowards. There were demonstrations and riots. The country was whipped into a fighting frenzy and paranoia. And as they swept aside democracy at home, President Wilson asked Congress to declare war on Germany, in order "to make the world safe for democracy."

For the next few days Americans waited while Congress debated. And no one could talk about anything but the war that was about to come. They lingered on streetcorners. They gathered in saloons and living rooms. They devoured newspapers before the ink was dry.

At the Cafe Savarese, on the third of April, the day after President Wilson's speech, men came and went all day long. There were newspapers in English and Italian. There were coffee cups and wine glasses and unemptied ashtrays. And on one table there was a bottle of brandy, provided by Silvio "for the crisis."

Even on the street outside there was an excitement of activity. Women in kerchiefs and aprons huddled to talk. A car backfired. The women turned in unison to look, their hands pressed to their bosoms. Children ran. Dogs barked. A peddler led his horse and wagon down the street, shouting out his wares. A junkman's dull bells announced his trade.

At noon, Primo Gentile, the butcher, came to the Cafe Savarese for lunch. He was a short, fat man with an impressive belly, a rotund face, and a bald head. He moved with surprising quickness, his thick arms held out from his body as though for balance. He was greeted by Gaetano, who was sitting at a table with Antonio and Stefano. Silvio was standing beside them, reading aloud from *Il Progresso*. Primo sat down heavily and wiped his perspiring face with a large handkerchief. "What is it?" he said in a wheezing whisper. "Has it come?"

Gaetano motioned for him to be quiet and listen. Silvio read: " 'In spite of opposition from a vocal minority, from La Follette, Norris, and Bryan, there is every reason to believe that the declaration of war will be passed by an overwhelming margin. Furthermore, there is already in preparation a conscription bill that will more than triple the size of the armed forces of the United States in the very near future. Debate over this bill promises to be more heated than the debate over the war itself. Many officials and military leaders still believe that only a volunteer army can be truly dedicated. Others feel that the call to arms may not be heeded by sufficient numbers. "Full-scale war requires full-scale mobilization," said Senator Loren, after listening to the president's speech. . . .' "

"*Dio santo!* The draft," said Primo. "They are going to make the draft."

"Sure," said Silvio. "What do you think? You think everybody's going to run out just like that and get themselves killed?"

"There will be enough who want to go," said Primo. "And plenty who can't wait to get over there."

"It's a big war now. They will take everybody. Except you. They don't have a uniform big enough."

They all laughed.

"I don't need a draft," said Antonio. "I'm ready to go right now."

"Never mind," said Gaetano. "You go if they take you. Not before. And you too." He made a gesture to Stefano.

"Who me?" said Stefano. "I don't volunteer for nothing."

"But if they call you?" said Silvio.

He looked at his father.

"If they call you, you go," said Gaetano. "Or else you go to jail."

"In jail they don't kill you."

"Where they send you, you will wish you were dead."

"It's war now, and we have a duty," said Antonio. His seriousness surprised them. "I wouldn't feel right if I didn't go. Two of my friends have already enlisted—Tony Balsamo and Jimmy Preston."

Gaetano took a deep breath and shook his head. "God damn them all for making this war! But Antonio is right. America has been good to us. We take, and we give back. When I was young I would never have said that. I was very cynical, very selfish. Now I feel different. When I went to war years ago it was without conviction. You remember how it was, Silvio."

"Eh, do I remember!"

"We were young and crazy. We didn't know what it was all about. But this war is different. It is the old tyranny of the kings and the new democracy. I never thought I would talk this way, but I believe it. I believe that Germany is our enemy—our personal enemy. If I were younger I would go."

Primo Gentile frowned. "Sergio says it is Wall Street that wants the war, that the poor will die for their profits. He says that if there is a draft he will refuse to sign up."

Gaetano's face hardened. "It is those anarchist bastards he goes with."

"Sergio has his own way of looking at things," said Stefano. "I don't agree with him, but—"

"But what?" said Gaetano. "You want to be loyal to your brother, naturally. And he's my son, but I tell you he's crazy. These ideas have ruined his mind. These people are using him. He gives them all his time. He doesn't even go to Renato's shop anymore. And he doesn't support his wife and kid. You know who supports them? Ask Primo. He does. And I do. It's a disgrace. He gives them meat. Your mother brings clothes for the baby. She asks me for money for them. I shouldn't do it, but I do. For Felice and my grandson, Marco, not for him. He talks in such big words about his idealism, but what about his own family?" Gaetano's fist came down on the table and was followed by an awkward silence.

Silvio cleared his throat. "Well," he said, "if he doesn't register for the draft, he's going to be in big trouble. Maybe it will bring him to his senses."

Gaetano looked grim. "Maybe!" he said. "But I doubt it."

With the declaration of war only a matter of days or even hours away the patriots took to the streets. There was a gathering in Washington Square around the Arch of Triumph, and an impromptu march up Fifth Avenue. Veterans of the Civil War and the Spanish-American War turned out in patched and ill-fitting uniforms. Flags appeared at windows and blossomed in the crowd. There was a fife-and-drum corps and a marching band as loud as it was unrehearsed. Open cars carried dignitaries, gray-haired men in fedoras and derbies, and mounted police cleared the way for them.

At Union Square the American Defense League held a rally. Long before this momentous decision they had been preaching preparedness and participation in the "great crusade." They had been rooting out German sympathizers and antiwar anarchists. They had harassed and blacklisted anyone who was un-American enough to suggest that the country should not go to war. Jubilant speakers, one after another, shouted their message from a makeshift platform that looked like an immense gallows. The crowd responded with hysterical approval. They sang. They chanted. "Liberty or Death!" "We'll hang Bill Bryan to a sour apple tree." "America, America . . ."

"We'll teach the bloody Hun what freedom's all about," said the tall orator with windblown hair and a tailored coat. He had been introduced as "your friend and mine . . ." He waved his fist in the air. "They will regret the day that ever they did dare to tread on us." The crowd roared. The drums rolled. A pair of cymbals punctuated every paragraph. The startled pigeons fluttered into the air and took refuge in the upper stories of the Bank of the Metropolis and the Mercantile Building. A few braver birds retreated only to the statue of George Washington on horseback. One perched on his head. Another on his outstretched hand.

The Broadway trolley came down along the square, clanging its bell to clear a way through the growing crowd that had spilled over into the broad avenue.

On a corner opposite the square and not far from the statue of Washington another group gathered, infinitely smaller and without trumpets or drums. Three men carried wooden boxes, which they put together to form a little pyramid, a platform for a speaker that would raise him perhaps three feet above whatever crowd he could attract. Two other men unfurled a crude banner, perhaps ten feet wide, looking suspiciously like sewn-together bedsheets: "Rich Man's War—Poor Man's Blood."

They were all badly dressed to the point of looking downright ragged. Three of the five wore caps. The speaker was bareheaded, as was Sergio, who held a bundle of leaflets in the crook of his arm. He was unshaven and his face was gaunt. He shoved his leaflets at those who went by. Some people took them; others brushed him aside. A few gave him angry looks or even cursed.

The speaker was Emile Muro, a man with the face of a killer-martyr. His black eyes were set deep in a well-defined skull. They were the eyes of a man in love with a vision and enraged by those who would prevent it from becoming reality. His mouth was thin and ambiguous, turning down in one corner and up in the other, so one could not tell whether he was angry or amused. His body was a mere frame of bone and flesh, but he gave the impression of being strong, as if his strength came from some psychic or spiritual source.

No one knew anything for sure about Emile Muro, but he himself seemed immensely well informed, and he gave the impression of having secret, important connections with a whole underground world of syndicalists, anarchists, and workers' organizations. He was rumored to have been in Buffalo in 1901 when President McKinley was assassinated. And over the years in Boston, New Orleans, Milan, and Paris. He revealed nothing, not even his age. He might have been thirty-five, or forty, or even forty-five. He called his own group *The Twenty-first of December*. When asked about the significance of the date he would only smile and say: "It is the winter solstice, the shortest, darkest day of the year."

His followers were content to believe that it was a reference to the decay of the state and capitalism. In that dark moment the workers would rise and seize power, the syndicalist dream. His mission was clearly sinister—to encourage decay, to create chaos, to destroy the very structure of society so that from the rubble a new world could be built.

Now he mounted the little platform to defy the patriotic mob across the way—a fly on the flank of a bull. His shirt was open at the neck and he wore only a vest. It was tightly buttoned, so he looked somewhat like a matador. "Come closer, comrades, and hear the truth," he shouted. "It's a rich man's war, fought with workers' blood. It is a conspiracy of the trusts, who own the government and the Church and the whole educational system. You have been robbed of your minds. You are slaves in a system that will exploit you in its factories and kill you on its battlefields. . . ."

Sergio felt a chill of admiration at the sound of Muro's voice. It had an urgency and resonance that made passersby stop. Some paused briefly and then moved away, as though from lepers. Others lingered. In a few minutes there were some twenty or thirty people in Muro's audience. But the noise of the larger rally drowned him out. He raised his voice and the veins in his neck became thick and visible. "See, see where your masters call. And you go crawling to them like beaten dogs. You are trained to bark and trained to beg. . . ."

How he wished he could talk like that, thought Sergio. With the magic of words he would lead mankind out of the grip of kings and capitalists into a new dawn—a world in which all men were truly equal. A world in which they were all brothers and owned in common all the riches of the earth. No profit. No private property. No poverty. No despair. No death on the battlefields of Europe.

His leaflets echoed the banner: "Rich Man's War—Poor Man's Blood." He himself had written the text. And he had run it off on Renato's press, in spite of their recent disagreements over Emile Muro. But it was to be the last time—absolutely the last time. "That man is a dangerous demagogue," Renato had said. "I advise you to have nothing to do with him. He is an extremist who distorts our principles. He will go down and he will take you with him. The Socialists have denounced him. Even the IWP."

Sergio felt the pangs of hunger as he moved quickly among the people who paused. He was insistent. He pleaded. He forced his literature on them. His head swam in the blaring of trumpets and the banging of drums. The noise of the crowd was a howling wind in his ears. He had not been eating well. He had not had anything at all since the morning of the previous day. It made everything seem strange and somewhat distant. Even his own voice sounded to him at times like the voice of another person.

At first he did not notice the large man in the derby hat who marched angrily across Broadway in his direction. He did not notice him until the man was shouting: "What the hell do you think you're doing here? That's a meeting of the American Defense League over there. Now, get the hell out of here before we have the police cart you away. Goddamned un-American sons-of-bitches!"

"We have a right to talk," said Sergio. "It's still a free country."

"Oh, yeah? Not for you, you dago bastard. It's not your country. It's our country."

"I'm a citizen, just like you."

"I don't care what you are. We don't want you here. Understand? Now, beat it!"

Emile Muro ignored the exchange and went on talking. Sergio turned away and continued to hand out leaflets. One of the other men said: "Maybe we'd better go. It's a big crowd. Too much noise."

"No," said Sergio. "We're staying. We have a right—"

"We'll see about that," said the man in the derby. He turned around and shouted to someone across the street. "Hey, Jack, Bill. Get some of the boys. We've got a little problem here."

"Your problem is not here," shouted Muro. "Your problem is over there on that platform. You will all have blood on your hands if we go to war."

"I'll have blood on my hands, all right, and it'll be yours, you scum." He charged at Muro and dragged him by the vest to the ground. Then, hovering over him, he punched him in the face. When Muro fell down he kicked at him. The other men shoved him away, but in a moment reinforcements arrived and there was a general scuffle that attracted the attention of the fringes of the larger crowd as well as a mounted policeman. Someone grabbed Sergio around the neck from behind. His leaflets went flying. He was hit in the side of the face and kicked in the leg. Finally, he jabbed his elbow hard

into the gut of the man who was holding him and got away.
Suddenly, they were swallowed up by a mob and everything
was confused. Fists were flying. Men were cursing. The
policeman tried to force his horse through the crowd. From a
kneeling position Sergio caught a glimpse of Muro. There
was blood on his face and a knife in his hand. He drove it
into a hefty man's back and then, moving like a snake,
slithered away into the crowd. Sergio followed, leaving the
other three men behind.

Felice Gentile, now Felice Adamo, was a plain woman
with the face and the hands of a peasant. But she was also
attractive, as such people often are. She was close to the great
simplicities and uncomplicated by modern problems. There
was a calm sureness in her movements and a quiet intelligence in her soft brown eyes. Gaetano had been right when
he predicted that she would make a good wife and mother.
She did not struggle to understand the mystery of the man.
She instinctively moved with his moods without surrendering
anything that was hers. She did not think in terms of love but
of life. They were making a life together. They would raise a
family. There would be joy and sorrow. They would grow old
and eventually die. God would look after the rest. She continued to go to church and Sergio, who was himself an atheist,
did not try to stop her. When she became pregnant, she
prayed for a boy, and three days before Christmas in 1915
Marco Adamo had been born. He was now fifteen months
old.

They lived in an apartment on East 112th Street, a four-
room railroad flat, which meant that one had to pass through
each room to get to the one beyond. There were no hallways.
Most of the tenements were built that way. Not all of them
had heat and hot water. This one did. It was Primo Gentile
who saw to it that the young couple were settled in comfort
and close to his own home. And it was Primo who provided
the dowry that furnished the apartment with furniture heavy
enough to outlast several generations of Gentiles. Sergio did
not interfere. He had become quite passive about his domestic
life. The home was Felice's province. He himself had business in the world to attend to—battles to fight. Wars to win.
At times it seemed to him that his marriage, his home, his
wife, his child, all belonged to someone else, some shadow

of Sergio that had to go on living after something inside of him had died.

It was almost dark by the time he got home. Felice was sitting in the kitchen, where the door to the apartment was. On the table were pieces of cloth cut from a paper pattern. She looked up from her sewing. She could see that his face was bruised and his shirt torn. "What happened?" she said.

"Nothing! It was nothing. Don't worry about it." He took off his jacket and handed it to her.

"Was there a fight?"

"They tried to stop us from talking, but we wouldn't leave."

"Oh." She carried his coat into the next room. She came back and cleared the table without saying anything else. Then she went into the bathroom and ran water in the tub.

Sergio sat at the table and had a glass of wine. It was warm in his empty stomach and he felt it in his head. He looked blankly at his wife, who now stood by the stove, heating up his supper. "There's going to be a war," he said.

"I know," she said. "My father was here today. He brought the meat. A veal roast and some sausage."

Sergio looked up and frowned. "I said there is going to be a war. How can you talk about meat?"

"What can I do about the war? And we have to eat, don't we? I hate to take from him, but until you get a job—"

"I can't get a job now. I'm too busy. We are organizing another demonstration against the war. There are many who are against it. Someone has to speak out."

"It won't do any good."

"How do you know?"

"My father told me. He said you're wasting your time. You should think of your family."

"I *am* thinking of my family. Why should my son be brought up in a world of bosses and slaves and then be sent to war?"

"Your son is only a baby."

"Yes, but there will always be wars as long as the poor people let themselves be pushed around. They must wake up. They must rise up."

"Please, Sergio, don't get so excited. It's not good for you. And you'll wake up the baby."

"I'm sorry, but it has been a very bad day. A day we will all remember. And the months and years to come. The men marching, dying.'' He looked up. ''Do you know how many have already died in Europe? It is a madness beyond comprehension. Now America wants to join the slaughter. And for what? For power. For money. For the profits of the industries that make the weapons of death.''

She came to him and stroked his hair and shoulders. ''You're tired and hungry. Come, have a bath and something to eat. You'll feel better.''

He gave in. He rose slowly and went into the bathroom. Later, when he was in bed with Felice, he felt the coolness of the clean sheets and the warmth of the wine and food, and he wondered whether or not he was the one who was mad, after all. How easy it would be, he thought, to turn one's back on the world, to lose oneself in the embrace of one's own small life. Too easy! His wife's body was close to his. A permanent offering. He draped an arm across her. He felt her generous breasts. And then, instead of making love to her, he fell asleep.

The next day Sergio stopped by the shop. He had remained on good terms with both Renato and Fanny in spite of their hostility to Emile Muro.

''Good Lord, you look awful,'' said Fanny. ''What have you been up to?''

''I can imagine,'' said Renato.

''Haven't you seen the papers?'' said Sergio. He unfolded the newspaper under his arm and pointed to a small item on page three.

Renato read aloud: '' 'Disturbance in Union Square. A fight broke out yesterday when a small group of political extremists, presumably antiwar anarchists, tried to disrupt the American Defense League's rally in Union Square. One man was hospitalized with a knife wound, and three other men were arrested. The suspects were questioned by the police and later released. They claimed they were merely spectators and that two other men, whose identities are not known, were making speeches and handing out leaflets. Witnesses said that the two men disappeared into the crowd, leaving behind an antiwar banner and hundreds of leaflets.' ''

''So that was you,'' said Fanny.

''And undoubtedly the mysterious Emile Muro,'' said Renato.

''Why are you so critical? We are all fighting for the same thing. You go to antiwar rallies. You even make speeches.''

"Yes, but it's not the same. This Muro, I think, is a real assassin, a terrorist."

Sergio shrugged. "Well, perhaps he's right. Perhaps one must fight violence with violence."

"Violence only leads to brutality and injustice," said Renato. "In the end we will wind up with a police state. As long as we have a free society we have a chance for a peaceful revolution."

"Ah, peace, peace! That beautiful dove is dead. What are we supposed to do now? Go quietly into the trenches, obediently to our little deaths? Well, I for one will not. If there is a draft I will not go."

"You have a family. They probably won't take you anyway. You would be a fool not to register."

"No, I will not register. I will not cooperate in any way with a law that I consider to be a form of slavery. If necessary I will run away."

"Be reasonable," said Fanny. "We are all against the war and the draft, but there are better ways around it."

"It is the principle of the thing!" He spoke with nervous intensity and seemed unable to stand still in the small shop.

"I am all in favor of principles," said Renato, "but one must also be practical. In prison you would do no one any good. And dead martyrs are never around to hear the adulation."

"I don't intend to be a dead martyr. Nor do I intend to be a live coward. I have my convictions. Without them I am nothing."

Fanny tried to smile, but she looked patronizing. "If you don't take care of yourself, you're going to waste away to nothing."

"I haven't got time to think about such things."

Renato and Fanny exchanged an understanding look. "Why don't you come back to work?" he said. "Maybe a few hours a day. You must need the money. Besides, it would do you good."

He looked away and shook his head. "No, not right now. Maybe in a week or two. I'll see."

"Well, at least stay for a cup of coffee. I'll put the pot on," said Fanny.

Again he shook his head and looked distracted. He smiled, then frowned, then blinked his eyes rapidly. "I must go."

\* \* \*

The Selective Draft Act was signed into law on May 18, 1917. And June 5 was designated the day of registration for all men between the ages of twenty-one and thirty. For his newspaper Renato wrote: ''All across this nation municipal buildings, schools, and churches have flung wide their doors to help accommodate the God of War, whose thirst for young blood seems insatiable. How sad it is to see these lads line up in response to this call to arms. And all for the mystique of nationalism . . .'' At the risk of antagonizing the patriots, he would put out a special edition denouncing the draft as a violation of human rights.

On the morning of June 5 Sergio was pale with rage and fear. At dawn he was pacing through the apartment like a trapped animal. Renato's advice echoed in his mind: ''Fill out the registration form, but ask for an exemption. There is a place on the form for it. They will give you your green card and they will leave you alone.'' He went into the small bedroom beyond his own and looked at his son, Marco. He was sleeping peacefully, his little fist clenched near his soft round cheek. In that moment he felt like a fool for imagining that he could make a stand against the government, the military, an entire society that had decided his life was theirs and not his own. He did not hear his wife come into the room, but suddenly she was beside him. She was barefoot and in her nightgown. Her hair was drawn back into a wide braid and her face was still soft with sleep. She took his hand and looked down at the baby. ''You will do it for him—for us. Don't let them put you in jail. It would be such a terrible disgrace.''

A sudden wave of tears threatened to burst from his eyes. He choked back a sob and for a moment could not speak. ''I don't know,'' he muttered. ''I just don't know what to do. I don't want to hurt you and the baby.''

''Then go to the school. Go with the others today and sign the papers. What harm can it do? With luck they will leave us alone.''

''And if they don't?''

''Then you will go to the army. You will go like your father—with honor. And we will not be accused.''

''With honor!'' he said quietly. He went to the window and lifted the shade. He looked down into a backyard where an old tree was dying for lack of sunshine. It was like the ghost of a dinosaur surrounded by tenement houses. "If we live for honor," he said, "then I should be true to myself."

"Yes," she said, "but the family—"

"Ah, the family. How they drummed that into us when we were kids. The family comes first. The family is holy. Without the family you are nothing."

"But Sergio," she said, pleading with him to believe. "It's true! It's true! Alone we are nothing. Politics is just a game that men play for power. It means nothing to me—to us. We have each other. We have our son. And our fathers and mothers. And we are all bound by blood. We are all of one blood. It is more than politics. It is—it is—I don't know. It is as if we were one. You and me in him, in Marco. He is of my body—and yours. What you do now you do for all of us. You will break our hearts to follow some madman in the streets."

"That's enough!" he said. "You know about your family, but about the rest you don't know anything. There are some duties and loyalties that go beyond even the family."

"No," she said firmly. "No! There are none."

"Be quiet. You don't know what you're talking about."

"But I do. I do!" She began to cry and sat down on the edge of the bed. The baby stirred in his crib.

"Now see what you've done," he said.

She went instinctively to her child, picked him up, and bundled him to her breast. She sat down again and began to nurse and comfort him.

Sergio stood there, suddenly feeling excluded. Then he went into the kitchen and heated up the coffee that was left from the night before.

After a while he went out. He went down to the river, to a place where he often sat on an old pier, a place once busy with sailing vessels, old packets, and barges, no longer used except sometimes by a tugboat. The sky was overcast, a kind of endless morning that made the river seem wide and dark and full of sadness. He sat on timbers split by age and held together by giant bolts. He liked the smell of tar and wood and water. He longed sometimes to be far, far out at sea and away from all the turmoil of New York and America and everything. His mind was like a cluttered drawer. He wanted to empty it into the sea and take a deep breath of freedom. But he felt himself hopelessly anchored to the shore, to his life. One never sails away from that, he thought. Even if he fled to some remote island in the Indian Ocean he would still have a son, a wife, a country, and a conscience. One always lived somewhere. He thought of Emile Muro and of how utterly disconnected he seemed from all the ordinary things in life. Surely, that was the price he paid for his devotion to the higher things. But even as Sergio thought this he hesitated, and a little breeze of doubt disturbed him.

It was still early when he wandered up to the Cafe Savarese. Somehow he knew that his father and brothers would all be there. It was an important day, and on days like this men always gathered to talk. There was something ancient and tribal about this instinct to gather, to talk, to confront a crisis collectively. The instinct was in Sergio too, though it conflicted with another part of him that wanted to break away, that wanted him to assert his independence from family, tribe, country, everything, so that he could be free to speak the truth. *Ah, but what is truth?* It was the voice of his uncle Pietro, that gaunt, ascetic priest who seemed to have such confidence in an entirely different kind of reality.

When Sergio walked into the cafe, some of the men stopped talking and looked at him as though he were a stranger. Silvio nudged Gaetano. "Eh, *compare*, look who's here. Maybe he changed his mind after all."

Gaetano said nothing. He looked at his son, and for a moment their eyes met across the room. Sergio took off his cap and ran his fingers through his long hair. It was Stefano who first talked to him. "Come on over. Sit down and have a coffee with us. Aldo Lascano is here. He has come already from the registration. He has his card and everything."

Sergio nodded at the young man in the oversized suit and green tie that had slipped a few inches from the collar button. He was a silly-looking lad with big ears and a broad grin. A real *cafone*. That's what Gaetano would have called him. But not today. Today he was something of a hero. "The first one on the line. Seven o'clock this morning," said Stefano. "Isn't that right, Aldo?"

"Yeah! I wanted to be first. Nobody's going to call me a coward. See, here's my card." He held out his green card.

"And what did you have to do?" said Stefano.

"They gave me a paper with questions, that's all. And a pen. I put in my name, my address, height, weight, race, stuff like that. And if I want to be excused and for what reason. And then I signed. It was easy."

"You see?" said Stefano. "There's nothing to it. And they don't even take everybody. They draw numbers, like the lottery. And who the hell ever wins in the lottery? And you, they wouldn't even put your number in, because of Felice and the baby. You should go. You should come with me and Tony. He has to make deliveries this morning, but after lunch we are going to the school on 110th Street."

Sergio shook his head. "You're all making a big mistake," he said. "You think it's so simple. Answer a few questions and sign your name. Don't you realize that when you sign that form you sign away your life?"

"That's enough out of you," said Gaetano. "Why did you come here? To start trouble? You should have stayed home."

Maria came to the table with a tray of coffee. "All right, all right," she said. "So much noise so early in the morning. Who wants coffee? Who wants something to eat?"

"Please, Maria, mind your own business," said Silvio.

Maria, who had grown quite sturdy in her maturity, gave Silvio a dirty look that made him wince. "This is no place for family arguments. We got customers. And what are you doing? Are you making the lasagna or the politics?"

"*Porca Madonna!* One of these days—" he muttered as he got up and went back to the kitchen.

Stefano, who was supposed to be waiting on tables, looked around to see if he was needed. Then he held out a chair for Sergio. "Come on, sit down. Have some coffee. Papa, let him talk. He has a right to talk like anybody else."

"Sure, let him talk," said Antonio. "He's not going to change anybody's mind. We've heard it all before." He was in his green denim work clothes. The sleeves of his shirt were rolled up, revealing his sun-brown, muscular arms. He was the tallest and strongest of the sons. On the plate in front of him were the remnants of an omelet and sausage.

"I thought you were going to do the deliveries this morning," said Gaetano. "When are you going to start?"

"Maybe we should go to the registration first. What do you think, Stefano?"

"It's all right with me. I don't care."

Stefano looked at Sergio. "What do you say? We all go down."

Gaetano looked at Sergio with angry hope in his eyes, as if he thought for a moment that his oldest son might actually change his mind. Sergio stared at his coffee, his shoulders bent under all this pressure. Then he looked up slowly and said: "You know, it is not an easy thing for me to do. I wish I could go. I want to go. My wife wants me to go. There is a voice in me that says I *must* go. And yet, I know in my heart that it is not right."

"What do you mean not right?" said Gaetano.

"Because of my principles. Because of what I believe."

"Oh, to hell with your principles. Do it for us. For me."

"For you?" said Sergio, the sardonic question informing his whole face.

"Yes, for me. For all of us."

"But why? This war doesn't mean anything to you."

"That's not the point," said Gaetano. He leaned forward patiently. "Look, let me explain something to you. You are so full of your idealism that you have lost sight of the practical things in life. We have a good thing here in America, but there are lots of people who don't like us, see? They call us *dago* and *wop*. They say we steal their jobs. They say we are dirty. They say we are corrupt. You should hear some of the things they say. They think that we are cowards, that we have no loyalty. There is a big suspicion and hatred of foreigners right now, especially Italians. I don't want to be part of that. I don't want them talking about us. I have important connections. I have the political club now with Malzone. We do a little business with Tammany Hall. We deliver the neighborhood votes. How would it look to them if my own son was thrown in jail because he refused to sign for the draft or because he talked against the war?"

"Ah, so you would have me go against my principles just to save your reputation. You don't give a damn what I think, what I believe."

Gaetano's face grew red with anger. "No, because those idiots have robbed your mind. You are confused. You don't even know what the hell you think anymore."

Sergio stood up suddenly and his chair fell over behind him. "I know exactly what I think. And half the people right here in this restaurant would agree with me if they had the guts to speak out against the system."

"Shut up, you fool. Sit down."

"No, I won't shut up, and I won't sit down."

There were people at half-a-dozen tables. They had stopped talking and were staring in Sergio's direction. Gaetano was also on his feet. "You sit down or I'll knock you down!" he shouted.

"Sure, go ahead, if that's your only way of proving me wrong. Just like the rest of them. Like the police. Like the army." He raised his voice to address the whole room. "But I say to all of you that this is an immoral war, that it is a war for profit and power."

Antonio stood up and grabbed him roughly by the arm. "Do what he says."

"That's right. Do what he says. Just like you, eh? It's you who are the coward, not me. Afraid of the system. Afraid of your own father."

Antonio stopped him with a blow to the face. Sergio went down backward against the chair. He raised himself into a sitting position and, holding his cheek, staring up at Antonio, stayed on the floor.

Gaetano intervened. "All right," he said, "that's enough."

"No," said Antonio, "it is not enough. He owes you an apology. And me too."

"I owe you nothing," said Sergio. He got to his feet slowly.

Gaetano had to struggle with Antonio to keep him from hitting his brother again. "He's a filthy coward, that's what he is."

"All right, all right, I said that's enough." Gaetano fixed his eyes on Sergio. "I want you out of here. And if by the end of today you have not done the right thing, I don't want to ever see you anymore. Do you understand?"

When Sergio removed his hand from his face, they could see that there was a thin trail of blood from the corner of his mouth. But the look of pain in his eyes was more than physical. He seemed wounded in his very soul, wounded beyond tears. So awful was his expression that all those who saw him were silent. He did not stop to find his cap. He simply turned and walked away. Only when he was beyond the door and out of sight could voices be heard again. They were quiet and embarrassed, because the men had witnessed a terrible thing—brother against brother, father against son. It was the worst kind of fight. Worse even than war.

# 8

"This is the winter of our discontent," wrote Renato in his diary. "In these dark times it is easy to lose one's faith in mankind and to fear for the future of the world. The country is in the grip of a terrible hysteria. Even President Wilson is concerned, though he won't allow himself to be quoted on the subject. Free speech is dead. Anyone with a German name is suspect. Socialists are beaten and arrested, just for being socialists. One sentence against the war will earn a sentence of five or ten years in jail. Theodore Roosevelt has called opponents of the war 'copperheads' and 'unhung traitors.' Samuel Gompers, who pretends to speak for the worker, has been quoted in the *Times* as saying: 'Opposition to the war declared by constituted authority becomes treason.' And that wonderful gentleman Dr. Henry Van Dyke would have war resisters executed.

"So it has come to this, with the snow falling over the city like a white shroud. I feel my spirit crack. My darling wife lies in bed with a deep cough and a fever. There is fear of influenza. I no longer publish my newspaper. A month ago a rock was thrown through the window of the shop. Then came the blue card in the mail from some defense league or other. It was a warning, like the old Black Hand. Afterward there would be the red card and a report to the Secret Service. What could I do? To stay in business—what business I have left—I must pretend to conform.

"If Sergio were here he would say that I have sold out to save myself. Perhaps he is right. But I believe it is the sensible thing to do. Have I grown cautious now that I am no longer young?

"We do not know what has become of Sergio. Last week the Secret Service men came and took him away.

118

He is being held somewhere for trial. That is all the authorities will say. We have been with Felice to inquire. They are abrupt and evasive. We will have to find a lawyer who will handle the case. It is a matter not only of money, but of finding someone who is willing. Felice has been to Gaetano, but he has refused to use his influence. He has washed his hands and turned away. And Primo Gentile has nothing to offer except to suggest that Felice and the baby come home to him and forget about Sergio. She has, naturally, refused.

"Antonio and Stefano were both called up early in the draft and are now in training somewhere in New Jersey. Their mother weeps and prays for all her sons. . . ."

There was an iron grill in the only opening of the heavy, metal-banded door. The opening was small and at eye level. Outside was a dim, subterranean corridor with stone walls and a cement floor, much the same as the cell itself, which was not much bigger than a grave. Or so it seemed to Sergio after ten days of confinement.

For nine hours each day he was shackled to the iron grill and forced to stand. The equivalent of a day's work, Sergeant Bassett had explained. At five o'clock they put a tin bowl of slop in the cell and a cup of water. Then they unchained him and gave him "the freedom of his cell" until eight o'clock the next morning. He was allowed no clothing but his underwear, and no facilities but a metal pail. High on one wall was a narrow slot with iron bars like teeth. It grinned down at him with dull light for a few hours a day and then disappeared for the night. It was winter, and the days were short. Most of his time was spent in absolute darkness. It was very cold and damp, but all he was given was a rough blanket. He slept on the hard floor, which smelled of urine and rat leavings.

By the eleventh day reality was slipping away and time was collapsing. He was leaning against the door. His eyes were closed. He wanted to sleep, but he knew that if he did his legs would give way and the wide metal cuffs would cut into his hands and wrists again. They were swollen and bruised and there was pus in the scabs. Any motion was accompanied by pain. He tried to hold still. His head nodded forward. He heard voices, but they were only ghostly echoes of earlier interrogations. Every day they talked to him. They turned the

key in the door and another key in the shackles. They watched
him sink to the cold floor. They laughed. They cursed.
Sometimes they kicked him as he lay there. They were Sergeant Bassett and Corporal Cutter. They never came alone,
always together. At first he argued with them, even demanded to see the commander of the prison, but it did no
good. Now their voices were hollow echoes in his semidream,
and they were subsiding, receding like slow waves along the
shore. A warm breeze came across the water out of his childhood and embraced him like a mother. He saw the Bay of
Naples, the masts of fishing boats in the dusk, and old Vesuvius
brooding in the distance. He was barefoot on the docks. His
friends were there. They were eating oranges and their faces
were wet with joy. His mouth moved and his dry lips cracked.
He felt the pain, but it was already too familiar to wake him
from his dream. The boys were fighting. They were naked and
in the water, fighting, laughing, and someone was slapping at
him, wrestling, choking him around the neck. Then he was in
church. Old women in black were weeping. Christ was bleeding
on the cross. His father was trying to cut off his hands with
a dull cleaver. He was pounding, pounding. . . .

Someone screamed. It was a stranger's voice, but it came
from his throat. His legs had given way. The shackles cut into
his wrists. He grabbed the chain and hauled himself up. He
was nauseated. His stomach went into spasms, but there was
nothing to throw up, only a trickle in the corner of his mouth,
warm like the blood from Antonio's blow. "Oh, God!" he
cried out, forgetting that there was no God, "kill me! Be
done with it, and kill me!"

The darkness whispered around him, denying him even this
final comfort. He opened his eyes, but it was as if he were
blind. He could not remember where he was or why. There
was a distant scraping sound. An outer door opened slowly,
on rusty hinges. A dull square of light appeared in front of
him, like an eye in the darkness. There were heavy footsteps.
They came closer. A grotesque face appeared at the window
in the door. He should have known who it was, but for a
moment he could not remember. The face was a shadow, two
points of light, a cap, a badge, a mustache. "Hey, Adamo,"
the face shouted. "Wake up. It's time to eat." The key was
in the door. It opened. He was dragged back. He saw the
buttons of a uniform and smelled the body of another beast.
There were hands on the chain. They yanked him forward.
The hands moved awkwardly, pushing metal into metal. A

second man held a light in a small cage. "Goddamn these rusty locks." The voice was close to his face now. "There! Your day's work is done. Time to rest and enjoy your evening meal. Caviar and steak and champagne tonight." The beast laughed. Sergio allowed himself to slump to the floor. Just to be able to fall down was a luxury. "Hey, Cutter," said the beast, "give the man his bath."

The other man put down the lantern and stepped back out into the corridor. He returned with a pail of water and dumped it over Sergio's head. It was ice cold. Sergio gasped and jerked into a sitting position. With a rush it all came back. He was in solitary confinement in the disciplinary barracks at Fort Jay on Governor's Island. And these men were Sergeant Bassett and Corporal Cutter. Bassett was a big man with a heavy gut and a face with prominent bones that seemed marked out with charcoal. Under his once-broken nose was a wide black mustache that almost concealed his upper lip. Cutter was wiry and frog-eyed, the silent partner in the unofficial inquisition. Bassett obviously loved his job, and those who put him in charge of the "political prisoners" knew full well what they were doing.

"What's the matter, Adamo? Had a hard day?" asked Bassett. He looked immense in the eerie light. The shadows made a fat skull of his face. Cutter stood behind him and to one side, as if to assist at the ritual. "Here's your food." He put down the bowl and cup at Sergio's feet. Sergio was hunched forward, hugging his knees and shivering from the cold water. "Go ahead, eat. Don't be shy. Don't mind us. We'll keep you company. A little dinner-table conversation. They say it makes everything taste better. Helps the digestion too."

Sergio reached for the bowl. There were times when he had considered a hunger strike to get his rights, but he was always haunted by stories of how they would force-feed prisoners who would not eat. They shoved a rubber tube down your throat with a funnel at the end. Into it they poured a soupy mush. They had done it to a friend of his. One day the man tore his clothes into shreds, made a rope, and hanged himself in his cell.

The food was still lukewarm, and, though he could not have described what it was, it served its purpose. He felt a bit stronger and more aware of what was happening. But he knew that with food would come the inevitable questions.

"That's a good fella," said Bassett. "Eat it all up. Good

and good for you, as my sainted mother used to say. And for dessert I have a little proposition. You give us the right answers, and we'll give you some clothes and send you upstairs with the good boys.''

Sergio said nothing. He just stared into the empty bowl, wishing that repulsive as the food was, he had some more. He knew it would be useless to ask.

"What is your name?" said Bassett.

"You know my name."

Bassett circled around Sergio until he was almost behind him. "Now, now, don't get insolent. Don't you remember what happens?"

"My name is Sergio Adamo."

"Your address."

"Three twenty-four East 112th Street."

"Have you got that, Cutter?"

The corporal nodded. He was writing on a clipboard.

"What is he doing?" said Sergio.

"He's doing something that you forgot to do. He's filling out your registration form. Perhaps you would like to request an exemption. Let's see, on what grounds? You are married. You are a C.O. You are a coward. What shall it be?"

"Whatever you want. I'm not signing anything."

Bassett continued his circle until he was standing in front of Sergio again. His voice became rougher. "Look, Adamo, they give me people like you for fourteen days. Misfits and fanatics. Nine times out of ten I send them back a soldier. You can go before the judge and say that you made a mistake, that you have reconsidered, and that you are willing to register. What's more, you can offer your cooperation in locating other draft dodgers. You must have plenty of friends who are trying to avoid the draft. All those socialists and anarchists.''

Sergio shook his head. "I don't know anybody."

"Did you ever hear of Vito Torio?"

Sergio shook his head.

"Paul Moretti?"

He continued to shake his head.

"Carl Bonner, Peter Ross, Emile Muro?"

Sergio looked up.

"Ah, did you hear a little bell ring? Was it Emile Muro?"

"No. I never heard of him, or any of the others. And I want to know why you are keeping me here, why I have not been able to see my wife or a lawyer or anybody."

"This is a federal installation. You are being processed."

"I am being tortured."

"Nonsense, Adamo. You have food and shelter, all the basic essentials of life. In due time you will have your hearing, and if my guess is right you'll be sent to Leavenworth for a long, long time."

"I'll tell them what you do here."

"Without witnesses, Adamo, you're just another lying sonofabitch traitor, that's all. Who would believe you? And who would care? If you were smart you would cooperate. I could fix you up with a job in the kitchen. And if they send you away I will put down on your report that you were a model prisoner. . . ."

"Why don't you just shoot me and get it over with."

"Listen, scum, if it was up to me, you would have been dead long ago. This is the goddamn army. Either you fight or we put you up against the wall. How the hell are we supposed to win the war with people like you undermining our boys?"

"I don't believe in war."

"Yeah, well, I do. What if some bastard broke into your house and started to rape your wife and kill your kid? What would you do?"

"That's different."

"It's not different. It's the same goddamn thing. My country is my home. I would lay down my life to defend it. It's as simple as that, Adamo. Can't you see it? What's the matter with you, man? You're not stupid. You're not German. You're a fucking I-talian. They're supposed to be on our side, aren't they?"

Sergio looked down again at the damp cement, as though his logic were failing him and his arguments beginning to dissolve.

"Here, give me that," said Bassett to the corporal. He took the form and the pencil and shoved them at Sergio. "Come on, sign it. Get it over with. Then we'll go upstairs and have a nice long talk with the captain. He's a nice fella. He's been waiting to see you."

Sergio said nothing. He looked away from the forms that were handed him.

After a long moment Bassett backed away, his face tight with anger. "All right, Adamo, have it your own way. But remember we only have three more days, and, by God, they are going to be the three worst days of your life. Cutter! Clear out this cell. Take that blanket. And that slop pail over there. But empty it first.''

The corporal turned the pail over and tapped it against the cement. Sergio looked away from the mess and closed his eyes. At that moment he was tempted to throw himself at the feet of Sergeant Bassett and plead for forgiveness. He wanted to cry, but something prevented him. He wanted to talk, but he could not. He had reached some terrible impasse inside of him that he did not understand. He no longer knew why he was doing what he was doing. His reasons seemed ridiculous. But then he didn't really have any reasons anymore—only the stubborn resistance. The refusal. That became an end in itself. Just to say *no, no, no* to everything.

They went out. The door was slammed shut and locked. The light faded from the small opening along with the sound of their boots in the corridor. Then it was dark again and he was alone.

In his diary Renato made these entries over a period of several weeks in January and February of 1918:

At last we have found a lawyer who thinks he will be able to help us. It was through my wife's cousin Benjamin. At first she went to her brother, but he refused to have anything to do with the situation. He talked about "guilt by association" and bluntly asked us not to come to the house anymore. The lawyer's name is Milton Levine. He is not particularly sympathetic to war resisters, but he has a certain passion for the law and is willing to take the case for less than his usual fee. Felice has been able to borrow fifty dollars from her mother, without her father knowing anything about it. And we have been able to raise twenty dollars by putting off the rent on the shop for a month. . . .

Mr. Levine has been in touch with the authorities and has discovered that Sergio is being held on Governor's Island without visiting privileges, and that his trial is scheduled for next Tuesday in the federal courthouse downtown. The presiding judge, he says, will be Sanford B. Hunt, which is the worst possible luck for us, because the man has no patience with C.O.s or draft dodgers. He is of the old school. And what's more he is a bigot—anti-Semitic, anti-Italian, anti-everything foreign.

He has recently handed out a sentence of ten years to an IWW organizer who made a speech in which he voiced his opposition to the war. Mr. Levine has suggested that our best approach is to get permission for Felice to visit Sergio so that she might persuade him to throw himself on the mercy of the court. . . .

At last we were able to arrange it, because Sergio was brought to New York the day before his trial and held overnight in the Tombs. Only Felice was allowed to see him, besides his lawyer, of course. She said that she barely recognized him, that they had cut his hair short, and that he had lost twenty pounds. As she talked she kept breaking down and weeping uncontrollably. She kept saying, over and over again: "I can't believe what they have done to him. They have destroyed him. He has no feelings left. No thoughts. Nothing. He did not let me kiss him. He did not ask for his son. But still he is my husband, and I pray to God that one day he will be himself again." As I listened to her I had to fight back my own tears. What cruelties are committed in the name of justice. . . .

It is Wednesday now, and it is all over. There really was no defense and Sergio would not agree to show remorse. Feeble as he was, he tried to make a speech on the witness stand. The judge ruled him in contempt. Then he overruled Levine time and time again. The jury was without compassion. Sergio was only one of twelve people who would be rushed through these trials. It was a disaster. No hope! He was sentenced to five years at Leavenworth. Levine says that only if the war ends soon will there be a chance for mitigation. . . .

# 9

In the fall of 1917 the war was not going well for the Allies. The Italians were routed at Caporetto. There was a Bolshevik revolution in Russia, which meant that the Russians would soon pull out of the war, allowing German troops to be moved from the eastern to the western front, which had bogged down in a stalemated war of attrition. From the Channel to the Swiss border the whole northeastern region of France was bathed in blood. And in blood the places where the battles were fought were written into history: Flanders, Ypres, Bethune, Lens, Arras, Cambrai, Amiens, St. Quentin, Cantigny, Noyon, Soissons, Château-Thierry, Reims, Verdun, St. Mihiel, Luneville, Epinal. . . .

In France "all roads led to Paris." For four years the whole thrust of the German strategy was to strike at the heart of the nation. They knew—everybody knew—that if Paris fell, France would fall.

Only in certain farflung arenas of the war was there some success in these dark days. The British and Japanese moved successfully against German colonies. T. E. Lawrence stirred the Arabs to revolt. Bagdad was taken. And in December, Field Marshal Allenby took Jerusalem. The Turks were crumbling. The once-great Ottoman Empire was in chaos and disarray.

But all of this happened as if in another world, another war. Center stage was in France, and there the terrible opera of "man's inhumanity to man" was staggering to a cruel conclusion. The British were decimated. The French were exhausted. The German dream of victory had become a nightmare. The only innocents on the western front were the Americans. They came like children, singing songs and playing at war. Soon they would learn what the others already knew— that it was no game.

In the spring of 1918 matters grew worse for the Allies.

126

The Germans launched a major new offensive all along the line. The British retreated to the Somme and the French fell back to the Marne. At Château-Thierry the Americans fought beside the French to prevent the Germans from crossing the river. Still, it was possible that Paris might fall. The casualties were enormous. It seemed, finally, a question of which side would bleed to death first.

At 12:10 A.M. on July 15 German artillery opened up a ferocious bombardment on the whole front from Château-Thierry to Massigès. Thunder from the bowels of hell split the darkness and made a madness of mankind. The noise was beyond human endurance. The ravaged landscape danced in fiery daylight.

At 4:15 A.M. the German infantry began to move up. For three days and three nights they moved forward against stiff resistance. There was no sleep and little food. Only discipline and death. The Allied generals waited in their headquarters, convinced that the German drive would soon run out of steam. Already they had plans drawn up for a counteroffensive, scheduled to begin on the eighteenth.

The main attack was led by the French Tenth Army, which had ten divisions in the front line, including the American first and second divisions. They were placed on the flanks of the French Colonials, the Moroccans, and the Senegalese. The Tenth Army was under the command of General Charles Emmanuel Mangin, sometimes referred to as "the butcher." The very name of Mangin struck fear in the hearts of the German soldiers. He had spent twenty-six years in Africa. His colonial troops were fearless and brutal. They never took prisoners, but they often took "trophies." They were fond of collecting ears and even genitals, though the practice was officially discouraged.

General Mangin was a tough, professional soldier. He understood his men, black and white, and his attacks were bold and confident. For the 18th of July his orders read: "Objective: to break through the enemy front between the Aisne River and the Ourcq River and push straight on in the direction of Fère-en-Tardenois in liaison with the offensive of the Sixth Army. . . ." The distance between these two rivers was about twelve miles. There was a large stretch of woods called the Forest of Villers. And there was a plateau in the forest that had to be taken early on. Later there would be the Butte Chalmont, on the other side of the main road to Soissons.

All this action took place in the triangle formed by Soissons, Reims, and Château-Thierry, which was only about fifty miles from Paris.

Among the thousands of Americans who took part in this phase of the Second Battle of the Marne were Sergeant Antonio Adamo and his brother Corporal Stefano Adamo.

They came by way of Paris. The city was alive with women and wine and soldiers, many of whom had been to the front, many of whom were wounded.

The French girls liked the Americans, perhaps because of their broad-shouldered boyishness, and Antonio and his brother had a good time across the river and, finally, in a small hotel on the Rue Bonaparte.

In a few days they were moving out in an endless line of camions that looked at times like old covered wagons with their ribs and canvas. The tops were rolled forward because of the heat, and the troops sat in rows facing each other on wooden benches. The air was heavy with gasoline fumes and noise and dust. They were on the road from Paris to Soissons, but Soissons was still in the hands of the enemy, and they knew they would have to leave the trucks and the road eventually and make their way on foot. They did not know for sure what their destination was. All they were told was that they were "moving up."

There was a lot of activity on the highway in both directions. There were armored trucks and supply trucks and artillery pieces and ambulances. Some of the vehicles were camouflaged in colors of earth and leaf; others were as drab as mud except for their insignias. There were horses and mules and men on foot, who exchanged greetings with the men in the camions. They were French troops, and they made jokes that Antonio and his brother did not understand. Some of the trucks returning from the front were damaged, and some of the men in them did not look up at all.

About twenty miles from Paris the road crossed the railway tracks and ran parallel to them for a while. Long trains crept by. They too carried troops, but also tanks on flatcars and heavy artillery.

By midafternoon it was very warm and there were many delays because of the congestion up ahead and the poor condition of the road. The men in the trucks cursed at the heat and the roughness of the ride and wondered how long it would be before they could get out to refill their canteens and relieve themselves. "We won't have no kidneys left by the time we get to wherever the hell we're going," said Joe Walsh. He was a pale kid from Syracuse, New York, whose face had been ravaged by adolescent pimples.

"Where you're going you won't need no kidneys," said Willie Fox, a Pennsylvania farmboy whose red hair and name were always good for provoking a comment or a wisecrack.

After a while the convoy of trucks stopped completely and the men were ordered out. They got down stiffly, dragging their packs and rifles with them. They groaned. They undid and did up belts and buttons. Some drifted a few yards off the road to urinate with their backs to the trucks and their faces toward a scene of gently rolling wheat fields in which blood-red poppies also grew. A gentle breeze wafted through the wheat, which turned to gold when the sun broke through the clouds. Beyond the fields, in the hazy blue distance, was a forest.

Antonio heard the orders down the line and echoed them to his own platoon. His men shouldered their packs. They adjusted the straps. They hefted and shrugged to settle them comfortably. But it was hot, and the packs were heavy. The cartridge belts and rifles also seemed heavy, and many of the men were already sweating before they started out on the dirt road that led away from the highway toward a place called Villers-Cotterets. Company after company, battalion after battalion, moved on this road, raising more dust than the trucks had raised on the highway. Antonio could not see where it began or ended. They were somewhere in the middle of a massive troop movement.

Mules were used to carry machine guns and teams of mules to haul the small artillery pieces. The sun came and went as white and gray clouds moved across the blue sky like a parade of animals and other images from childhood. Dust settled on the faces of the men and stuck to the sweat, creating odd masks that made them look primitive or dead.

Some of the officers were on horseback, but their own second lieutenant walked with his men. He was Lieutenant John Harrison Reeves, a blond-haired, blue-eyed lad who seemed too young to be anything but a college boy. He had a clean, neat look. He was from a very good Philadelphia family, a family rich enough to have bought him an exemption from the draft, but he was too idealistic for that, too eager to do his duty. He was given a commission, though he was only a year out of Lafayette College. Sometimes Antonio felt sorry for him, because they had all heard jokes about these young officers, about how they had gotten their commissions and about how they lasted maybe three hours in combat at the forefront of the attack.

They marched through a place where there had been some fighting. It was hard to tell when. There were shellholes across a wide meadow, but the grass and weeds had started to grow back in an unhealthy way so that the whole landscape looked diseased, especially along the edge of a forest where many of the trees had been destroyed and stood like scorched and broken sentinels. "We must be getting close to the front," said Stefano.

"It's hard to tell," said Antonio. "Perhaps the front is getting close to us. They say the Germans have been on the move."

"You scared?"

"I don't know yet. Wait until something happens."

On the left was a cluster of buildings that had been shelled into ruins. There was a rubble of stones and a broken wagon with one large wheel still intact. Beyond the abandoned ruins one telegraph pole was still standing, with one crossbar, which made it look like a tall, brooding cross.

The men, who had been talkative at first, now grew silent. The column slowed and the troops bunched together. It was impossible to see what was going on. Then the lieutenant was blowing his whistle and men were falling out. "What is it?" said Antonio.

"Supply trucks at an intersection," said the young lieutenant. "Fall out and rest, but be ready to move. We are behind schedule already."

They saw the troops beyond the intersection moving away from them, leaving a gap through which a line of trucks passed, lurching over the rough ground. Not far off, in a clearing, were massive piles of matériel. Cases of shells for the artillery. Metal canisters and wooden crates with black stenciled markings on them in French. The trucks were being unloaded as they moved into the clearing.

"There will be a depot here, I suppose, for the action further up," said Lieutenant Reeves. He paused beside Antonio and took out a cigarette. He offered the pack to Antonio, who took one and nodded his thanks. He noticed how slender the officer's hands were, and how they seemed to tremble when he tried to strike a match.

Antonio quickly lit a match and held his cupped hands out. "How much further will it be?"

"I'm not sure," said the lieutenant. "Perhaps fifteen or twenty miles."

"Will we go right into the line?"

"We are supposed to be in position on the right flank of General Mangin's colonials by no later than an hour before dawn. At this rate we may have to march all night."

As they stood there smoking and talking they could hear a very distant rumble of guns, which was almost drowned out in the noise of trucks and the sudden new noise, a terrible clanking, grinding sound, of several tanks that crawled into view. They looked grotesque and clumsy, like prehistoric creatures.

"There are more troops coming in up ahead," the lieutenant said to Antonio. "I think they're French. They'll be moving up with us single-file on the left. They want to keep the center open, if possible."

The troops who joined them were black colonials in mustard-colored uniforms and khaki-covered helmets. They smiled good-natured greetings, and their white teeth flashed in the waning light. They carried small packs and rifles that were longer than the Springfields the Americans carried. They had bandoliers of cartridges and broad knives almost the size of machetes at their sides. They looked lean and quick.

When Harvey Cooper, a lanky Southerner with an Adam's apple like a vulture's, saw them, his eyes went wide and he poked the man in front of him, who was Willie Fox. "Hey," he said, "they ain't Frenchies; they're niggers! What's niggers doin' in the goddamn French army?"

"I don't know, Harv, and I don't care," said Willie, "just so long as they're on our side."

When the ambulances and trucks came back through the center, both columns had to move further to the side of the road. There were more delays. In some of these vehicles there were wounded soldiers, all Frenchmen, and the new troops looked at them silently as they went by.

They moved on slowly. At dusk they passed a large group of French soldiers who had pulled off the road to cook and eat. The men were making their own meals on small open fires. The smell of their cooking wafted back along the road, and the Americans wondered when the hell they themselves were going to eat. "Eating for them is like going to church," said Sam Rosen. "They all know how to cook."

"Yeah," said Cooper, "well Ah know how to eat, and if we don't git somethin' soon, Ah'm gonna wander off and find me a cafe."

Sam Rosen smiled and cleaned his glasses. He was a little man, almost thirty years old and, unfortunately, still a bachelor when the draft came along. His father could not convince the authorities that his little corset factory was an essential industry and that his son should be exempted from service. So off he went.

When they were beyond the field in which the French soldiers were cooking, the landscape turned very bleak. There was no color in it, and everything seemed ripped and scorched, as if there had been some serious fighting there not so long ago. The dying light only added to the grimness. There were shellholes and torn stretches of barbed wire, and most of the trenches were jagged and collapsing. A few were shorn up with logs and railway ties. Here and there the ground humped up, as if there might be something built under it.

The sky closed in with sweeping, billowing clouds. There were flashes of light on the horizon beyond another stretch of woods. And there was a sound of thunder that might have been the sound of guns. Antonio could not tell which. Veins of lightning suddenly fractured the billowing sky with lingering cracking sounds that made the men wince and lean forward.

Again they stopped. An officer galloped up the middle of the road alongside the trucks. He was shouting orders, which Antonio could not make out. Stefano moved closer to his brother and said: "What's going on?"

"Who the hell knows?" said Antonio, more angry than frightened at the sudden confusion.

Lieutenant Reeves appeared, streaks of sweat and dust on his face, which looked strangely old in the thickening darkness. "There's a mess up ahead," he said. "A stalled tank. Nothing can move. They're sending us across that field and through the woods. We'll pick up the road again a mile or two ahead."

The heat of the day and the heavy humidity were resolving themselves into a sudden thunderstorm. The wind picked up. The rain came down. It washed the dust from the soldiers' faces and soaked into their uniforms, easing the pain of the straps that had been cutting into their shoulders. The whole sky seemed to be boiling in anger.

It was a violent storm that would not let up. It mingled with the sound of battle and masked it so that, after a while, they could not tell which was which. They were blinded by darkness and rain, and underfoot the earth turned to mud. Their feet grew heavy and their steps were slow and uncertain in the pathless, rutted terrain. The blind led the blind as each man took hold of the pack of the man in front of him. The wheels of the caissons and guns slid this way and that or tilted into a rut and stalled. The mule drivers cursed and beat the animals in rage and frustration. When a machine-gun mule went down near Antonio he could hear the muleskinner shouting in the darkness: "Goddamned, fucking beast. Get up, you bastard. Get up!" And there was a sound of struggling in the sucking mud.

For a while they went along a fence and it served to guide them, but it ended abruptly in a ditch, into which several men had fallen and hurt themselves. They had been dragged up by their comrades and were sitting there in the darkness with some men around them when Antonio went by. One was moaning, "Oh, Christ. Oh, Christ," over and over again.

The woods were worse. If there was a path, they had lost it. Lieutenant Reeves came along the line: "Stay close," he said. "Don't stray. Just keep moving. We'll be back on the road soon."

Antonio echoed these commands to his own platoon. He held on to the man in front of him. He didn't know who the man was, but he knew that Stefano was behind him, and he could feel desperation in his brother's grip. It was impossible to talk. The thunder continued to roll but seemed to be moving away to the south. A bolt of lightning made a sudden silhouette of the struggling column. How stupid it all was, Antonio thought. Grown men subjecting themselves to this torment when they could be sitting in a cafe sipping wine or lying in bed in the arms of a woman. Slender white arms. Perfume. Laughter like blossoms falling from a tree in spring.

In his headquarters at Bonneuil-en-Valois, General Mangin gave frantic orders to his officers: "There can be no further delay. We must coordinate with the Sixth. Try again to confirm the position of the Americans. The British are already in reserve near Point Sainte-Maxence and Senlis, and my Moroccans have arrived. At four thirty-five A.M., our artillery will open up all along the line. We must catch them by surprise. The whole operation has come down from Pétain and Fayolle. The German offensive is over. Do you understand? Our center has held. And we have every reason to believe that the enemy does not yet know that our movements are for a counteroffensive. Every minute we lose puts us in jeopardy. . . ."

When they finally got back to the road they found that it was almost as jammed up as when they had left it. Now everything was moving forward. Men and machines made an artery through which blood was pumped into the wound that was called the front line. By three o'clock in the morning the rain had stopped and the sky began to clear. Some stars and a waning moon were visible. They could see again, and it made them talkative. Antonio noticed how quiet it had become. No thunder. No distant guns. Even the trucks and tanks had fallen back, as if to a rear position. In the eerie, predawn light they could see that everything about them was scarred with battle. They were on land where men had died. There was a bitter, rotten smell in the air. Gunpowder and blood. Ashes and rotting wood. A hint of the mustard gas they all feared. The rain had not been sufficient to wash it away. And they also smelled their own damp clothing, which was gradually drying out from the heat of their own bodies. And there was something else that most of them could smell but not name. Not sweat or urine, but something animal, something that came from themselves. Those who had been there before called it the smell of fear.

Word was passed along the line to proceed as quietly as possible. They moved into their position about 4:00 A.M. It was a ruined field that might once have been rich with golden wheat.

"We'll go forward until we make contact with the French," said Lieutenant Reeves, "and then to the right, but only to those stumps, and then wait."

"How far are we from the front?" said Antonio.

"You're looking at it," said Reeves.

Antonio's puzzled eyes swept over the dead, quiet landscape. "This?" he said. "But there's nothing here."

"We are less than a kilometer from the enemy. There's been a pullback, but they are probably dug in again."

There was no more forward motion. The men shifted and shuffled uneasily without talking. There was a labyrinth of old trenches off to their right, and some splintered woods on the left.

"Why is it so quiet?" whispered Stefano.

Antonio's mouth was dry. "I don't know," he said, "but it won't be for long." He stood very close to his younger, smaller brother and talked to him in a fatherly way. His voice was almost a whisper and there was an urgency in it. "Remember, be careful. Protect yourself. Don't do anything foolish."

"You too," said Stefano.

They could hear some of the men relieving themselves nearby. And they could hear the heavy whisper of Harvey Cooper: "Christ, I'm so hungry I could eat my own foot."

The quieter it got the more terrifying the whole scene became. Down the line someone was being sick to his stomach.

Suddenly someone said in a firm voice that startled them: "Fix bayonets!" The sound of blades being drawn and clicked into place resounded in the murky silence. A ghostly mist was rising from the ground and the air went dead.

Most of the men had no idea what was going to happen next. They moved obediently, convinced, as those who believe in God, that there was an invisible intelligence somewhere that had everything under control.

And then it began, at precisely 4:35 A.M. From somewhere behind them, beside them, above them, beyond them, came the artillery barrage. Their hearts seemed to burst with the bursting shells. Their senses were assaulted. Some men screamed. Some cursed. Many hugged the ground and felt it shake. Every Allied gun for miles and miles was fired repeatedly as fast as the gun crews could reload. It was as if the world were one immense volcano that was exploding itself out of existence. There were a thousand flashes of light within a matter of seconds, and the smoke that rose from the exploding shells aborted the dawn.

"*Madonna mia!*" muttered Antonio, conjuring up in his moment of panic the language of his parents. He made a quick sign of the cross, as he had been taught to do as a child even before he was taken across the sea to the country he would eventually think of as home. Images hurtled in with the rushing blood that filled his head, but the only clear thought he had was that his father had wanted him to do this, and he heard himself whisper aloud: "Why? Why?"

This fantastic insult to their sanity seemed to last forever. In actual time it only lasted five minutes. Then it tapered off to the larger guns. Orders were shouted that could barely be heard. The silhouetted figure of Lieutenant Reeves danced before them, waving frantically to the troops deployed to the right and left. With a .45 pistol in his hand he ordered them forward. The men moved with a rush and screams they could not control. No one was shooting at them yet, but they ran forward in a crouch, as they were taught to do. Their bayonets reflected the flashes of light. The soft ground sucked at their feet, as though the earth were trying to swallow them up.

Antonio's limbs were heavy at first. It was like trying to run underwater. But the mere act of moving made motion more possible, and soon they were running with confidence and even believing that it was possible to stay alive.

The illusion did not last long. From somewhere in that no-man's land, where nothing could have survived the artillery barrage, came the coughing and chattering of machine-gun fire. In the first light of dawn Antonio saw his first death. Not forty feet from him a man stiffened into an upright position and then, arms outspread, fell forward and lay still.

Volleys of riflefire thickened as they continued forward. At last they could actually see the enemy, shadowy, hunch-backed figures darting here and there, faceless in the strange light, elusive behind rolls of barbed wire. They went down on their knees or bellies to fire, then were urged forward again by rows and rows of soldiers behind them. It was necessary to get up, to advance, to stay together with one's platoon, one's company. It had been drummed into them. Maintain contact. Do not fall back. Do not try to hide. When your unit moves, move with them.

Antonio began shouting to his men by name, urging them to keep low and to keep moving. "Come on, Cooper! Get up, Rosen! Forward! Forward!" He kept his eye on the lieutenant, who was being incredibly brave. It was the way it was, he thought, with those who have class. They would rather die than disgrace themselves. And he was suddenly afraid that any moment his reckless young lieutenant would be blown to pieces. He rushed forward and grabbed him by the arm. "We are coming to a line of old trenches,'' he said. ''Why don't we dig in? We can concentrate our fire—''

On the lieutenant's face was the strangest, most horrible expression, as though he already knew he could not survive this attack. ''Our orders are to advance,'' he said. ''Keep your men moving.'' And again he waved the troops forward.

They were soon at very close range and the firing became intense. There were hand-grenades and small mortars and the larger guns of the remaining German artillery. The air hummed and cracked with gunfire. And mingled with it were the sounds of human beings, growling, shouting, crying out in pain.

Up and down the line men were dropping. They would fall and writhe in pain or just lie silent. A grenade tore away a man's face. A machine gun slapped another man's chest with a terrible *thud, thud, thud*. Antonio passed a man who was weeping facedown. He grabbed him by the shoulder and turned him over. His guts were spilling out through his torn uniform.

Still they inched forward, crawling now more than running. Antonio came over the rim of a shellhole and was about to slide in for cover when he was startled to see a German soldier there, staring up at him and unable to reach the rifle that had fallen from his wounded hand. Before he could think of what else to do, Antonio had fired at him point-blank and ripped a hole in his chest. He felt dizzy and sick suddenly. It was Stefano who dragged him away from the awful sight.

A few yards further on they were pinned down by heavy machine-gun fire. ''Take cover!'' was the order that reached them. Antonio saw Lieutenant Reeves conferring with another officer. They were pointing toward a crude bunker that looked like a bulge of earth. Reeves crept back toward Antonio. ''We've got to get rid of that damn gun,'' he said. ''It's tearing us to pieces.''

''There's too much wire,'' said Antonio, ''and they're being covered by riflefire from over there.'' He nodded toward the edge of a blasted forest, where the stumps made a ghoulish graveyard. ''We need some field artillery or a tank. We can hold here and send a runner back to the C.O.''

''Our orders are to advance.''

''But lieutenant, it would be suicide to move head-on into that position.''

Reeves looked confused. His eyes were wild with indecision.

A mortar shell exploded nearby and the two men dove for cover in shallow ground. When they looked up again they were covered with mud and there was a body on the rim of the old crater. Shrapnel had taken off the man's helmet and the back of his skull, killing him instantly. Antonio looked around and shouted: "Stefano!" He crawled to the dead man and dragged him back into the shellhole. The corpse tumbled down, rolling over several times, limp and heavy, and landed face-up at their feet. It was not Stefano. It was Joe Walsh, the kid from Syracuse with the bad complexion.

"Listen," said the lieutenant, "maybe we can outflank that bunker with a few men and wire-cutters and get close enough to use our grenades. We can hold this position for a while and draw their fire."

"Sure, but who will go?"

"Damn it, I'll go myself. Somebody's got to do it."

"No, you fool. You're supposed to be running this unit. Nobody else here knows what's going on. I'll go. I'll take Fox and Goldin and Szabo. Keep an eye out for my brother, will you? I don't know where the hell he's gone to."

Szabo and Fox crept forward into the rolls of barbed wire and used their clippers. Over their heads came the sharp and constant rattle of the German machine guns from the bunker. There were two of them. One fired while the other reloaded. Returning their fire were the now entrenched men of the Twenty-third. It was a fierce exchange. Antonio could tell that his advance men had not yet been spotted. He and Goldin armed themselves with half-a-dozen grenades, which were attached to their belts. As the wire opened they followed, crawling in the damp, muddy ground, almost invisible, since they were themselves already so covered with mud. They had left their rifles behind. Their mission was very specific.

The fighting went on. The small squad inched forward, avoiding sudden movements, keeping facedown, hoping to look like benign lumps of earth.

Stefano located Lieutenant Reeves. "Where's my brother?" he said.

"He's out there."

"My God! What the hell is he doing out there?"

"They're going to take that bunker."

Stefano started forward, but Reeves grabbed him by the arm. "Get down, you idiot!"

"But I want to go with him."

"I said get down, Adamo, and that's an order."

Suddenly there was activity on their right flank. Rows of men wearing the mustard-colored uniforms of the colonials were moving toward the fringe of the woods from which the covering fire was coming. Cooper came up and said: "Hey, lieutenant, them nigger soldiers is here."

Reeves went out to locate an officer. He found a Frenchman. He was a white lieutenant, who talked rapidly and pointed first here then there. Reeves couldn't understand what he was trying to say. He shouted and his face turned red. "The Boche, the Boche! They go! *Regardez!* In the *bois. Vite!* We this side. You there." He made circling motions with his hands.

Reeves looked again and saw a whole line of Germans moving toward the woods. Then he understood. They were falling back for shelter. Their lines were giving ground under pressure, except for this bunker and several others who kept up constant fire and might very well have been ordered to fight to the death to give their comrades time.

"My men are out there," said Reeves. He tried to explain, but the impatient officer waved his arm in disgust and ran off to his black troops, shouting orders in French at the top of his voice.

The wires were cut clear up to the bunker. All four men were within ten yards of the sinister hump in the ground with its single slot, barely a foot wide, through which two guns chattered away frantically, blindly, in the direction of the enemy. Antonio crawled beside Szabo. "That's close enough," he said. "Now, get back, and for God's sake keep down. Don't try to run." Szabo stared at him, his face wet with muddy perspiration, his eyes steady and hard. He moved away slowly, back through the wire.

Antonio readied a grenade. Goldin was only a few feet away. He too had a grenade in his hand. Antonio pulled out the pin and slowly counted—one, two, three, four. Then he tossed it toward the slot. It disappeared inside. There was a long and terrible moment in which nothing happened, then an explosion, muffled by the mound of earth. One of the guns stopped instantly, but the other went on erratically. Goldin's grenade followed and also hit its mark. Smoke poured from the slot. A hand and arm appeared, clawing at the air. Then it went limp and it was all over.

They started back. Szabo and Fox were already twenty yards ahead of them. Antonio looked over his shoulder and saw several German soldiers rushing toward the bunker. He could hear one of them shout, then they opened up with riflefire.

"Jesus Christ!" he said aloud, and he and Goldin got up and started to run, zigzagging and crouching as bullets struck the ground all around them. They almost ran into the arms of the advancing Moroccans. Antonio was startled by a black face and the flashing blade of a knife. The colonials swept past them and on into the teeth of the fusillade. They seemed utterly fearless. Their fierce voices were not like the voices of his own men. He rolled into a shellhole and looked back. The Moroccans never stopped. One dropped. The others overran the position. They met the last remaining Germans hand-to-hand. It was no match. The last thing Antonio saw was a group of mustard-colored uniforms, some flashing knives, and a German soldier crawling on all fours to escape. He was struck from behind in the back of the neck.

The slow advance continued, and by midmorning the Tenth Army had gained a foothold on the plateau northeast of the forest of Villers. There were some tanks in the front line now with Antonio's unit, and teams of mules struggled up the slope with field pieces.

The fighting went on all day, and there was no time to eat or sleep until after dark, when there was a brief lull. Then it all began again. German artillery opened up on the plateau. There were orders to move on. The advantage had to be pressed. They fought their way forward in open, ruined country between Louâtre and Chouy. To their left was the Sixth Army, finding it rough going against very stubborn resistance in the Louâtre area.

Lieutenant Reeves consulted the crude copy he had made of Captain Hansen's map. "Here is the road to Soissons," he said to Antonio. "When we have crossed that we will have the Butte Chalmont on our right, a very high place, well fortified. We will have our work cut out for us."

For another day and another night the fighting continued without letting up. The Tenth Army was on one wing of the attack. The Fifth Army was on the other. The objective was to pinch off the Germans in the Marne pocket before they could evacuate their equipment and troops. Fully aware of what was happening, the Germans put up their stiffest resistance on both flanks to buy time.

On the twentieth of July, the third day of the campaign, an unfavorable shift in the wind made possible the use of gas against the American divisions. The men were warned not to be on the alert and to check their equipment. In spite of the heat they were expected to cover all surfaces of their body. Mustard gas had first been used by the Germans at Ypres the year before. It took a terrible toll among the British troops. They had all heard horror stories about the gas, and it was the weapon they feared most. It was, in fact, not a gas at all, but an oily mist with a sweet, even agreeable odor. It caused severe blistering on contact and could lead to blindness. If inhaled, it destroyed the respiratory tract and lungs. The effects were often delayed. Even days after exposure a man could die.

In the late afternoon the wind died and then shifted. It was only the gentlest of breezes, but one could see by the drifting white clouds in the fairy-tale blue sky that it was moving in their direction.

They were coming across a wasteland that had once been part of the road to Soissons. It had been wiped out by repeated bombardments and could no longer be distinguished from the rest of the battlefield. The struggle had moved back and forth all day long within about two hundred yards. It was difficult terrain, and both sides seemed weary and cautious.

Antonio fought off waves of fatigue that made his eyelids sticky and his mind heavy and hazy. It was as if he were still awake but slipping into dreams, even hallucinations. Things wavered in front of him in the startling sunshine. The forest in the distance seemed to move. Scenes of horror came back like a regurgitation. Quick images of butchery and death. The bloody hand-to-hand fighting of the day before. The face of another German he had been forced to kill with his bayonet. Stanley Szabo so severely wounded in the leg that he was sure to lose it. When they cut away the shredded khaki they could see that the whole knee was shattered and he was bleeding to death. It was Jonathan Goldin who had had the presence of mind to make a tourniquet of Szabo's belt to stop the hemorrhage. The tough Polish kid from Chicago refused to cry, but before he passed out he grabbed Goldin by the arm and said, ''Don't let them take it off. Kill me, but don't let

them take it off—'' The corpsmen carried him away on a
stretcher.

There were guns in the battered forest to the north of them,
a strong position, impossible to assault. The guns kept up a
methodical shelling of the area that made it difficult for them
to do anything but dig in.

About three o'clock they brought in two prisoners. If anything they looked more weary than the men of the Twenty-
third. Their uniforms seemed too large for them, as though
they had lost a great deal of weight since they were issued.
Their shoes were worn through. Their faces were gaunt and
unshaven. They glanced with nervous, shifting eyes at their
captors. They were neither arrogant nor humble. They were
disciplined, but still afraid. They were ordinary young men,
no doubt, but they had grown old in the war.

They were taken down the line and questioned by Captain
Hansen, who had a makeshift headquarters underground in an
elaborated trench. Later, Lieutenant Reeves reported that the
prisoners were made to talk. ''How?'' said Antonio.

''Captain Hansen put a gun to their heads and told them that
it was their only other choice.''

''Would he have used it?''

''Probably.''

''Could you do that?''

''No,'' said Reeves. ''No, I couldn't do that. Could you?''

''I don't think so. I don't know.''

''In any case, it worked. And the bad news is that the
Germans are planning to move out of the woods in our direction.
If the shelling picks up, we'll know they're telling the truth.''

The shelling did increase, and at about seven o'clock one
explosion blossomed into a curious yellow mist that expanded,
snakelike, and drifted toward their position. ''Gas!'' someone
shouted. And the warning was repeated down the line with
growing hysteria. They wrestled with their gasmasks and in a
few moments were converted to monsters, creatures that might
have arrived from another planet, creatures with large eyes
and little elephantine snouts.

Another gas shell landed. Then another. The oily clouds
hugged the ground in the almost dead air. They moved slowly,
irrevocably. Someone screamed. The troops all began firing
into the mist, in case the enemy was advancing with it. There
was a momentary panic in the ranks. Some men began to fall
back and Lieutenant Reeves ordered them to hold their ground.

He had his pistol in his hand. Once he had to fire over their heads. Some 105s opened up. Then there was heavy machine-gun fire. A gust of wind swirled the gas and it seemed to be sucked up from the ground. Someone yelled about a broken mask. A man without helmet, rifle, or mask panicked and started to run. He went the wrong way and was swallowed in the mist. They saw him crawling along the ground. Then they saw his face go pale and blue. He slumped forward. Lieutenant Reeves ran out to drag him in. It was too late. The man came to for a moment but was in terrible agony. He was vomiting and his face was wet with tears. He could not breathe. They found another mask for him, but before they could get it on the man was dead. Lieutenant Reeves withdrew from him, as if he was now handling not a man but a piece of garbage. He was still disgusted by death.

The next day they got the news that Château Thierry had been retaken, and that the American Third Division had crossed the Marne. That put them in the Barbillon wood on the other side of the Butte Chalmont. The German position was clearly disintegrating. It was only July 21, the fourth day of the battle, and it seemed to them all that they had been there forever. They had lived with such intensity that it was hard to imagine they had ever had a life before this one—or ever would again.

In a rare quiet moment Antonio and Stefano sat on the ground near what might once have been a tree. They smoked cigarettes and kept their eyes on the pickets and wire and low stone wall a hundred yards away. Off to the right, a wagon, horse-drawn, was bringing back dead bodies. They could hear one of the grave-registry boys laughing with a kind of snort. He was Jenkins, the one they called "the undertaker." The sun was hot, and the smell of rotting flesh drifted back in their direction.

Stefano had long ago lost his lightness of heart, and whatever faith he had in anything was gone. In a quiet voice he said, "I think Sergio was right not to have come."

"He did not have to come; he only had to sign up for the draft."

"I think he was right not to have signed, not to have done anything that would connect him with this. Had I known what it was going to be like, I would have let them put me in jail. But how could *he* have known? Tell me that, Tony. How? What is all this for? What are we doing here?"

"The president says it is to make the world safe for democracy."

"Democracy, my ass! I don't believe it. I don't believe any of it anymore. There is no reason good enough for—for this."

"We don't know, Stefano. We just don't know. What if the French and British lost? Without our help they might have lost."

"Oh, fuck the French and fuck the British. Who cares?"

Antonio looked around. "Not so loud. Keep your voice down. I understand how you feel, but maybe some of the others do not."

"Well, then, fuck them too. I'm sick of it. If I knew where to go I would run away."

"Don't say that, Stefano. You would be sorry."

"Yes, but maybe I would be alive."

"They would court-martial you. They would shoot you. Don't be a fool."

"Don't worry. I'm not going to do it. But how do we get out of this, eh? Tell me that."

"I don't know. With luck. With the help of God."

"Fuck God. Fuck everybody."

"Stefano, don't say that."

Stefano was leaning forward and looking at the ground. Then, suddenly, he was sobbing. His whole body shook and he buried his face in his hands.

"Oh, Christ!" said Antonio. "Don't crack up on me now. We've come this far." He moved closer and put his arm around his brother, partly to comfort him and partly to hide him from the other men, some of whom sat only a few yards away.

Through his tears Stefano said: "I'll be all right. But oh, my God! Oh, my God!"

For the next few days there was serious fighting, but by the twenty-fifth the Butte Chalmont was under siege, as was the Orme du Grand Rozoy, the heights dominating the Ourcq valley from the north. On the twenty-eighth one was taken. On the twenty-ninth the other fell. The men were worn down. The ranks were depleted. General Mangin ordered a two-day rest, July 30 and 31. Reinforcements were brought up. Some units were relieved, but not Antonio's.

On August 2 dawn broke over a quiet battlefield. There

was no sign of the enemy. No movement. No gunfire. Nothing.
"They've pulled back," said Lieutenant Reeves.

"Thank God," said Antonio.

Stefano simply stared into the emptiness and said nothing.
After his outburst he seemed grim and fatalistic.

In the next few days they advanced easily to the Aisne and
Vesle rivers. Many towns were retaken, including Soissons.
At the Vesle River they were met with heavy artillery fire,
and it was clear that the Germans would make a strong stand
there. Still, they moved quickly, hoping that an advance
patrol would take a bridge and establish a foothold that could
be exploited on the other side.

They took a small, abandoned village on the river, but it
was of no real use. It had long ago been leveled by repeated
bombardments. Near this village was a narrow stone bridge
over which the Germans had retreated, though oddly enough
there was no activity at all on the other side. Lieutenant
Reeves conferred with Captain Hansen. "Our orders were to
maintain contact with the enemy and move into all areas
abandoned by them."

"But we were led to believe, sir, that the Germans had
pulled back to the other side of the Vesle, and that they would
make every effort to hold that line."

"They probably will. And what's more, it is Colonel Moran's
opinion that Foch will decide to conclude this offensive right
here—at least for the time being. But that decision has not yet
been made."

"But surely, sir, it would be risky to cross over at this
point. I mean, without a general plan of attack on their
position, a small unit could easily be caught in a pocket with
their backs to the river."

"That's right, Reeves. But it is just possible that they may
not want to defend this portion of the river, for fear of being
outflanked from Soissons. We don't know, and there's only
one way to find out—make contact with them. That means
crossing the river."

"But sir, we know their artillery is active just a mile or two
from here."

"Yes, Reeves, but we happen to be *here*." Hansen was a
square-jawed man with heavy features and a receding hairline.
He had the reputation of being colorless and cold, but a good
soldier. He laid out a map and tapped at it with a pencil. "We
have reports of action here and here, but nothing here." He

drew a little semicircle around the area across the river from the village.

"It doesn't make sense," said Reeves.

"A lot of things in this war don't make sense, but orders are orders. Take a patrol across the bridge. Find out what you can. I'll see if we can get some air reconnaissance from Colonel Moran."

Reeves stood up and saluted. "Yes, sir!" He went out, almost choking on his objections.

Outside he found Antonio smoking a cigarette and looking out across the river at the docile field on the other side. "Look at that, lieutenant," he said, "like an ordinary summer day over there. You wouldn't know there was a war."

"Well, there is a war, damn it," said Reeves, "and who the hell knows what's really over there?"

"What did Hansen say?"

"What do you think he said?"

"I think he said we cross the river."

"He wants me to take a patrol over. If we meet no resistance, the rest of the company will follow."

"I'll go with you."

"Listen, Tony, you don't have to do this. Your boys have had a rough time."

"We've all had a rough time. What the hell! Besides, it looks so peaceful over there. Maybe we can find ourselves some girls and go for a picnic."

Reeves smiled at him affectionately, but his eyes were sad. "All right, then, let's get it over with."

They moved out double-file in broad daylight. The bridge was made of very old stones, except where it had recently been repaired by the Germans. There were some new timbers in the middle span, and their boots sounded hollow as they crossed. Below them were gentle arches, through which the clear, indifferent water moved.

On the other side were fields of wheat, but under the wheat they could see that the ground was uneven from earlier shelling. It was as if nature were trying to hide the scars of old wounds.

The road they followed was unpaved but almost as hard as stone, having been packed down over the years by wagons carrying crops to the mill on the other side and by farmers going to and from the little marketplace in the village. Now everything was gone—the marketplace, the village, the people. Only the stubborn wheat had returned.

They passed a farmhouse, still miraculously half intact. They paused to go through it but found nothing. They moved on, using a hand-drawn map. "There should be another path off to the left," said Lieutenant Reeves. "It parallels the river, then swings off north to join a large road to a town called Vailly. We'll double back on that path to the riverbank. We'll complete the circle and then do the same to the right. We'll work back and forth that way and see how far we get. There may be stragglers or an ambush."

"How far are we going to go?" said Antonio.

"If our forward clearance is more than a mile, we'll send a message back to Captain Hansen. What he does about it is up to him. He may move the company in, or he may decide to recall us after all."

"If the Germans are anywhere around here," said Antonio, "there's no way we're going to hold this pocket on the wrong side of the river."

"Don't worry. As soon as we make contact we'll withdraw."

There was the sound of steady artillery fire in the far distance, and in the blue sky they could see drifting smoke. They came to a stone wall and looked down a slope to a patch of woods. It was startling in the sunshine, because it was in full bloom and undamaged. Lieutenant Reeves held up his hand for the column to halt. He motioned for them to deploy along the wall. In a hushed voice he said: "I don't like the looks of that." He was nodding toward the woods. "You could hide a whole army in there."

"What are we going to do?"

He looked down the slope and then to the right, where the shallow meadow softened into a marsh. They heard the sound of birds, and the whole scene was strangely quiet except for the distant guns. Reeves was sweating. His thin, handsome face was drawn and tight. "We'll go forward slowly, another hundred yards or so. If we draw enemy fire, we can head back to the bridge."

"If the Germans are in those woods in force, we'll never make it back to the bridge."

"All right, then, send someone back for a unit to support our rear. Tell them we think we've sighted the enemy."

"I'll send Stefano."

"All right."

Antonio conferred with Stefano, and he started back along the dirt road. He got no more than fifty yards from the wall when the shelling began. Guns opened up from the woods and shells ripped up the ground all around them. Stefano turned and started back, but his brother was yelling at him: "Go!" He hesitated, then broke into a run. He turned again at a rise and looked back. The platoon was under heavy fire and trying to use the wall for protection. To their left they could not see what he could see—a line of German soldiers skirting the woods so that they would come up behind the patrol.

The firing grew very loud. Stefano shouted a warning back, but they could not hear him. He saw his brother waving frantically for him to go on. Then he saw him twist, his hand still in the air. And he saw him fall forward against the stone wall. He screamed: "Tony! Tony!" but his screams were drowned in the roar of guns. His heart sank. His hands went cold as ice. For a moment, eyes wide, he could not move. Then a bullet sang past him and chipped off the rocks behind him. Instinctively he ran, dropping his pack and gun as an animal lightens himself against the hunter by emptying his bowels. He did not look back again.

By the time he reached the bridge his lungs were bursting. Everything wavered in front of him, and he was afraid he would pass out before he could cross over. He saw a column of troops getting ready to move on the other side. He staggered across. A man came out to meet him and kept him from collapsing. Stefano was gasping for air and could hardly speak. "In the woods . . . ambush . . . They killed us. . . . My brother . . . my brother . . ."

They took him to Captain Hansen, who gave him some brandy. When he was calmer he explained what had happened. His voice was dull and subdued. His eyes were cast down.

"I see," said Captain Hansen coldly. And then as an afterthought he added: "I'm sorry about your brother."

# 10

In prison Sergio kept a diary. It was a schoolboy's notebook
sent to him by his wife. He wrote in pencil and sharpened the
pencil by rubbing it against the cement floor. He was in
Leavenworth until a full year after the war. As a draft evader
in a time of patriotic fervor he was not treated with any
special compassion. He kept to himself in the prison yard. He
did his work in the steamy atmosphere of the prison laundry.
And in his free time, before the lights went out, he read
whatever books he could find and scribbled in his diary. The
prevailing theory about prison systems was that it was best to
keep the inmates isolated from one another as much as possible.
Hence the small, dark, lonely cells in which a man could
easily go mad, and often did. But for Sergio this isolation was
a blessing. In his diary he referred to himself as a true
"alien," not because he had been born in Italy and had come
to America, but because he belonged to no nation at all. "I
am a human being. I have the right of any animal to exist and
to associate with whomever I please. I have the right to live
anywhere. What do national boundaries mean to me? Nothing.
They are artificial ways of separating the peoples of the world
and controlling them and making wars for territory. It is
cooperation we need, not conflict. . . ."

He wrote in his notebook in a very small, careful script that
grew even smaller as the pages became fewer. He asked his
wife for another notebook, but it did not come for a long
time.

In the early days of his confinement he made a major
decision. "They have the power to destroy me," he wrote.
"I must have the cunning to survive. I have tried complete
resistance and it has failed. I have seen raw cruelty in my
captors. I have looked into the eyes of men who have killed
other men and who are capable of killing me. In those
sadistic, simian eyes one can read the whole history of mankind.

149

Stupidity, cruelty, the lust for power. These are the darker things. They must be overcome. . . ."

There were many conscientious objectors at Leavenworth. They came from all over the country. "There are some Russians here," he wrote. "They call them 'Holy Jumpers,' because of their religion. They came from Arizona. What they were doing there I don't know. They refuse everything, even to eat. Two of them were beaten so badly that we thought they would die. There was a rumor that one of the guards would be brought to trial, but of course nothing happened."

Many of Sergio's early entries were descriptive observations, as though his curiosity survived in spite of his ordeal:

When we arrived at the train station it was already dusk and it was very cold. I did not know where I was. A town in the Midwest. Low houses. Brick and wood. A truck outside the station. And a wagon with a team of horses. Soldiers stamping their feet and blowing steam. They were our guards. We had chains on. After a while, they forced us into a crude formation and marched us toward the prison. This meant going through the town, with people on the sidewalks looking at us as though a circus had arrived. It was a humiliation that I will never forget. Worse even than the physical abuses at Fort Jay . . .

There are many kinds of work here. I myself have been assigned to the laundry. Others work in a machine shop or in construction gangs. None of us is paid. Proof again of the exploitation of labor. It is one thing to be punished by imprisonment. After all, the idea is to remove a criminal from society. But it is another thing to use that man's labor for the benefit of the capitalist. And that is what often happens. I am sure that the officials who make the arrangements get their share of the profits, but I have taken vows of silence and will say nothing. Since I cannot offer physical resistance, I will have to be true to myself in the dungeon of my heart. . . .

We hear now that the hunger strike has spread to seven hundred prisoners. They have begun to force-feed some of them. This is a terrible process. They stick a rubber tube down your throat. On the end of it there is a funnel, into which they put some semiliquid mixture that already looks like vomit. . . .

Some of the guards in this prison could easily be on the other side of the bars. They have criminal personalities. They use their position of power like bullies. They are especially hard on the C.O.s, because these prisoners have become the whipping boys of the whole prison. A man who has committed rape or murder or armed robbery gets more respect than a man who does not believe in violence or war and has been true to his principles. . . .

There is a boy named Andrew who talks to me sometimes in the yard. I say little, but I listen, because he is in despair. He is a Mennonite and, in his innocence, followed the instructions of his faith. He is no more than nineteen, fair-haired and thin to the point of being fragile. He says that he has been sexually abused by some of the hardened criminals. It is a common enough thing here. There are even some effeminate men who sell their services. How grotesque it all is! This Andrew tried to complain to the warden, but nothing was done, and later he was badly beaten up by two men in the yard while the guards looked the other way. . . .

I have not seen it, but they say there is an insane ward where they send the prisoners they cannot control. Those who will not eat or work are sometimes sent there. They say it is even worse than the "hole." A nightmare. Political prisoners mixed with real madmen. . . .

Alienation. Isolation. I sometimes feel invisible, as if I really don't exist at all—a pair of eyes and ears. That's all. What's more, it may be true. . . .

There are religious services here, but I do not go. Many of the men who go do not believe in God. It is just something to do. A few have become fanatical in their faith. In a place like this it is a real temptation to give over one's self to some great mystery and look for life after this misery. . . .

Another letter from Felice. Always the same. She talks about my son. He is well. He talks like an American. He plays in the hallway with the boy across the way. And about my father, who will not come to visit. And her mother and sister, who do. She is without ideas, but full of the details of life. Women are like that. It brings back to me so sharply the whole neighborhood, the whole outside world. I can smell the food. I can hear the noises in the street. . . .

It was Felice who first told him about his brother's death. For three days he made no entries and wrote no letters. Then he scribbled in a tiny, uncertain hand:

My brother is dead! How can I contain this thought? Antonio. Dead. I write it down to make it real, because I have developed the habit of removing myself from pain. When the letter came the other day, it was as if I had known it all along. As if I knew he would die in the war. I lie awake at night and try to imagine him there on some battlefield. I wonder how it happened. Was it a bullet or a bayonet? Was it a bursting bomb? How was his body broken and torn? I see his blood. I see his face. Antonio! And I see him as he was, so strong and beautiful in the sharp sunlight, lusting after women, laughing and full of life. Oh, Christ, how horrible! How impossible. Of the three of us sons, he should have lived, he who was so much more suited for life than me, or even Stefano. He who was strong and arrogant. What was I beside him? Nothing. Nothing. Nothing . . .

From time to time there were letters, but never from his father. News of Gaetano came only through other people, through his mother, or Renato, or even Natalia, who had the boldness and generosity to write to him in spite of everything that had gone before. But only Renato wrote with any regularity and remained, in his feelings and sense of duty, more of a father than Sergio's own father had ever been. Sometimes in the night, when he could not sleep, Sergio remembered in vivid detail the day he spent with Fanny, and he wondered whether, in spite of all their radical ideas, he had betrayed Renato. The thought haunted him. The memory aroused him. He wrestled with his confusion.

His mother's letters were full of grief and death. He could imagine her in her black clothes now, having joined the old women who gathered on the stoops of the tenements and in the market, much as they did in the old country, in the narrow streets of La Fontana. And she wasn't even fifty years old yet. How incredible, he thought. Some old cultural habit, some old love affair with pain and death.

She wrote in Italian, because, even after almost twenty years in America, it came to her more naturally. "It is a time of death," she wrote. "A month after my Antonio there was the son of Signora Buscemi, and now Aldo Lascano. We stayed with his mother for a whole day. We brought the food and the bread, as if there was to be a wake and a funeral. But of course there was nothing, only the mass and the tears. It is bad enough to lose a son, but to have him buried so far away in a foreign country is unbearable. A mother wants a final kiss, a final embrace, to put her child to sleep for one last time. . . .

"And, as if the war was not enough, we have had another death. Your grandfather's brother, Zio Luigi, passed away suddenly in his sleep just a few days ago. He was seventy-five, not really very old, and never sick in his whole life. Your father was very generous with his widow, Philomena. They have never had much, and it was a long time since Luigi worked. Your father paid for everything. God will bless him for that. Since Antonio, he has been so sad, so quiet that I do not know what to think. I try to talk to him about it, but he refuses. And he refuses to talk about you. I plead with him to forgive you. He says only that for him, you died when Antonio died. Every day I go to church to ask the Mother of God to comfort him in his pain and to open his heart to forgiveness. But what a terrible thing it was for him to lose his son. What a terrible thing for all of us. . . ."

From several people came news of his sister, Laura, who at twenty was not only beautiful, but restless and rebellious. "After all," wrote Fanny, "she was only two years old when she was brought to this country. She is really an American. I can understand her conflict with the old values. She wants to run her own life. Your father will not allow it. Your mother is more sympathetic, but she is afraid that her daughter will be ruined. It's the same old thing. The old morality. The old ways. The trouble began when Laura went to work for that shop that makes costumes for the theater. The shop is owned by Adolph Steiner. I remember his uncle when we lived downtown. He owned the shop my mother worked in. Adolph is a simple enough man, but his brother Morris is a madman. He is obsessed with the movies. With a partner he has started a studio in Queens for making two-reelers. And now he is talking about going to Hollywood, California, which is becoming a big center for the production of moving pictures. Well, Morris discovered Laura sewing costumes and convinced her that she was much too beautiful to be doing such an ordinary thing. He's right, of course. He has given her parts in two of his movies. Not big parts, but a beginning. Your father thinks that all actresses are whores, especially those who act in movies. Your mother doesn't know what to think. She is afraid that Morris Steiner will take advantage of Laura. He is a man in his mid-forties with a fat wife. Perhaps he will take advantage of her. On the other hand, perhaps Laura will take advantage of him. She's a clever girl, and very spirited. I envy her for her sense of adventure. Sitting here in this dreary shop, I can easily envy anybody who gets out into the world. . . ."

Natalia's letter came as a surprise. It came in a blue envelope and was written in a firm, feminine script that was so much like the woman herself. "We are busier than ever in the shop. I have hired two new girls. We are thinking of buying a small building on 117th Street that has a loft. It would give us much more space for the machines, and we could keep the shop exclusively for stock and sales. But I am talking too much about my own business. I am sure you would rather hear about other things. I went upstate not long ago to see Mariana. She is quite happy with the Sisters of Mercy, though she has lost some weight and seems to me a little overworked. They get up very early, and I do not think they eat very well. For them food is only a necessity, not an enjoyment. Still, she seems content and dedicated. She will be teaching in a small school in the fall. I think she will do well. She likes children. What a pity she will never have any of her own. She asked for you. I gave her what news I had. She said she will pray for you. I hope it is not too terrible for you, Sergio, and that you will be out soon and reestablish yourself. Your wife and child need you. And your mother—I don't mean to alarm you, but she does not look well. I passed her on the street one day and I hardly recognized her. She has not recovered from Antonio's death. And she worries about you and Laura, and even Stefano, who came back from the war in a very poor state of mind. It is his nerves, your father says. He has bad dreams. He looks away when you talk to him. He is working again at the cafe, but only in the kitchen, where he does the most ordinary things. . . ."

Renato's letters were long and leisurely, as though he were lonely and therefore appreciated the loneliness of Sergio. Taken altogether, they were a chronicle of the wartime oppression, the hysteria over aliens and radicals. There was the harassment of the Defense League. His decision to stop publishing the newspaper. And finally his decision to close the shop for a while. When the war ended he reopened, but did not republish the newspaper. It was too controversial, he said in his careful way, suspecting that Sergio's letters might be read before he received them. He used only first names when he referred to certain people. "Emile has reappeared. Guido saw him in Mexico, where he had gone during the war. He is active again, but I do not know much about it and, as you know, I am not sympathetic to his ideas. . . ."

In the summer of 1919, Renato commented on the bombing of Attorney General Palmer's house: "It is unfortunate in a way, because there is so much talk of revolutionaries and deportations. There is the Lusk Committee of New York, about which the less said the better. They make lists of radicals. It is very dangerous to say anything these days. It has made a docile man of me, and I am a bit ashamed, but I must make a living. I do not get much business. Sometimes I work as a typesetter for Luigi Ponti downtown. And so it goes. . . ."

In spite of his falling-out with Gaetano, Renato still visited the Cafe Savarese. He and Silvio remained on good terms. Of one of his visits he said: "I ran into your father, who is there very often, of course. I had not seen him, even from a distance, for some time. He looks older and more serious, but otherwise well. The death of Antonio, of course, he took very hard. It is no secret that Antonio was his favorite. He was forced to say hello to me, but he did not invite me to sit with him, so I guess there will be no reconciliation for a while. He is very bitter against both of us. I guess he feels that we have betrayed him in some way. I don't fully understand it. But of course, he went to war himself, for whatever reasons. And he uses this to justify Antonio's going to war. He doesn't really remember how different it was for him, and maybe he wants to feel that Antonio did not die for nothing. It is not simple, Sergio, and you must try not to be wounded by what he does. The more I think about it, the more I think there is some fundamental difference in values and attitudes between him and us. Years ago he laughed at me because of my idealism.

He has always been a violent individualist—and now a little bit of a capitalist and political figure (he and Joe Malzone have started the Italian-American Political Club). We have been devoted to another view of society, a view in which there is cooperation and not conflict and competition. He used to say he had no philosophy except to live and let live, but really he does. It is the 'survival of the fittest' in a world that is 'red in tooth and claw.' And so he has come to terms with his grief in his own way. He has shared it with no one, and everyone in the neighborhood is impressed with his strength, because he goes about his business. But those who can see inside of him know that there is a wound that will never heal. . . .''

At his parole hearing, Sergio said all the right things. He was brought into a room where five serious men with stiff collars sat around a table. There was an American flag in one corner. And on the wall was a picture of President Wilson. Sergio felt like a disease being examined by a team of doctors. He said that he had been politically naive. Yes, he said, he loved his country. Yes, he believed in democracy. Yes, he would be willing now to die for America. For the profiteers and pigs, he thought. In his imagination he was pushing the plunger on a bomb that blasted his inquisitors into oblivion. The whole interview was an exercise in deception. He would tell them exactly what they wanted to hear, and they would send him back to his comrades, to Emile Muro and the Twenty-first of December Movement—and to his wife and child. Yes, to them too, because he missed them very much. His imprisonment had sharpened his awareness of many things. He emerged angrier but wiser. The scope of the problem was even more immense than he had ever imagined. There was not only the social system to contend with; there was the whole twisted nature of man. Cruelty, corruption, the lust for power. The struggle between good and evil. It sounded, even to him, like a religious view. Dark forces within us dragging us down, manifesting themselves in oppressive governments and laws. Even the ideals of the Russian Revolution had been betrayed.

In his last days at Leavenworth he thought about many things, as though it were time to draw conclusions about his experience and make plans for the future. But his plans remained obscure. Even on the long train ride home. Even as he walked up the street with a bundle under his arm that represented his personal belongings. Even as he plunged from stark daylight into the gloomy darkness of the hallway that would lead him to his unsuspecting family.

Felice was in the kitchen, washing clothes. The washtub sloped inward to accommodate a washboard. The enamel-coated metal top for the tub leaned against the wall. Felice wore an apron over a drab gray dress. Her sleeves were rolled up. The kitchen smelled of brown soap. On the corrugated metal of the washboard she scrubbed each piece of clothing. She turned it and scrubbed, turned it and scrubbed. Then she dipped it back into the water and twisted it. She used the sink beside her. There, waiting to be rinsed clean, was a small pile of washed clothes. Under the sink was a small maze of pipes. The floor was covered with linoleum, with a pattern that vaguely suggested pale green flowers and leaves. In places one could see the outlines of the floorboards where the linoleum was worn thin. Though the late November sun was still shining outside, the electric light was on. The only window in the kitchen was half blocked by a window box in which Felice kept food from spoiling. In the cold weather it was cheaper than buying ice. She brushed back some strands of loose hair with the back of her hand to avoid getting soap in her eyes. She seemed lost in her work and her thoughts, but from time to time she looked behind her to see what Marco was doing. He was in the next room, playing on the floor with blocks and toy soldiers and a tin truck. He, too, was lost in his thoughts. He wore short pants and high shoes, the laces of which were always coming undone. And he had the same large brown eyes that his mother had. His dark hair had only recently been cut in the style of the ''little man.'' It took from him his baby look, and Felice was sorry she had been talked into it by her mother.

The knock at the door startled her from the rhythm of her work. She looked up at the door and wiped her soapy hands on her apron. She did not recognize the knock, and no one called out to her, but still she felt something and her heart beat faster. She knew about the parole, but she did not know when he was coming. She dared not think it was him—but she knew.

She opened the door without asking who was there. Before her was a man who might have been Sergio, or who might have been a stranger. A gaunt man, unshaven, with his shirt buttoned to the neck but no tie. A man in a limp black suit, wrinkled from the two-day journey by train. He no longer had a mustache, and his hair was very short. Under his arm he carried a bundle wrapped in brown paper and string. She was unable to speak.

"Well," he said, "what are you looking at? I'm back."

"But you didn't tell me. Nobody told me anything."

"It was to be a surprise."

She backed away to let him in. Her hands seemed to be tearing at her apron, and her eyes blinked rapidly to hold back the tears. Then she gave way. "Oh, God!" she cried, and threw herself at him. He let the bundle fall and held her in his arms. Over her shoulder he could see young Marco, who was staring back at them with a frightened expression on his face.

Felice kissed him several times and pressed her soft face against his unshaven cheek, as if the small pain of it were an exquisite pleasure to her. He wanted to respond more passionately, but the habit of affection had not yet returned to him. What he felt was a kind of pleasant numbness, as though he had surprised himself more than his wife.

Poor Marco did not understand. He began to cry. Felice pulled away and went to him. She swept him into her arms and presented him to his father. "Marco, Marco, don't cry. It's your papa. He's home. Don't you remember him?"

"How big he is," said Sergio. "Not a baby anymore."

"He was less than two when you went away. Pretty soon he will be four."

"Hello, Marco," he said. "Why are you crying?"

There was something in Sergio's voice that reassured his son. He stopped crying. His frown relaxed, as though he were remembering after all, though that memory must have been very dim, something more emotional than visual—something.

"Every day I told him about you, about how you were working in another place, how you were coming home, maybe for Christmas." And then to Marco. "Don't you remember, Marco? Papa is coming home. How we sang that song? And now he is here. . . ."

Suddenly Marco smiled, echoing his mother's joy. "Papa!" he said in a shy voice. And Sergio grabbed him into his arms and gave him a strong squeeze that brought tears into his own eyes. He kissed his son, who drew back from the bristles of his face.

"Be careful," she said. "Your beard is rough."

Sergio put Marco down and looked around at the apartment. "It looks the same," he said.

"Yes, everything is the same. Everything."

"And you?"

"Yes, me too. I am the same. The same for you."

When his mother saw him she cried. Her tears were real, but also a learned ritual. Her gestures, too, were learned. He had seen them in the older women when he was a boy. Hands clasped together. Eyes rolling heavenward with gratitude. Hands outspread—receiving, grasping. The offer of mother-love. But God, how old she looked, how old and weary and ill! She was in black. Her hair was half gray. Her eyes looked permanently red and swollen, though her face was pale.

She took him to her bosom. "Sergio! Sergio!" she said in an exhausted voice. "I thought I would never see you again. My darling son. I thought they would kill you." And with her dry lips she kissed him as though he were once again a small child.

He was embarrassed, but he let her have her way for a few moments. Then he stiffened and drew away, gently. "I'm all right now," he said. "It's good to be home."

"But what have they done to you? You look so skinny. Didn't they feed you?"

"Sure they fed me, but not like you. Only American food. Soup and bread. Meat and potatoes. Then more soup and bread and more meat and potatoes. Every day. At night I dreamed of pasta and minestrone and smoked eels. I could smell the market on First Avenue."

She smiled. "Ah, how good it is to have you back. I was so worried. And after Antonio—" The tears came again.

He put his arm around her and comforted her. She seemed smaller, more fragile. "And Stefano. How is he?"

She shook her head and held her handkerchief to her mouth. "He was always such a happy boy, so carefree. And now so serious, so nervous. I pray to God to give him back his joy, but there is always a cloud over him, as if he still hears the war. They say many are like that, and he goes to a doctor where they send them. Once a week he goes, but he never tells us what they do or what exactly is wrong. I don't understand—"

"I do. The war was too much of a shock for his mind. And then his own brother—"

"They sent us a telegram. That's all we ever got from them—a telegram. We sent them a son; they sent us back a piece of paper. . . ." Her mouth grew thin and bitter. Her eyes were a permanent mist of tears.

"And Papa? Is he all right?"

"Yes, he's all right. But at first it was terrible. He was like a ghost in the house. He would say nothing. But inside it was as if they had killed him. I could feel him bleeding—inside. In his heart."

"Do you think he will see me?"

"No, don't try to see him. Not yet. It would only give you pain. He's not ready yet. There has been too much anger. He says he cannot look at you without remembering Antonio."

"I wish it had been me, not Antonio."

"No, no, Sergio, don't say that. Whatever happened was God's will. We will all go on. We will do what we can. Come into the kitchen. I will make you something good to eat. Come!"

Laura, he learned, had moved out of the house. As soon as she turned twenty-one she had defied her father and declared herself independent. She was learning fast. Morris Steiner explained her rights to her. And Gaetano threatened to kill Morris Steiner. But the storm passed, and soon Laura was settled in an apartment downtown with a girl named Mary West, a bosomy blonde who had worked for Mack Sennett. When Laura's first film appeared in the nickelodeon on 116th Street, everybody in the neighborhood went to see it—except Gaetano, of course. They were disappointed, because her part was so brief. But she had promises of better things, and she believed them. Her mother was not at all sure. "I know it is the American way. And I know it is the good times. But it seems so cheap to show yourself that way. To have the men look. And then God knows what troubles a girl can have when she lives in a house without a man. There should always be a father or a husband or a brother—"

By the time Sergio came to the shop to see Renato and Fanny they had already heard he was back. In many ways it was the best homecoming of all, because here, at last, were people who understood him, people to whom he could talk as an equal about things that were important to him. But through the smiles and happy greetings he could see that they had both aged. The wartime pressures had taken their toll. Fanny was almost forty and looked it. Renato was his father's age. It was in his eyes that Sergio could see how close to disaster he had come.

"They broke up the shop," he said. "They threatened me with sedition and espionage under the new laws. They were putting people in jail right and left."

"I know," said Sergio with a smile.

"You didn't have to go," said Fanny.

Sergio shook his head slowly. "No," he said, "I had to. I wanted to. Perhaps it was foolish, but now I feel better for having done it. I owe them nothing."

"I admire you for what you have done," said Renato. "But we are different that way. I am not a coward, but I have a practical streak. As long as I have my freedom I can be useful to the cause."

"Then why don't you begin the newspaper again?"

"I will, Sergio. I will. But you have been away. You don't quite understand what has been happening. It is a big Red scare. They say that what happened in Russia can happen here. They say it is all the foreigners who are bringing in the radical ideas. Attorney General A. Mitchell Palmer, he's a madman. His list contains the names of sixty thousand people. Undesirables, he calls them. Almost all are foreigners. Many are aliens without American papers. There have been raids already, and arrests and deportation proceedings. There is a ship—the *Buford*. They call it the 'Soviet Ark,' because it carries off radicals who have been deported."

"Are you two on the list?"

Renato shrugged. "Maybe. But so far nothing more has happened."

"So you will keep quiet."

"Yes. But only until the panic passes. And you, too, should watch yourself. Don't think you are immune just because you served time. They will take Emile Muro for sure. And Sullivan and Arnaboldi. Maybe Bernardo and Andrea Salsedo."

"They won't take Muro. He's too clever for them. He will do his work in hiding, and he will make them pay."

"Yes, and he will kill innocent people."

"He will fight violence with violence."

"They will shoot him down in the street. Palmer is on a rampage."

"We'll see."

"You're not going to try to get in touch with him—"

"We'll see."

"Sergio, don't," said Fanny. "Please don't. Stay out of it for now. Later on we will work together."

"How can I stay out of it? The war is now. And this is my war, not that slaughter in France where my brother died."

"Things will change."

"Things will change only if we change them. There must be resistance. There must be agitation."

# 11

On December 24, 1919, at about 7:15 A.M., a Ford truck was parked in front of the Bridgewater Trust Company on Summer Street. Bridgewater was about thirty miles south of Boston. Located there was the L. Q. White Shoe Company. The paymaster for the company was Alfred E. Cox. At the bank he was given three metal boxes containing $33,000 in cash. In the truck there was a larger metal box secured to the floor. He put these cash boxes into it and locked it up. Then he sat on it with his back to the driver as the truck drove away along Summer Street to Broad Street, where it made a right turn. The driver of the truck was Earl Graves. Beside him was a policeman, serving as guard. His name was Benjamin F. Bowles. The truck drove along Broad Street behind a trolley car, which slowed to a stop as it approached Hale Street. Parked near the corner was a black touring car. Suddenly, three men emerged from it. One held a shotgun. The others had handguns. When the truck was within twenty yards of them they began to fire. Bowles fired back. Earl Graves swerved to the left and passed the trolley so that it came between the truck and the bandits. They were in the middle of the street, still firing after the truck as it sped away erratically, only barely under control. The three men got back into their black touring car and drove away. The truck jumped the curb and hit a telephone pole. Fortunately, no one was injured in the accident, no one was shot in the attempted holdup, and the payroll reached the L. Q. White Shoe Company.

Not content with a police investigation, the company immediately telephoned the Pinkerton Detective Agency in Boston. About 1:00 P.M. that same day J. J. Hayes arrived in Bridgewater and went to work on the case. He questioned everyone who was in the truck and a few eyewitnesses who were on the street at the time. Earl Graves said that the man with the shotgun was about five foot six, weighed about 145 pounds, and was about thirty-five years old. He had a dark complexion, a black mustache, and looked like a Greek. Alfred E. Cox thought he looked like a Russian, a Pole, or maybe an Austrian. Bowles said that the man's mustache was black and closely cropped, that he looked like an Italian or Portuguese, and that he had red cheeks and a slim face. Frank W. Harding, who saw the incident from the street, said the car was a seven-passenger Hudson with license number 01173C. The man with the shotgun looked to him like a Pole, but the other two men he thought were Italians.

The Pinkerton man filed his report and the police continued to investigate the case, but no arrests were made.

On January 2, 1920, Attorney General Palmer conducted his biggest raid on radicals. In thirty-three cities across the country twenty-five hundred suspects were arrested. Warrants were issued without "probable cause." Suspects were held incommunicado and brutally interrogated. The bail asked for by the Justice Department was $10,000. In a general press release Palmer said: "My one desire is to acquaint people like you with the real menace of evil thinking, which is the foundation of the Red movement."

In an editorial a few days after the massive raid, William Allen White said: "The attorney general seems to be seeing red. He is rounding up every manner of radical in the country— every man who hopes for a better world is in danger of deportation by the attorney general. The whole business is un-American."

Palmer was undaunted by criticism. "Each and every adherent of this radical movement," he said, "is a potential murderer or a potential thief and deserves no consideration."

\* \* \*

One of the names on Palmer's list was Andrea Salsedo. Early in March he was picked up by detectives from the Department of Justice. Though he was an alien, his arrest was not reported to the Department of Labor, which was in charge of deportations, nor was it reported to anyone else. He was taken secretly to a building on Park Row in New York. There he was repeatedly questioned over a long period of time. He was not allowed to contact an attorney or relatives. No one, in fact, knew where he was. The detectives knew what had to be done. The point was not to prosecute Salsedo but to make him talk. He was rumored to have extensive connections in anarchist circles.

The room in which they held him was bare except for two chairs and a wooden table. On the ceiling there was a single light fixture, which at night tinted everything a dull yellow. From the narrow window Salsedo could see that they were perhaps eight or ten stories above a busy street. He was guarded around the clock and questioned at irregular intervals, sometimes in the middle of the night, sometimes at dawn when he might be weary and offguard. But he said nothing. "Did you know Luigi Galleani?" they asked. "Do you know the whereabouts of Emile Muro? What do you know about the bombings of June third of last year? Where were you? What were you doing? Have you ever been to Boston?" He shook his head and refused to answer. They tied him to a chair and punched him in the face. They beat him on the arms and in the groin with a piece of rubber hose. They threatened to castrate him. "Nobody knows you're here," they said. "We could kill you and no one would ever know." For several days they gave him no food or water. Then they put a bucket of water just out of reach. Later on they began to feed him again, because his mind seemed to be slipping away. When he was sufficiently recovered they offered him bribes and amnesty for his information. Still he refused to cooperate. In their frustration they beat him again, and used more refined tortures. There were burns on his body that became infected. They gave him no medical treatment. . . .

On April 15, about nine-thirty in the morning, an agent of the American Railway Express Company picked up an iron box at the railroad station in South Braintree, Massachusetts, twelve miles south of Boston. It contained the payroll for the Slater and Morrill shoe factory, nearly $16,000. The agent took the iron box to the company's number-one building, which was just west of the railroad tracks. The paymistress divided out the money and put it in pay envelopes for the employees. Then she put the envelopes into two wooden boxes, each of which was then put into a steel box. Just before 3:00 P.M. that afternoon, Frederick A. Parmenter, the assistant paymaster, took the boxes from building number one to the factory building, which was just beyond the tracks on Pearl Street. With him was an armed guard, Alessandro Berardelli. About halfway to the factory building, two men who had been leaning against a fence opened fire on them. Berardelli was hit four times and died almost immediately. Parmenter was wounded twice and died fifteen hours later. A getaway car picked up the bandits, who threw the metal boxes into the backseat. There was more firing from the car as it sped away. From the street or surrounding buildings, eight people actually saw the shooting. Most of them described the bandits as short and dark and probably Italians, but there was much confusion at the scene and they could not agree on the details. . . .

On April 27 Sergio was asked to come to a secret meeting in the back room of a restaurant in Little Italy. There he shook hands with Emile Muro. And he was pleased to see Guido Arnaboldi, who had been successfully evading Palmer's detectives. They talked about the old IWP and how it had been virtually destroyed by the Red raids. "And how is our friend Renato Benario?" said Arnaboldi.

"He's scared," said Sergio.

"We're all scared, but we carry on. I had hoped that *La Cronaca* would come out again, maybe underground."

They drank some wine. The room had no windows, only the glass panel of a door in the rear. There were wall lamps and a faded mural that might have been of the Bay of Naples. The table was not set up for food. There was only the bare checkered tablecloth, the glasses, and the bottle of wine. There were also two large clamshells for ashtrays and soon the small room was filled with smoke.

Two more men arrived and were introduced as friends of Salsedo. They shook hands and talked quietly. "We know he is still being held," said one of the men, "but we do not know where. We have a lawyer now."

"What good can a lawyer do," said Emile Muro, "when there are no charges and there is no trial?"

"There are some influential people who do not like Palmer's methods. There may be some legal action that we can take, if we can get to the right judges. There are serious questions of civil rights."

"In this climate you will get nowhere," said Muro. "Direct action is what you need."

A sixth man came in. They looked up when the door opened and they saw the man chatting with the waiter, who nodded in their direction. He took off his hat and held it in his hand as he greeted those he knew and was introduced to the others. "This is Bartolomeo Vanzetti. He has been collecting money among our friends in Boston for Andrea Salsedo. And he has come to New York for a few days to see what can be done. He is with some of Galleani's people. But now, of course, Galleani is gone. How long has it been? Almost nine months now since he was deported. But still the work goes on."

Vanzetti sat down and someone poured him a glass of wine. It was the man they called Bernardo. He seemed to be well acquainted with the visitor from Massachusetts. He was also an old IWP organizer turned syndicalist, then anarchist. He sat down beside Sergio and put his hand on his shoulder. "This fellow," he said to Vanzetti, "was in jail until a few months ago. He did a couple of years in Leavenworth."

"Because of the draft?"

"Yes," said Sergio. "I refused to register."

"You should have gone to Mexico. There were many of us there. My friend Nicola Sacco went with me. We met some very interesting people. Some from the West Coast of the IWW."

"How long did you stay?"

"Only four months. Nicola came back because of his family. He has a wife and two nice kids. I was single, so I stayed away until the summer of 1918, but not in Mexico. I went to St. Louis and Youngstown and Farrell, Pennsylvania. I picked up odd jobs, mostly in the country. I like the country. I have a bit of a chest and it's easier for me there. The good air and all. Now I sell fish. It's not bad. I have some freedom. I order wholesale and then make the rounds to my customers. I can be done in a few hours. Some days I don't have to work. My overhead is a barrel, a wagon, and a piece of ice. That's all. It's better than working in a factory. I will never do that.''

"I don't blame you," said Sergio. "I went to Lawrence for the big strike in 1912. It was unbelievable. Textile workers in rags. How ironic! Were you there?"

"We came for a few days. I had the honor of meeting Carlo Tresca." He turned to Arnaboldi. "I thought he was to be here today."

"He said he would come for a few minutes if he could manage it. He has been trying for some time now to help Salsedo. We are hoping that he will have some new information."

No sooner was his name mentioned than the man himself arrived. He was a dramatic figure in his black suit, broad-brimmed hat, and generous tie. He had come from an aristo-cratic family and was a man of much education and talent. His energy and intensity filled the room. He was clearly in a hurry. He hesitated and eyed the men he did not know with a certain suspicion. "Is everyone all right?" he said to Arnaboldi.

"Oh, yes. Everyone is known. We are all concerned about Salsedo. And we are all here to help."

Tresca smiled at the familiar face of Emile Muro. "And what do you think we should do, Emile? Blow up the Depart-ment of Justice?"

"Of course," said Muro with an appreciative smile. The others laughed.

Tresca raised his eyebrows. "Don't laugh. He means it— unfortunately. For this Salsedo business, however, we must be very careful. He knows a great deal. If he can be made to talk, he will implicate a lot of people."

"He won't talk," said Muro. "I know him very well."

"On the other hand," said Tresca, "if we can prove a case against Palmer and his detectives, I know where to send the information. There is a group of lawyers and congressmen who are out to get Palmer. Some of them have personal reasons. Some of them are idealistic. More violence at this point would only play into Palmer's hands. Give me a chance to talk to some people. Perhaps we should organize a defense committee and make a fuss in the newspapers."

They talked for an hour, agreeing on some points, disagree-ing on others. When the wine was gone, they ordered another bottle. Carlo Tresca's last advice to the others before they broke up was to get rid of their literature as quickly as possible. "It would be foolish at this point to be caught with anything incriminating. If they pick you up, let the burden of proof fall on them."

"If they pick me up, something else will fall on them," said Muro, flashing a .38 automatic.

Tresca shook his head. "If they pick *you* up, you're going to need more than that. Who else is armed?"

They looked at each other. Finally, Bernardo raised his hand, then Vanzetti. "I don't want to make it easy for them, but don't worry. I'm not going to kill anybody."

"I can't tell any of you what to do, but for the next few months I think you should be very careful. There is some hope that in due time the political climate will change."

They shook hands warmly and quietly dispersed. Riding back uptown on the elevated subway Sergio thought about the men with whom he had the privilege of meeting. He was very impressed by Vanzetti's humanity and by Tresca's style and intelligence. They immediately became his heroes in what he called the "real war."

Two days later he met with Muro and discovered that Vanzetti was on his way back to Boston. He also found out that the whereabouts of Salsedo were now known to his friends. "He is being held in a building on Park Row by Palmer's operatives," said Muro. "We should set off a bomb there just to let them know that *we* know." Sergio was against it, and Muro was persuaded to wait—"But only until we hear again from Tresca."

On May 3, less than a week later, Andrea Salsedo was dead. He had fallen from one of the upper stories of a fourteen-story building on Park Row. Most reports described the incident as "an apparent suicide." Emile Muro insisted that it was murder. "I think they killed him because of what Tresca said, because a case was going to be made against Palmer and his detectives."

"But why would they attract attention to themselves like that?" said Sergio. "They could have taken him for a ride somewhere. No, I think he killed himself because of what they were doing to him up there, and maybe to keep himself from talking."

"Maybe, but we will never know. And now he's dead.

What are we going to do about it? Are we going to let them get away with it?"

"What can we do?"

"Every time they kill one of us, we should kill one of them. Or we should set off a bomb. We should send a present to Palmer—a few pounds of dynamite."

"It would never reach him."

"I know. But I have had in mind some more interesting possibilities. I have been thinking about Wall Street, that great symbol of capitalism. What a great demonstration it would be to plant a bomb in the Stock Exchange itself. Eh, what do you think of that, Sergio? Can you picture it? Can you see the confusion? The bodies writhing on the floor, their hands still clutching buy and sell orders—trying to make one last deal before they expire." He laughed, revealing small, tobacco-stained teeth.

Sergio did not laugh. His face was pale. "You're not serious."

"No? Why not? You see what they have done to Salsedo. They would do it to me and to you and to all of us. They would kill us. They *have* killed us. Doesn't that justify revenge? Even their Bible says it does. 'An eye for an eye'—"

"I don't know. I need time to think about it."

"Well, think fast, my friend. Time is running out. But say nothing to anyone. Do you understand? Not even to your closest friends. Palmer's agents are everywhere."

On May 5 Bartolomeo Vanzetti and Nicola Sacco got on an electric trolley near Sacco's house about 7:20 in the evening. They got off at Main Street in Brockton and stopped at a luncheonette for coffee. The day before, they had heard about the death of Salsedo. It was now clearly urgent that they get rid of the substantial supplies of radical literature that they and their friends had in their possession. For this purpose they needed an automobile. They had discussed the matter earlier at Sacco's house with Mike Boda and another friend named Orciani. Mike had an automobile and was willing to lend it to them, but it was in a repair shop in West Bridgewater, a shop owned by Simon Johnson. The car was a 1914 five-passenger Overland. Orciani had a motorcycle with a sidecar. He said he would take Mike Boda to West Bridgewater and that Sacco and Vanzetti could go by trolley and meet them there.

There was some confusion about where exactly they would

meet. After they had their coffee in Brockton, Sacco and Vanzetti took a streetcar to Elm Square in West Bridgewater. They waited around a while, but their friends did not show up. They decided to walk toward the garage.

At the Johnson house there was a knock at the door about 9:20 P.M. Mrs. Johnson answered the door. She saw Mike Boda, and the headlight of a motorcycle beyond him. There was a man on the motorcycle and, further up the street, two more men walking toward the house. She called her husband, Simon, who came to the door and talked with Boda. While the two men were talking, Ruth Johnson went to her neighbor's house and called the police. A police alert had been circulated among garage owners in the area to be on the lookout for suspicious-looking foreigners who had an interest in automobiles.

Simon Johnson told Mike Boda that his car had been repaired but that he didn't think it was a good idea to take it, because it had no 1920 plates. Mike didn't argue with him. He went back up the street to the motorcycle, beside which the two other men were standing. The four men conferred briefly and decided that it would be too risky to drive the car without proper plates. Mike got into the sidecar of the motorcycle and he and Orciani drove away. Sacco and Vanzetti walked back to the streetcar stop.

A few minutes later they were arrested. They offered no resistance. At the time of their arrest Vanzetti was carrying a .38 revolver that was fully loaded. He also had several shotgun shells in his pocket. Sacco was carrying a .32 automatic with nine cartridges in it and twenty-three additional rounds of ammunition in his back pocket.

That night they were questioned by Michael E. Stewart, the Bridgewater chief of police. He had been asked to cooperate with federal authorities in the roundup of undesirable aliens. He asked them why they were armed and whether or not they were anarchists and believed in overthrowing the government by force.

The next day District Attorney Katzmann interrogated the prisoners. He was more interested in solving the attempted robbery at Bridgewater and the killings at South Braintree. He asked them in detail about these events. The answers they gave about their weapons and whereabouts were sometimes evasive and false. Later they explained that they lied because they were afraid of being persecuted for their politics and because they did not want to implicate their radical friends. The District Attorney was not convinced.

When Sergio heard about the arrest of Vanzetti and Sacco he was very upset. "This is terrible," he said. "They're going to be railroaded because they are Italian aliens."

"Not just aliens," said Fanny, "but self-confessed anarchists."

"It is not yet a crime to be an anarchist," said Renato, "unless you believe in the violent overthrow of the government. But you are right, of course. In the minds of most Americans today, if you are an Italian alien, chances are you are a dangerous radical. Unfortunately, Sacco and Vanzetti not only freely admit that they are anarchists, but they were heavily armed when they were arrested. Palmer could easily have had them deported. But this—this accusation is very bad. They are talking about armed robbery and murder."

"That's right," said Sergio. "And some local D.A. wants a feather in his cap for getting a prosecution in a couple of serious criminal cases. In this climate, what jury is going to acquit them? They are as good as dead."

A few days later he talked with Emile Muro. "Now, wait a minute," Muro said. "Suppose they are actually guilty. Now, don't get me wrong. I didn't say they were. I have no evidence either way, and we will probably never know for sure. But just suppose! They were armed. They were in the area. They lied to the police. There was a lot of money at stake. It would have made a nice contribution to the cause."

"No," said Sergio, "it's impossible. The crimes were clearly the work of professional bandits. It was not their style. Sacco, I understand, is a family man with a good trade and a good income. A simple man with a house and a garden, with pure ideas—"

"Yes, and with a thirty-two automatic stuffed in his belt."

"It's not unusual."

"And even Vanzetti. He was armed when we saw him here in New York."

"Yes, but did he look like a man who had committed armed robbery and murder? When we saw him it was almost two weeks after the South Braintree job. He was going about his business. He was worried about Salsedo and the Palmer

raids. I don't believe he had anything to do with those
killings—nothing at all.''

Emile Muro nodded. ''You're probably right.'' He narrowed his eyes and nodded. ''Yes, it is probably what you
say it is. And they will no doubt kill them. If they are found
guilty, they go to the chair.''

''What can we do? There must be something—''

''It's like the case of Salsedo. We did nothing. But not this
time.''

''Then what?''

''I haven't made up my mind yet, but even if I had I
wouldn't tell you—unless, of course, you were with me.'' He
paused. ''Are you?''

Sergio looked from side to side as though he were confused.
And then he looked into the eyes of Emile Muro and found
there the cold, steady gaze of a man capable of violence. A
chill of horror went through him. He measured it against the
greater horror of that injustice in Boston, and then slowly
nodded his head.

There were two crimes, and there were to be two trials.
Sergio followed the details of these trials with such intensity
that at times it seemed as though he were incapable of thinking about anything else. He helped with the defense committee,
which was set up almost immediately by Carlo Tresca. One
day he staggered home, partly exhausted, partly drunk, after
collecting money door-to-door all over Little Italy. *"Per
l'amore di Dio!"* said Felice, echoing her mother on such
occasions. ''What have you been up to now? You look
terrible.''

''I've been working,'' said Sergio. He took off his black
jacket. The sweat showed through his shirt. His tie was
undone. It was June, and it had suddenly gotten very warm.

''Working? You call that work? Your crazy politics. Does
it put bread on the table? Does it buy clothes for your son?''

Sergio sat at the kitchen table looking like a beleaguered
animal. He was still thinking about the nickels and dimes he
had collected, and about all the people who had said *no* in
spite of his passionate explanation of the case. Over and over
he had made the same speech, until his throat became sore
and his voice grew thin and strained.

Felice went on. ''And I bet you didn't eat all day. Just a
wine here and a wine there with your stupid friends. And in

this heat. You'll get a stroke if you keep that up. You'll wind up in the hospital, and we'll wind up in the street. How long do you think my father is going to support us? How long is he going to put up with all this? Every day he fights with my mother, because he says it's a shame what is happening. He wants to stop helping us so that we will help ourselves. If it wasn't for my mother—''

"Please, Felice, be quiet," he said finally. "You don't understand what's happening. Yesterday they handed down an indictment against Vanzetti. Two charges: intent to rob and intent to murder. That D.A. is very clever. He has nothing on Sacco in the Bridgewater case, so he indicts Vanzetti. Then later he will indict Sacco in the South Braintree case. And what's more, he will strengthen his case by saying that Sacco was in the company of a convicted criminal. Maybe he will try to get them both for that one—''

"Sergio!" she said, raising her voice. "Who are you talking to? I'm your wife. I'm not a political meeting. This is our home. I don't want to hear these things."

"Yes, yes, I understand," he said impatiently. "I have to get some work. I have to bring in some money. Renato would take me back, but he doesn't have enough business right now. He can hardly make ends meet himself. But he says he will try to get me in with Luigi Ponti downtown. He has a big press. He does trade papers, everything."

"But when, Sergio? We can't live in a dream like this. Tomorrow and tomorrow. And maybe this and maybe that. What about today?" She went to him and put a hand on his slumping shoulder. Her voice softened. "I know you feel bad about these men, but please, Sergio, it's not your fault. And you can't fight this battle for them. They are in trouble and I feel sorry for them. But I don't know them. Many people these days are in trouble. We, too, are in trouble. Listen to me—''

He turned his head, looked up at her, saw her tear-stained cheeks and the shadows under her eyes. And he saw something else—the female animal defending her home. The mother. The wife. It was suddenly a force that filled the room. It overwhelmed him and calmed him all at once. He knew it was pointless to go on about the trial.

She sat down beside him at the table. When he was calm she took his hand and said: "Listen to me, Sergio. I have something important to tell you."

Her seriousness reached him. His large brown eyes were receptive. He could feel the stranger of human affection come into the room, and he became aware of the dull yellow light, the covered tub, the painted wall, the linoleum, the icebox—everything. It was his home. He was home, and this was his wife, and in the back bedroom his son was sleeping.

"We are going to have a baby," she said. Then she waited for her meaning to sink in.

He looked at her. He frowned. The significance of her announcement blossomed slowly in his mind like a flower, but a flower with thorns. He moved his lips first and then he said: "A baby? But—"

"Yes," she said.

His confusion rounded into a smile. "But that's good, Felice. That's wonderful!" He held her hand very tight in his and almost cried.

"Now do you understand?" she said.

"Of course! Of course! I'll have to get some work right away. We'll manage. Don't worry. One way or another we'll manage. How long is it? When?"

"My mother took me to Dr. Pedrino. It's more than three months already. Maybe November or December . . ."

He drew her to him and kissed her on the cheek and then on the mouth. "And what do you want this time? A girl?"

"No," she said, "another son."

"But why?"

"Because if you only have one son and something happens, it is a terrible thing. But if you have another son—"

"I understand," he said. "But after that we will have a girl, a beautiful girl like you."

A touch of color returned to her cheeks. "I'm not a girl anymore."

"You're only twenty-six."

"Sometimes I feel like a hundred."

"I'm sorry, Felice. I have not been a good husband and father. But I will do better—I promise. First thing tomorrow I will go out and look for work."

She smiled, but there was still a touch of sadness and uncertainty in her smile.

The Sacco and Vanzetti case became a *cause célèbre*. It attracted the attention of Italian organizations, labor organizations, journalists, and even the Italian government. By July,

1920, Carlo Tresca's defense committee had raised over five thousand dollars. It was only the beginning. Support came not only from radicals, but from moderate sources. Fred Moore was hired to defend them. He had successfully defended Ettor and Giovannitti after the Lawrence strike. The journalist Eugene Lyons went to Rome and stirred up the Italian press. Art Shields wrote the first propaganda pamphlet. It was called: *Are They Doomed?* Professors Dentomoro and Guadagni of Boston traveled around New England giving talks and raising money. The Workers Defense Union of New York made a series of healthy contributions. Donations were also made by the unions of the butchers, the hotel workers, and the tailors. Eventually, some sixty-four union locals gave money, some of them from as far away as California and Colorado and Texas. Carlo Tresca's mistress, Elizabeth Gurley Flynn, joined the battle, along with other influential radicals like Feliciani, Biedenkapp, and Lopez. Even the more conservative New England Civil Liberties Committee decided that the trial would not be fair and came up with five hundred dollars and other kinds of support. Through the influence of Elizabeth Glendower Evans, individual contributions began to come in from such prominent people as Louis Brandeis, H. L. Mencken, and Samuel E. Morrison. Many writers and artists and college professors were sympathetic.

Meanwhile, Sergio worked in the trenches and behind the scenes. He also went to work for Luigi Ponti, at least for a while. When he was fired for missing too many days, he found a job in another print shop downtown. He lied about his prison record, about his politics, about everything. Through Emile Muro he produced false documents and letters of recommendation. He worked at night, and during the day he gave himself to the cause.

"But what exactly is the cause?" said Emile Muro. "Our anarchist friends have become the darlings of the liberal establishment. Are they any better than the people who are trying to convict Sacco and Vanzetti? I say they are all the same. They own the power structures, the institutions, the government. They should be reminded that our colleagues are against all these things. That the state must be dissolved. That capitalism must be destroyed."

Sergio was weary and disillusioned. Emile Muro's arguments made sense. "Yes," he said "they are stealing our heroes.

They must all be violently reminded what the war is all about.'' He agreed to carry out the plan that Muro had devised some months earlier. They had stolen a delivery truck and hidden it in a friend's garage in Brooklyn. And from a construction site in New Jersey they had acquired a considerable amount of dynamite. The plan was simple, but it was repeatedly postponed. The idea was to park the van in the Wall Street area, set the fuse, and walk away.

Vanzetti's trial in the Superior Court at Plymouth, Massachusetts, had been swift. It began on June 22 before Judge Webster Thayer. Vanzetti was found guilty on July 1. On August 16 he was given twelve to fifteen years.

On September 11 Sacco and Vanzetti were indicted in the South Braintree murders. The trial would be held in Dedham before the same judge.

On September 16 a violent explosion shook Wall Street, leaving thirty-three people dead and many injured.

Sergio trembled as he read the newspapers the next day. He left his house early, but he did not go to see Muro or anyone. Nor did he go to work that night. He was almost insane with confusion. But at the core of it was a sense of triumph. He had done the right thing. Yes, it was war and he had done the right thing. But the demon of doubt kept whispering in his ear. What if Sacco and Vanzetti were guilty after all? Then he was wrong. Then he should be executed with them. But they were not guilty. Everybody knew that. All his friends. All the right-thinking people in the world knew that. And yet—and yet, what if they were all wrong?

Renato sought him out. It was no accident that he met Sergio on the street one day. ''Come and have a coffee,'' he said.

In the cafe Sergio said: ''I know what you are going to say—that I am neglecting my family. That I have lost my mind.''

''You look terrible. You should take better care of yourself. Ever since you got mixed up with Emile Muro and that crowd you have not been the same.''

''Let's not talk about all that again. At least we are doing something. People like you—what do you do? You just talk.''

''And what exactly have you done, Sergio?''

''None of your business.''

Renato looked wounded. ''There was a time—''

''I'm sorry. I can't talk about it.''

"About what?"

"Nothing." He started to get up. "I have to go."

"Wait. Sit down, Sergio. I won't insist. I don't even want to know. But listen to me, son. Whatever you have done, it is not too late to make a new start. Come back and work with me. Perhaps we will start up the newspaper again. We are all concerned. We are all on the same side. Don't throw away your life. There is a larger cause. And there is your family. Your children. Don't be a martyr—be a man."

Sergio looked with confusion and agony at this man who was a father to him. And he listened to this voice full of reason and love. He wanted to break down. He wanted to cry and confess everything and beg for forgiveness, but instead, at the last moment, he stood up and shouted: "I have done nothing wrong! Don't accuse me. Don't try to change me now."

Renato reached out to take him by the arm, but it was too late. Sergio pulled away and walked quickly out of the cafe.

"Sergio!" he called out in a pleading, helpless voice. It was no use. Sergio was gone. Renato knew there was no point in following him. Suddenly he was overwhelmed by a terrible sadness and foreboding that made him feel that somehow he had failed.

In the days and months that followed, Sergio became obsessed with proving that Sacco and Vanzetti were innocent. He needed the proof not for a court of law but for the court of his own conscience. They had to be innocent. They had to!

On November 30 his second child was born. Felice insisted on the name Lorenzo. "After your grandfather," she said. "It's only right."

"I never even knew him. He died before I was born."

"It doesn't matter. I'm sure he was a good man."

"He was a man with principles. He went with Garibaldi in the liberation."

The child was almost nine pounds and already seemed a sturdy, broad-shouldered boy to Sergio. "He looks like my father," said Felice.

"*Dio santo!* Let's hope not," said Sergio. He looked down at the broad red face, the flat nose, the soft black hair. His smile waned. "It's hard to imagine," he said, "that someday this little creature will be a grown man."

"God willing," she said, and took the baby to her breast.

*     *     *

The second trial did not begin until May 31, 1921. Almost seven hundred people had to be screened to find a jury of twelve. The district attorney built his case on circumstantial evidence and on the testimony of eyewitnesses who thought they could identify the accused as having been at or near the scene of the crime. On July 14 both men were found guilty. There followed a long series of motions for a new trial, motions that impeached the character of certain witnesses, motions that questioned the evidence, especially the ballistic evidence, and even motions that questioned the impartiality of the judge himself. On more than one occasion Judge Thayer had made hostile and indiscreet remarks about Italians and aliens and anarchists. The flames of the controversy were fanned by these disclosures, but nothing was done to save the accused. Slowly but surely they were being moved along on the conveyer belt of injustice toward their executions.

Sergio followed every newspaper report, every rumor, every inside piece of information he could get his hands on. He read law books in the library. He kept scrapbooks of headlines and pictures. He wrote letters; he made streetcorner speeches at public rallies. His obsession became a kind of madness. He grew thin and ghostly. Even his friends were afraid that he had carried his concern too far. They tried to discourage him from making public appearances. He looked too awful, like some caricature of the crazy anarchist. Some of them even avoided him when they saw him on the street. But he was unaware of all this. He grew more and more convinced that his efforts were important and that he alone might succeed where the rest of the world had failed.

Through all of this he tried to work for his family too. He lost his job at the print shop. He took to haunting the union halls for day labor in restaurants or on construction jobs. He washed dishes. He dug ditches. He shoveled coal. But he barely made a living, and soon Felice was having to accept help from her family again. They were resentful. They argued among themselves. They confronted Sergio, who tried to explain his position, but they did not understand. They said to Felice: "Your husband will wind up in Bellevue one of these days." And Felice cried and went to church to light candles and pray.

*     *     *

On November 18, 1925, Sacco received a note from another prisoner in the Dedham jail. It said: "I hereby confess to being in the South Braintree shoe company crime and Sacco and Vanzetti was not in said crime." The note was signed by Celestino F. Madeiros, a man already convicted of murder and under a sentence of death. Madeiros was willing to describe the crime but unwilling to name his accomplices. A great deal of legal activity followed, but in the end Judge Thayer ruled that the confession was unconvincing and insufficient grounds for a dismissal or a new trial.

When the news of the confession broke, Sergio was overjoyed. No matter what the courts did with the information, he was determined to follow up the lead and personally prove that the accused were innocent. He would have to find out who Madeiros was working with, and he would have to bring in another member of the gang, perhaps the leader himself. He might even have to force a confession from him. Toward this end, he armed himself with an automatic pistol and forty rounds of ammunition. When he explained to Emile Muro what he wanted to do, Muro said: "Forget it, Adamo. You'll never pin anything on those guys, whoever they are. And if you try, they'll kill you."

But it seemed to him the only hope. He tracked down some people who knew Madeiros. He got to the lawyer who had defended him, and to some relatives and friends. One acquaintance was willing to suggest that in those days Celestino had been working for the Morelli gang of Providence, Rhode Island.

Sergio told his wife that he had a chance of a good job out of town. She pleaded with him not to go, but he packed a bag and got on the train to Providence. He told her he was going to Hartford, where he had a friend. His own trail would end there. Nobody knew where he was, not even Emile Muro.

In the middle of winter, Providence was a dreary town. Red brick, cold rain, soot from a thousand chimneys. The January sky was heavy and gray. The cheap hotel he stayed in was only a notch or two better than a flophouse for derelicts. No questions asked. A dollar a day. No hot water. A toilet and a tub down the hall. In his narrow room there was a single bed. Beside it was a table with a lamp on it. There was a chair over which he could hang his damp clothes when he came in from the rain. It snowed two days after he arrived.

There was a minimum amount of heat. The radiator hissed

in the evening but went cold in the day. "Most people work in the day," said the clerk at the desk when Sergio complained.

He kept his coat on in his room and made notes in a small notebook. It reminded him of the diary he had kept while he was in prison. This, he thought, was another kind of prison. He had done a terrible thing and now he had to prove that it was justified.

He made the rounds of the local bars. He visited the Italian neighborhoods. He asked a lot of questions. He found out that there was a Mike Morelli and a Frank Morelli and a Joe Morelli, but nobody had seen them around for some time. There was also a man they called "Steve the Pole" Benkoski. And another man connected with the gang named Tony Mancini. It took three weeks to put together enough information to get a picture of the group. Joe Morelli was apparently the leader of the gang. "Don't fool with him," he was warned in the dim light of a bar. "And don't cross him."

After a month in Providence, Sergio was almost broke and in despair. He was down to his last four dollars, without a ticket home and without any definite clues to the whereabouts of the Morellis. He was ready to give up. That night it snowed again. He sat in his room and stared out the window into the street. He heard the scraping of a shovel on the sidewalk. There was a shadowy figure shoveling snow toward the white-gray dunes along the curb. In the middle of the street the trolley tracks glistened where a streetcar had just gone by. As he looked out on this scene he remembered the story that his father had often told him when he was a boy, the story of how his grandfather Lorenzo had died in the great blizzard of 1888 while he was shoveling snow. Now, for the first time, the loneliness and agony of that man he had never known became real for him.

Suddenly there was a pounding on his door. He was startled from his reverie and could feel the skin contract on the back of his neck. He reached for the gun that was in his coat pocket. He slipped it into the back pocket of his pants. "Who is it?" he called out.

"Just open the door," someone said.

He didn't know what to do. His heart was beating so fast that it made him dizzy. "What do you want?" he said.

The answer this time was a splintering crash that sent the door flying open. Before him were two men in black overcoats and soft-brimmed hats that shaded their faces. "Is your name Adamo?" said the first man.

"Yes," said Sergio, his mouth dry.

"My name is Joe Morelli. I understand you been asking around for me. Well, here I am. What do you want?"

"I–I–I'm a friend of Celestino Madeiros."

"Madeiros? That stool pigeon. What the hell does he want? I can't do nothing for him now. He's going to the chair."

"It's about the Sacco and Vanzetti case."

"What about it?"

"Madeiros says he was in the shooting at South Braintree."

"Yeah, so what's that to me?"

"He told some friends of mine that he was with your gang."

"Is that right? Well, now, ain't that interesting." He turned to the other man. "Come on in, Frank, and close the door. This fella here is trying to say that we pulled the South Braintree job and killed a couple of people."

"No kiddin'," said the second man.

"And why are you bothering yourself with all this, Adamo? What's in it for you? You a cop or something?"

"No, no, I'm no cop. I'm a friend of Vanzetti's. I'm trying to help him out."

Morelli pushed his hat back and revealed more of his face. He had a dark complexion and a mustache and was built somewhat like Nicola Sacco. He took a few steps forward and then sat down on the bed. Sergio was standing by the window, and Frank Morelli was standing by the door. "So you want to help your friend, eh?" said Joe Morelli.

"That's right."

"And how, exactly?"

"All I want from you is to put it in writing that Sacco and Vanzetti are not guilty."

"And that we are?"

"Yes. But they won't get you."

He burst out laughing. "This kid has got to be crazy, eh, Frank? Where do you come from anyhow, kid?"

"I come from New York."

"All the way from New York. How about that? Vanzetti must be some good friend of yours."

Sergio shrugged. He was suddenly conscious of the gun in his back pocket.

"So you want me to save the ass of some anarchist fish peddler?"

Sergio nodded. He felt his muscles growing stiff with fear.

"All right," said Joe Morelli, standing up. "Only I don't know how to write." From his coat pocket he drew a large revolver, perhaps a .45. "This is how I make my statements. What do you want me to say?"

The room seemed suddenly small and airless, like a dungeon. Outside he could hear the scraping of the snow shovel on the sidewalk. In that strange moment he realized that he had done it all wrong. All wrong! He started to shake his head, as though to deny something. Then he reached for the gun in his back pocket. A single shot shook the room. It knocked Sergio back against the wall and tore a hole in his chest. He saw the men turn to shadows. Then the floor was rising to meet him and the light went out.

The two men left the hotel. They went out past the clerk, who did not even look up from his magazine. Later he would tell the police that he heard nothing. Nothing at all.

# II

---

# New York 1933

". . . America can break your heart."

—W. H. Auden

# 1

It was early March, and heavy clouds swept through the five-o'clock sky. "What if it rains tomorrow?" said Joe Lucci. He was seventeen, like all the others, except Diego Hernandez, who was a year older.

Marco Adamo was on the roof of his five-story tenement house with four of his friends. The house was near Lexington Avenue on 112th Street. They had lived there since his father's death, some eight years earlier.

"It's not going to rain," said Marco. His friends called him Marc.

"How do you know?" said Joe Lucci. He looked small in his father's tattered hand-me-down jacket. It was heavy wool with a broken zipper and frayed cuffs. His father worked on the docks when he worked at all.

"Because I heard it on the radio," said Marc.

"Anyhow, it don't matter," said Marty Fischer. They called him "Fish." He was short and fat, with skin like sour cream and with glasses that made his eyes look too big. "It ain't a ballgame; it's an inauguration. They don't call it on account of rain, you jerk."

"I didn't say they were going to call it. I was just thinking about what Mr. Rosen said in school today. He said there was going to be a crowd of a hundred thousand people."

"So what?" said Marty.

"So nothing. It's just a lot of people. More than a World Series game," said Joe Lucci.

"Sure, because it's a big deal," said Marty.

"But why? The new president takes an oath and makes a speech. Who wants to watch that? And they come from all over the country? I wouldn't walk across town to watch that. Anyhow, it's going to be on the radio."

"Maybe you're not interested," said Marc, "but a lot of people are. It's history in the making. Later on they can tell their kids and grandchildren that they were there when Roosevelt was inaugurated.''

"My father says it ain't going to make no difference who's president. He says they're all a bunch of rich sons-of-bitches who don't give a damn about the poor.''

"If your father didn't drink so much, he wouldn't be so poor,'' said Marty.

"Hey, watch what you say, Fish. You're talking about my father.'' Joe's Sicilian eyes darkened, and he half rose from the pile of bricks that had once been a chimney.

"All right, all right,'' said Marty, backing off. "But I think anybody who wants to make a living can make it. My father sells potatoes and onions in the market. He's never been out of work because he works for himself.''

"My father's been out for over a year,'' said Diego Hernandez. "He don't do nothing. He sits around the house all day and drinks coffee. He talks about going back to Cuba. He says he'd rather starve to death down there, where it's warm in the winter. He hates the cold weather.''

"What about you?'' said Marc. "You want to go to Cuba?''

"Me? I was born here. I ain't never been to Cuba. How do I know?'' He was tall and angular, with a kind of El Greco figure and soft Latin eyes. He could draw and paint with a natural ability that mystified everyone in the high school, including himself. They had asked him to do a big mural in the auditorium, and he was trying to finish it before he graduated in June. They were all graduating together: Marc, Marty, Diego, Joe, and Kevin Flanagan, called "Red" because of his hair.

It was the "gang," "the club," "the boys." But not a gang in the usual sense. Not violent. Not a street gang, like those Italians or the Irish or the Negroes in nearby Harlem. There were even Puerto Ricans now, moving in near Madison and Park. Still, it was good to have a gang, because to go alone in the streets was dangerous.

The light was fading in the gray sky. It was getting colder. The rooftop was black tar. There was the sooty smell of smoke that drifted across the whole dismal scene. There were hundreds of such rooftops, some lower, very few a story or so higher, so one could see for miles. On each rooftop there were chimneys and a small housing for the door. Everything was tarred over. Everything was black or gray or sooty red. On some there were clotheslines and wires that served as radio antennae. On a few there were pigeon coops, especially east of Third Avenue, in the Italian neighborhood. Flying pigeons was a popular hobby. The birds flew together as a flock and were trained to return. One used a long bamboo pole to send them aloft and give them certain signals. Sometimes the boys found a dead pigeon on their roof, though there was no coop.

Marc was restless. He wandered around while the others talked about their fathers. Flanagan's father was a boozer and a wife beater. Red Flanagan hated him and had even had a fistfight with him in the street one day. He was thinking of joining the navy when he got out of school, "just to get the hell out of the house and the neighborhood."

Their voices drifted away on the March wind that drove the clouds toward the river. Marc thought briefly of his own father and of the mystery surrounding his death. He did not like to talk about him, nor did his mother. Marc had been only nine when Sergio died. He remembered him well, but always as a brooding, unhappy man who had been different from other men—Marc could not say in exactly what way. Different! A man with a secret. A man who in spite of his poverty had seemed connected with major things in the world. He had read a lot. He had seemed to know what was going on. He had talked about important people as if he knew them. Perhaps his father had been mad, he sometimes thought, and no one would tell him. "He liked the politics too much," was all that his mother would offer. "But don't ask me what it was all about. I don't know. I only hope that God has forgiven him and that now he is at peace. In this world he never was."

Marc looked toward the East River, and beyond, to the flat stretch of Queens that disappeared into the smoky late-afternoon sky. On this side of the river he saw the tanks of the gas company, the gray-green patch that was Jefferson Park, the barges tied up to the piers, one of them loaded with coal and leaning at an odd angle. To the north he could see the Harlem River and the South Bronx. To the south there was a great stretch of tenements until the buildings got taller and became the familiar skyline of Manhattan. There was the Chrysler Building and the Empire State Building. He had seen it being built. Joe Lucci's uncle, who was a mason, had worked on it. And to the west there was Park Avenue, where the market was, under the tracks of the New York Central Railroad, and then more tenement houses and a ridge of higher ground and some taller buildings. He could not see the Hudson River, but he knew it was there.

On a cloudy day like this everything seemed dim and faraway. He stood by a low brick wall capped with roof tiles and looked down into an airshaft. It was narrow and dark, and windows looked out into the dingy space. It made him dizzy to look down. He did not like heights and could never do the daring things that the other boys did when they played roof tag. But that was when they had been younger. Left over from those days was the crude shed they called their clubhouse. It was built with uneven boards against the housing for the roof door. By now it was abandoned and half collapsed, but on it one could still see the name they had chosen: *The Fugitives*. It was painted in red, now badly faded and only barely legible. In those days they spent hours and hours on the roof, talking, arguing, planning secret societies and comic-book gangs: *The Vampires*, *The Sky Hawks*, *The Raiders*, *The Spies*. The roof gave them a sense of freedom, because there they could feel invulnerable, as though the place were a fort. There they could be alone. And from there they could see out of East Harlem toward another world. It gave them the visible proof they needed that there was a place to escape to. Down at the street level one often felt that the neighborhood was all there was, and all there would ever be.

For Marc especially, East Harlem was a kind of prison from which he longed to escape. He knew all its boundaries and every block in it. For a while he delivered newspapers on foot. Then he had done some work at the settlement house for Mr. Lang, and for the first time thought of the place as a community, a slum. It gave him a sense of distance, a certain perspective. There it all was. And it was home.

East Harlem. Two hundred thousand people of over thirty different nationalities and all the races of mankind jammed into the most densely populated blocks in New York City. Its unofficial boundaries were Fifth Avenue, the Harlem River, the East River, and 96th Street. There had once been 150,000 Jews in Harlem and East Harlem, but barely 10,000 remained. It was now dominated by the Italians. There were pockets of Poles and Russians and Spaniards and Germans and Irish. Even white-haired Finns and gypsies and a handful of Orientals. The people of the great melting pot, melting and sweltering, struggling with one another and the hard facts of ghetto life.

It was a city within a city with 160 square blocks, 600 grocery stories, 500 candy stores, 378 restaurants, 156 bars, 230 tailor shops, 26 junkyards, 300 doctors, 14 pawnshops, 42 churches, and 11 funeral parlors.

Mr. Lang had told him all this—and more. Mr. Lang was a socialist, but not a radical. He believed in social and economic planning. He hated Hoover, but he thought maybe Mr. Roosevelt could do something to solve the nation's desperate problems. "He may be rich, but he understands the poor. Let's hope he doesn't sell out to big business. The time has come for the welfare state. There has to be an equalization of wealth. There has to be an end to poverty and suffering, to economic depression, to inequality and injustice. If things don't get better they will get worse, and if they get bad enough there will be a real revolution." Mr. Lang did not want to see that. He believed in the democratic process and a society run by laws. He even had faith in human nature, though working in East Harlem had often shaken that faith. He was a stocky man with a bald head and rimless glasses and a vaguely foreign accent. For Marc he was a link with the world of ideas.

It was Mr. Lang who had taken him aside only a few weeks earlier to ask him what he planned to do after high school. He urged Marc passionately to go on to college and offered what help he could. Marc didn't know what to say. He explained about his mother and his brother, who was only twelve. He explained about how hard times had fallen on his mother's family, how her father had lost his money in the collapse of the local bank, how he had suffered a stroke and then lost the butcher shop and everything. From the other side of his family there came nothing. He didn't know why. Some old dispute. Another mystery. And so his mother took in piecework and made maybe six or seven dollars a week, and he himself worked on Saturdays as a delivery boy for a drugstore on 73rd Street. There was a little help from Uncle Stefano, and that was it. They had been denied welfare, but they stayed off the breadlines. That was something at least. Now he was graduating, and maybe he'd get a job. Maybe!

What exactly he would do he didn't know. It bothered him to think about it. The clouds were getting thicker. The sky was getting darker. His friends were in a shouting argument about something or other. Someone was calling his name. He went back to them. "What do you guys want, anyway?" he said. "What are you fighting about now?"

"This jerk says that Jack Sharkey will put away Primo Carnera before the tenth round," said Joe Lucci. "He's got to be crazy."

"Oh, yeah?" said Marty. "You want to put some money on it? How much? How much you want to bet?"

"Fifty cents. I bet you fifty cents Carnera knocks his brains out."

"Yeah? Show me the fifty cents."

"Don't worry about it. I'll get it if I lose."

"Get the money first. Then we'll bet."

"Why the fuck don't you guys make a bet and shut up?" said Red Flanagan. "All you ever do is argue. What I want to know is are we going to the movies tonight or not?"

"What's playing?" said Diego.

"*Public Enemy*, with James Cagney, and a Bob Steele western."

"I seen it twice already."

"Well, what the fuck do you want to do, anyway?"

"I don't know. What do you want to do, Marc?"

"I want to go somewhere about a million miles away from you guys, so I don't have to listen to this shit anymore."

The apartment was on the third floor. It was warm. The radiator hissed and sometimes banged metallically, as if there were messages being sent from some other part of the building, a desperate man hammering away at the pipes.

There were three rooms, all in a row. From the dark hallway you went into the kitchen. The door was heavy. There was a metal number on the outside—3B. And there was a little circular bell that no longer worked. The hallway was cold, because the janitor refused to heat it. The radiators had been turned off and the valves jammed. It did no good to complain. The landlord lived in Queens. Nobody ever saw him. An agent collected the rent.

There was linoleum in the kitchen, scrubbed clean by Marc's mother. He hated to see her down on her hands and knees like that, making swirls of soap with that stiff wooden-backed brush—the scrub brush that every women in the neighborhood had. The mop, the scrub brush, and the washboard. Symbols of their calling. They were the mothers; they were the housewives. And they were poor. All Marc's friends had

mothers like that, with ill-fitting apron-dresses, with wisps of
hair escaping from hairpins and combs and kerchiefs. They
gathered on the stoop to talk. They went shopping with their
shopping bags. They climbed the stairs slowly, stopping to
rest at the landings. On pillows, they leaned out windows.
They called to the iceman and the potato peddler, and to their
kids: "Joey! Watch out for the cars! Angela! Be nice to your
sister!"

Marc's head was full of echoes and memories, undigested
observations, the unresolved arguments of his friends. He
didn't want to go home. He wanted to take a long walk.
Whenever his mind was cluttered that way, he tried to walk it
off. He would walk for miles sometimes, along the river,
across town, downtown, through Central Park—anywhere. It
didn't matter. It was as if he were walking away from all the
confusion. But he always came back. And there always was
this three-room apartment, with its shiny linoleum and dim
yellow light, with its cockroaches under the damp sink, its
narrow bathroom with no tub—they had to use the washtub
to take a bath—and a chain to flush the toilet.

They were in the kitchen when he came in. His mother was
at the gas stove. She glanced up at him and seemed momentar-
ily startled, as if she saw in Marc her dead husband. He was
now just as tall and lean and dark, but better-looking and
sturdier across the shoulders. It was the Gentile blood, more
pronounced in Larry (Americanized from Lorenzo), who was
broader in every way, like his grandfather Primo. He was
only twelve, but almost full-grown. He had hands and feet
like a man. He had a full, round face that was getting less
chubby as he stretched out a bit. But it was still oddly
cherubic and sweet, though, all in all, he looked like a
miniature truck driver. He was a strong kid and a tough kid
and all the boys on the block admired him. His brother,
Marc, also admired him, even envied him at times for his
courage and confidence. By comparison Marc was a kind of
Hamlet character, who worried his way through everything,
turning things over and over in his mind. Larry seemed totally
free of meditation. Even in his anger there was joy. And he
always seemed to be almost smiling, which only added to his
good looks.

Steam rose from the pot that Felice stirred. "Wash up. It's
almost ready," she said.

Marc looked at his hands. They were as black as the

rooftop. For some reason that he didn't understand his hands were always dirty when he came home, no matter where he'd been or what he'd been doing. It was the fine, invisible soot that fell like dust or death on all of East Harlem—on the rest of the city and perhaps on the whole world.

Larry was already at the table, slouching in his chair and playing with his fork. "Don't do that," his mother said when he made a scraping sound against the empty plate. "If you can't wait, then have a piece of bread."

For dinner there was spaghetti with a fish sauce that was made with tomatoes and codfish. Not Marc's favorite meal. It reminded him that it was Friday. His mother clung to her religion and her old ways, but she had long ago given up trying to get the boys to go to church. She did not make an issue of it, did not even discuss it anymore. Things were changing. With her children she spoke only English now. They barely knew Italian. And she herself had been brought to America as a young girl and didn't know what she was. She was Italian. She was American. She was Catholic. She was a widow, but she no longer wore black. She lived on a certain block in a certain city, but her neighbors were Irish and German and Jewish, as well as Italian. Their ways were different. It was all very confusing. When she was a child it was much simpler. There was only one way, the way of her father. The old way. But now her father was in a wheelchair and could hardly speak. His left side was paralyzed. His arm hung limp like the dead meat that he used to hang in his butcher shop. He was old and sick and bitter. He waited for death with a blanket across his legs in his wheelchair in front of the building in which they still lived. "I should send him back to the old country to die," her mother said. "I should go with him. But even there we have nothing. It has been such a long time. *Madonna mia!* I wish I knew what to do. What to do." And she would rock back and forth and dab at her eyes with her handkerchief.

Felice served out the steaming, soupy pasta. A white cloth hung over the enamel top of the kitchen table. There was a round loaf of bread, from which several slices had already been cut. The three of them ate like that almost every night, sometimes in silence, sometimes full of talk about something that had happened during the day. It was the "family," or whatever was left of it, and Felice held on to it, instinctively, joylessly. It was not until her husband died that she realized how much she missed having a daughter. She needed another woman in the house—mother, sister, daughter. It was only between women that certain things could pass. It had always been that way. Between women and men there was a distance, no matter how great the love. And here she was with these boys who were becoming men. What's more, they were becoming men in America. They learned things in school she did not understand. She sometimes glanced at their homework and shrugged her shoulders. And they had friends, whose families she did not know, friends who were not even Italian. It had never been that way before.

"Why does it always have to be fish on Friday?" said Larry. "We don't even go to church."

"I go to church," said Felice. "And you should too. It would keep you out of trouble." She turned to Marc. "Do you know what your brother did today? He had another fight. Right in the street. It was a disgrace. The boy's mother came out screaming."

"He hit me first," said Larry. "What was I supposed to do?"

"He was smaller than you."

"Yeah, but he's thirteen."

"It doesn't matter. Marc, tell him. Talk to him. You're the oldest—"

It made Marc uneasy when his mother talked to him that way, as if now he were the father. She had the old habit of referring certain things to her husband, and now he was the husband—the male figure. She could not get beyond that. It was too much a part of the way she had lived, and she would never change. But Marc did not want to play the father. He did not want to scold his brother. He did not want to go to work to support this family. He only wanted to live his own life. It was like the neighborhood itself. It was part of his prison—these demands, these obligations from another world, another way of life, from which he was breaking away. He could feel things inside of him tearing and cracking. He could feel his own resistance, an inner voice announcing freedom. Still, there was no freedom. Still, he was here in these three small rooms, at this small table with his brother and his mother and the smell of codfish and Clorox.

"What happened?" said Marc, looking at his brother.

"We were playing stoopball with Fritz and some other kid. What's-his-name, Stevie Malone. He said I cheated, I didn't touch the base. But I did. I swear I did. So he pushed me, and I hit him. That's all.''

"That's not all," said Felice. "He beat him up." Once again she appealed to Marc, and waited for him to scold his brother.

He knew what she wanted to hear. He didn't want to say it, but finally he did. "Listen, Larry, I'm warning you. You'd better watch your step. You understand? You don't fight unless you have to defend yourself. I don't want you to be a bully. If I hear that you're pushing the kids around, you're going to be sorry." That was as far as he could go.

His mother was satisfied, and so was his brother. The duty had been performed. Larry needed the voice of a man in the house as much as his mother did. They went on eating in silence. Outside there was the sound of rain against the windows.

After dinner Marc listened to the radio in the living room. It was another connection with the outside world. Through static and interference Marc brought in voices from hundreds of miles away. They came through the New York stations and the new network. Marc knew all about it. He read magazines in the library. He studied the listings in the newspaper. He knew all the frequencies, all the call letters: WOR, WJZ, WHN. The little cabinet was made of wood and looked like a miniature Gothic cathedral on the mahogany buffet by the window. A wire ran to the fire escape and then up the brick wall to the roof.

It was Uncle Stefano who had given them the radio, over a year ago. And what a revelation it had been for Marc. There was music. Popular music and classical music. He had heard phonograph records of people like Bing Crosby before, but not the other kind of music. He listened for hours without knowing what it was all about, absorbing it, solving it like a savage who sees a mirror or a camera or an airplane for the first time. And there was sometimes opera. That was more familiar. He had been with his father once to the Metropolitan Opera. They had sat high up, miles away from the stage, and they had heard the full, sweet sound and seen the sadness on the stage. His father had wept. Marc had been very young and did not understand. It had frightened him to see his father in tears. Now on the radio he understood. They had talked about opera in school. Mrs. Grasso had played records of

Enrico Caruso, and she, too, had gone misty-eyed as she listened. Marc's world was getting clearer and clearer, larger and larger. There was not only the radio, but there were books. There was the branch of the public library on 110th Street. It was one of the places where he and his friends would hang out when they had nothing else to do. They would browse and read and argue and fool around. Sometimes they would be kicked out for making too much noise. Marty Fischer was the big reader and the most passionate arguer. He could argue about anything from Einstein's theory of relativity to the effectiveness of Dazzy Vance, who pitched for the Brooklyn Dodgers. And always he was willing to put his money where his mouth was. "You want to bet? I'll bet you anything. Fifty cents. A dollar. Put up or shut up!"

Marc found the news broadcast he wanted. The deep, prophetic voice of Gabriel Heater filled the living room. He sat face to face with the radio, as though they were carrying on an intimate conversation. His brother sat on the daybed that opened up at night to accommodate both of them. His mother was in the kitchen folding laundry. The ironing board was up, and he could hear the tick-tick of the heating electric iron.

"There's good news tonight," said the commentator. "On the eve of the inauguration there is widespread hope all across the length and breadth of this beleaguered nation that the new president will be able to find a solution to the economic difficulties that have closed our banks and left millions without jobs. . . ."

The prophet of hope and doom went on, moving from domestic affairs to international developments. In Germany there was the burning of the Reichstag. The new chancellor, Adolf Hitler, and his Nazi party blamed the disaster on Jews and Communists. In Cuba, President Machado and his secret police, the *Porra*, were accused of more murders as resistance to his iron rule mounted. In China, the Japanese moved out of their puppet state in Manchuria into Jehol province, ruled by the opium-rich warlord Tang Yu-lin. Yu-lin was quoted by newsmen as saying: "The Japanese can have this province when all the Chinese are dead!"

After the news came Major Bowes's Amateur Hour. Marc's mother came in to listen for a while. With her quick hands she made small, neat bundles of their socks. Those with holes she sewed. Sometimes she paused to laugh. Marc was pleased when she did, because it happened so rarely.

It stopped raining. Larry wanted to play checkers. Marc said all right and allowed him to win one game. He pretended to be upset at the loss. Later he read a book and listened to music. Uncle Stefano came over, as he often did, and sat with his mother in the kitchen and drank coffee and talked in Italian. Marc and Larry paid little attention to them. About nine-thirty they went to bed, and in less than a minute Larry was asleep. Marc just lay there in the dark, hearing the voices in the kitchen but slipping away to other things. He and his friends had all been talking about what they would do after they got out of school. None of them really knew, except Red Flanagan, who wanted to join the navy, and Marty Fischer, who had applied to City College. He had urged Marc to do the same. It was easy to get to, he argued, and it was free. The trolley car went right up Third Avenue, across 125th Street, and then, with a transfer, up Broadway to 136th Street. But every time Marc thought of college, he also thought of his mother and brother. It wasn't fair to let her work like that. And even if they got on relief, they would be off again when he was eighteen, in December, because he would be expected to work. He was becoming the father of his father's family. And he resented it. It wasn't fair. It just wasn't fair. And it wasn't fair of his grandfather Gaetano, who could easily have helped them. If it weren't for the old fight—whatever it was.

By some strange coincidence his mother and Uncle Stefano were talking about the same thing in their quiet voices in the kitchen. They often talked about it, about the past, and about other problems in the family. "You could go to him even now," said Stefano.

"And do what? Beg? No, I will never do that. I will never take anything from that man. He destroyed his son, my husband. He turned his back on him when he was in need. He disowned him. You remember at the funeral how he came to me, a man with guilt on his back, blood on his hands, offering money. You remember what I did."

"Yes, you did a foolish thing. You spit on him and his money. You did not allow him to say he was sorry. Do you know how deep a hurt that was for him? Maybe deeper than the death of Antonio. Now a lot of time has passed, and you no longer get help from your family. Your poor father—'' He made a gesture with his hand. "For the sake of the boys you should go to him. He will not refuse you. But I know him. He will never come to you."

She shook her head slowly. "No, I can't, Stefano. I can't do it. We'll manage. One way or another we'll manage. Marc will get work after his graduation. He will have a diploma. He will get something good."

"There is no work. There is nothing. He will be standing on lines. He will be hanging out in the streets. He's a smart boy. He should go to college or something."

For a moment she said nothing. She aimlessly stirred the coffee that remained in her cup. "I can't go to him," she said in a fading whisper.

He reached across the table to touch her hand. "Then let's do the other thing that I have wanted to do for a long time. Let me be the father."

"But how can we do that? How can I marry my husband's brother?"

"It has been done before. There is nothing against it."

"What will everybody think? What will your family say?"

"Eh, and what do you suppose they think now? You think they don't know? You think the old ladies don't talk?"

"It would be the end of everything between you and your father."

"But what is there between me and my father? Ever since the war he has looked at me as if I was a cripple. It wasn't my fault. I had the war nerves. There were things I couldn't do. I could feel his contempt because I was unable to follow in his footsteps, because I had—you know—the episodes, the bad times. But . . . but I am much better now. I make a few dollars. I have my own place. And between us . . . well, you know how it is."

She looked at him with sad eyes. "Stefano," she said, "I don't love you. I don't know if I can be a wife to you."

"But we have slept together. We have been like a man and wife."

"That's different. We have been alone and there has been a desire. But there are other things."

"Love will come in time."

"How stupid of us to talk this way. In a year I'll be forty. What is love to me? A dead dream. A toy that a girl plays with."

"I'll also be forty, and I want to do something with my

life. I feel useless, except for you and the boys. They are of my blood, my brother's blood. It would not be like an ordinary stepfather. They would accept me."

"Of course they would." It was she now who was patting his hand. "But let me think about it. I'm too tired now. There is so much happening. My poor father is so sick. . . ."

In the darkness of the living room Marc became aware of the tone of their conversation, though not what they were saying. How soft and intimate it suddenly was. He wondered whether what one of his friends had suggested one day was true—that maybe they were lovers. He had buried the thought, because he did not know how to feel about it. Was he jealous? Was he angry? Should he somehow, as the man of the family, protect his mother? Or should he be pleased? All those feelings crowded in and then slipped away as sleep came to carry him off into dreams, those nightly wild and whirling dreams that seemed to be his other life.

# 2

Marc loved the morning, any morning, even one like this, which was cloudy and chilly. Morning meant a new beginning, new life, a new day. Anything was possible in the morning. Nothing was possible at night—that other death. There was danger in darkness, and there were bad dreams.

He almost always woke up with the first light of day, even this dim, misty light. As the days grew longer he woke up earlier. Sometimes he would read in bed. Sometimes he would go down to the empty streets and walk around, feeling superior because there was no one else there and, for a change, it was quiet. Sometimes he would imagine that everyone else in the city had died and that he had been left in complete possession of the place. But inevitably another person would appear. An old man with a junk cart. Somebody walking a dog. Another kid with a sense of adventure. And once a slender man with a mustache who said: "Come to my place. I'll give you a nice hot cup of coffee. Come on, we'll have a little fun.'' The man's desperate eyes were frightening. Marc did not even answer. He crossed the street and walked rapidly away. He had learned to sense trouble, to smell danger, and his impulse was not to fight but to run. His own fear embarrassed him. He did not want to think of himself as a coward. He was almost a man, and he should not be afraid. But through fear he learned to survive—the name of the game in East Harlem. Already three of his earlier friends were dead. Lou Cardona while hitching a ride on the back of a trolley under the Third Avenue el, Carl Hagerman from rheumatic fever, and Sal Buscemi, who was just fourteen when he died, from a knife wound. This death was the worst for Marc, because they had been good friends. It left him with a horrible sense of reality—the knowledge that death was real and inevitable. It was a cold thought that often kept him awake at night. But in the morning, ah, in the morning, all things seemed possible again!

And on this morning he would carry with him the added excitement of the inauguration of a new president. It was in the air. Everybody was talking about it. With fading hope the people had turned to Roosevelt. He was already something special in their eyes, a father for the whole nation. And for Marc, too, as he walked to the corner to wait for the Lexington Avenue trolley. He wore a short woolen coat and a cap. Under his coat he wore a school shirt and a tie, because Mr. Schneider wanted him to look presentable when he made his deliveries. The drugstore was in a very good neighborhood, a neat establishment with old apothecary glass in the windows and antique instruments on display.

Marc started work at eight and finished at seven. For his eleven hours he earned two dollars. He carried a sandwich and an orange in a brown paper bag and took fifteen minutes off for lunch. His carfare was a nickel each way, and sometimes he spent a nickel on a Coca-Cola. But there were occasionally tips, nickels and dimes that could add up to as much as eighty cents or even a dollar near the Christmas season. It was a good job and he felt lucky to have it. He felt lucky too because he got to walk around among taller apartment buildings and even along Fifth Avenue and Central Park. He rode in elevators sometimes, usually the service elevators. He rang doorbells. He saw other people. And then there was the shop itself, with all its medicines and chemicals and health aids—a fascinating place that had been there on 73rd Street for almost fifty years. At home he had a chemistry set, and Mr. Schneider gave him a few things to "experiment" with. Mr. Schneider was already an old man, and he had a nice smile. "You could do worse," he had said, "than to be a pharmacist. It's a good life. A good living." He had a Jewish accent. He was clean and meticulous and moved around the shop with a wonderful fussiness. He had a middle-aged assistant who spent most of his time in the back making up prescriptions. Marc sat on a stool behind the counter and waited for deliveries to go out. When he had nothing else to do, Mr. Schneider made him dust the already immaculate shelves or move boxes around in the little storeroom.

Marc arrived early. It didn't matter. Mr. Schneider was always there before him, no matter how early he arrived. Marc had the impression that he was always there, that he had no other life aside from this drugstore. He never saw him in anything but his white coat or anywhere but in the shop. And Mr. Schneider never talked about his private life. Marc often wondered whether or not he had children, but never had the courage to ask.

"Well, today is the great day," said Mr. Schneider. "We get a new president. What do you think of this Roosevelt? You think he is any good?"

"I think he will be better than Hoover," said Marc.

"Even I would be better than Hoover," said Mr. Schneider with a smile. "But that's one job I wouldn't want for anything in the world, especially right now. What a mess, eh? What a mess!"

"My history teacher, Mr. Rosen, thinks that Roosevelt will get us on the road to recovery."

"Well, we'll have to wait and see, won't we? You know what they say about promises, promises. The inauguration will be on the radio. If we are not too busy we'll listen later on. We'll see what the man has to say."

Millions of other people would also listen to the special broadcast, among them Gaetano Adamo, at sixty-three the influential leader of the Italian-American Political Club on 116th Street.

He was getting ready to go out. He stood before the full-length mirror in his bedroom and did up his striped tie. His white shirt had a starched collar. Over his shirt he wore suspenders and then a gray vest that went with his new gray suit. He buttoned his vest snugly about his middle and patted himself. He still looked sturdy and trim. He had taken off a few pounds around the middle and he felt good—very good, he thought, for a man of sixty-three. A touch of white in the temples and in the mustache, but all in all distinguished, maybe even handsome. At least there was a woman of thirty who thought so. "Just an acquaintance," he said to Silvio. "Nothing serious."

"Married?"

"Yes, but her husband travels a lot."

"Be careful he doesn't come home unexpectedly one night."

"He should thank me for looking after her. If it wasn't for me, she would have left him long ago."

They laughed in the old way.

He brushed his hair and then put on his jacket. He turned this way and that to see how he would appear to the world, and then he nodded, as if satisfied, and went down to the kitchen.

His wife and daughter were there. Francesca was three years younger than he but looked ten years older. She had not been well for a long time, and in the black clothes that she had vowed to wear forever she looked not only old but unhappy. She had never really recovered from the death of her sons. And then there were other deaths, some in the old country, some here. Her parents, her brother, a cousin. She rarely left the house except to go to church. Now that Laura was back she did most of the shopping. She had come home from California without a husband but with a three-year-old daughter named Lisa Martin. Mr. Martin, she had explained, had left her suddenly for another woman, and his whereabouts were unknown. Gaetano had never believed her story. Her mother did not seem to care especially, having assumed from the time her daughter left the house that she was ruined anyway. And what was she to do but take her back when she was in trouble, disgrace and all? It deepened her bitterness, but she was moved by the baby, Lisa, and spent many hours with her, talking to her in English and Italian, sometimes singing to her—songs from her own childhood and from her youth when she was first a mother.

Laura was thirty-five, still attractive, but obviously worn by her experiences in the hard world of entertainment. She had made a few films, but never the big time. She had involvements and betrayals. She had compromised. She had taken jobs she didn't want. She had lived with a man for a while. Then one drunken night she had married the man called Bill Martin. She had hardly known him. It wasn't even his real name. And he hadn't been at all what he seemed. He had been drunk a great deal. He had been cruel. And he had not been an assistant director at Twentieth-Century Fox. He had been nothing. A lounge lizard. A partygoer peddling his decaying good looks. He had gotten her a job in a speakeasy on Sunset Boulevard. He had gambled, and finally, he had disappeared.

"Are you going to eat before you go out?" said Francesca. She noticed his neat appearance but said nothing. She had long ago resigned herself to the fact that she had lost her youth, her looks, and even her health. She had nothing with which to hold him, except her position as his wife. And that, she knew by now, nothing would take away from her, except maybe death. As for the rest—well, what was she going to do? He was still vital, still handsome. Let him do what he had to do. She would keep his house and mourn for his sons. Perhaps in the next life they would be lovers again. For this she prayed on her sore knees in the church before the Virgin Mary. And sometimes in the night, when he was a long time coming home, she even prayed for death, for an end to the misery and the pain.

"I will have lunch at the cafe," said Gaetano. "And then I will go to the club to hear the speech."

"What speech?"

"The speech of the new president. It is the inauguration today. It will be on the radio. You should listen. And you too," he said to Laura, who sat at the kitchen table with Lisa on her lap.

"I'm not interested in politics," said Laura.

"You're not interested in this. You're not interested in that. What the hell are you interested in, anyway? Lipstick? Cigarettes?"

"Please, Papa, don't start."

"And when are you coming home?" said Francesca.

"I'll be home when I get home," he said.

She smiled sadly, remembering how he used to say that when they were first married. That was more than forty years ago. She held back the tears with tight lips and urged him toward the door. "Go, go," she said. "Enjoy yourself. Don't drink too much. It makes you get up in the night."

The Italian-American Political Club was housed in a three-story building that was owned by Gaetano. On the ground floor there was a storefront meeting room, with card tables and folding chairs and a private bar. Upstairs there were several offices with desks and telephones and metal filing cases. Here the people of the neighborhood came with their problems. Many wanted jobs. Many hoped to get on home relief. Sometimes a landlord raised the rent or refused to paint or to fix the heat. Sometimes a boy was in trouble with the police. At the club they could always get somebody to listen, and almost always they could get help. They showed their appreciation by voting the right way at election time. There were many who were not well educated and did not understand politics. They waited for someone to come from the club to tell them the right thing to do. It was the old system all over again. The *padrones*, the bosses. They knew best. They were the middlemen. They had influence higher up—in this case with Tammany Hall. "It's simple," Gaetano often explained. "We give them the votes; they give us the jobs. Street cleaning, construction, you name it. We got a foot in the door at City Hall. You know what I mean?"

By the time Gaetano got to the club there were already about forty men there—no women. The tables were all full, and extra chairs had been set up all around the rim of the room. The big radio had been put up on the little platform, as though it were human and would deliver a speech. "Hey, Gaetano!" someone called out. "Hey, *compare!*" said someone else. There were many greetings. Gaetano shook hands. "Look at him. What are you doing, running for governor? Look at that suit. A hundred-dollar suit!"

He nodded. He strutted. He took out a cigar and lit it, blowing smoke into the already smoke-filled room. But it was not a celebration—not entirely, because at the 1932 Democratic convention Tammany Hall had backed Al Smith again. Their favorite, Mayor Jimmy Walker, had resigned under pressure, after the Seabury Report recommended to Governor Roosevelt that he remove the dapper darling of the Tammany Tigers.

On the other hand, Roosevelt was a Democrat, and that

was something. Besides, there were other elements in the city with which it was possible to do business. Ed Flynn, for instance, of the Bronx, backed Roosevelt. In Rockland County it was James Farley. "One has to see which way the wind is blowing," said Gaetano. "When the price is right, we can deliver the vote. Let *them* decide who the candidates will be. When we want a candidate of our own we will make some noise. Like for the congressman of the twentieth district—that's what we worry about, eh?" And the mayor. It was beginning to look as though LaGuardia would run in the fall. That made a difference to many members of the club. To get Italians in office—that was important. But he would not be the candidate of Tammany Hall. Curry would insist on John O'Brien. "A big mistake," some of them said. "A very big mistake."

It was a noisy, smoky crowd. There was free wine, compliments of Priola, and free beer, compliments of Rocco D'Angelo. They could afford it. Prohibition had made them rich. And there had never been any problem in the neighborhood with the police or the government men. That had all been taken care of.

It was almost time. Some men fiddled with the radio to find the right station. Everyone seemed to be talking at once about Roosevelt. There were loud remarks on both sides, and many gestures of the hands, not all of them decent.

"Quiet!" someone shouted. "It is beginning."

A hush fell over the room. On the wall behind the platform were two flags, one American, the other Italian. The voice of the announcer was garbled at first. Then they heard the swearing of the oath and the new president spoke to more people at one time than had ever heard a president before. The announcer described him standing there in the chill wind without a hat or overcoat, his defiant chin thrust forward against the invisible enemies of the nation.

"My friends, this is a day of national consecration," he began. And then the powerful lines: "The only thing we have to fear is fear itself—nameless, unreasoning, unjustified terror which paralyzes needed efforts to convert retreat into advance. Our common difficulties concern, thank God, only material things. . . . Only a foolish optimist can deny the dark realities of the moment. Primarily, this is because the rulers of the exchange of mankind's goods have failed through their own stubbornness and their own incompetence. . . . This nation asks for action, and action now. Our greatest primary task is to put people to work. . . . May God guide me in the days to come!"

They could hear the roar of the crowd. The people had come in silence and uncertainty. They would go away with new hope. "An incredible display of enthusiasm," said the announcer. "This man already seems to have captured the hearts of those who have heard him speak. And indeed, ladies and gentlemen, it was a powerful and inspirational speech, one that will be long remembered. . . ."

Back at the drugstore Mr. Schneider was wiping tears from his eyes and trying to hide the fact from Marc. "Good! Good!" he kept saying. "Perhaps we will have a future after all. For you, I mean, for the young. You should have it better than us. You should have a better world." Then, suddenly, he cleared his throat. "All right, now, back to work, back to work!"

But later, just before closing time, Mr. Schneider gave Marc a long, serious look. "So tell me, sonny, what are you going to do with your life? You're graduating from high school. You should have plans already. What are your plans?"

Marc shrugged. "I guess I will look for a full-time job." He explained about his family, even about Gaetano. "But he gives us nothing, because he disowned my father."

"Why? What was the matter with your father?"

"He was against the war. He refused to register." Marc hesitated. "He went to prison. When I was nine years old he died."

"And you mean to tell me that your own grandfather has done nothing for you? Impossible. Disgraceful. Why, if I had a grandson—"

"My mother refuses his help."

"Nonsense! Your mother has nothing to do with it. Your grandfather owes it to you. Listen to me, sonny. Go to your grandfather. You say he is an important man, a man with money and property. Go to him. Be bold. Tell him that you want to go to college and that he must pay for it. Believe me, he will admire you for your courage. Don't be afraid. You won't get anywhere with a high school diploma. Everybody goes to high school these days. It's no big deal like it used to be. But you are a smart boy. You can be something. All you need is a little *chutzpah*. You know what is *chutzpah*? *Ach*, never mind. Just do what I say. Go to your grandfather. Do it right away. Tomorrow. Sunday is a good day for such things. He will be home. He will eat well. He will be in a generous mood. I know how you Italians are. Deep down, softhearted and all family.''

Mr. Schneider locked up and then went back to the cash register. He took out two dollars and handed them to Marc. Then he hesitated before taking out another bill. He handed this to him also. Marc looked at it. It was a five-dollar bill. He started to say something. "Never mind! Never mind," said Mr. Schneider. "Just take it and shut up! Now, go. Go home. And remember what I said."

Marc did not forget. It was as if he were under orders. After all, Mr. Schneider was his boss. But he also knew it was the right thing to do. He woke up to a clear and beautiful morning and took a bath while his mother and brother were still asleep. He put on clean clothes, even a tie and his best sweater and his only jacket, so he looked quite dressed up. Later, when his mother saw him, she said: "What's this all about?"

"It's Sunday."

"Sunday you usually knock around with your friends."

"Maybe I'm going to church for a change."

"For you that would be a very big change."

"All right, then, maybe I have a girl friend."

"A girl friend? What are you talking about? You're only seventeen. Don't start with the girls. There will be plenty of time for that."

"What's the matter? You jealous?" He teased her.

She smiled. "All right, then, don't tell me what you're doing. I don't care. I don't want to know." She started to make breakfast.

"I'm going to buy the newspaper," he said. "I'll be right back."

On the street he felt good in his leather shoes. The bright sun made everything seem doubly alive and sharp. There was a special quiet, clean quality about Sunday mornings. The Department of Sanitation truck had been by, and the street was damp where it had been sprayed down. Rivulets ran along the curb, carrying away the waste of the past. The bell was ringing at the Protestant church around the corner. He bought the paper at the candy store, the *Daily News*. It carried a bold headline about F.D.R. Inside, there were comics and sports and advertisements. He enjoyed the smell of the candy store—the blend of tobacco and sweets and stacks of paper—the soda fountain, the magazines, the model airplanes. The kits were ten cents. From them he had built a Spad and a Fokker Triplane, the kind that had been flown by Baron von Richtofen.

When he came back his mother scolded him for going out without a coat. "It's not as warm as it looks," she said. "It's only the beginning of March."

He sat down to breakfast. She served him. Husband, son, or father, she would have instinctively waited on him. The old way was profoundly etched in her mind. What was a duty was also a privilege. She didn't even have to think about it. "I made you something special," she said. She presented him with a plate of French toast and sausage.

As he ate she sat opposite him, having only coffee. She seemed to take more pleasure in watching him eat than in eating. "You look nice all dressed up like that," she said. "But you don't have to tell me where you are going. If you were a girl it would be different."

He said nothing for a while, but when he was finished eating he said: "Do you want to know what I am going to do today?"

"Only if you want to tell me."

"I'm going to see my grandfather."

She frowned. "My father?"

"No, my grandfather Adamo."

Her frown deepened. "But why? We never go there. You know that."

"I want to see him. I want to talk to him."

"About what?"

"I'll tell you after I see him."

"I can't stop you. It's your right, but—"

"Don't worry about it, Ma. I know what I'm doing."

She said nothing further. She cleared away the dishes, then went into her bedroom to dress for church. When she came back he kissed her for the first time in years. She tried to smile, but she looked confused. "Will you be back for dinner? We have a chicken."

"Yes, Ma, I'll be back," he said, and went out.

As he approached the house on 116th Street his courage almost failed him. He had not been there since his father died. A few times he had seen his grandfather on the street, and for a long time his grandmother came by to visit them— but less and less frequently, until she stopped coming altogether, except on holidays.

He found the house, a sturdy brownstone. He went up the front steps and into the hallway. It smelled of polish. There was a big carved door with a piece of heavy cut glass in it and a curtain on the glass. There was a brass mailbox and a little overhead chandelier. His heart was pounding as he pushed the electric bell. He could hear it ring inside. Through the curtain he could make out someone coming to answer. The door opened. An attractive woman stood there. At first he wasn't sure who she was. She also was slow to recognize him. Then she broke into a broad smile and said: "Marco. Is that you? My God! Look at you." And she called back: "Papa! Guess who's here? It's your grandson Marco." And then to Marc, after the ritual kiss, "Come in! Come in. What a surprise!"

Francesca's eyes immediately grew moist. She embraced him and muttered something in Italian that he didn't understand.

They were in the kitchen. Gaetano came in, not yet fully dressed. He was adjusting his suspenders and his still half-buttoned-up shirt. He paused in the doorway and looked Marc up and down, as though he were trying to find in him the nine-year-old boy he had last known. Then he smiled diplomatically and shook his head. "I can't believe it," he said. "You're all grown up. Look at you. And you finally come to see us, eh? Finally. What took you so long? Come on, sit down, have a cup of coffee. Is anything wrong?"

"No, no, I just wanted to talk to you, that's all."

"Eh, Laura, don't just stand there. Get him something. Get us some coffee. *Dio santo!* I can't believe it."

"We were just getting ready to go to church," she said.

"All right, then, go, go!"

"We will see you when we come back," she said.

Francesca stood there with her hands pressed together as though in the presence of a miracle.

"Come on, Mama, we're going to be late," said Laura. And she took her mother by the arm.

When they were alone Gaetano shook his head and said: "These women! More trouble than they're worth. When you want to eat, they want to go to church. When you want something else, they have a headache."

"I hope you don't mind my coming here like this," said Marc.

"What do you mean *mind*? What are you talking about? I'm your grandfather. No matter what has happened in the past. You should tell that to your mother. She's been a very stubborn woman. When your father died I offered to help. I offered to forgive."

"I know," said Marc.

"But she refused. And even worse. What fights we had in this house because of your mother."

"And my father."

Gaetano lowered his voice and looked away for a moment, as if into the past. "Yes. He was very difficult. You know the story?"

"More or less. But I didn't come here to talk about all that."

"No, we mustn't rake over the ashes. What's done is done. We were all wrong in our own ways. We were all foolish. I sometimes think that getting old and wise is just a matter of finding out what a fool you have been. I hope you don't make all the mistakes I made. But I imagine you will find a few of your own to make." He brightened. "Ah, but you look fine. So grown up! Such a young man all of a sudden. Where does the time go? How long has it been? Eight years now since your father died. You are in high school, no?"

"Yes, my last year."

"I know. I don't come around to see you, but I know what's happening. I always hear. I hear from your grandmother, and from other people in the neighborhood. I keep my eye on things. I even know about your job downtown." He looked around, as if for a woman to pour his coffee. Then he shook his head. "They are never here when you want them. We should go to the cafe."

"I've eaten already," said Marc. "I just came to ask something of you. I can't stay long."

Gaetano got up and went to the stove. He found a pot of freshly made coffee. He put out two cups and filled them. It was as if they could not get serious without the ritual of food or drink. It was not until he had made the symbolic gesture and sipped his coffee that he could say: "All right, then, tell me what it is that you want. A job, maybe, after you graduate from the high school?"

"No, I want to go to college," Marc blurted out.

"Mmm!" said Gaetano. "College, eh? And what for?"

"I don't know yet. But I don't want to waste my life. I don't want to work yet, just to support my mother and brother. I want to get an education. I want to be something."

"I don't blame you. If I had to live my life over again, I would feel the same way. I would have gone to school and the university. And you know what I would have been? I would have been a lawyer. That's right, a lawyer. And do you know why? Because I could have gone into politics. Instead, I went to the army. And when I came out I was nothing. And by then it was too late to do anything but look for work. I was married. I had kids. For me it was too late to think about anything except how to survive. In the old country when you were poor you didn't even think about going to the university. Maybe you could become a priest, like my brother, but that was different. I didn't want to be a priest. I was wild. I didn't believe in nothing." He shook his head. "The things I did you wouldn't believe. Me and Silvio and our other friends." He paused and looked wistful. "Now some of them are dead, and we're all getting old."

"When I was a little kid my father told me about the war you were in in Africa. You were a lieutenant."

"Yes. It was a terrible war, like all wars, but it was also different. Not like this last war. It was . . . it was . . . I don't know. Different! Let's hope you will never have to go."

"Do you think there will be another war?"

"I don't know. Strange things are happening in Europe. You know, I went to Italy last year when my mother died. She was very old, eighty-eight. I brought back my sister Angela with me. There was nothing there for her anymore. Nothing for me either. I didn't know anybody. It had been what? Thirty-two years. And the whole country is different. This Mussolini has changed everything. These Fascists. I don't know. Some people here think he's wonderful. But you have to go there to see. Everybody in uniform. Police everywhere. No freedom. I don't like it. And now in Germany this madman Hitler. God knows what he will do. I'm afraid there's going to be trouble, big trouble. Let's hope that this time America will stay out of it. Those people over there, they don't know when to stop killing each other. Sometimes I think your father was right not to go. But at the time I did not want my sons to be called cowards. Now I would give anything to have them back." He tightened his lips and blinked his eyes as if to hold back the tears. "Ah, but what are we talking about? The past is done. We live now and for the future, eh? Life is only real when you're alive. I'm alive and you're alive, and here we are. You have come to me, and I understand. Believe me, Marco, I understand. You want me to help you, and, of course, I will. The only problem is your mother. She will not take help from me. I would gladly give it. If not for her, then for you and your brother. But how are we to do it?"

"I don't know. I thought maybe you would find a way. I just want to go to school with a free mind."

"And what college do you want to go to?"

"Some of my friends are going to City College. I suppose I could go there. It's free. But I would like to get away from home. I would like to live on my own."

"Yes, that's a good idea. Get out. See something of the world. Meet people. Perhaps you will be a lawyer, eh? That would be wonderful if you could be a lawyer. And then, later on, if you wanted to get into politics, maybe I could help you. I'm not without influence, you know. I have the political club. I have connections. Yes, yes, we could make something of you. You have the looks. You have the intelligence. And you have the Adamo blood. By God, we *will* make something of you. And never mind about the college of the city. We will put you in a big university with the rich boys. We will give you some class. You leave it to me. I have friends. I can fix it. I know a professor at Columbia University. He's Italian, very big in his field. I will talk to him. And as for your mother—well, don't worry about that. I will manage it somehow."

Marc didn't know what to say. He stood up awkwardly. "I should get home. I hope you didn't mind my coming here like this. I just didn't know what else to do."

Gaetano walked him to the door. "Of course I don't mind. It was a good thing you did to come here. Good for both of us. And I expect you to come again, often. Do you understand?"

Marc smiled. "Yes, sir!" he said.

At the door Gaetano extended his large hand. Marc took it. Then suddenly, the old man embraced his grandson as if some dam of feeling in him had broken. He held him for a long moment, kissed him on the cheek, and, just as suddenly, pulled back. "All right, then, go. You have things to do."

As Marc walked away along 116th Street there were tears in his eyes. He did not acknowledge them, because he had denied the habit years ago. Only children cried, and he was not a child anymore. He was a man.

# 3

Like a walled city within a city Columbia University dominates Morningside Heights. It looks west to the Hudson River and the Palisades of New Jersey and east over the bleak clutter of tenements in Harlem and East Harlem. Its outer rectangle of attached buildings is penetrated only by arches and 116th Street, which is private where it passes through the heart of the campus. Though the style of the structures varies from classical to turn-of-the-century modern, there is something medieval about the way this great center of learning defends itself from the city surrounding it. It has the advantage of the high ground on one side and the river on the other. Though cosmopolitan in the vastness of its resources, it is still oddly monastic in design. Crime and commercialism flourish on the outside like marauding bands of vandals and barbarians, while inside professors and students guard history and ideas and literature against the death of civilization.

From the very first moment that Marc set foot on campus, a special excitement gripped him that heightened his perception. With hungry eyes he saw everything, and for him everything was new. On a clear, sunny day in spring he wandered among buildings and lawns and churches like a creature from another planet. He stood outside Hamilton Hall, where, his guidebook told him, most of the undergraduate classes were held. He walked through Van Am quad. He looked at statues and read inscriptions carved in stone. He studied the very bricks in the paths and followed the flight of pigeons as though he had never seen pigeons before. Surely, they were not the same species that settled on the black rooftops of East Harlem.

He was conscious of his own feet, his newly shined shoes,

his clothes, his appearance as a stranger—perhaps an intruder—
in the eyes of those who already belonged. He walked slowly,
turning this way and that, looking up the high facade of
Livingston Hall and Hartley Hall, and across to Furnald and
the Journalism building, and beyond to Kent and Schermerhorn
and the chapel. There were stone benches and alcoves and
memorials to great men who had made their mark here and in
the outside world. Ivy climbed the redbrick walls. There were
actually trees! And here and there, in the startling sunlight of
the first spring of his new life, were arrangements of flowers.
He absorbed them with such appreciation that it was a wonder
they were still there after he had passed by. There were no
flowers in East Harlem, except those few that grew in stingy
boxes on windowsills that faced the sun. Here there were
hundreds. Thousands! Untrampled and unrobbed.

It was this, perhaps, more than anything else about the
place that impressed him—that so much grandeur and beauty
could exist and not be violated It was clearly a safe place,
possibly even a sacred place. He had never known such a
place before. In his world there was no safety. Nothing was
beautiful. Nothing was sacred. When he was anywhere outside of his apartment he moved instinctively with catlike
caution, because the streets and parks and hallways were
dangerous.

He had his interview with the dean in Hamilton Hall, a
special arrangement made by Professor Gian-Battista Clemente,
of the Italian department. At University Hall he registered one
day. He ate his lunch at a wooden table on the lawn and was
approached by squirrels. He was shown his room, a small,
narrow space with a desk, a bed, and a closet—all his own.
Incredible! It would be the first time in his life he had ever
had a room all to himself. He was even proud of the number
on the door: 324. It was a better number than any of the
others! It had a special ring to it. He repeated it to himself as
he wandered around the campus and over to the great Cathedral of St. John. "Three twenty-four. I live at three twenty-
four Livingston Hall. I am a student at Columbia University."
He was trying on his new identity as one might try on a new
suit of clothes. And he was turning this way and that way to
see himself in a mirror in his mind.

When he left home he assured his mother and brother that
he was only going across town and that he would come back

often. Even in that emotion-filled moment as they walked him
to the trolley they looked vaguely betrayed, as though he
were deserting them. He secretly believed that all his
promises to return were lies, because he wanted to go and
never come back. Somebody had unlocked the prison door,
and he was going to get out before the door slammed in
his face.

It was a hasty farewell. A quick kiss, a handshake, a brief
struggle to get his suitcase onto the trolley. Then a wave from
the rear window and a strange sinking feeling in the pit of his
stomach as his mother and brother grew smaller and smaller
and finally disappeared.

His first day and night in Livingston Hall were filled with
confusion and apprehension. He was never quite sure that he
was doing what he should be doing or acting the way he
should be acting. He had taken on a whole new identity. Even
his own voice sounded odd as he talked with other young men
on the third floor. There was a lot of activity and noise. There
were many parents in the hall, helping their sons move in.
There were suitcases and trunks. There were tennis rackets
and musical instruments, radios and typewriters. He caught a
glimpse of a three-room suite furnished not with standard
college furniture but with plush chairs and rugs and drapes
that could only have been privately provided. His own room,
by comparison, suddenly seemed monkish and drab, with its
institutional mahogany stain and its bare floor, but he loved
it.

He wandered in and out, upstairs and downstairs. He sat at
his desk, a simple, austere table with a tarnished student
lamp. He arranged his few papers and his catalogue. Then he
rearranged them. He imagined a shelf of books. He scribbled
nothing in particular on a yellow pad. Then he tore out the
page, crumpled it up and dropped it into the small metal
wastepaper basket. It was the first time he had done that in
his own room at Columbia College, and therefore it was a
wonderful act.

The boy next door introduced himself as Howard Porter,
from Little Rock, Arkansas. Marc was astounded. He had
heard of Little Rock, but he never really believed that anyone
lived there. "And where are you from?" said the neat boy
with the short hair and the face of a young businessman.

"Oh, I'm from right here in New York," said Marc.

"How about that," said Howard Porter. He spoke with a

peculiar accent, not quite like the southern accent one heard in the movies. "You must have had an interesting life."

"Well, sort of," said Marc, afraid to elaborate.

"Little Rock's all right, but it sure can get dull at times."

The conversation faltered. Other boys came down the hall. Several of them seemed to be old friends already, though they had only met that day. There were introductions: Alexander Sheffield, Arnold Gross, Franklin Dobbs, Douglas Weems, Leslie Perrin, Pierre Gerrard. Marc had some difficulty remembering who was who, except for two foreign students: Reinaldo Ramos, who was from the Philippines; and Koji Nakamura, who was from Nagasaki, Japan. Koji was only two doors down from Marc. He was a pleasant fellow, but slender and silent, with a permanent polite smile.

Marc felt lost in some of the conversation. Most of the students seemed to know an awful lot about the college. They mentioned faculty members, fraternities, meetings they had been to, plans for that night and the next day. Even the names of girls at Barnard College.

He retreated to his room. He was suddenly tired. He sat at his desk, which was by the window, and looked out into the quad. A September cloud dimmed the scene. Colors softened and faded. A little swirl of dust swept across South Field from the running track that circled it. Groups of students walked by, laughing, chattering. He had no idea where they were going or where, in fact, there was to go. He had not yet been to the Lion's Den or any of the dining halls. He had taken in too much too soon and wanted to be quiet for a while. He sat there until the cloudy sky turned into an orange-gray sunset and made silhouettes of the buildings across the way. What now? he thought. His clothes were in the closet. His empty suitcase was shoved under the bed. He couldn't just sit there like that in his room. He put on a sweater and went out.

He found the Lion's Den, the college bar, one flight down and without windows but with polished wood and pennants, tables and booths, and the fragrance of beer and food. It was crowded. Someone was playing the piano. There seemed to be a party going on. He watched for a while, but was too shy to intrude himself into the gaiety.

He went back upstairs and then outside into the growing darkness. He wandered through the campus, through circles of light made by lampposts. Some of the buildings were dark, but the dormitories were blazing with light. He walked to the corner of 116th Street and Broadway, and then south on Broadway, which was wide and lined with shops. Suddenly he was out of the citadel and in the ordinary city again. He felt naked and lonely.

He became aware of his hunger and looked for a restaurant or a grocery store—something. He still had the ten dollars his grandfather had given him for spending money in his pocket, but he was determined to make it last as long as possible, just as he was determined to take as little as possible from anyone. He had already been told that he would be eligible to work on campus, and he had chosen a kitchen job in one of the dining halls. His hours would be six to nine in the morning, when his classes would begin.

At a delicatessen he bought two hot dogs and ate them as he continued down Broadway. Before he reached 96th Street he had passed several movie houses, and it occurred to him that he might get through the evening by going to the movies. He went to the Thalia and saw a film called *Shanghai Express*, with Marlene Dietrich. He lost himself in the exotic setting and was moved by the beauty of Dietrich. He had seen her before, in *Blue Angel*. He enjoyed being there in the dark, an anonymous participant in the fantasy on the screen, but soon it was over and reality returned in the form of a newsreel. An urgent voice talked of the negotiations between Chancellor Dolfuss of Austria and Mussolini of Italy, *il duce*, who had proposed an Italo-Austrian-Hungarian bloc. In the next sequence were roaring crowds of Nazis in uniform, and Hitler himself, delivering a frantic speech in German, which the announcer translated simply as: "There can be no peace and stability in Europe until Germany and Austria are united!"

Marc walked back to the campus along Riverside Park. Across the wide, dark river he could see points of light, like stars, along the Palisades.

Back in his room again, he prepared himself for the great adventure of sleeping alone for the first time in his life. He had never been away from his family. He had never traveled farther west than New Jersey or farther north than Westchester County. He took off his clothes, except for his underwear, and got into bed without the ceremony of washing or praying. He pulled the covers to his chin and lay there for a while with the light on. Then he turned the light off and lay in the dark. Through the window shade came a hint of campus lights.

There were distant sounds of traffic, and voices from other parts of the building.

His mind wandered. He thought of his friends and wondered whether or not they would come to see him as they had promised. He missed them already, even more than he missed his mother and brother. He had been with them all the time, every day. He suddenly realized how important they were to him—or *had been* to him. And he realized also, with something like fear, that all that was over, that things would never be the same again. They might very well not come. How could they? They had lives of their own. And even if they did, it would only be for a visit. It could not be as it had been before. And then he wondered what they were doing that very night, whether or not they were talking about him or thinking about him. They were all still there, still together. Marty had not gone to college after all, because his father had gotten sick and he had to take over the stall in the market. Joe Lucci was waiting around for his uncle to get him a PWA job. And Diego was hiring himself out as a house painter when he could have been painting the *Mona Lisa*.

A wave of sadness swept over Marc and turned to drowsiness. For a while he fell into an uneasy sleep. A few hours later he woke up in a sweat. He had had a nightmare in which he had been on the rooftop of his house and had fallen into that airshaft that went down, down, down, but had no bottom. He fell into darkness past windows like blind eyes.

He got up and put on the light. He did not know what time it was, because he had no watch or clock. He dowsed his face with cold water at the sink, and then put on his clothes. He was afraid to go back to bed. Instead, he sat at his desk and wrote a long letter to his grandfather, thanking him for all he had done and telling him how wonderful his first day at college had been.

In the days that followed, many things happened. A whole world of ideas and books came flying at him. He sat in classrooms with his tie and jacket, as all the others did. He read into the night and fell asleep over unfinished assignments. He worked in the kitchen; he joined the freshman track team. There was no time to think about the past. He made some friends but kept much to himself, still somewhat out of step with how the other students lived. He was drawn to two of his professors and sometimes stayed after class to talk with them.

There was Professor Gian-Battista Clemente, to whom his grandfather had first referred him, who remained his unofficial adviser and mentor. He was a leisurely, elderly man, a product of the universities of Europe, a scholar of considerable reputation, a humanist with a human touch. His office was a wonderful clutter of books and papers and pictures and smelled of the same cigar smoke that Marc remembered from the old cafes of the Italian neighborhood—the cigars, in fact, that his grandfather Gentile had smoked until his stroke.

Professor Clemente had a great shock of gray hair and an elegant mustache that curled whimsically at the ends so that he seemed always to be amused. "Tell me," he would say, "what you are reading these days. What you like and dislike." And they would talk about Plato and Aristotle and the Greek plays, which were all part of Marc's Humanities course. And they would talk about the direction in which Marc might go. "You like the science, eh? Yes, yes, very impressive to the modern eye. But a seduction too. Science is wonderful, but it is not always the same as wisdom. Remember that. There are many ways to reach the truth. Art is very important. Very important indeed. But we are in an age of great materialism. It is *things* we want. Machines. I, personally, am very suspicious of the machine. We make the aeroplane"—he pronounced it with four syllables—"and then what do we do with it? We drop a bomb on our enemies. But who are the enemies? We are. They are. Somebody else is. We are all enemies. And what a pity it is."

"I thought I might be a doctor," said Marc one day.

"Yes, yes," said Professor Clemente. "A doctor. A mechanic of the human body. Such people are, of course, necessary. I have known many doctors. I am always amazed that they are so incapable of abstract thought after so many years of study. I find them remarkably dull. But don't let me dissuade you. If you feel you have a calling in this direction, by all means pursue it."

Some months later Marc decided that he did not want to be a doctor after all and would not continue as a premed student. "I think I am interested in broader things," he said. "Ideas. Philosophy, maybe."

"There was a time, of course, when all things were philosophy. In the ancient world. Even in the Renaissance. To understand the universe. How noble. How grand. But today if you are a philosopher you can starve to death, unless you become a teacher. It is all one can do. It has been cut off at both ends, the political and the scientific. The practical applications have been carried off by the men of action. Soon it will be only a little academic enclave of fussy old men.''

Still another time Marc arrived with a manuscript in hand. ''I've written a story,'' he said. ''Do you think you would have the time to read it?'' He was considering literature. Perhaps he would be a writer.

''It is the best and the worst of all the ways to spend one's life,'' said Professor Clemente. ''If you can write like Shakespeare or Dante you will be a God, you will be immortal. But if you are a commercial storyteller or a cheap journalist, you will squander yourself to amuse your readers.'' After reading Marc's story he said: ''You have some talent, but it is very, very rough. You must learn the forms. You must read. You must practice.''

It was not until his sophomore year that Marc began to think seriously about becoming a lawyer. Pressure from Gaetano made it almost impossible for him to arrive at a decision without some confusion and resentment. He did not like being pushed. He wanted to find his own way. Sometimes Gaetano came by unannounced and took him to lunch. Marc could not say no. He felt like a child in his grandfather's presence. And he felt a little embarrassed in the dorms. Gaetano was clearly not well educated and obviously an immigrant. He still had an accent. Marc thought of himself as an American, and he was unconsciously disconnecting himself from everything in his past, because his past was a nightmare from which he was trying to escape.

But aside from Gaetano's expectations, Marc felt himself drawn to the study of political science and law. Not petty legalistic matters, but the broader questions. ''Man is a social animal,'' said Aristotle. ''What is justice?'' asked Plato in the *Republic*. Marc became fascinated by political and social structures, by history, by the ways in which the human race tried to find happiness. ''If you are not careful,'' said Professor Clemente, ''you will wind up in politics. That can be dangerous, especially these days.''

And in that moment, with the sun pouring through the arched and leaded window, illuminating the books and papers and the gray hair of the smiling professor, Marc realized that something was drawing him irrevocably in that direction. Was it the influence of his grandfather, the ghost of his father, or some natural predilection to be where the power was? "I don't want to be a voice crying in the wilderness," he said, having just recently heard the expression in another course. "I would like to do something significant in the world, something for the people, all the people."

"You sound like a socialist. Arrogance and impatience makes us all revolutionaries when we are young. Later we realize that history is not a dead cat to be put out in the garbage, that tradition is not just a prison but sometimes the very foundation of the house."

"I'm not a socialist."

"What are you, then?"

"I don't know."

Professor Clemente leaned back in his large chair and lit a cigar. The smoke wafted into the beams of sunlight. "Tell me, Marco," he said. "Do you know what is going on in Italy these days? Do you know about Mussolini?"

"A little. He's very popular in the neighborhood I came from. You see many Italian flags there. And there is a feeling of pride, because Mussolini has put Italy on the map again. But I don't know about men like that. About Hitler and *il duce*. I am for democracy."

"National pride can be a very dangerous thing. Let me tell you about this man. I was there when he came to power, in 1922. It was, in fact, one of the reasons I left. There were many of us who opposed him, even when he first formed the *Fasci d'Azione Revoluzionaria*. We could see the trouble coming. He believed in force. He talked about 'a bath of blood.' He is a great demagogue, an emotional speaker, a strong leader. We Italians have always had a weakness for such men. Men who could talk. Men who reminded us of the ancient glories of Rome. But did you know that in the beginning he was a socialist?"

"No," said Marc.

"Yes, an honest socialist. A schoolteacher. A journalist. He was named after Benito Juarez, the Mexican revolutionary. I think it was the *irredentism* that started him on another course—to recover certain lost territories. The idea of national destiny. He was influenced by Cesare Battisti and the reading of Nietzsche. He was against the church. He even wrote a novel called *The Cardinal's Mistress*. But he has gotten much support from the church. And do you know why? Because he finally destroyed the socialists, and also the communists, and even the republicans. He destroyed them with armed gangs before he ever achieved power. The government looked the other way, because they wanted the radicals wiped out, and *il duce* was a convenient instrument. Little did they know the price they would have to pay. From the *squadre d'azione* there came the party itself, the *Partito Nazionale Fascista*. Under pressure, King Victor Emmanuel asked him to form a cabinet in 1922. After that—well, after that everything changed. By 1925 he was virtual dictator of Italy. And now we are in the grip of a passionate patriotism that I am afraid will prove fatal. While millions cheer, many of us weep for Italy. There are no real elections. There is no real justice. There are no unions, only the *corporazioni*. Everything is controlled. But you see, our people here do not understand. All this noise and music and flag-waving appeals to them. To them it is all a big pageant, an opera. I don't mean to be insulting, but they are naive; they are stupid. If only they knew. It is up to your generation to enlighten them. Get your education. Go back among them. Tell them the truth."

Marc looked down at the faded rug, away from the piercing eyes of the professor. "I don't think I will ever go back," he said.

"But why? They are the people who need you. They are your people."

"I want to be an American, not an Italian. I was born here. And besides—" He hesitated. "I don't know. It was oppressive. I never felt free of the old values. Their ways are so rigid. Their thinking is so narrow."

"Are you ashamed of them?"

"Not exactly."

"I think you are. It is a pity. It is the influence of the prejudice. Americans have disliked the Italian immigrants ever since they started to come here in great numbers. They have had contempt for them because they are different, because they are poor and uneducated, because they speak a foreign language and keep to themselves and have strange ways. They call them dago and wop. They laugh at them. It is a crime, really, what they have done to us here. But the worst crime of all is when they rob the young of their self-respect. Believe me, Marco, it is not a disgrace to be an Italian-American. You must never feel ashamed. In time it will pass. But only if we believe in ourselves. We are of a great culture, and the old ways have much to commend them. Don't you ever forget that. The love of art and music. The adoration of the family. The sensitivity to life. You must never lose these things because they call you names. They call this country the 'melting pot,' but when finally they have melted us all down, when they have boiled away our culture and history, what will we have?''

Marc was left speechless by the outburst. He was moved yet uneasy. He suddenly wanted to leave the smoke-filled office. He wanted to be out in the sunshine. He wanted to be running around the track, feeling the cool breeze against his sweating skin.

"I'm sorry," said Professor Clemente. "I didn't mean to be carried away. You will not forget to come to *Il Circolo Italiano* on Wednesday. We have a very interesting speaker. I insist that you come. Now, go. I have work to do.''

Once in a while Marc went to see his mother and brother. He brought with him a bag of dirty laundry, not because he could not find another way to do it but because his mother expected it, desired it. It was her way of participating in this new phase in her son's life. He brought home his laundry as a kind of gift to his mother. He allowed her to do it and thus share in his new life. He came home but never spent the night. Even in the summer he took a course and kept his room.

At home they thought he looked different, even talked different. "I don't know; it just don't sound like you," said Larry.

"You're crazy," said Marc, slipping back for a moment into the Italian-American sound, with its distinctive rhythms and slurrings. He had not consciously changed his speech, but on his infrequent trips home he became more and more aware of how his friends and relatives talked. And it began to offend him, because he was falling in love with formal English. He was reading good literature and listening to the accents of other people. There was a student from England who would have been called a faggot by Marc's old friends, because he spoke in the precise, almost effeminate way that the English have. Marc was fascinated. The guy actually pronounced every syllable, every consonant and vowel. What's more, he came out for track, and they often worked out together. His name was Andrew Moore. He had blond hair and blue eyes and was almost too handsome.

When his old friends finally came to visit him, Marc was glad that they did not meet Andy Moore. They might have laughed or made fun of him. The whole visit was something of a failure, as Marc had feared it might be. They came to the dorm without calling and had to wait around in the lobby. There were three of them: Marty, Diego, and Joe. They came on an impulse. They were not used to planning things. They had been sitting around, as usual, when one of them said: "Eh, let's go see Marc, what do you say?" And they were off. They took the crosstown trolley at 116th Street and got off when it turned south on St. Nicholas Avenue. They walked up through Morningside Park and found their way to Livingston Hall. In their street clothes they looked out of place. In the lobby, students glanced at them with curiosity. When Marc came in he wasn't at all sure that he was glad to see them.

"So this is it," said Marty. "This is where you live?"

"Yeah," said Marc, trying for the old rapport. "Come on, I'll show you my room."

They went up in the slow elevator and crowded into the narrow room, which seemed smaller than ever with four of them in it. There was only the one chair and the edge of the bed. "Not bad!" said Marty, who sat at Marc's desk. "You really got it made."

"You meet a lot of girls around here?" said Joe.

"The girls are at Barnard College, on the other side of Broadway."

"Just across the street?" said Joe.

"So, come on, tell us. You get laid yet?" said Marty.

"That's none of your fucking business," said Diego on Marc's behalf.

Marc thanked him with a smile. "You want to see the campus? I'll show you around."

"Sure," said Diego.

"I don't know," said Joe. "Maybe you got things to do. Maybe we should go."

"But you just got here."

He took them down and showed them around the various buildings, museums, and churches. Cautiously, with what they imagined was reverence, they lowered their voices, but could not alter their language: "Holy shit! Look at that dome," said Marty. Joe Lucci whistled to express his awe.

They went down to the Lion's Den and had a beer. Marc could tell they were uneasy, perhaps even envious and resentful. There was a special sadness in Marty's eyes. "How's your father?" said Marc.

"About the same," said Marty.

"Any chance of going to college next year?"

"I don't know. My mother says she can handle the business herself, but I just don't know."

They went back up to the quad and stood around. Then Marc said: "Hey, I have to go to a meeting of the Italian Club. You want to hang around for a while or come back later? Maybe we can have something to eat." It was a lie, and later he was angry at himself. Of course, they didn't stay. And they never came back again. He saw them occasionally in the old neighborhood when he went to visit his family. Then less and less frequently. Then not at all.

There was a lot of social activity on campus, but Marc was generally not part of it, except for the Italian Club. He had no extra money to spend on dates. And he had no dates. What's more, he was unfamiliar with dating rituals, and that made him shy. He just worked in the kitchen, went to classes, studied, and worked out with the track team. Sometimes he was entered in a meet, but he never did very well. He was good, but not quite good enough. But he went on running, because the physical exercise was exhausting and exhilarating. It also helped to keep his mind off sex. But still it intruded, and his desire was a kind of agony because it could never be satisfied by fantasy and by what he did in the night in the privacy of his room. There were no girls in the college, but there were quite a few in the rest of the university. He looked at them longingly from a distance, at the way they walked and the way the wind played in their hair and in the folds of their skirts. He had an occasional encounter—a smile, a conversation, a cup of coffee—but nothing ever became more than an acquaintance. Opportunities came and went. He scolded himself for not being bolder, and he listened with envy to the stories of other students who had been to dances, to fraternity parties, to weekends of skiing and hayrides. He felt removed from it all, and he didn't quite understand why. It wasn't just the money, he finally decided. It was a lingering feeling that he didn't quite "belong." He found himself in a curious no-man's land. He had broken away from his old life, but he had not really broken into his new life. It left him feeling desperately lonely.

Then something happened. The something was someone: Alyson Whitney Harper.

In the spring of his sophomore year he was working out with the track team, hoping to earn a place on the mile relay team so that he could make the trip to the Penn Relays. He wanted to go not because he thought he could win a medal but because he had never been anywhere and he had an urge to travel.

Track is not really a team sport. One runs alone. One struggles more against one's own limitations than against the opposition. Perhaps that's why Marc was drawn to it. There was very little interaction with others, very little conversation. The coach suggested exercises and sometimes assigned specific distances during the workouts, but a runner was almost always on his own.

Marc wore ordinary gray sweats over his blue and white uniform. His soft leather shoes were spiked up front and without heels. They forced him to run on his toes. He was really a sprinter trying to stretch out to the quarter-mile. He had good speed off the mark, could do the 100 in ten-flat and about twenty-three for the 220. But he had yet to break fifty-four for the quarter, and that wasn't quite good enough, even for the weak second or third leg. It was a question of endurance, and the coach had him doing some half-miles to build up his wind. Marc loved to watch the distance runners, those lanky, shallow-chested, gaunt, and lonely men. How light they seemed, how inward-looking and brave. The long-distance runner knew pain. He needed special determination. The sprinter only needed speed.

Sun after rain brought out the green of the infield. Toy white clouds played in the blue sky. The buildings of the campus looked clean and sharp. After the long winter, spring had come like an immense seduction to soften the whole world and drive the students half insane. They stayed up too late. They drank too much beer. They wandered, like lovesick troubadours, to the dorms of Barnard College.

Marc lost himself in his running. He had taken off his sweats and was warming up with a slow half-mile. His legs felt good. His breathing was steady. The air conspired with a thin film of perspiration to keep him cool. He enjoyed the motion—needed it, in fact, after the long hours of study, of sitting still. *That* was the real discipline, he thought.

The first time he passed the girl in the red sweater he didn't really notice her. She was a blur of red and blond, a hint of beauty behind the veil of his meditations. But the second time he went by, breathing more heavily, he saw her very clearly. She was just standing there, holding some notebooks against her chest. She was looking at him. She was watching him run and she was smiling. He went by, glanced back briefly, and saw that she was still staring at him. He was embarrassed and confused. Perhaps she had mistaken him for someone else, he thought. He slowed to a jog and went once more around the track.

When he passed her again he was just walking. "Hello!" she said. "Are you a tracker?"

"A what?" he said.

"You know, a runner—whatever you call it."

"Well, what do I look like?"

"A little silly in those shorts. And going around and around like that."

"Why were you looking at me?"

"Actually, I was looking for a friend of mine. A boy named Alex Sheffield. Do you know him?"

"Yes, do you want me to get him for you?"

"No, no, that's all right. He told me he was on the team. I thought I'd come down and watch."

"Then why were you looking at me?"

"I don't know. You went by and you had this serious look on your face. What could you have been thinking about?"

He blushed and laughed. "I really don't know. I was just running. Listen, Alex is right over there, if you want him. I—"

"No, I don't *want* him, tracker. I just wanted to watch him. I wanted to see how he looks in his uniform. They're kind of cute."

"What?"

"The shorts. They have little slits in the side."

"Yes. For freer motion."

"I'm all for that," she said, and made a motion of her own that was oddly suggestive. Her clothes were collegiate and expensive. She wore them like a model in a magazine, and she was very beautiful. She had blue eyes and fine, precise features. She seemed animated by some special intensity and boldness. A little feverish, in fact, so that her soft, white skin was touched with the color of roses. She was the all-American Anglo-Saxon girl, of that northern European blood that in those stern climates produced fine skin and fair hair and an elegant frame.

Marc was disturbed. She was more attractive than any woman he had ever talked to, and he felt suddenly clumsy and a bit stupid.

"Well," he said, "I guess I'd better—I mean, I'm supposed to be—"

"Running around in circles?"

"Well, yes, I guess you can say that."

"Isn't it rather silly?"

"What?"

"Running in circles. I mean, it seems awfully pointless. I can understand football. And baseball makes sense, I guess. But this seems ridiculous."

"It's not really. You see—"

"Oh, don't try to explain it. Just tell me your name."

"My name is Marc Adamo."

"That's a nice name. Would you like to know mine?"

"Well, I—"

"My name is Alyson Harper. Alyson Whitney Harper. Isn't that a horrible name?"

"I think it's very nice."

"I think it sounds stuffy. I'd like to have a simple name, like Mary or Ellen or Jane."

Marc shifted uneasily from foot to foot and glanced back across the infield to where the coach was standing. "I'm supposed to be working out," he said.

"Not forever, I hope."

"Only until about five."

"Good, then we can have a cup of coffee or something, can't we?"

"I guess."

"I'll be in front of the library. Don't be late. I hate to be kept waiting."

He was too puzzled to do anything but nod his head and start back up the track.

"Hey!" she called out after him. "I didn't come to watch Alex Sheffield run around in circles. I came to watch you."

*     *     *

Alyson did not settle for coffee. She insisted on going down to the West End, which was practically a campus bar. She no longer had books with her. She did not even have a purse. And she had changed into a dress that buttoned tightly up the front and descended to her calves. It revealed her delicate shoulders, her perfect bosom and narrow waist. Everything about her was extremely feminine—her slender fingers, her slightly high-pitched voice, her sensual mouth.

"You're not wearing the same clothes," he said when he met her.

"Neither are you." She ordered a beer.

"I'm not supposed to drink when I'm in training," he said.

"But beer is good for you. Irish women drink it when they're nursing their babies. It's full of malt and hops."

He laughed and ordered a beer. They sat in a booth. For a few moments he looked at her without knowing what to say.

"What's the matter, tracker? Lost for words?"

"I don't know. It's just a little strange, that's all."

"You mean *I'm* strange. Just because I come to watch you run."

"But you don't even know me."

"I've seen you around."

"Where?"

"None of your business. I saw you and I wanted to meet you. I'm notoriously spoiled, and I usually get what I want."

"Does that mean you're also rich?"

"*Stinking* is the word. Daddy's got bales of money. It's disgraceful, in a way, with so many people out of work and standing on breadlines and all that. But I don't feel guilty. Why should I? I had nothing to do with it either way."

"Where does it all come from?"

"I really don't know. Banks and things. He has an office on Wall Street. They say he was a genius to survive the crash. While other people were jumping out windows, Daddy was quietly taking over things. He was not in the stock market, though. Something else. Much too complicated for mere mortals to understand. But he's not a bad old teddy bear. He's very generous with us all."

"And who's *us all*?"

"Moms and Babs and Miles. Moms is the garden club."

"You mean she belongs to it?"

"No, she *is* the garden club. Very, very proper. She

doesn't approve of me at all. Everything I do shocks her. It's kind of fun.''

"Like what?"

"Like wearing tennis shoes to her charity ball. She was not amused. She keeps telling me I should be more like my sister, Babs, who is married to the son of Loomis and Loomis, Incorporated, perhaps the ugliest man in Westchester County. Moms is terribly afraid that I will take after my brother, Miles, who is the real black sheep of the family.''

"What does he do?"

"Miles? Nothing. He's been in Europe for a year or so. He says he's writing a novel. but we all know that he's drinking a great deal and gambling and doing all those fun things. You know, like the Fitzgeralds and the Murphys. He's almost thirty and I don't think he's ever written a line or earned a dollar. But he's very pretty and everybody adores him.''

Marc stared at her across the table as though he were in the presence of a new species of animal. He studied her. He absorbed her. He tried to solve her. But that was not easy. She talked a great deal, but she was elusive. She dodged in and out with flippancy and wit. But Marc imagined that he could see in her pale blue eyes a more serious person, a girl, a woman with real feelings. A little sad, perhaps. Or was he only finding there what he preferred to find? It was even possible that the sadness he saw in her eyes was his own. This girl was more than a challenge for him—she was impossible. Worlds away. Modern with a vengeance. Self-centered. Sure of her beauty. Careless! His own views of men and women had been forged in the crucible of his family. It mattered little that he had denied the old ways. They lingered in him, not sharp and absolute as in his grandfather, but like shadows and echoes. Women were not supposed to act this way. They were not supposed to be sexually aggressive. They were not even supposed to be witty. Wit was a weapon in a man's arsenal. A man was supposed to amuse a woman, and she was supposed to be a passive and appreciative audience. She was supposed to guard her virtue with coyness and practical morality. But she was supposed to seethe with repressed passion and have a burning desire for marriage and babies. He knew that all this was nonsense, that the world was changing very rapidly, and that he was no longer even altogether Italian, but he could still not escape the shadows and echoes.

"We're all going abroad this summer," said Alyson. She talked in a quick, slightly detached way. Her eyes were not fixed on him. They caught him as if in passing, then she glanced here and there around the bar and then at him again. "We're going on the new *Queen Mary*. It was just launched last year, and Daddy says she's going to try for a new record. He wants to be there when it happens. Somebody or other at Cunard is a very good friend of his. And he doesn't much like the French."

"What does that have to do with it?" said Marc.

"They hold the record, with the *Normandie*. But Daddy thinks they're awfully arrogant, and we're not going to Paris this time, which is really too bad, because it's such a beautiful city and my brother is there making a very bad reputation for himself. So he will have to meet us in Italy or Majorca or someplace. I'm really dying to see Italy. All that art, and all those mysterious Italians." There was mischief in her smile, and Marc didn't know whether to be pleased or offended.

"Do you like Italians?" he said.

"I've never met any. Daddy says they're all a bunch of anarchists. And Moms thinks they're dirty. But I hear the men are very handsome and very interested in women, especially foreign women. My aunt Jessica fell in love with an Italian in Naples ten years ago, and I don't think she ever recovered from it. He was married, of course. They all are."

"I'm not," said Marc.

She looked at him suddenly as though he were really there. "What do you mean?"

"I mean I'm Italian and not married. But then, I'm only nineteen."

"You're joking. You're not really Italian, are you?"

"My father was born in Naples. My parents are both Italian, but I was born here in New York. I guess I'm what they call an Italian-American."

"Oh! I'm sorry if I said anything nasty. I didn't know. I mean, you look so American."

"And how exactly does an American look?"

"Oh, you know! It's more in the manner than the looks." She smiled. "I think that's really neat."

"What?"

"That you should be Italian. I knew there was something about you I liked."

"I thought it was my legs."

"Well, as a matter of fact—"

They laughed. She leaned back and drank from the cool, sweating glass of beer. A thin line of foam clung to her damp upper lip. She licked at it with her tongue.

"Your legs aren't bad either," he said.

"Do you really think so?" she said. "I always thought they were a bit too shapeless. You know, when I was twelve I was just as tall as I am now. But what a stick! Daddy used to say that I was as graceful as a young giraffe."

"Well, something must have happened since then, because I think you're very beautiful." He said it before he knew he was saying it, and he suddenly sounded too serious.

Her gaze no longer wandered from his face. He could almost feel her mind at work. For a moment the pose was gone. She even spoke differently. "You mean it, don't you?" she said. She was not even smiling.

"Yes," he said.

She was silent for a second or two. And then the curtain rose, and there she was on stage again—Alyson Whitney Harper, the rich girl without a care in the world. "I meant to go to the library, I really did. But it's such a quiet, boring place. I have to write a term paper about Machiavelli. We were given a list to choose from. I don't know why I chose Machiavelli. I don't know anything about him, except that he wrote a book called *The Prince*. It sounded sort of like a fairy tale, I guess."

"It's not," said Marc.

"You've read it?"

"Yes. It's a very important book."

"Good. Then you can tell me all about it and save me the trouble. Is that cheating? I don't think so, do you?"

That night Marc could not sleep. He could not quite believe that he had been singled out by this rich, beautiful girl, who could undoubtedly have anyone she wanted. But what exactly did she want from him? he wondered. He dared to think of sex. But where? How? He couldn't visualize it. And he was worried about his inexperience. Nervousness heightened and dampened his desire all at once. He lay there in the dark, thinking of naked bodies, reviewing incidental adventures that had never gone all the way, and he tried to persuade himself that it was, indeed, possible to make love to Alyson, that behind that fancy facade she was just another girl. But she was not ordinary. Perhaps she was a nymphomaniac. He and his friends made jokes about such girls. And the shadows and echoes said that any girl who announced her desire was not normal.

The next day they met at the library to talk about Machiavelli. Marc tried to be serious. Alyson listened as though she were impressed, but she could not take the fifteenth century seriously. "You know," she said, "you have a very nice voice. Can you speak Italian?"

"Yes, but not very well. After my father died—"

"Oh, is your father dead? How sad! What happened?"

He hesitated. "I'll tell you some other time. You have a term paper to write. Remember?"

"I have a horrible habit of putting things off until the last minute. Then I stay up all night and work like a demon. You probably think that I'm a bit of an idiot, but really I'm not. I get reasonably good grades. God knows how! I mean, sometimes it's all so boring I could scream. I wish I had you around in the middle of the night. To study with, I mean," she hastily added, but she was smiling, and he saw again that lively devil in her eyes.

The next day was Friday and they went to the movies to see *King Kong*. She grabbed his arm and seemed genuinely frightened. They held hands. He was so conscious of sitting next to her that he almost lost track of the film. But it was difficult to ignore a fifty-foot ape, and it was impossible not to feel sorry for him as he was kidnapped from nature and chained to a stage in New York for the amusement of the heartless crowd. When he made his final, tragic stand atop the Empire State Building, Alyson cried. He could feel the stifled sobs and, in the flickering light that came from the screen, could see the tears that dampened her cheek. He put his arm around her and drew her toward him in a comforting way. "It's only a movie," he whispered.

But later, outside, as they walked back along the park, she almost cried again. "It was so sad," she said. "They didn't understand. They were so cruel."

"Beauty and the beast," said Marc.

"I'm sorry," she said. "I should have warned you. I always cry in the movies."

"How about in real life? Do you ever really cry?"

"Not very often. When I get depressed, I usually wind up doing something silly."

"Like what?"

"Like wearing tennis shoes to the charity ball."

They laughed. They paused to look down at the river and the moon's reflection on the water. "Would you like to kiss me?" she said.

"Yes," he said.

She tilted her face to his. He kissed her innocently. "That was nice," she said, but she would not let him go on. They walked hand in hand in silence.

When he was leaving her at the dorm, she turned to him, as though in midthought. "Besides," she said, "it would never have worked out."

"What?"

"King Kong and Fay Wray. I mean, talk about mixed marriages . . ."

In that instant, he almost fell in love with her. Almost. But there were still the shadows and echoes.

In the days that followed, Marc imagined that he was getting to know Alyson better. He sometimes thought of himself as a hunter. He was stalking her, trying to catch her in a clearing, unprotected, so that he could see exactly what she was. But every time he cornered her she slipped away. Sometimes he became the prey. One day they passed a line of ragged men, waiting for some kind of public relief. The line moved slowly. The men shuffled in old shoes, their shoulders bent in a posture of defeat and failure. Marc felt a stab of pity, then anger. He turned to Alyson. "How can you say you don't care when you see things like that? Are you sure that being rich doesn't bother you just a little bit?"

Her reply was like a counterpunch. "You know, you're awfully sentimental about poverty. Are you poor? If you are, what are you doing at Columbia?"

He didn't know how to answer. He had told her very little about his life, and she hadn't really asked. "I don't think that has anything to do with it," he said.

"Of course it does. If being rich is such a sin, then how come all those virtuous poor people want to be rich?"

"I didn't say the poor were virtuous."

"They certainly aren't. They're ugly and vicious!"

"Don't say that."

"It's a free country. I'll say whatever I please. I suppose you find those men attractive. Look at them. They are the dregs, the failures in a competitive society."

"They are the victims."

"Oh, nonsense, Marc. That's what I mean by sentimentality."

"I'm talking about compassion."

She paused to stare at him. "You *are* poor, aren't you?"

"I don't know."

There was a touch of cruelty in her laugh. "How can you not know? Either you've got it or you haven't."

"You mean money?"

"Yes, money."

"We never had very much. Yes, I suppose we were poor, but I have a grandfather who came as an immigrant from Italy and did quite well."

"Ah, the rich grandfather rescues the poor boy from the slums and sends him to the university. How touching!"

He could not explain the meanness in her mood, and they did not seem to get along at all that day. But the next day she called, not to apologize but to say that her car, which had been in for repairs, was ready. She insisted that he come with her. "We'll take a ride. You'll love it. It's a yellow Buick roadster. The top goes down and everything." She was full of girlish delight. It was as if their serious conversation had never taken place.

He tried to understand her inconsistencies. He made amusing laws and categories: the Alyson Shift (a sudden change of mood), the Alyson Freeze-out (three consecutive days of inaccessibility), and the First Law of Thermo-Alyson Dynamics (passion after detachment, often in the dark by the river). He responded with a wide range of feelings, from resentment to affection to physical desire. The desire was difficult to deal with. He was absolutely convinced that there was an understanding between them, that sooner or later they would make love—but he had no idea when, and the choice seemed to be hers.

Then one day he decided that she was just toying with him, using him until she could go back to whatever boyfriend or fiancé she had waiting for her in Scarsdale.

He confronted her directly. "Is there a man in your life?" he said, feeling foolish.

"I thought you'd never ask," she said.

"You mean you *hoped* I wouldn't."

"It's not in very good taste, you know. Moms wouldn't approve at all."

"I'm sorry. I suppose I have no right."

"I don't mind," she said. "I take it as a compliment. It probably means you like me."

"Of course I like you."

"But do you love me?" It was a glancing sort of question, not altogether serious.

"Do you want me to?"

"No. It would only complicate things. Daddy wants me to marry Terrence Morley. Isn't that ridiculous?"

"I don't know. Who's Terrence Morley?"

"Oh, just somebody we've known for a thousand years. It doesn't really matter. The point is, his name is Terrence. How can I marry somebody with a name like that?"

Marc smiled. "Are you engaged?"

"Oh, no, nothing like that."

"I mean is it serious?"

"Oh, I don't know. He comes from a very good family, and he has horses. What more could a girl want? Moms would be delighted."

"Do you like him?"

"Everybody likes Terrence. He's tall and handsome and playful."

"Do you love him?"

"Good grief, no! But I'm not sure I believe in love anyway."

Marc hesitated. "Has he—have you—"

"What are you trying to say, you poor, tongue-tied boy?"

"Never mind."

"You mean, have we made love?"

He answered with a positive shrug.

"What a charming question."

"Well, have you?"

"It's not a question I care to answer."

"Oh."

"As a matter of fact, we haven't. There, does that make you feel better?"

"Yes, but have you ever—with anyone?"

She addressed an invisible third party. "Good Lord! Now he wants to know whether or not I'm a virgin. You Italians are really terribly inquisitive."

She avoided answering, and he did not ask her again.
He did not have to. Before the summer separated them, he
knew.

It was early June. Classes and exams were over and students were packing to leave. Once more Marc was planning
to stay on. He could not imagine moving back in with his
family, especially in the summer. He remembered the sweltering nights, the damp sheets, the feeling of suffocation. The
slant of light from the kitchen where his mother and uncle
talked in whispers. It would always be like that, he thought.
A dead end for his mother. A convenient impasse for Uncle
Stefano. He hated it all, and he hated it even more because of
Alyson.

It was a sad time. He would walk down the hall of the
dorm, and suddenly there would be an empty room with the
door open, the mattress rolled back, the sheets in a pile on
the floor. Someone would have left, almost as if he had died.
Eventually, almost everyone would go home except for a
handful of students, most of them foreigners, who would
attend the summer session. The dining room would be closed.
The building would be ghostly.

Alyson, too, was packing. In a week or so she would be
off to Europe with her family. There had been a series of
farewell parties, and she looked tired and confused. She
blamed it all on Lucy Lowell, who had smuggled a bottle of
bourbon into the dorms. "It's all so juvenile," said Alyson.
"I have a good mind to go away and never come back. I'm
glad I'm going to Europe."

"I'm not," said Marc. "I'll miss you."

"Will you?"

"Of course. I wish I could go with you."

"I wish you could too, but the whole family would have a
massive stroke."

He laughed. She was in one of her warmer, wittier moods.
"Maybe someday we'll take a trip together," he said. "To
somewhere, anywhere."

"That's a marvelous idea. Let's do it, Marc. Let's do it
right now."

"What do you mean?"

"Oh, not a big trip. Let's get in the car. Let's go
somewhere. Let's pretend—"

"Pretend what?"

"I don't know. We'll pretend that we're running away, that we're wanted by the police, that we've eloped with the family jewels."

"Why not?" he said, and before they knew it they were driving up Riverside Drive and across the George Washington Bridge into the greenery of New Jersey. The top was down. The wind blew their hair back and made them feel free. The motor of the Buick hummed.

"I'll change my name to Irma Jones, and we'll trade the car in for a Model A. They'll never find us. We'll lose ourselves in the wilderness and survive on berries and weeds."

"You have a wonderful imagination, but you wouldn't last long on berries and weeds."

"We'll wash them down with champagne. The primitive life."

She drove. He sat beside her, his arm across the back of her seat. They went very fast and the tires squealed on the curves. "Slow down," he said. "You'll get us killed."

"Would it matter?"

"Of course, you fool!"

She slowed down. Then she pulled over to the side of the road and stopped. She pouted girlishly. "You shouted at me," she said.

"You were driving too fast."

"I'm sorry. I wanted to get away."

"From what?"

"From all that back there."

"But where are we?"

"I don't know."

"Are you planning to go anywhere in particular?"

"Yes. To the ocean. I always go to the ocean, because then I know where I am."

"But how do we get there?"

"Instinct! It never fails." She started the car and they were off again, this time less frantically.

A few hours later they were on the Jersey shore, watching the lazy waves wash up on a wide stretch of sand. They carried their shoes and walked along the water's edge, leaving footprints behind. In the distance was a row of summer houses, bungalows on stilts with screened-in porches and weathered decks. On the sand were scattered chairs and umbrellas, and beyond them another stretch of empty beach.

Marc looked back at the long track of footprints in the

sand, and then at their lengthening shadows. "We should probably start back," he said.

"No, I want to stay right here until the sun goes down."

"Won't they be looking for you at school?"

"I don't care. Let them look. When I get back I'll tell them I was kidnapped by gypsies."

They sat in the smooth white sand that sloped up to a dune that was tufted with long grass. The sky deepened. There was a ship on the horizon and a wisp of smoke. After a while, Alyson stretched out and looked straight up as though to lose herself in the sky. Marc leaned on one elbow beside her and studied her face. "What are you thinking?" he said.

"I was just wondering how far it is from here to there, and when you were going to kiss me."

He leaned over her and touched her lips with his. She put her slender arms around him and held him there. Their lips parted. They kissed again, in a lingering, passionate way. He could feel her breathing, and he could see that her eyes were closed. He leaned against her breasts. He felt the outline of her body with his hand. Her skirt had moved above her knees. In the dying light he saw her white thighs. He touched her. She sighed. Her flesh was soft and cool. "How nice that feels," she whispered.

He caressed her thighs and moved farther up. Then he hesitated, excited and afraid.

"It's all right," she said. Her hand moved along his back. He felt the warmth and dampness of that secret place through a film of silk. She parted her thighs. She invited him. "Take them off," she said in a pleading, dreamy voice.

He did, and saw her nakedness for the first time. He was bursting to be free of his own clothes, but didn't know what to do. He looked down the dark stretch of beach. There was no one there. The breeze played over them. The surf rose and fell like the heartbeat of the world. He kissed her again on the mouth and then opened her blouse to kiss her breasts. She rose to him like the sea and said: "Please!" Her hand undid the buckle of his pants. He did the rest.

Half undressed, they made love in a simple way, and he could feel that it was also the first time for her. They were children in the hands of nature, and Marc was amazed that he had ever been afraid. They stayed together and nearly slept in their embrace. Night covered them and the stars came out.

After a while Alyson sat up and pulled down her skirt. "My hair is a mess," she said.

He adjusted his clothes and sat down beside her. "Are you all right?" he said.

"Of course I'm all right. It was bound to happen sooner or later, and I'm glad it was you."

"Was that what you had in mind when you first stopped to talk to me that day?"

"How did you know?"

"I didn't. But now I do."

"And now my secret's out. You see, I'm not so sophisticated after all. It's just an act. I was afraid that I would never be able to make love—oh, I can't explain. Let's not talk about it."

"I hope that's not all you wanted."

"God, you sound like a girl. Do you think I've taken advantage of you or something?"

"No. It was something I wanted too."

"Good! That makes us even."

"Except for one thing."

"What's that?"

"I've fallen in love with you."

He waited for her to echo the feeling, but she just stood up, brushed the sand from her skirt, and said: "It's getting awfully late. We really have to get back."

Before she left for Europe she said: "You can write to me at the Hotel Russell in London. Russell Square. It's very simple. They'll forward our mail. I'm not sure exactly where we'll be. We're sort of waiting to hear from Miles. He's being very bohemian about the whole thing."

Her first letter did not come for several weeks, but then there were a half-a-dozen letters before the summer was over. There was rarely anything personal in them. A brief reference to the incident at the beach. And a wish-you-were-here.

Marc wrote back to Alyson from time to time, but he found he had little to say. The more personal things, he decided, would have to wait until the fall. And he certainly didn't want to talk about his family or even the college. "The summer, thus far, has been uneventful, except that I am almost suicidal with envy. Perhaps someday I, too, will get to Europe, especially to Italy. I hate you for being there without me. . . ."

*        *        *

By the fall Marc had imagined himself into a love affair
that proved to be a little less than he thought it was. His
symptoms were classic: jealousy, possessiveness, distraction.
She was meant for him. She was his other self. He couldn't
live without her. A mysterious magnetism drew him to her.
He ran the gamut of all the cliches. He even wrote poetry. He
reread *A Farewell to Arms* and almost cried at the end.
He haunted the movies and discovered Garbo in *Grand Hotel*. He
wrote letters to Alyson that he never delivered. And he called
her too often. At times she seemed distant and annoyed. She
told him to stay away for a week or two to give her a chance
to breathe. And then he saw her at a football game with
Franklin Dobbs. It was time for a serious conversation, he
thought, without knowing exactly what it was he wanted to
say to her.

One gorgeous October weekend he drove to Scarsdale with
her, but only for the ride. She could drop him at the railroad
station, he said, and he'd catch a train back to New York.
She did not invite him to the house. He talked. She drove.
Her hair was swept back by the wind in the open car. She
looked like an advertisement for the American Dream. He
said: "I've been thinking a lot about us lately."

"What's there to think about?" she said.

"Well, you know—"

"No, I don't know."

"Don't you think it's about time we came to an understanding?"

"I don't understand what you mean by an *understanding*."

"You know how I feel about you."

She turned off the main road onto a smaller road and then
onto a dirt road that led to a lake. They got out and sat on the
grass. He threw pebbles into the lake as he talked. "I'm crazy
about you, and I don't know what to do. I thought if you felt
the same way, well, we could sort of go together or
something."

"You mean, you don't want me to see other boys."

"It's only natural, isn't it?"

She tore idly at the grass. "I think it's barbaric. What do
you think I am, anyway, a slave girl or some Italian peasant?
I'm sorry, Marc. I don't want to be pinned down by anyone. I
need my freedom. I want to go everywhere and do everything
before I get married. And when I get married, I want to live
in disgraceful luxury. So you see, it would never work out."

His smile was bitter. "Like King Kong and Fay Wray," he said.

"Well, not exactly. But almost as impossible. I do like you an awful lot. You're very special to me. But you're so terribly serious, and sometimes it makes me uncomfortable. You're always making plans, and I never know what I'm doing. You want commitments, and I'm irresponsible. I could tell you I love you, but it would be a lie. I could say that I would be faithful, but I really wouldn't. I know me too well. I'm not very good at these things. Besides, there's all the rest."

"What do you mean?"

"Come, I'll show you." She went back to the car. He followed. They drove to the outskirts of Scarsdale. The houses were large and the lawns were neat. They followed a narrow, winding road. When they came to a high wall, she said: "That's our wall." It went on for a quarter of a mile and was punctuated by an elaborate iron gate that might have been imported from a Medici palace. The sign said *Seven Oaks*. "Not very original, is it?" she said.

"You mean you live here?"

"Yes."

"Is that the house?"

"That, my dear boy, is the gatekeeper's house."

Marc's mouth went dry and he tried to swallow. She waved to a man with a pipe and drove on through, but she stopped short of the big house. "God!" was all that Marc could say. It was a mansion worthy of Newport, an imitation French *château* that could have housed a medieval army.

"Now do you understand what I've been talking about all these months? It's my freedom and my prison all at once. As long as I play the game I can have anything I want. Now that we're here, would you like to see the inside? I'm sure I can explain you, one way or another."

"No thanks. I've seen enough. And I don't want to be explained. I get the point."

She touched his arm. "Please don't be hurt, Marc. And please don't stop calling me. I think you're very sweet."

He had to wrestle with the idea that she would never be entirely his, that she would see other men and perhaps even sleep with them, but he could not break away. He went on seeing her, on her terms, until the end of his senior year.

And then something happened that cut even deeper than the unrequited love. Alyson announced that she was pregnant and that he was the father.

"It's all too stupid for words," she said. "It's going to ruin my summer."

"My God! What are we going to do?"

"*We* aren't going to do anything."

"I don't understand. Do your parents know?"

"Of course."

"How did they find out?"

"I told them, you idiot."

"And what did they say?"

"Moms had to sit down and have a glass of water, and Daddy almost had a stroke. But they know how to deal with these things."

"What are they going to do?"

"They're sending me to Switzerland for a little 'holiday.' "

"What does that mean?"

"That means I will go to a very expensive clinic, a kind of country-club sanitarium, where they will cure me of my boring condition."

He frowned. "You mean, you're going to have an abortion?"

"Of course. You don't think I'm going to mess up my life by having a baby, do you?"

"But how can you be so cold-blooded about it? So . . . so businesslike?"

"What do you expect me to do? Cry for my dead baby? As far as I'm concerned it doesn't exist and it never will."

"But damn it, don't I have anything to say about it? Why didn't you come to me first?"

"And what could you have done?"

"I don't know. We could have gotten married, I suppose."

"And live on what? Berries and weeds? Besides, I don't want to get married."

"Then why did you tell me at all? Why didn't you just go?"

"I thought it was only fair—"

"You call that fair? Alyson, you are incredible. You are all the things you always said you were."

"You can't say I didn't warn you. Now, why don't you just go away and stay out of my life?"

They were walking on Morningside Drive and could look out over the sprawl of tenements below. He was angry and wounded, but he saw in her face not only the hardness that was her mask but the girl who would not cry. He felt torn and helpless. "Alyson!" he said, as though to reach across the gulf between them.

She shook her head and half shouted, half moaned: "No!" Then she turned and ran. He did not go after her. He watched her go up the street and disappear around the corner.

He sat for a long time on a park bench and looked toward the bleakness of East Harlem, as though it were the bleakness of his own heart. He was there again on the rim, on the razor's edge between two worlds. He felt empty and alone, unable to go back, unable to go forward. It began to get dark. There was a chill in the air. Finally, he got up and walked slowly back to his room at the dorm.

# 4

Three years later he was handed a law degree in the commencement exercises on the steps of Kent Hall, while once more the world was in flames. Marc was deeply concerned. "A hell of a time to graduate," he said to one of his classmates. "We'll all be in the army before we can pass the bar exams." The events of his senior year paraded before him in headlines: "Germany Invades Poland." "Blitzkrieg." "England and France Declare War." "Reds Attack Poles." "Warsaw Falls." "Soviets Strike Finland." "Graf Spee Scuttled." "Neutral Denmark Invaded." "Norway Fights Back." "Chamberlain Resigns." "Paratroopers in Holland." "Belgium Falls." "Panzas Split Allies." "Disaster at Dunkirk." "Paris Weeps!"

That was just the other day. The news on the radio still echoed in his mind. It had all happened so quickly. Marc glanced around at the other young lawyers. They were somber. They listened to predictions of more difficult times to come. "The democratic process . . . the humanistic tradition . . . the very survival of civilization as we know it . . ." The June breeze that waved the swastika over Europe here played in the folds of the black medieval robe of the speaker. Everything around them contradicted the knowledge that the world was in crisis—the sunlight, the pigeons, the placid buildings. No one doubted that Hitler's aim was global conquest, but here there were only words—no festering corpses, no screaming Stukas, no women weeping for the dead.

Marc's mind wandered. *What are your plans? What are your plans?* his grandfather kept asking him. From the very beginning he was protective—intrusive. After his wife's death, he was worse. Marc began to feel uneasy. Gaetano was trying to get from him something he could not give, something that only his own sons could have given him. A hundred times Marc wanted to tell him that he could not make up for the tragedy of Antonio and the disappointment of Sergio. But he never did. Gaetano was too full of pride, too full of dreams for Marc's future. He would never forget the look on the old man's face at Francesca's funeral. He couldn't bear to hurt him, not now. But sooner or later he would have to assert himself, make his own plans, take his own direction. And once again he was convinced that the direction had to be away from the old life, the family, the neighborhood. To go back would be suffocation.

"We must never lose sight of the traditions that built this nation . . ." said the speaker. And Marc thought of the first Adamo who came to America and died in the Great Blizzard of '88, shoveling snow for a few cents an hour. And he thought of his father, and of that day in 1927 when the world held its breath as the switch was thrown on Sacco and Vanzetti. It was Renato who told him about his father, about his principles and his obsessions. "He was a very sensitive man, like a son to me. Nobody knows for sure why he was killed. The murder was never solved. He had nothing worth stealing, and why he was in Providence I don't know." The body never came home—only a police officer to tell them what had happened and to ask some questions. Marc had been standing behind his mother when she answered the door. The moment she saw the officer, she knew. Her cry came back to him, that ancient wailing sound that women make when a part of them has died.

The speaker was talking about "the current Machiavellian disregard for justice. . . ." And Marc thought about the term paper he had helped Alyson write. He had never seen her again or heard anything about her. He avoided her friends. He didn't want to know. He could not be sure she was even alive.

He thought of the confrontation that was sure to come with his grandfather. He had not dared to tell him that he had been offered a position in the midtown firm of Mandel and Berger. And Gaetano's gift to his grandson—a surprise—was a fully furnished office in a building once owned by Johnny DeMarco. "All you have to do is hang out a shingle. We need you here. We need each other. There will be plenty of work for you. Don't worry. I'll see to it personally."

Commencement was over. The music played. The faculty marched out. Then the students. There were handshakes and kisses. The cameras clicked. And then they dispersed. They went forth. . . .

There was a reception at the Cafe Savarese for Marc, all arranged by Gaetano, of course. There was champagne and wine and an elaborate arrangement of food. "Nothing but the best!" said Gaetano, beaming at his grandson.

The whole family was there: Marc's mother, who had moved back to an apartment near First Avenue; his brother, Larry, who was now twenty years old and well on his way to a boxing career; his great aunt Angela, who now shared a house with Natalia. Aunts and uncles on both sides, and great-aunts and uncles. Maria and Silvio, and their three daughters—all married, with eight children among them. His grandmother Gentile, a widow now. And her aging sister Carmela, also a widow. His aunt Laura, married to a man named Paul Arno, who was not Italian in spite of his name. Her daughter, Lisa, who was twelve and beginning to bosom out. Children whose names he didn't know scampered about. Old ladies with yellow skin and hair on their faces kissed him. Gaetano, who was seventy, drank a bit too much and introduced Marc elaborately to his friends. Everyone agreed that it was a wonderful occasion, but Marc's feelings were mixed. He welcomed the affection and the admiration, but he was not sure that he could pay the price.

Marc spent the night at his mother's apartment. He had his own room. "It's here for you whenever you want it," she said. Through Stefano she had accepted Gaetano's help, and now Larry was making some money fighting four- and six-rounders in New Jersey and New York. He was generous. He had taken over as man of the house.

Marc's reaction was a mixture of guilt and relief. He was even secretly envious at times. "You're doing good," he said to his brother one day. "I want you to know that I appreciate the way you've been taking care of Mom and the house. I should be doing more, but—"

"Don't even talk about it," said big-hearted Larry. "We all know how it is. You got important things to do. Someday you'll be famous. You got the brains in this family. All I got is a good left hook." And he jabbed playfully at Marc, who was no match for his broader, stronger brother.

Felice worried about her younger son. "I don't want him to get hurt," she said. "I don't want him to get in with a bad crowd. *Madonna mia!* If his father knew, he would turn over in his grave."

It was very late by the time the party was over at the Cafe Savarese. It was only four blocks to the apartment, but Silvio insisted on driving them home. Marc had never spent a night in the new place, and didn't really want to even now, but there was no way around it. It was spacious and comfortable, but outside there were the same sounds that had haunted him all his life. Even the same smells: soot and tar and the stench of the river.

Long after his mother and brother were asleep he lay awake in his bed, staring out the window, past a fire escape to silhouetted forms in a dim blend of lamppost light and moonlight. He fought against the tide of memories that threatened to drown him. They seeped in against his will. Toy soldiers and worn linoleum. The smell of brown soap. The sound of the washboard over which his mother scrubbed.

It was almost dawn by the time he fell asleep. The next day, he had promised himself, he would have his talk with Gaetano.

It did not come until late in the afternoon. When Marc arrived he found his grandfather in front of his building, talking with some friends. They were smoking cigars and arguing about the war. The sun was bright and the breeze was fresh. Across the street, hanging from a fire escape, was a large Italian flag. It belonged to Franco Fusari, who was pro-Mussolini. He was arguing, in Italian, that America should mind its own business and stay out of the war. "Eh, and *il duce* should mind his own business too,'' said Mario Coriano. On June 10 Italy had declared war on England and France. It was not a happy day in the neighborhood. Many of those who had flown Italian flags removed them from their windows and fire escapes.

Fusari was red in the face. ''And what was he going to do? I ask you. What? He has gone with the strong. Can you blame him for that? If he did not go with Germany, then Germany would have gone against him. And you see how it is with France, with all of them. If America stays out, then Germany and Italy will rule Europe. It is all one can hope for now.''

''Sure,'' said Gaetano. ''And if we get into it, We will have to fight our own.''

''What then?'' said Coriano. ''Will you take the flag down?''

''No,'' said Fusari. ''I am for *Italia*. It is my blood.''

''But America is your country now. You would be a traitor.''

''Ah, America, America! I don't give a damn about America.''

''Then why don't you go back?''

''Maybe I will.''

''You're crazy to talk that way,'' said Gaetano. ''I don't believe the Italian people want to go with Hitler. Last time they were with us, and a good thing too. It is only *il duce* and the Fascists. It is the national socialism, or whatever the hell they call it. . . .''

As Marc came up the street he saw them talking and smoking and waving their hands about. Gaetano was leaning against the railing of the stoop. He saw his grandson and broke away. ''Marco!'' he said. ''I'm glad you came around. In all that confusion yesterday we didn't get a chance to talk. Come on upstairs and we'll have something.''

Marco followed him up the stairs. He noticed that Gaetano went slowly and with that certain cautiousness that older men get. He remembered that his grandfather had turned seventy. Still, from across the street, he looked ten years younger.

Gaetano opened the door with a brass key. ''Hey,'' he called out, ''who's home?'' Nobody answered. They went in. He called out again. ''How do you like that?'' he said. ''When you need them, they're never here. We'll have to make our own coffee. Or would you like a glass of wine?'' They went into the kitchen. Gaetano looked confused for a moment. "You know, I keep expecting to find my wife here when I come home. She was always here, always ready to get me whatever I wanted. I miss her. But at the end she was so sick, so weak, that I was almost glad when she died. I shouldn't complain. There are plenty of women around to look after me. My sisters, my daughter, my nieces. They are always coming by. They clean the place. They make sure I get something to eat. It's only me and Stefano now. My sister Angela says I should think about getting married again."

"And have you thought about it?" said Marc.

"Yes, I've thought about it, but I have to think some more. It is one thing when you are young and you will have children. It is a natural thing to do. But at my age—I don't know. It doesn't seem necessary. I could take a housekeeper." He smiled. "A nice young one. But old enough to avoid a scandal. Maybe forty, forty-five. He put two glasses on the table and found a bottle of wine. "To hell with the coffee. Too much trouble. Somebody will come later to make supper. Maybe you will stay."

"My mother is expecting me. But I wanted to talk to you. It's about the office. It's beautiful. I can't tell you how grateful I am for that, and for all the other things you have done for me."

"You like it then, eh?"

"Complete with law books. It was more than I expected. More than anyone right out of law school could expect."

"Ah, on that I had the advice of Attilio Giordano, who has been my own lawyer. But soon he will retire. And then *you* will be my lawyer, eh?"

"Well . . . yes, but—"

"What's the matter? Why do you look like that?"

"I wanted to talk to you, *Nonno*, because I am not sure yet what I will be doing."

"What do you mean? I thought it was all settled. We got you all the way through college, and through the law school. So now you will be a lawyer, no?"

"I still have to pass my bar examinations."

Gaetano made an impatient gesture with his hand and said: "I don't know what is the bar examinations, but whatever it is, I am sure that you will have no trouble with it. You get your license. You hang out your shingle."

"But you see, *Nonno*, I can't really practice law until I

pass those examinations. I may have to work for a while as a law clerk. They all do it.''

''But they gave you the paper, the diploma. I saw it with my own eyes.''

''It's hard to explain, but it's something I have to do.''

''All right, all right, so you do it. So you move into the office and do whatever you have to do. You know best.''

Marc looked down at the white tablecloth. ''I've had a good offer from a law firm downtown. I think I'm going to take it.''

''What kind of an offer?''

''Just a clerk for now, but it could develop into something very good.''

Gaetano was frowning and looking at his grandson as though he did not quite understand. ''You mean you want to go to work for somebody else? For strangers?''

''*Nonno*, it's a very important law firm.''

''Who are they?''

''Mandel and Berger.''

''What are they? Jews? You would rather work for Jews than to have your own office with your own people? What's the matter with you? I don't understand. There's plenty of business here. Plenty! And then I thought maybe you wanted to get into politics. With that I could certainly help you. In fact, it has always been my dream that you would run for political office one day.''

''I know. I realize that you have planned out my life for me, but it's *my* life. *I* have to live it. And I have to do it my own way.'' He was struggling to assert himself. His voice rose, but then softened again. His stomach seemed to be melting. He wanted to jump up and shout: *Leave me alone!* But he couldn't. He felt sorry for his grandfather and sorry for himself.

''What's the matter, we're not good enough for you, eh? I work with you on this all these years, and now you tell me *thank you, good-bye*. I thought I was doing you a favor to arrange that office. It was my gift. I thought it was all settled, that there was, in fact, nothing to settle. It's the old way. . . .''

''That's just the point,'' said Marc. ''It *is* the old way. The family arranges everything. The father makes all the decisions. Or the grandfather. I have been on my own for a long time. I have been with Americans. I was born in this country. My thinking is not the same as yours. I need more freedom.''

Gaetano nodded his head slowly, sadly. "I see. You need more freedom. From what? From me? I'm not telling you what to do."

"But you are."

"Because I gave you a gift?"

"It's more than that."

"Well, I'm sorry if I interfered. I was only trying to help you out."

"I know. And I really appreciate it. It's a beautiful office. But let me take this other offer for now. Just for a while, until the examinations. Then—well, then we'll see."

"All right, all right! But I'm going to hold it for you, just as it is. And when you find out how it is out there, you'll come back. I'm sure of it."

Marc weakened. "I'm pretty sure, too, *Nonno*. I just have to find out for myself, that's all."

Gaetano raised his eyebrows philosophically. "I guess we all do. When I was your age nobody could tell me anything. And what a mess I made of my life." He smiled, remembering incidents from the past. He refilled their glasses, and Marc could see that his grandfather was about to begin one of his long, rambling stories. He felt better about the whole thing, and Gaetano did too, because Marc had asked his permission and he had granted it. *That* was the way things should be.

Before long Gaetano was explaining to friends and relatives that it was his own decision that Marc should get some experience in another firm before opening his own practice in East Harlem. It was important to give the impression that he was still in control of the situation, and this need for control extended into more personal matters. It was time, Gaetano decided, that Marc had a wife. After all, he was twenty-five years old. He arranged to introduce him to Piera Cesario, the daughter of a friend of his. His recommendation was hardly subtle. "She is beautiful and unspoiled," he said. "She has been strictly brought up. I can vouch for that. And she does not have that contradictory way about her that some women have. She will make a very good wife."

Marc did not commit himself, nor did he object to the introduction. She was indeed beautiful—dark-haired and wide-eyed, and her figure suggested a ripeness that might one day broaden into sturdiness. He agreed to take her out. They went to the movies and to dinner. It was all very pleasant, but after a while it was clear that they did not have much in common. She was interested in marriage. He was interested in companionship. She had less than a high school education and knew nothing about what was going on in the world. Even the war did not interest her. She smiled when he talked about it, but her mind was clearly somewhere else. "What a handsome couple they make," said Piera's father. "When do you think we can set the date?"

"Don't rush them," said Gaetano. "Remember that this is America, and that these young people have to make up their own minds."

"*Porco Dio!*" said Pietro Cesario. "You talk like an American yourself. In the old country we would have had them at the church by now. And the grandmothers would be knitting clothes for the first baby."

But there was to be no wedding and no baby—not for Marc, at any rate. Not after Piera met Larry Adamo, who was her own age and her own idea of what a man should be.

Larry's first appearance at Madison Square Garden was in a four-round preliminary match, a middleweight contest in which he met, by careful arrangement, a more experienced but frequently defeated fighter named Billy Moran. Losing did not seem to diminish Moran's value as a steppingstone for up-and-coming young fighters. He always put on a good show. He was tough and a bit of a bleeder.

There was a good crowd at the Garden. The headliner was Billy Conn, a potential contender for Joe Louis's title. The overhead lights made a stage of the ring. By comparison, the crowd looked lost in semidarkness, receding away in ringside rows and then steeply upward in the grandstands. From the farthest seats the ring looked very small and one could see the clouds of smoke rising from the spectators, as if the whole place were smoldering. The audience was almost all men, and they all seemed to be smoking.

Gaetano had bought half-a-dozen ringside seats. With him were Marc and Piera, Piera's brother and his girl friend, and Gaetano's old friend Joe Malzone, who was a big fight fan.

Marc had only seen his brother fight once before. He thought he was very good, but did not much like the atmosphere at the St. Nicholas Arena. There was more drama here, a bit more glitter, but still he found the whole spectacle a little depressing. The animal noises of the masculine crowd reminded him that man was an aggressive beast. He dimly remembered arguments at Columbia in Philosophy courses. And he remembered more vividly that there was a war going on in Europe. "The paragon of animals," said Shakespeare. "Between the angel and the brute!" said Pascal. But when the bell sounded and the fight began, Marc felt his muscles tense and his heart beat faster.

Joe Malzone had a deep, rusty voice. He kept yelling: "Hit him! Hit him! Kill the bum!" His tie was undone and his shirt unbuttoned at his thick neck. Gaetano smoked a cigar and watched with great concentration. Sometimes his head moved, as if to duck a punch for Larry, and sometimes his fists were clenched. Piera looked neither frightened nor terribly interested, but she watched quietly. It was as if the men were doing something that she did not quite understand and did not want to interfere with.

Her mother had not approved at all of her going to the fights, even if her brother was there. "It's no place for a girl," she had said before being overruled by her husband.

In the program the fight was listed as a middleweight contest. Larry had to train down to get under the 160-pound limit. He was only five foot eight, two inches shorter than Marc, but almost ten pounds heavier. He was stocky and strong, with a broad chest and a thick neck. He still had a round face, dark curly hair, and an oddly innocent expression; boyish and bullish all at once. Marc, on the other hand, had the slender, ascetic look of his father, with deep, serious eyes and a sensitive mouth. His mother looked at him sometimes as though she were remembering her dead husband. Marc was conscious of the similarity and glad of it. The more he learned about his father over the years the more he admired him and made him something of a tragic hero. Over and over again he invented scenarios for Sergio's death in Providence. The plots were political and criminal. There were government agents and anarchists; there were members of the Mafia and Murder Incorporated. Whatever it was all about, he was sure that his father had been on the right side and that what he had been doing was important.

In the first round, the fighters felt each other out with jabs and clinches. Moran was listed in the program as thirty-two, but he was rumored to be older. He had a hard look. His hair was cut very short. His eyes were small and quick, his cheekbones prominent, and his nose had obviously been broken more than once. He was about Larry's height but came into the fight a few pounds lighter. He had, in fact, started his career as a welterweight. "He's a bum," said Gaetano, "but he's a good bum. He was once a number-four contender. Sometimes he takes a dive, but they like him to win one for every one he loses, just to make him worth beating. Tony's got it all figured out. We talked it all over before he booked the fight."

There it was again, thought Marc, the old man behind the scenes trying to manage things. He was talking about Tony Manzella, who had a contract with Larry and a dozen other fighters. He was a shrewd promoter, with friends in the underworld. Marc did not particularly care for him, but he had produced a couple of titles, and Gaetano was convinced that he could bring Larry along for a shot at the middleweight crown. "Maybe in a couple of years or so. After all, he's only twenty years old."

By the end of the first round the crowd was unimpressed and restless. Larry went to his corner. He was glistening with perspiration, but he wasn't even breathing hard. The place was warm, and the smoke did not help. The two men in his corner were Sammy King, an ageless Negro who worked at Rudman's Gym, and the wiry trainer Rudy Wills, who had been, in his earlier days, a pretty tough little lightweight. His career had ended when he went blind in his right eye.

They worked on Larry routinely. The bell sounded. They shoved his mouthpiece back in and sent him out. He had been given whispered instructions to open up.

Moran must have been given the same instructions. They came out swinging. Moran was accurate with three quick jabs and a hard right hook to the head. Larry countered with a right and a left and an uppercut to the body before being tied up. Moran butted him in the chin with his head and kept his hands moving in the clinch. The crowd loved it. They began to shout and whistle. The fighters came at each other again. They looked angry. There was a rapid flurry of punches, most of which missed. Then Larry walked into a right hand that staggered him. Gaetano was suddenly on his feet. "Move to your right," he shouted. "To your right." Moran came after him and tried to corner him. There was no style in his attack. He was just throwing punches as fast as he could, as though he smelled blood and was going in for the kill. Larry slipped away along the ropes. Moran lunged and almost went down.

The referee automatically wiped his gloves. When they squared off again Larry seemed fully recovered. He had himself under control and allowed Moran to come to him. By the end of the round Moran looked tired and puzzled. Larry was too young and too fast. He had weathered the lucky punch and now seemed the stronger of the two. The bell sounded.

By the third round Marc had forgotten all about philosophy and was standing and roaring with the rest of the fans. Larry had opened a cut over Moran's left eye and the blood dripped down his cheek. He went into a defensive crouch. One could see that his vision was imparied, because his counterpunches were wild. Larry stalked him, dancing lightly to the left and right, then came right into him flatfooted and opened up a barrage of punches that left Moran helpless on the ropes. Still he would not go down. He did not even look afraid. He took his punishment; it was all part of the job. It was not until it was all over that Marc felt anything but contempt for Moran. He was the opponent. He had to be beaten. And he was. A right and a left to the body brought Moran's guard down. A left jab set him up. And a right hook jolted his head back so violently that he lost his mouthpiece. He was already on his way down when Larry finished him off with another left. The crowd roared its approval as the veteran sagged to his knees, then pitched forward onto his face. It was smeared with blood. The referee counted over him. Moran made a feeble effort to rise. He got to all fours and looked dumbly out into the crowd in Marc's direction. He was a pathetic sight, but he was the enemy and he had been defeated.

Later, Gaetano and Marc went to the dressing room while the others waited outside. Gaetano hugged his grandson and actually kissed him on each cheek. Larry had the pleased look of a child-warrior. Marc could see that he enjoyed what he was doing, and that he had found a way to be more than just another ordinary kid from the old neighborhood.

They celebrated at a restaurant on Forty-fourth Street. Larry was introduced to Piera and her brother and the brother's girl friend. From the very beginning it was clear that there was an attraction between them. Larry's eyes kept going back to her. And she blushed as if she had been caught secretly wishing that he would make love to her. Marc was amused and even a little jealous. Not specifically because of Piera, but because of that kind of animal attraction. It had not been like that between him and any woman, not even Alyson, whom he imagined he had loved. It was so basic, so simple. For him love was always so damned complicated.

The next day Larry came to his brother and said: "What's the story with Piera?"

"There's no story with Piera," said Marc. "If you want to take her out, it's all right with me. The old man tried to fix me up with her, but it didn't take. She's a nice girl, beautiful, unspoiled, and strictly brought up—" He smiled to hear himself all of a sudden sounding just like his grandfather.

"What's the matter?" said Larry.

"Nothing! It's too hard to explain. Take Piera out. She likes you. I can tell. Do you want me to talk to the old man?"

"Yeah, maybe you'd better."

# 5

Everybody knew that it was only a matter of time before America would get into the war. Americans knew it, and that knowledge haunted their increasing prosperity. There was guilt for hanging back. There was outrage at the brutalities of the aggressors. But there was also fear and resistance, and the memory of the first World War. The Axis nations also knew that it was only a matter of time. They saw the industrial giant rousing itself from the Great Depression and flexing its muscles with growing awareness.

Meanwhile, the war went very badly for the Allies. Practically all of Europe was in German hands. Only a few neutral nations stayed out of it. The rest were conquered or frightened into collaboration. From Norway to Greece, from the English Channel to the gates of Moscow, the Nazi war machine rolled on. The only bright moments for the Allies were provided by the Italians, who had no heart for this war. In North Africa, in Ethiopia, in Greece—they proved themselves inept. A furious Hitler sent in German troops to do what the Italians could not do. Greece and Yugoslavia were overrun, and General Rommel, "The Desert Fox," was threatening the Suez Canal, which could have provided a link with the Japanese, who had dreams of ruling the eastern half of the new world. The dream of world conquest was rapidly becoming a reality. There was no point in allowing America to wait any longer. And there was a great advantage to be had in striking the first blow.

On November 26, 1941, a secret strike force under Admiral Chuichi Nagumo set sail from Tankan Bay in the Kurile Islands. Avoiding the usual routes and fighting foul weather, they made their way toward Pearl Harbor, where the bulk of the American Pacific fleet was gathered: eight battleships, five cruisers, and twenty-six destroyers and other ships. Included in the Japanese strike force were six modern aircraft carriers that could put over four hundred planes aloft.

It was Sunday morning when the attack came on Pearl Harbor. One-third of the men were on leave. Many other crewmen were ashore. Some were still asleep. Others were on their way to church. There was no warning. When the day that would live in infamy was over, virtually every American ship and plane had been destroyed and over three thousand men were dead. Billows of smoke rose into the once peaceful sky and formed a great shroud. The world was shocked. America was plunged into war.

In the months that followed, the news was grim. The Japanese flag was planted on island after island, in the Philippines and all of Southeast Asia. The Germans advanced in Russia. And Rommel was within striking distance of Cairo. Then came the crucial battle of El Alamein. There General Montgomery turned back the *Afrika Korps*. And in November, 1942, the Americans landed in North Africa.

The tide had turned. By the summer of 1943 North Africa was in Allied hands and Sicily had been invaded. The next stop was the mainland itself, the soft underbelly of Europe, as Churchill called it.

On September 3 the British Eighth Army crossed the narrow Straits of Messina and landed at Reggio di Calabria. A few days later the American Fifth Army was gathered in a massive invasion force off the beaches of Salerno. Mussolini had fallen, and Marshal Badoglio had just surrendered his country to the Allies. But the fighting went on. The Germans, under Field Marshal von Kesselring, took over and established a defense line south of Naples.

Hundreds of ships seemed to reach to the horizon, troopships, warships, support craft. Before them lay the ancient and beautiful beaches between Paestum and Salerno, and beyond those beaches the chaos of a country in collapse. The Germans, who had come to Italy to fight beside the Italians, now became an army of occupation. Their weaker brother had failed them utterly, and they were full of contempt and rage at the Fascists and all the Italians. They had no guts, no honor, no will to fight. They were a short, inferior breed, not at all like the Aryans, who would one day rule the world.

On one of the troopships in the invading fleet was Lieutenant Marc Adamo, a Civil Affairs officer with the Allied Military Government. His unit would not go in with the first wave, but they would be needed early in the campaign to establish some kind of order among the confused civilians.

It was early evening when the U.S.S. *John Thompson* came within sight of the shore. It was a mere hint of hills and a gentle sweep of beach that soon disappeared again as the light faded behind them in the west. There was no moon, and the convoy inched forward in silence. The other ships became silhouettes, then whispers in the night. There was a strange perfume in the balmy darkness, full of legends and history, sea nymphs and myths.

Marc stood at the rail with several other men. They wore helmets and battlegear. At any moment they might be ordered ashore. The landing crafts had been made ready for lowering, but no one knew for sure exactly when and where they would be going in. They looked toward the distant, disappearing shore and the dim clusters of light that showed where the villages were. "Do you think it'll be long?" said Marc to the officer beside him.

"I imagine they'll begin the bombardment sometime before dawn," said Captain John Ross. He was no older than Marc, about twenty-seven, and about as American as freckles and the main street of Madison, Wisconsin. "Nothing's going to happen before that. They always soften them up first, just in case."

"Don't we have any intelligence ashore?"

"Not a hell of a lot. We're getting some help from the British. They seem to be better in that department than we are."

The deck was full of men, just standing around or sitting in groups. Smoking was only allowed down below, where some of the men were playing cards or writing last-minute letters to kill time.

"Waiting is the worst part of it, isn't it?" said Marc.

"You've never been in a landing before?" said Captain Ross.

"No."

"I first hit the beach at Oran in North Africa. We were all green and scared to death. By the time we landed in Sicily it wasn't so bad. But this time I have a feeling we're not going to get off so easily."

"Why not?"

"Well, they say that now that the Italians are out of it, von Kesselring is going to make us pay for every inch. A slow, tough, defensive strategy. At least that's Colonel Whitmore's opinion. And it figures."

Marc looked out over the calm sea. "What a hell of a way to come home," he said.

"Home?" said Ross. "What do you mean?"

"My father was born in Naples," said Marc.

"Is that right? You know, I wouldn't have taken you for Italian. You got any relatives here?"

"Some—not many."

"You going to try to look them up?"

"Yeah, I guess so. If they're still alive. I really don't know much about them, except for a great-uncle who's a monsignor or a bishop or something."

"How about that!" said Captain Ross. Then he started chewing his gum a little faster, as though he didn't know what else to say.

The bombardment began in the darkest hours before dawn and made blossoms of fire and streaks of light almost continuous enough to turn the darkness into hellish day. The noise was deafening and strange on the otherwise silent sea. In the flashing gunfire Marc could see the formation of warships in the convoy. The arc they formed echoed the arc of the shore. And soon there were other echoes as the German shore batteries in the far hills answered the barrage with sporadic fire.

With the first light of day there was a lull. From the deck of the *John Thompson* they could see the small landing craft of the first wave. First a few specks of white foam, then scores, then hundreds, line after line. And here and there the larger LSTs that carried in tons of supplies and tanks and artillery pieces. It was the largest invasion from the sea in history.

Now and then an FW 190 flew over the convoy and chattered away with its machine guns at the landing craft, but it was only a gesture, a token attack. "They'll wait until the men are on the beaches," said Captain Ross. "That's when they're most vulnerable. Especially if they haven't got their antiaircraft units set up. There's always a lot of confusion at first. No communications. A little panic. Men crawling around looking for their outfits, or maybe just trying to hide."

"Sounds like fun," said Marc.

"Oh, yeah!" said the veteran, chewing his gum with an air of superiority. "But don't worry. They won't be sending us in until the beachhead is secure."

A golden morning spread itself over the scene like a diaphanous veil trying to conceal an ugly wound. The sun rose behind the gentle hills and over a rim of ancient ruins. Its light caught the ships and gilded them. The water turned from gray to blue and moved against Marc's ship with a lazy breathing motion. *Poseidon*, he thought. The god of the sea.

All day long the small craft moved in. Men waded ashore along miles of beaches. Steel mesh was flung down to provide traction for trucks and tanks. The shelling continued off and on. Through his binoculars Marc watched a cruiser. Fire flashed from its long guns and the sight reached him before the sound. It was like an old movie in which the timing is off between the actor's lips and the words he speaks. On the shore, puffs of smoke came from the hills where the shells landed. As the day wore on, more planes were strafing the beaches, and enemy fire was increasing all along the coast. From offshore they could tell that resistance was stiffening. The men who had not yet gone in looked quiet and worried.

In the afternoon the officers were briefed by Colonel Holmes. He also looked worried. "There was supposed to be an element of surprise," he said, "but I guess it was too much to hope for. They're taking a hell of a beating in there. It may be another day or two before we can go in. We've been ordered to sit tight until at least oh-six-hundred tomorrow. They're calling now for some heavy air support, but it will have to come from Palermo, maybe Tunis. The enemy has the high ground and more guns than we thought possible.

They must have known about this operation from the very beginning.''

Until the briefing Marc had felt oddly detached from all the action and noise, as though he were a visitor or an invisible observer. But now the reality of it all was beginning to reach him. There were men dying on those beaches, even though he couldn't see them. A cold little arrow of fear made his stomach tighten and his heart skip a beat. His mouth and lips were dry.

He went back up on deck. The sun had just set and the sky was getting dark. But over the beachhead there was an eerie, pulsating glow, as if the whole coast were ablaze.

The next day they were told that the situation had improved and that forward lines had been secured and stabilized. The *John Thompson* was ordered to move in closer to shore and lower its landing craft.

Once in motion the men seemed less nervous. It was the waiting that gave them time to think. Marc, too, was relieved in a way. It was better to be doing something, anything. Besides, he wanted to get it over with—whatever was waiting for them on the beach.

Normally, the AMG men have nothing to do with combat, but on this occasion Marc and the others were handed carbines—just in case. They crouched in the bargelike metal landing craft with regular infantrymen. The whole vessel vibrated as the noisy engines shoved them forward. Marc could smell the man beside him. He must have been sweating badly. And he could smell the sea as the air wafted over them.

Suddenly, with a grinding, crunching sound, the flat-bottomed craft was run ashore and the forward ramp was lowered like a drawbridge. They scrambled up the beach, wading at first in water up to their knees. There was no gunfire, only the sound of distant fighting. Marc wasn't sure exactly what he was expected to do. His only orders were to keep in touch with his own men—about half a dozen of them, mostly noncoms—and report to Captain Wiggins for further orders. First, of course, he would have to *find* Captain Wiggins, who was, theoretically, in touch with Major Sykes, who would, again theoretically, know all about how to set up an AMG unit.

Marc and his men wandered aimlessly up the beach. Though

there wasn't much fighting, there was considerable confusion. There were pyramids of supplies: crates of ammunition, foodstuffs, even office equipment. Everything seemed to have been dumped there. And there were jeeps and trucks and motorcycles. A tank came ashore, bobbing and nodding like a giant turtle. There was a lot of activity.

"So what do we do now?" said Sergeant Munch.

"I don't know," said Marc. "Move forward, I suppose, until we find HQ and locate Captain Wiggins."

Several sandy roads had been created by the heavy traffic. Men and vehicles moved along these, but men were also spread out all along the beach and moved toward a wooded slope. An officer behind Marc was shouting: "Get off the beach! Keep moving! Take cover and dig in!"

They had to move aside for a truck that was coming the wrong way. Everything else was moving forward. It alone was coming back toward the beach. As it went by Marc could see why. He went pale and he could hear himself gasp. "Jesus Christ!" said Sergeant Munch. The truck was full of bodies, heaped in like so many sacks of potatoes.

When they reached the woods, they decided to dig in and wait until things were clarified. "There's no point in going any further right now," said Marc. "We're only liable to get into trouble."

It was a beautiful evening, except for the rumbling of what might have been distant thunder. "Somebody must be catching it up near Salerno," said Munch. He was a homely-looking farmboy who had spent a couple of years on a small-town police force before joining up.

From the slope they could see the vast convoy in the dying light and the flashes of the guns that were still shelling the hills further up the coast. As it grew dark, more and more headlights went on down on the beach. They were like the wandering eyes of some lost and luminous creatures. Marc fell asleep without deciding to do so.

The next day they located a field headquarters, but it didn't do them any good. The officers there didn't know anything about Captain Wiggins or the AMG or anything else, apparently. There was a lot of cursing and telephoning and more people asking questions than answering them.

"It looks like we've arrived a little early for work," said Marc. "We might as well find a place to hole up for a few days."

From an infantry captain they learned that considerable ground had been taken up forward and that the beachhead seemed secure all along the line. There had been some casualties, but it hadn't been as bad as it looked.

The following day, just when it seemed as though some order were emerging out of the chaos, the Germans launched a counterattack designed to drive them all into the sea. Von Kesselring brought out his tanks, his artillery, and his best troops. He threw everything into the battle. Holes were punched in the fragile American line. Some units were cut off and surrounded. But the heaviest fighting was a few miles away from where Marc and his men had landed, though shells exploded in the woods and there were skirmishes less than half a mile forward of their position.

For a day and a half there was nothing but noise and the movement of troops. Then the air support finally arrived, in the form of B-25s from North Africa. German fighters came out to meet them, but they were badly outnumbered. Enemy positions in the hills were bombed repeatedly as squadron after squadron made its run and headed back. Von Kesselring almost accomplished what he had promised, but not quite. He was forced to pull back. The great Salerno beachhead was saved.

Two and a half weeks later the Fifth Army marched into Naples. Ragged crowds of Neapolitans greeted the American troops with wild enthusiasm. Not because they really cared who occupied the city, but they had heard that the Americans had plenty of food and were generous. Considering the massive inefficiency of the whole operation it was a wonder they had any food at all, and a small miracle that they ever took Naples. Marc could not believe some of the things he saw and heard. Supplies were openly looted by soldiers who seemed, at times, totally without discipline. Antiaircraft batteries shot down their own planes. And some of the planes bombed their own men. Most of the officers knew nothing about the geography of the place they had been sent in to occupy. And no one that Marc talked to knew any Italian. The elusive Captain Wiggins, it turned out, had fallen off the ramp of a landing craft and broken his arm. He was immediately put back on board and taken to the troopship. He would probably get a purple heart for his valiant accident. Marc was left completely on his own. He was told by another officer that his best bet was to follow the infantry into Naples, where he was sure to run into Major Sykes sooner or later. So he and the others tagged along, picking up rides wherever they could. By the time they reached Naples only Marc and Sergeant Munch were still together. On the road they saw many Italian soldiers, their uniforms filthy and torn, their feet bleeding in split shoes or wrapped in rags. They didn't know where to go or who to surrender to, so they were simply walking home. They had walked away from the Germans and now they were walking away from the Americans, and nobody seemed to care one way or the other. But they were a cheerful lot, because the war was over for them. They sometimes broke into song or called out greetings. The Americans threw them cigarettes and K-rations.

The city of Naples was an incredible mess. It had been bombed and shelled by both sides. And when the Germans pulled out they had been determined to destroy anything that might be of use to the Allies and to cripple the port as well. They blew up telephone and telegraph centers. They scuttled ships in the harbor. They set fire to warehouses and depots and even to the university, which seemed to Marc an act of gratuitous cruelty. And they left behind hundreds of mines and explosives with timing devices. There was no food supply, no water supply, and no public transportation. There was malaria and typhus and dysentery and virtually no medical help for most of the sick and wounded. There was a municipal government, but it wasn't functioning. Many of the officials who had been Fascists had gone into hiding.

Marc rode to Naples in the backseat of a jeep. He watched the crowds that greeted them. There were soldiers on foot and slow-moving tanks in his column. People were dressed in odd combinations of clothing. Most of the children were barefoot. There were gaunt faces and desperate eyes, but everywhere the Americans went they heard cheering and whistling and applauding. So this was going to be his job, Marc thought. Civil Affairs officer for hungry people in a crippled city. Impossible! It would take a whole army of CAO personnel to rescue them from this chaos. And he and Sergeant Munch couldn't even find their commanding officer.

Eventually they did. Major Benjamin Sykes was a large man in his mid-forties. He liked good food, good whiskey, and bad women. He wore a red mustache that made him look rather British, but he was actually from New York. He was a lawyer and a politician. When the war broke out, his Tammany Hall connections got him a commission in AMGOT. Logically, his municipal experience would have suited him for the post in Naples, but his Italian was rather primitive and he did not seem to understand the nature of his mission. The problems were staggering, but they didn't seem to bother Major Sykes. In fact, he did a little staggering of his own—just about every night. When the best meat in the shops was chicken gizzards and the best wine tasted like bad vinegar, Major Sykes was eating like a king and drinking vintage Orvieto and Valpolicella. While most of the military personnel were moving into the Piazza del Municipio, Major Sykes managed to get assigned to one of the palatial mansions on the Riviera di Chiaia. It was very important, he said, to impress these people. "Appearance is very important to them." The grand house not only impressed the Neapolitans; it also impressed Major Sykes. The gilded furniture and frames, the mirrors, the chandeliers, and the enormous staircase might all have come from a movie set for a film about Louis XVI and Marie Antoinette. When he was in his cups the major chuckled and said to his friends: "We've got it made here."

When it came to the work itself he was very good at delegating responsibility. "See what you can do about the food supply and the markets," he said to Marc one day. He gave him no guidelines, no background, nothing—and only Sergeant Munch as an assistant. But there was some advantage in the loose arrangement. It gave Marc the freedom to tackle the problem in his own way. He had plenty of office space, a battery of empty file cabinets, and a typewriter. At first he had no telephone and no transportation, but then, through the magic of Major Sykes's influence, he had put at his disposal a jeep and a driver, a kid from Brooklyn named Tony Amato, who could even speak a kind of street Italian that consisted almost entirely of curse words. Marc liked him, but Sergeant Munch thought he looked like a cheap hood from a gangster movie.

Whenever an office was opened by the military in Naples it was almost immediately swamped with Italians who had problems or confidential information or services to sell. It didn't matter whether it was an office of the AMG or the CID or the CIC or whatever. The city was crowded with people. They milled about in the streets, they stood on lines, and they waited to see anybody in authority. Why not? They had nothing else to do. They were hungry and unemployed and the city had come to a standstill.

Marc talked to an odd assortment of characters. One old man was convinced that his house was haunted by the ghosts of dead German soldiers. An investigation revealed nothing more than rats crawling in the rubble of the portion of the house that had caved in during an air raid. One day a hunchback came in to offer the magic of his hump to the American army—for a price, of course. Marc knew the old superstition that rubbing the hump would bring luck. He was amused, but the grotesque little man was dead serious.

A woman came in and actually confessed to killing her husband in an argument over the funeral arrangements for their dead child. The Neapolitans were obsessed with elaborate funerals and would sacrifice anything to make a good showing. The woman was almost hysterical. Marc didn't know what to make of the story or what to do with the woman. After a while she said: "Aren't you going to arrest me?"

"No," he said. "If you want to be arrested, you must go to the police."

She looked insulted. She stood up, cursed him, and stalked out of the office. It was the last he ever saw of her.

It wasn't long before Marc learned the first principle of the Neapolitan way of life: *Never tell the truth*. The most important virtue was *deception*. People lied about everything. They pretended to be rich when they were poor. They pretended to be friendly. They pretended to be angry. They created facades that were misleading, using borrowed clothes and business cards. They introduced themselves as professors and lawyers and engineers, when most of them were nothing of the sort. And it was apparently not a quality that had developed with the war. They had apparently always been that way. Through centuries of foreign occupation the city had learned to live with conquerors and to ignore them or deceive them. The city had a life of its own, a culture of its own that had never really been conquered. And the people were strangely affectionate and dishonest at the same time. They were full of contradictions. Marc was fascinated and frustrated. It was almost impossible to get anything done in such a city. And for the most part, nothing much did get done.

Ever since he arrived in Naples, Marc knew that he would

have to visit La Fontana, the place from which his family had come. He wanted very much to go there, and yet it bothered him, because it might be personal and he was shy. He was not sure he wanted to talk to old relatives of his grandparents, people he never knew. He preferred the impersonality of his official role. Being a relative would somehow make him vulnerable, he thought. He was afraid they would make a fuss, or that they would try to take advantage of him. And his Italian had changed. There were traces of the old accent, but it was overlaid with the formal Italian he had studied in college. Perhaps it would embarrass them. In any case, the problem was, here and back in America, that he and his family no longer spoke the same language—in any sense. Still, he had to go.

It was mid-November. A cold, gray day with occasional rain. In his uniform and raincoat he looked very military, very handsome. He did not tell his driver, Tony Amato, where he was going. He simply said: "It's a private matter," and Tony winked.

Marc drove up the Via Roma and then along the Corso Umberto I to the Piazza Garibaldi. Sometimes the street scenes looked normal; sometimes the devastation was painfully obvious. There was a military ambulance at a scene where a building had collapsed. He circled around the confusion and went on. He caught a glimpse of one of the public markets he was hoping to reopen, but it would be a long time, he thought. Besides, there still wasn't much to sell. Almost everything that was marketable was finding its way to the black market. The situation was already a scandal, but nobody seemed to be doing anything about it.

He made his way to the Piazza del Mercato and parked his jeep. He would walk from there, following the pencil-drawn map that had been given to him by Gaetano. He also had with him a list of names given to him by his grandfather and Silvio and other members of the family. It was not a long list, and few of them had been heard from in years. "Most of them are probably dead by now," said Gaetano, "but try to find them, and let me know. Write to me, and don't get into any trouble, eh?"

Marc found the church of Santa Maria del Mare. It had been damaged in one of the air raids on the port. Some of the windows were boarded up, but the door was open and a few old women in black, supporting each other by the arm, climbed the steps and went into the dark, damp interior. He went in after them. The place was musty and almost empty. There were no candles. Some of the wooden benches were missing. But the bleeding, weeping statues were there. They struck him as vulgar, almost ludicrous. He remembered the elegance of St. John's Cathedral in New York.

Outside again he consulted his crude map. He found the Porta Greca and wandered into the narrow streets. The rain had stopped and there were many people outside. They looked hungry and stunned, and it occurred to him that it was like walking back into the Middle Ages during a plague. The *scugnizzi* were almost naked, but for a few shredded rags. Their skin was crusty with scabs and filth. Their eyes were sad and wild, not the eyes of children. He saw some of them in an alleyway playing indecently with themselves. When they caught sight of him they cursed and shoved their genitals at him defiantly.

At the door of one house lingered three teenage girls who were trying to look like women. They beckoned to him with ghostly smiles. There was a foul smell at the open door, as though it were a diseased mouth. He tried not to imagine what was inside. He had heard and seen enough already of the rampant prostitution in the city that involved, he was told, maybe a third or more of all the women, even young girls only nine or ten years old. Sex was sold in cafes and alleyways and even in the cemetery. Privacy was a luxury, and the troops were learning to do without it. And there was something about this city that seemed to heighten desire, as if in the face of starvation and death making love was an act of heroic desperation. Marc felt it himself but had avoided doing anything about it.

The narrow street glistened with the recent rain and the dampness only gave a rotten edge to the stench. There was uncollected garbage, sorted through a dozen times by scavengers. There were heaps of fly-infested manure. There was the smell of human excrement and urine. And the smell of filthy and unhealthy human flesh. He had the impression that there might be dead bodies rotting away in some of the houses. He half expected a wagon of corpses to appear as if from the thirteenth century.

The shops and the cafe were closed. In front of the boarded-up cafe a few men sat on old chairs, unable to break the habit of congregating in that place. They did not look unfriendly, just curious. He went up to them and said: "I am looking for anybody named Adamo or Rosatti."

"What for?" said one of the older men. His head was a skull and his lips disappeared into his toothless mouth, but his voice was strong and his eyes were clear.

"My grandfather is Gaetano Adamo. He's in America. He asked me to visit some people here."

The old man looked at the man next to him, as if for permission to speak. Then he said to Marc: "They have all gone away, or they are dead. There are no more Adamos here. I remember him, your grandfather. He lived down there on the right. There by those stones. It was a long time ago. The old lady was the last one. She died. A sister came with him for the funeral. But then they went away again."

"And there were some cousins," said the other man. "Two of the sons went into the army, but they never came back. The father died a long time ago."

A third man leaned forward and took a pipe from his mouth. "There is only Gino Rosatti from that family, but he's, you know—" He pointed to his head.

"Where can I find him?" said Marc.

"It's better you don't find him," said the man.

"But there is also the one who was the priest," said the first man. "They say he is very high up. Maybe he went to Rome."

"Sorrento," said the second man. "I remember now. My wife said something one day. Her sister worked at the convent before the war."

"And where does this Gino Rosatti live?" said Marc.

The gaunt old man shook his head. "I told you, he don't remember nothing."

Marc insisted and the second man pointed out a house. "In the back," he said. "There is a Donna Maria, an old woman with a purple mark like wine on her face."

He found Donna Maria in a miserable *basso*. She was making something that smelled like dandelions on the stove. It was a pot of soup that seemed to be waiting for more ingredients. There was no wooden furniture in the room except for the table. He suspected that she had broken everything else up to use in the stove. In the place of chairs there were some cement blocks. And in one corner of the room, on a rotting mattress, was a very old man. He was propped up against the wall in a sitting position. His skin looked yellow

and his eyes moved in an odd, erratic way, as if he did not
have full control of them. His mouth moved and saliva dripped
from the corners into the bristles of his unshaven chin.

Marc explained why he was there, and immediately the
woman said: "Maybe you can get us something to eat. He is
my cousin and he has been very sick. He cannot speak. His
arm and his leg are dead. He had a stroke before the Americans came."

Marc did not even try to speak to the old man, who was,
after all, only a distant cousin on his grandmother's side. He
was overwhelmed by a feeling of revulsion. All he wanted to
do, suddenly, was get out of there. But Donna Maria grabbed
him by the arm and began to plead and weep. "Bring us
something to eat. Please! Bring us something. Anything!"

He took out his wallet and gave her several bills—more
money than she had seen in years. She tried to kiss his hand,
but he pulled away and walked quickly out the door without
another word.

Before he could escape through the Porta Greca he was
besieged by beggars and children who had apparently heard
that he was not there to arrest anybody and might be an easy
touch. He knew it was a mistake, but he threw a handful of
coins into the street and then actually broke into a run to get
away. Back at the Piazza del Mercato he jumped into the jeep
and drove away so quickly that he almost killed a mule. He
heard the driver's curses behind him.

It was a depressing winter for Marc. The hopelessness of
the situation was getting to him. The American troops behaved badly. The Italians behaved even worse. Everything
that was not actually bolted down seemed to disappear. Supplies were diverted. Civilian relief goods fell into the hands of
corrupt officials. And to make matters worse, the weather
was cold and unpleasant for longer than usual. In his letters to
his grandfather, Marc found himself slipping into true Neapolitan evasiveness. He said that he had been unable to locate any
of the friends or relatives on his list, but that he had reason to
believe that some of them had been evacuated to the country
and were probably all right. He didn't know why he avoided
the truth. It just, somehow, seemed easier that way.

The war went on elsewhere but sometimes reached them in
the form of a surprise air raid. The Germans were far from
defeated. In January they turned the landing at Anzio into a

nightmare that the Americans would never forget. In February the Americans decided to bomb the ancient monastery of Monte Casino. It had been founded in the year 529 by St. Benedict, and there was widespread hope that it might be spared. Two hundred and fifty-four American planes shattered that hope, but not the German position. They continued to hold out in that key hill of the Gustav line.

By early spring Marc was about to give up. He was convinced that nothing would ever be done about the wholesale corruption in this city. It was Dante's *Inferno* all over again. Circles of evil that embraced every vice, every crime, every form of human degradation.

Then he was drawn into an investigation being conducted by a few people over at CID, the Criminal Investigations Division. There were a couple of men there, working with considerable freedom and confidentiality, who actually thought they might crack the organization behind the black market. It was the wide-eyed optimism of Lieutenant Wayne Goodson that encouraged Marc. He liked the man instantly. He liked his innocence and courage. He was one of those handsome, straight guys who could have walked right out of the American Dream. He was a shiny crisp apple in a barrel of rotten fruit. How he stayed that way Marc had no idea, but it was more than just amusing. Ten minutes with Wayne Goodson could make a man feel clean again, even in a place like Naples.

It was March 15, the Ides of March. Wayne and Marc and one of Wayne's informers got together for lunch in an out-of-the-way restaurant up by the National Museum, which had not as yet been reopened. There was hardly anyone in the place, and hardly anything on the menu. "These are hard times," said the owner-waiter apologetically. They ordered the pasta and fish sauce, which proved to be a little thin, made probably from fishheads.

Emilio Faviano was not an ordinary informer. He had real credentials. He had been quietly starving to death with dignity when Lieutenant Goodson came across him. He had once been a professor of linguistics at the university. And he had served in the Italian army as a translator. He was proficient in many languages and in many Italian dialects. He was also something of a mimic and a performer, having taken part years ago in certain university productions. When he decided to offer his services to the military, it was quite by accident that he came to Wayne Goodson. He thought he had come to the offices of the AMG. He was in the wrong place but at the right time. He was a man in his early forties with a soft round face and eyes like an owl. He was very gracious and disarming. No one would have taken him for an undercover agent. But he could become almost anything with his linguistic and acting gifts. "You should have gone into the movies," said Marc. "You would be rich and famous by now."

"Do you think so?" said Faviano. There were several layers of satire in the little pose that he struck.

"Sure," said Marc. "You could have gone to Hollywood."

"No, no, they would have made me an organ grinder for sure. I have seen your American films."

"We have some interesting news," said Wayne.

Marc leaned forward to listen. Faviano looked pleased with himself.

"We have been tracing the affair of the seven trucks, as you know. We thought it would end with a man named Rocco Barone. But now we have proof that this Barone is only an underling of Vito Generoso himself."

"Vito Generoso?"

"Ah, you know the name, of course. He was very big in America, eh?" said Faviano.

"Yes, in the Mafia. But to escape a murder indictment before the war he left the country. We knew he came to Italy, but—"

"Let me tell you about this man," said Faviano. "He was born not far from here, in 1897. When he was sixteen years old he went to America. He was quick with the gun and completely ruthless. He came up fast in your country and was second to Luciano. Drugs, smuggling, gambling, extortion. All the usual things, eh? And then the murders and the trouble and the return to Italy. He came with a lot of money. Nobody knows how much. He contributed to the Fascists and became a good friend of Mussolini and Count Ciano. In different names he has had many business enterprises. In the *zona di camòrra* here he is one of the top bosses, maybe number one. But then there comes the war and the confusion and the armies of the Allies. And there comes the black market. Nobody wants to look into it, except the *tenènte* here and maybe one or two other people in his department. And do you know why?"

"I can guess."

"Because the military is into it up to the neck."

"It was very discouraging to find that out," said Wayne.
"And it has made our job much more difficult."

"Yes," said Faviano. "There are many important people,
military and civilian, who do not want this investigation.
Fortunately, most of them do not even know it is taking
place."

"But don't you file reports?" said Marc.

"Yes, but only to Major Summers, and I think he is being
very discreet."

Marc shook his head. "You're both lucky you haven't
been killed by now."

"I'm only doing my duty," said Wayne. "A lot of good
men have died in this war."

Marc looked at him. The man was strangely selfless and
fearless. It was hard to believe. It wasn't quite normal. "So
what is your next move?"

"My last instructions were to gather sufficient evidence
that Vito Generoso is, in fact, the man who runs the black
market in Naples, and perhaps in all of southern Italy. Then I
will ask permission from my superior to arrest him."

Marc put his hand across his forehead and eyes. "Wayne,
you don't know what you're getting into. You're talking
maybe about a lot of high-ranking officers in the Allied
Military Government."

"As a matter of fact," said Faviano, "did you know that
Mr. Generoso has been an official interpreter for certain
officers in the AMG?"

Marc shook his head. "What incredible arrogance!"

"He has what you might call friends in high places."

"I realize that he is a powerful man," said Wayne, "but
we are going to do our best to break him."

"Have you ever seen such confidence?" said Faviano. "I
would give my life for this man. He is a hero."

"Or a fool," said Marc. "I was merely hoping to get a few
legitimate food shipments into the city. I wasn't planning to
bust the Italian Mafia."

"Unless we do something," said Wayne, "your relief
shipments will wind up on the black market along with
everything else."

"Should we tell him about the *shed*?" said Faviano.

Marc looked from the professor to the lieutenant.

"We think we have located a very important depot of

theirs—about ten miles outside of town. Several large underground storehouses full of wheat and olive oil. Some of these things have undoubtedly come from the agencies you have been working with. They are intended for the relief of the starving people in Naples, but they never get there.''

"Yes, I know, but I didn't know exactly where they were going."

"Well, now we know."

"And what are you going to do?"

"We are going to seize the shed."

"You and who else?"

"Me and Faviano, and a few other people who work with us. We are making arrangements."

"Nonmilitary personnel?"

"Not entirely."

"Are you going to do this with or without authorization?"

"I have been authorized to gather evidence. I consider this valuable evidence. Would you like to come along?"

"Sure! I'll come along. Just keep me informed."

"It'll be a while. We are just setting the thing up."

"How long?"

"Weeks. Months. It's hard to say. We'll keep in touch."

On his way back to the Riviera di Chiaia, Marc scolded himself for being seduced by Wayne Goodson's innocence and heroism. What the hell am I getting myself into? he thought. And how do I get out of it? There was still time. He would think of something. But by the time he was back in his office he had decided that he did not want to get out of it after all. He wasn't sure why. Perhaps it was a chance to do something honest in this sink of dishonesty. Or perhaps it was the excitement of a little action. He decided to wait for further instructions.

Spring came. It was suddenly very warm. People took off their extra clothes. Boys stripped to nothing plunged into the bay, where the hulks of sunken ships still lay like dead leviathans. Everything moved more slowly, and the women seemed to move with a special rhythm and softness and often looked back over their shoulders to see who was looking at them.

Marc, too, felt the change, and it made him restless with desire. Since he came to Naples there had been a few incidents, but no involvements, and he would not deal with prostitutes. In the winter months he rediscovered in himself an ascetic streak and spent much of his time alone. He read a great deal and wrote many letters. It was easy in December and January. But by March, with warm breezes assaulting the bay from the south and wafting in all the mysteries of the Mediterranean world, it was impossible to stay indoors, impossible to avoid the siren songs. He walked the crowded streets. He lingered by the sea. He discovered new ways of understanding the very thrust of life. He saw it in the lean, hard hips of the men and in the abundant bosoms of the women. He saw it in the naked boys who scampered over the stones of the ruined docks and in the quick smiles of the young girls who flaunted their new breasts.

He was in the grip of all these feelings when Anna Liano came to see him. Sergeant Munch brought her in from the waiting room. He introduced her and handed Marc the usual form. Under *nature of business* was scribbled *confidential*. Munch lingered and continued to stare at the woman until Marc said: "All right, Sergeant, you can go now."

Anna Liano was one of those women who seem to be in touch with secrets that are at the very heart of the world. She was tall, five foot seven or eight, and slender, but with well-defined bones, which gave her a special elegance. She might have been English or Scandinavian. Marc thought of the Normans who had settlements in Sicily and the south of Italy. But her generous features were clearly Mediterranean, perhaps even Middle Eastern. Her skin was fair. Her hair was dark but alive with light. And the sun was streaming through the tall, undraped window. Her eyes—he had to look twice—were as blue as the sea. And her mouth could be seen in the ruined statues of the Acropolis. No wonder Sergeant Munch had been unable to leave the room, thought Marc. He himself stood there for several moments as though he had forgotten where he was or what he was supposed to say. Then he cleared his throat and said: "Please sit down. We are alone. You can speak freely."

He waited for her to take the chair beside his desk. Then he, too, sat down. He offered her a cigarette. She accepted. He leaned forward to light it for her. "Thank you," she said.

"My name is Lieutenant Adamo. I see that you are Anna Liano." He was glancing at the form on his desk. "And that you live on the Via Cimarossa. A very nice district. Very nice, indeed. And, if you don't mind my saying so, you seem to belong there."

"Thank you. The house is not what it used to be, but we manage to hold on to it. There was a time when——what shall I say?—it was well known, and the Lianos were important. But times have changed. Now there isn't much left but the name. My father is not well. I look after him. There are only the two of us."

"Then you are not married?"

"No." She said this with a special firmness. It was almost a denial.

Marc leaned back in his chair. "Why did you come here?"

She hesitated. He saw a slight tremor in her long, delicate fingers.

"Don't be afraid," he said, and he caught her eye. "You can trust me."

"Thank you," she said. "I was told that I could."

"Oh? By whom?"

"I would rather not say, if you don't mind."

"All right, then . . ."

She took a deep breath and said: "Three months ago my brother was murdered. Until then he had been taking care of the family. My father did not know where the money was coming from, but I did. My brother was involved in certain activities, certain arrangements that required contacts in high places. The buying and selling of goods."

"The black market."

"Yes," she said as though she herself could not mouth the words. "And there was a misunderstanding. I'm not sure exactly what it was. The people he was working with killed him."

"Are you sure it was them?"

"Yes, absolutely sure. He knew he was in danger. Shortly before he was killed he gave me a list of names. I would like you to have that list, but since it is the only thing of value I have—"

"I see. In other words, you want to sell me that list."

She looked away. "It is not an easy thing for me to do. It's very humiliating." Then she looked up more firmly and with a flash of anger in her eyes. "But what else can I do? We are desperate. Most of the furniture is already gone. All I have left is this list and . . . and myself. Should I go into the streets? Should I prostitute myself? I would rather die. This is bad enough.'' Her lips quivered, but she held back the tears.

Right there and then Marc wanted to take her in his arms and protect her from the brutes in the broken streets of Naples, but he controlled himself. ''Why didn't you go to the police?''

''Because they have no money, and because they are corrupt. They would do nothing for me.''

''We also have a Criminal Investigations Division.''

''I know, but I wasn't sure I could trust them. I took a chance with you because of certain things I have heard. That your family is Italian. That you have compassion.''

It was Marc's turn to be embarrassed. All his life he had been retreating from the crudeness and poverty of his own family. He did not think of himself as compassionate. He did not like to get involved. In the midst of all this chaos he searched for quietude. But first there came Wayne Goodson. And now there came Anna Liano. ''May I see the list?'' he said.

''And in return?''

''How much do you expect?''

''Fifty thousand lire.''

Marc made a whispering, whistling sound. ''That's a lot of money.''

''I hope to leave here as soon as the war is over. I am sick of Naples. Sick of Italy.''

''Where do you want to go?''

''I don't care. America. Argentina. Somewhere away from Europe. If my father is still alive I will take him with me.''

''Can you tell me something about your list? It might take some persuasion to raise the money.''

''There are some Italians and some Americans. Some camòrrista, some military. It goes very high up. And you probably know better than I do how much has been stolen.''

''Yes, we know. And we are trying to do something about it. We also have names. What we need is evidence.''

''What I have will help. With each name there are notations. Very revealing. It makes one sick.''

''Yes, I know. But aren't you afraid? I mean, if they found out—''

''If they found out that I had such a list, they would kill me, of course. I am depending on you. I don't want to see anyone else. And I don't want to come here again.''

"All right, then. I will see what I can do, and then I will
see you—where?"

"At the house. At night. Late. And only you, without your
uniform, if possible."

"I think I can manage it."

"Come after ten but before eleven. We have no telephone,
of course." She stood up and started to leave.

He came to her and extended his hand. "I'm glad you
came to me," he said. "I will try. Perhaps we can help each
other." He did not mean to be suggestive. Later he blamed it
on the weather.

Her handshake was firm but feminine. He did not want to
let her go. He read her reaction in her sea-blue eyes. There
was a chance, he thought. Or was he imagining things?

To raise the money he went to Wayne Goodson. It was not
easy. Major Summers came up with less than half the amount.
It was Emilio Faviano who arranged for the rest by "re-
circulating" certain confiscated items. "Think of it as an
investment," he said when his lieutenant looked hesitant.
Goodson drew up a receipt and wrote on it *Operation Vesuvio*.

It was the end of March by the time Marc had the money in
hand. In the meantime, he had checked out the dossiers of the
Lianos in the files on the top floor of the Questura. The
Fascist police, like their German counterparts, had kept track
of almost everyone. What Marc found corresponded, more or
less, with what Anna had told him, except that her father had
apparently been, at one time, a Fascist of sufficient importance to be in the black book that was kept by the AMG—
some said for blackmail purposes. An inconsistent attempt
was still being made to round up former officials.

On April 2 Marc decided to get in touch with Anna Liano
in the way she had insisted upon. Faviano had provided him
with some ill-fitting civilian clothes. To be sure he would be
able to find his way at night, he drove past the house that
same morning. It was a quiet, aristocratic neighborhood near
the Villa Floridiana, which was set in a lovely park on
Vomero hill and commanded a view of the city, the bay, and
Vesuvius. On a clear day one could see in the distance the
Isle of Capri. The area had not been damaged much by the
war, and in the early morning it looked much as it once had
in earlier years. The tragedies inside, the decadence and
despair, were not immediately visible. The Liano house re-

minded him of a formidable but somewhat disheveled old lady. The gardens were overgrown. The shutters were closed. One of the iron gates was missing. One went up a brick path past stone urns to steps guarded by weatherworn lions from the eighteenth century. They looked tired and benign.

That night there was an immense moon, surrealistic in its deep orange color. It cast an unsettling glow over the whole hill. And the air was heavy and moist and without so much as a whisper of a breeze.

Marc parked his jeep a few blocks away on the Via Cilea and made his way on foot. He was uncomfortable in his borrowed clothes—a yellow shirt, a dark blue jacket, and black pants. The colors were bad enough, but whoever they belonged to must have had very short arms and legs. There was plenty of room in the jacket to button it not only around himself but around the holster of his .38 automatic.

As he turned the corner into the Via Cimarosa a civilian car went by. It was an unusual sight and it made him wonder. A few pedestrians strolled in the soft moonlight of the humid evening. One old couple had a dog on a leash. A younger couple merged into one form as they walked toward the Castel Sant'Elmo. He sat on a stone bench and smoked a cigarette. A skeleton of a cat appeared briefly and then looked around nervously before leaping a low stone wall and disappearing. It reminded Marc of the jokes that he had heard when he first arrived in Naples. There were very few cats left, they said. "And never buy a rabbit from a butcher unless the head is still on."

He waited until a quarter past ten. Then he simply went to the house, walked up the path, and knocked gently on the heavy wooden door. It opened immediately, and there was Anna Liano in a blue silk dress that came below the knee. In this light and that dress she was even more beautiful than the first time he had seen her. He suddenly felt like a clown in his ridiculous disguise.

The hallway was lit only by candles, and the large living room was a dark cavity. "We have no electricity," said Anna. She beckoned for him to follow her. "We won't wake my father. He's not feeling well." She led him down a hallway. "We only use the kitchen and two bedrooms. I hope you don't mind if we go to my room. There is a table where we can sit by the window."

"Whatever you say."

The shutters were open in Anna's room. Outside the floor-to-ceiling window there was a little balcony with an iron railing. From the window one could see the whole, magnificent view—all the magic of Naples without the suffering, without the poverty. Anna blew out the candle. "We can talk by moonlight," she said. "Isn't it magnificent?"

"Incredible," he said. "I've never seen anything like it."

"There *is* nothing like it."

He could see that there was no rug on the floor and that in addition to the table and two chairs there was only a bed, but it was a magnificent bed. She saw him looking at it. "It was my mother's," she said. "It will be the last thing with which I part. Come, sit down. I can only offer you a little vermouth."

"That will be just fine," he said. "I should have brought something. I'm sorry."

"But I hope you *have* brought something."

"Oh—yes, that. Yes, I have."

She raised her glass. "Shall we drink to our little conspiracy?"

"By all means," he said.

From somewhere she produced several sheets of paper that were folded together. "Can you see? Or should I light a candle?"

"I think I can manage," he said.

She watched silently as he read. Twice he shook his head and said: "My God!" And then he said: "I don't believe it. Not Major Sykes."

"Yes, your own major. Read the rest of it and you will understand."

When he was done he dropped the papers on the table and stared out the window toward the bay. Vesuvius was suddenly a grim reminder of death, and he thought of Lieutenant Goodson's notation—*Operation Vesuvio*. "I had no idea that the rot had reached so far."

"It's very sad, isn't it?" she said. "It makes it very hard for one to believe in anything. And here I am—perhaps as bad as the rest."

"You mustn't think of it that way. It's a matter of survival. And perhaps some good will come of it."

"Survival? Ah, yes, in the name of survival what atrocities we can commit. We are such animals—all of us. You know, sometimes I sit here at night by this window and I think about a trip we all took with my father one year. I was fifteen years old. We went to Bolzano to ski. The snow was very white and clean. And the air was cold and pure. I fell in love with the ski instructor at the hotel. He was very amused. He told me that he was thirty-nine years old and that he had a daughter my age. I said it didn't matter. He said it did, and that one day I would realize that I was really in love with the snow and the mountains. He was right. And now it is the clean, cold whiteness that I think of on these hot, humid nights. The clean, cold whiteness of youth, of innocence, of a world at peace."

"What year was it when you went to Bolzano?"

"It was 1935."

"You're still very young."

"I don't feel very young."

"I would expect you to be married. You're very beautiful."

"Ah, on a night like this one might say almost anything. I must remember to save something for another time. Otherwise you will know everything, and perhaps you won't come back."

"Do you want me to come back?"

"I think so. Yes."

He hesitated. "And would you like me to stay now?"

She was staring out the window when she answered. "Yes. It is that kind of night, isn't it? A little madness in the air. Do you feel it?"

"Yes."

"They say it is the south wind."

"But there's no wind at all."

"It doesn't matter. This air is from Africa. On such nights it is impossible to sleep." She stood up and went to the little balcony. She seemed to be waiting for him. He went to her. He stood beside her but was afraid to touch her. She turned to look at him. For a moment they said nothing. Her eyelids seemed heavy. She offered her lips. He kissed her. Her lips were very warm. He could hear her breathing. She drew away.

"Is something wrong?" he said.

"I'm sorry you had to wear those idiotic clothes. You look much nicer in your uniform. Why don't you take them off?"

"Right here?"

"No. Inside." She took his hand and led him to the ancient bed. They got undressed without embarrassment and lay down together on the cool, stretched sheets. There was nothing over them but moonlight. She curled against him and said: "Hold me for a while."

For a long time they lay there in a silent embrace and looked toward the window and the sky. It seemed to him that he had known her forever, that he had never had another life. They were suspended in time in the magic of the moonlight. When he thought she was asleep, she whispered: "How good your body is—soft and strong." She raised herself to kiss and explore him. He moved from a dream of silence into a dream of passion.

They made love slowly. As the moon rose it grew smaller and whiter. There was an understanding in their kisses and in whatever they did. She covered him with her body. She was tall, but light and almost fragile. She kneeled over him and touched his almost bare chest with her long fingers. He liked having her there where he could see her and feel her. He came into her and her passion was revealed. She sighed and swayed and found her pleasure with head tossed back and closed eyes.

Later they made love again and she wanted him over her and in her. He could feel her desire, and she urged him with her hands to do it hard. They came together, and it was as he always imagined it could be. For a while they talked, and then they slept in each other's arms.

It was the beginning of the sort of thing that he had hoped to avoid. An affair was one thing, but he had to be careful not to fall in love. Not like this. Not here in some war-torn city in another country, where nothing is real except the loneliness and the suffering that drive people into one another's arms. It was very dangerous.

For a while they did not talk about that part of it. They went to restaurants. They rode out into the country. They walked. They talked. They made love. She introduced him to her father, who proved to be a charming man. His weakness did not rob him of his civilized ways, and he did not impose his condition on his guest. It was Anna who explained that he had a very bad heart and that he could die at any moment. But if he was careful—well, he might even improve. There was always hope. Now that she had some money she would find him a good doctor.

*Operation Vesuvio* was falling into place very slowly. There were complications. The Liano list had been very helpful, but in a way it had also complicated matters, because not even Lieutenant Goodson or Faviano knew of some of the names. There had to be adjustments. There was the possibility of an infiltration at the CID.

Marc was just as glad. April and May were marvelous, made for love, for dreams. For the old saying: *dolce far niente, how sweet to do nothing*. They went to Pompeii and to the island of Ischia. He did his CAO work in a perfunctory way and was praised by Major Sykes for holding the fort. The major himself was often away.

It was inevitable. Marc fell in love with Anna Liano. He knew it was happening even as he was refusing to admit it. Everything conspired against him—her beauty, her need, her acceptance of him. She was aristocratic and earthly. She had style and passion. And it was all real, unless she was the world's greatest actress. Doubts crept in. In Naples that was possible. Appearance and reality! The city of illusions. What was it that Faviano had told him? "Everybody in Naples is a liar."

He fought against the idea. There are certain feelings that cannot be faked. A woman could pretend to find pleasure in sex, but he did not think she could pretend to love someone. It was too delicate a matter, too subtle. It revealed itself in every movement, and in the eyes, which are "the windows of the soul," according to an old saying. In Anna's eyes he saw love.

Or was it desperation? Was she softened by the thought that she could become an American citizen by marrying an American officer? It was beginning to happen, and the AMG was taking a dim view of the number of requests that were pouring in. The official policy was not to prohibit but to discourage such marriages.

But no, she never even suggested such a thing. She seemed content with the friendship, the affair. She did not seem to want to know where it was going, as investment-minded women often do. "It's a beautiful day today," she would say. "Let's not worry about tomorrow." And off they would go to some lovely place to escape from the noise and confusion of Naples. They would go to Herculaneum or Amalfi or even to Paestum, which was fifty miles down the coast. There they could walk in startling sunshine among Doric temples so well preserved that one was instantly transported to another world. One day they wandered through the Temple of Neptune, built in 450 B.C. and almost completely intact, and then through the ruins of the Temple of Ceres. "It was built twenty-five hundred years ago," said Marc.

"Which only proves that nothing lasts. You see how time has taken its toll." There was an odd smile on her face. A breeze played in her veillike dress as she leaned against a fluted column. For a moment he saw her as though she were a vision of an ancient Greek goddess who had suddenly materialized out of the past.

"They were remarkable people," he said.

"How do you know? You weren't there. Perhaps they were no better or worse than us. These temples, like our cathedrals, tell us very little of ordinary life." Her smile disappeared. She looked sad.

Marc took her by the hand and they walked over the large worn stones that formed a path through the temple. He read aloud from a small guidebook: "Paestum was founded in the sixth century B.C. by the Sybarites, a people of Greek descent. It was given the name of Poseidonia. . . ."

"I thought a Sybarite was one who lived only for pleasure," she said.

"That's largely a myth, because the ancient city of Sybaris was wealthy. It was eventually destroyed."

"Not by God."

"No, not by God. By a mortal enemy."

"Like the Germans, you mean?"

"Yes."

They walked through the remains of the forum and over the Via Sacra. "How did you manage when the Germans were here?" he said.

She shrugged. "We managed. They weren't here for long."

"But they did a great deal of damage."

"Only to the city. Not to us. They took some of the houses on the Vomero. Some officers stayed with us. They were not uncivilized."

"What do you mean?"

She drew away. "Oh, let's not talk about the bloody war. Let's talk about the ancient Greeks. About temples and Sybarites. Let's go down to the sea and put our feet in the water."

And off they went, running, laughing, forgetting everything but the dazzling day and the cool sand of the beach—a beach not far from the one on which Marc had landed some eight months earlier.

On the third of June the Allies entered Rome. There was rejoicing in the streets of Naples, as there might have been at a *festa* or at the news twice a year that the blood of San Gennero had liquefied, that ritual miracle that protected the city from disaster. Feast or victory or the reception of a hero, it was all the same in Naples. Poverty made the Neapolitans ready to celebrate anything. It gave them a momentary escape, the illusion that all was well. And illusions were cheaper than bread or fish.

Two days later Lieutenant Wayne Goodson came to Marc's office and said: "Operation Vesuvio is on for tonight."

"That's awfully short notice, isn't it?" said Marc.

"We didn't know ourselves until early this morning," said Goodson. "It's not only the shed we want; it's certain people. Two of them will be there tonight. We need them alive. There must be witnesses. I have five men of my own, not including you. Faviano has half a dozen. There will be four M.P.s and two Englishmen who have been working with me. Eighteen men in all. Nineteen, if I count myself. I have a jeep, a truck, and an armored car."

"Good Lord! Where did you get all that stuff?"

"A CID investigator has certain advantages."

"I was supposed to be somewhere tonight."

"Unless it's a matter of life and death, you'll have to cancel it."

Marc thought for a moment. "What do you want me to do?"

"I want you to be on the main road to Caivano, where it branches off to Nola. We will rendezvous at midnight. From there it is only five kilometers. We will issue weapons, but we do not expect much resistance. There have, normally, been only six to ten of them there on such occasions, not all of them armed. They will be expecting three trucks from Bari."

"All right," said Marc, thinking that he would have to invent something to tell Anna. More secrets. More lies.

Shortly before midnight Marc pulled his jeep off the road and into an olive grove. Before long the lights of a truck appeared. He waited. Another vehicle came up the road. He backed out of the grove and pulled alongside of it. Wayne Goodson climbed out and came over to the jeep and got in. "I'll go with you," he said. "Faviano has my car. He will bring up the rear. We will lead." In another moment the last vehicle appeared. The whole operation seemed well rehearsed.

They drove on the highway toward Nola but stopped after a few miles. Lieutenant Goodson got out and went to confer with the driver of the armored car. There was no other traffic on the road. Marc waited, listening to the sound of the idling motors and looking out over a field toward some dark hills in the distance. The moon was less than full. The air was heavy and warm and there was the sound of insects. A mosquito sang in his ear. He brushed it away.

They started up again, but only went a hundred yards or so until they turned into a narrow dirt road. After a quarter of a mile the truck left the column and followed another dirt road that branched off to the right. "They will come up behind on the other side," said Goodson.

"What about the trucks from Bari?" said Marc.

"They have already gone in, about half an hour ago. We had a man posted back there where we stopped. They should be busy unloading by now."

Everything happened very quickly. There was a glow of light around a bend in the narrow road. They came to a clearing. They saw the trucks and several large humps of earth. "Pull over there and stop," commanded Goodson. The armored car rolled past, and the jeep skirted the left flank. The dust that was raised from the road wafted through their headlights and through the armored car's floodlight.

Several dark figures were frozen in their tracks near the trucks. Several others scampered from the cellarlike doors of the underground storerooms. A loud, magnified voice startled Marc. Through a bullhorn someone said: "You are surrounded and under arrest. Do not try to resist. Come forward together!"

"Follow me," said Goodson. They ran forward and took cover in the shadow of the armored car. Marc had a carbine and Goodson had what looked like a Thompson.

The first shot was fired from one of the trucks. They were camions with canvas tops. There was a rapid, loud exchange of shots. "Damn it!" shouted Goodson. He climbed into the armored car and grabbed the bullhorn from one of his men. "Cease fire!" he said in a loud voice. "Cease fire!" The shooting stopped on both sides. Almost all of it had come from the military. The enemy was clearly overwhelmed. The lights of the CID truck turned them into silhouettes. They were putting up their hands and huddling toward the light so they could be seen. Marc counted seven of them, but in the lesser light near one of the trucks there were two bodies on the ground.

Goodson and his men approached cautiously from both sides, their guns ready. Marc advanced with them, feeling more excitement than danger. His heart was beating rapidly. His palms were damp. One of the captured men was talking very rapidly in Italian. Goodson answered without the benefit of the bullhorn.

"All right," he said. "Line up there in the light. Throw out your weapons and take off your clothes." There were protests. He repeated the order more firmly. Reluctantly they obeyed, until all seven were stripped to their underwear. They looked naked and vulnerable and ridiculous.

"What about *them*?" said Marc, indicating the two bodies.

"See if they're still alive."

Marc hesitated.

"Celano! Fazio! Go with him," said Goodson.

Marc held back while the other two men rolled over the bodies. One was limp and covered with blood. His eyes were still open. "Dead as a stone," said Fazio. The other one moaned when they moved him. Celano opened his shirt. He was wounded in the gut and bleeding badly. "*Dio santo!*" Celano said, and then started ripping at the shirt to make bandages. "Get me some more of those things," he said to Marc, pointing to the clothes on the ground. That much he could do, but he could not touch the wounded man.

They searched the clothing of the captured men, then allowed them to get dressed. They handcuffed them and put them into the truck with several guards.

As they suspected, the bins and trucks from Bari were full of wheat and olive oil, and even some sacks of flour that still had the markings of a relief agency on them.

They left half-a-dozen men behind to watch over the storerooms and the trucks, and off they went back to the city as if the whole operation were merely routine.

"What will happen now?" said Marc.

"That remains to be seen," said Goodson. "But don't say anything to Sykes. Nobody knows you were here. I'll make my report to Major Summers."

"All right," said Marc.

"And don't say anything to Anna Liano."

"You know about her?"

"Of course. And maybe a few things *you* don't know. But that will have to keep."

Marc felt his heart sink, but he said nothing.

The next day Marc noticed that Major Sykes seemed distracted, but aside from that everything seemed normal and quiet. Perhaps too quiet, considering the events of the previous day. There was nothing in the newspapers. Nothing on the radio. No messages. No telephone calls. No one seemed to know anything at all about the incident on the road to Nola. As he had promised, Marc said nothing to Anna, and he decided that it might be wise not to get in touch with Goodson. He just sat tight and did his work.

That day went by, then another, then a third. His curiosity was an appetite that grew sharper by the hour, but there was really nothing he could do. He tried to put the incident out of his mind, but it kept coming back. And he wanted to spend some time with Anna. They had been talking about going to Capri for a couple of days, if he could get away and if she could get someone to look after her father.

It was ten days before Goodson finally got in touch with him. He sent one of his Italian operatives around with a message. Later he explained that he did not want to come in person to AMG headquarters as long as Sykes was still there. They met in a cafe off the Via Roma.

As soon as Marc saw Goodson coming down the street he could tell that something had gone wrong. He walked with a quick, stiff motion, as if he had been wounded in his principles. "Jesus Christ, Wayne, what's been happening?" said Marc even before he said hello.

Goodson sat down. His jaws were tight and the muscles were working as though he were chewing on his own teeth. "You won't believe what they've done," he said.

"What could they have done? You laid it all out for them, didn't you?"

"I made my report to Major Summers—in writing. He said it was a good job."

"Is that all he said?"

"He said he'd have to take it up the line. Two days later he said that the AMG was taking over the shed and that it would

prepare cases against the men in custody. I told him that I
didn't think it was wise to turn over the case to anyone.''

''Where did the pressure come from?''

''Some goddamn general had him on the blower for over
an hour, chewing his ass out. He wouldn't tell me who. He
said that he had no choice but that he was assured there would
be an appropriate follow-through, assuming that the evidence
was adequate for prosecution. Summers is okay. He means
well, but he's got a lot of other people to deal with. Anyway,
he told me to get my papers together and be prepared to
testify. So I spent a few days checking out everything and
getting up dossiers. I was able to link two of the men directly
with Generoso. I waited another two days before nudging
Summers. He said there were no new developments, so yesterday I drove out to the shed, just to see what the hell was
going on. And do you know what I found? Two infantrymen
walking up and down smoking cigarettes. I asked them what
was going on. They said they were guarding these here
bunkers. I asked them if they knew what they were. They
said no. The trucks were gone. When I looked inside the
storerooms they were completely empty. Not a grain of wheat.
Not a drop of olive oil. Nothing. It was pointless to ask any
more questions. I could see that all our work had been
undone.''

''Yeah, but what about the men in custody?''

''They were turned over to the civilian police, who released them the other day for lack of evidence. No charges
were filed. The dead man was put down as a robbery victim.
The wounded man died in the hospital from what they called
a self-inflicted wound.''

''Sons-of-bitches! I don't believe it. How can they get
away with that?''

''God, I don't know, Marc. Maybe everybody's on the
payroll except you and me.''

''Isn't there anything you can do?''

''I don't know. It's very big. Bigger than I thought. I don't
know who to go to. Summers is honest but fatalistic. He says
if I bring in Generoso the same thing will happen, unless we
can use the murder indictment in the States to start some
extradition proceedings. He's going to try to contact a State
Department official. We'll see what happens.''

Marc shook his head. ''Listen, Wayne,'' he said, ''maybe

you'd better leave it alone. If you push too hard—you know—they're liable to get to you."

"I'm sorry, Marc, but I just can't back off now. I won't involve you, but I have to do what I have to do."

The waiter came by, and they ordered another bottle of wine. After a while Marc looked meditatively into his glass and said: "What were you going to tell me about Anna Liano?"

"You don't want to know, Marc. Why don't you just take things as they are?"

Marc looked at him. Even Wayne was beginning to bury the truth. "No. I want to know what I'm getting into before it's too late."

"All right. I'll make easy to read. She was married to an Italian officer who went over to the Germans and retreated North with them. They all would have gone, but her father was too sick to make the trip. He was the number-three man in the Department of the Interior. He should have been picked up, but she bought him off the list with everything she owned."

Marc let out a sigh and rubbed his forehead. "So that was her secret," he said. "I knew it was something."

"I'm sorry!" said Goodson.

"It's all right," said Marc. "Just as well."

He did not mention his conversation with Goodson and did not cancel their scheduled visit to Capri. Anna had gone to see their old housekeeper, and she had agreed to come back to look after Signore Liano. Anna was very excited. "It has been years since I have been to Capri," she said. "It is the most beautiful place in the world. I think I would like to be buried there when I die, somewhere high on Monte Solario in a small churchyard, far from the noise and close to the sky."

Anna looked younger and more beautiful than ever as they boarded the boat. There was a freshness and a freedom in her face, as though she had just emerged from a storm into the sunlight. She was happy to leave the gloom of the old villa and be relieved of looking after her father. She wore her hair loose, as though to express her sense of freedom, and the warm breeze played in it so that it seemed alive. She laughed out loud and pointed to this and that as the boat pulled away from the shore. It was the old steamer ferry, and its gray smoke left a trail in the very blue sky. Anna leaned against the rail. She was wearing a loose white blouse that suited her slender shoulders and arms, and a blue skirt that was darker than the sky but lighter than the sea. Marc stood beside her, touched by her joy, though he carried with him the pain of her secret.

He had thought a good deal about what Wayne Goodson had told him. At first he was merely angry and hurt. Then he was sad. Then he was recklessly in love again and thought he didn't give a damn about the past. Then he did. Finally, he decided that he would put all his feelings aside until he had a chance to talk with Anna. Somewhere on Capri they would find the right place and the right time, but first he had another duty to perform. His great-uncle, Pietro Adamo, had returned from Rome to the archbishop's residence at the *duomo* in Sorrento. From there he had gone to the Carthusian monastery on Capri for a rest. He was now seventy-two years old and not in the best of health. His brief note said that he could be visited there. Marc was almost as nervous about that visit as he was about his impending confrontation with Anna.

It was eighteen miles across the bay to Capri, and the old boat took two hours to make the trip. The magic island became more distinct as they drew closer. Behind them the great sweep of the curving shore became almost as beautiful, and Naples faded from noise and poverty into an illusion of grandeur, its colors and churches and castles caught in the sunlight.

"It was called the island of the goats," said Anna.

"I can see why," said Marc, looking at the steep mountains that rose well over a thousand feet in places. "It's much bigger than I thought."

"About four miles by two miles," she said. "The emperor Tiberius built twelve villas here. There are wonderful stories of the luxury and orgies of those days, but of course they are exaggerated. I am sure that there is more sin in a single street of Naples than there was ever here in Capri, even in the days of Tiberius."

They came into a wide inlet and docked at the Marina Grande. The harbor was full of fishing boats. Behind the clustered white houses rose the gray cliffs. From the marina they walked up the steep road to the village of Capri. They came to the church of San Costanza, where the patron saint of the island was buried. Near the church there began the famous 159 Phoenecian steps that led to Anacapri, another settlement higher up than the main village. There were other men in uniform among the visitors, some of them with women. Off the Piazza Umberto I they went to their hotel, but only long enough to leave the single leather bag that they carried.

They walked at random about the lovely town and then decided to go up the Via Fuorlovado to the ruins of the Villa Tiberius. It was built, impossibly, into the very high rocks. It was a vast place, a palace really, with vestibules and baths and wide staircases. "I sometimes think I would have preferred to live in those days," said Anna. "But only if I could have been very rich."

After lunch they visited the Gardens of Augustus, with their terraces and view of the Marina Piccola. Nearby was the monastery where Marc's uncle was staying. "Do you want to come with me?" he said to Anna.

She thought for a moment. "I would like to meet your famous uncle, but I am not sure he would like to meet me. Besides, he is in seclusion here, and it might be an intrusion. I will go back to the hotel and wait for you." He kissed her and watched her go off. Then he turned to the old fourteenth-century monastery, the beautiful church, and the soothing cloister with its view of the sea.

He did not quite know how to approach the place. By its very structure it seemed protected from the world. He went into the cool interior of the church and walked around, hoping that a member of the order would appear.

It occurred to him that he did not know how to address a bishop of the church who just happened to be, also, a relative. Marc had been a very bad Catholic. He might very well have described himself as an atheist, but that struck him as arrogant. He felt more comfortable in the ranks of the agnostics.

After a while a monk came up the aisle and Marc made his inquiry. He showed him the letter from his uncle. The monk looked at him with soft, arched eyes and without speaking indicated that Marc should follow him.

He was made to wait in a bare *entrada* with black stone floors. Five minutes passed. Ten. Fifteen. Apparently these monks had no sense of time, thought Marc. Or else they imagined they had all of eternity.

Eventually, the sad-eyed fellow came back and took him into the cloister. They walked for what seemed a long way past rows of arches that enclosed a formal garden. Beyond the large cloister there was a smaller one and a smaller garden with a fountain. There a slender old man waited for him. His habit was as simple as any monk's. Protruding from his skullcap was a fringe of gray hair. A beaded crucifix dangled from his waist, and in his hand was a small book. He did not rise when Marc approached. He simply watched him with an impassive face.

Marc hesitated within a few feet of the frail figure. He made a little bow. "You will forgive me, sir, if I do not make the proper greeting. I have never met a bishop before."

"Don't worry about the formalities," he said. "This is a very simple place. I come here myself to escape the pomp and ritual of ceremony. Come, stand closer. Let me look at you. All men in uniform begin to look alike. So, you are Marco Adamo, the grandson of my brother. And how old are you, Marco?"

"Twenty-eight, sir. I will be twenty-nine in December."

"I see. And are you married?"

"No, sir."

"You needn't call me *sir*. I'm only a bishop, not a general. Come, sit down where we can talk. You can call me *zio* if you want. You know, of all the children in our family only Gaetano had sons. And how tragic that he should have lost two of them so young. I remember your father. He came to visit me a long time ago. But I cannot claim to have known him very well. My brother and I do not correspond very often—hardly ever now. The fault is as much mine as his. And then there was the war."

"I hope it will be over soon," said Marc.

"Yes, we pray for that."

They talked comfortably for a while about family matters and about Marc's career as a lawyer and officer. Then the old man asked him what he planned to do after the war.

"I'm not sure," said Marc. "My grandfather wants me to establish a practice in the Italian neighborhood in New York."

"And why are you uncertain?"

"Well, you must know how it is with lawyers. The work is very mundane. Petty squabbles and paperwork."

"Yes. Naples is full of lawyers. Most of them are out of work. Why they continue to study law I don't know. It is an old tradition. Very Roman. The conviction that man is a political animal and that he must take part in the political process. Even in the church we have lawyers. The world has become very legalistic. I was for a time in the Vatican. It is very political. Now I have withdrawn to a quieter duty and long for something simpler still. Perhaps I will retire to this place someday and devote my last years to meditation and prayer. It is very beautiful here, don't you think?''

"Oh, yes! Very beautiful. Very peaceful."

"But not boring, if you are attuned to the inner life. Some men are; some are not. Some need that vigorous involvement with the world. Ambition. Competition. As if there were a kind of salvation in earthly accomplishments."

"Perhaps there is," said Marc. "If one does good."

"There is nothing wrong with doing good, but there is no salvation in it. And there is always the danger that one will feel important. I do not mean to preach you a sermon, but you must be careful of that, my son. Self-importance, power, wealth—these are great seductions. I have felt them myself. When I was younger I had ambitions in the church. As I got older I saw the futility of the quest. I long now only for serenity, not even the glory of sacrifice. I know that you have not come for advice, but I will give it to you anyway. Seek the simple way and be true to yourself."

Marc was deeply moved by his meeting with Pietro Adamo, and the words of the old bishop echoed in his mind as he made his way back to the hotel in the village. Everywhere he looked there was the sea, and everywhere vineyards and flowers. By the time he reached the hotel he was thinking about a life of splendid isolation. Yes, he thought, he could very easily spend the rest of his life in Capri.

The time did not come for him to talk seriously to Anna until after dinner, after food and wine and a walk in the scented moonlight. It did not come, in fact, until it was almost time to make love. And then he was reminded of the harsh secrets that he carried with him like invisible luggage.

In their room she almost subverted him with a kiss. He had to force himself to pull away. "What's wrong?" she said. An edge of concern touched her joy.

He lit a cigarette, though he didn't smoke very much. He went to the window and looked out at the darkening sea. "I was told something about you that I think we should discuss."

"Oh!" she said. It wasn't a question. It was a confession. "So you know." She sat down on the bed. Her hands were folded tightly in her lap, and she stared down at them.

"Yes," he said.

"How long have you known?"

"Only since the other day. I had lunch with Lieutenant Goodson, CID. He picks up this sort of information."

"And now I suppose you want me to explain."

"Well, I thought we might talk about it."

"What is there to talk about?" A coldness had crept into her voice, but he could tell that it was from a feeling of hurt.

"I was beginning to imagine that we might make a life together."

"Were you?"

"Yes."

"I don't believe you. You can say that now because you think it's impossible."

"That's not true."

"Then why have you never mentioned it before?"

"You know as well as I do. Because there's a war, and when the war is over everything might be different. I didn't want that kind of involvement. I didn't even want to fall in love with you."

"Well, this should make it easier for you. A little contempt can go a long way."

"Damn it!" he said, flinging the cigarette out the window and crossing the room. He sat down beside her. "I didn't mean to accuse you, Anna. I don't want you to be hurt or angry. I just want you to tell me the truth. And I guess I'm disturbed because you didn't tell me the truth to begin with."

"I didn't know you."

"You said you trusted me. I believed you. You knew I was falling in love with you. I didn't have to tell you."

"And what about me? You think I am without feelings? You think it's not the same for me? Yes, I admit I lied to you at first."

"But why?"

"Because I knew you would be more interested in helping me if you thought I was not married. Afterward——"

"Afterward what?"

She looked up at him. Her voice was almost a whisper. "I lied to you because I didn't want to lose you. I also resisted the involvement, and I also failed." Her expression melted into a weak, sad smile. "So you see, we are both failures, and everything is a mess after all."

He took her hand. She did not resist. "Anna," he whispered.

"Yes?"

"Oh, Anna!" He took her suddenly in his arms and held her very tight. And he was in her arms too. He kissed her hair. Her cheek was warm against his. "I love you."

"I love you too. And God help us both."

"Is it so impossible?"

"Yes. No. I don't know."

He drew back to look at her. "Do you want to tell me about it?"

She looked away as though to escape the request. But then her gaze drifted back to his. "My father is not an evil man. He is very kind and very intelligent. It is a pity that he had to make his way in these disastrous times. He should have been a man of the Renaissance. A man of letters and science. He trained as an engineer. He was never very political. He joined the party because it was required of him. He had such visions of a new Italy. New roads, new industry. The eradication of poverty in the south. He admired *il duce* for a while, but then he was disillusioned, as many of his friends were. He kept still and he advanced. He was very good at his work. What was he to do? Rebel and be shot? Is he to be condemned for being a good Italian at a time when Italy was a legitimate Fascist state? It had diplomatic recognition. It conducted business—yes, even with America, that great bastion of democracy. We were a good family and we did well under Mussolini. Two years ago I married Enrico Cavalieri, whom I had known from childhood. He was a captain in the army. It was always understood by our families that we would marry."

"Did you love him?"

"I told myself I did. I have since learned a little more about love. But he was very handsome and gentle, almost like a brother. Yes, in a way, I loved him. To deny it would only be half a lie, but I won't deny it. We could have had a good life. We may still, if he ever comes back."

"Do you know where he is?"

"You took the city on the first of October. Two weeks before that the Germans had rescued Mussolini from his prison and used him to reestablish a government in the north. Enrico insisted that it was his duty to follow."

"And you have never heard from him?"

"No. It's been over eight months. I don't know whether he is alive or dead, but soldiers still come from the north. I keep thinking that any day now he is liable to appear. It's a foolish hope. He made his commitment, and he will honor it. I know him. If he is alive, I won't find out until the war is over."

"So you can't leave."

"You never asked me to."

"And if I had asked you, would you have come with me?"

"I lived in dread of that, because I would have wanted so much to say yes. Even now—but no, no, I don't suppose I could have. You have no idea how I have been torn—" She began to cry. He took her in his arms again to comfort her.

"Don't say any more. Don't think about it. It was you who taught me how to put aside tomorrow for today. Today we are here. Today we are on the Isle of Capri, and we will make a small eternity of these few days." He kissed her and she returned his kiss, full of warmth, and then suddenly, hungrily, full of passion. They made love as they had never made love before, because the barrier of lies was gone and they were closer than ever—and more desperate.

Three days later Marc was back at his desk in Naples. He came in at nine o'clock and found on his blotter an official envelope with his name on it. He opened it slowly, afraid of what might be in it. He recognized the transfer papers immediately. He was ordered to report to AMG headquarters in Rome no later than five o'clock that afternoon. He would be picked up at eleven and personally transported.

He marched into Major Sykes's office and threw the papers down on his desk. "What the hell is this all about?" he said.

"Can't you read, Adamo? You've been transferred to Rome."

"But why?"

"Your guess is as good as mine. They need some CAO personnel, and you're a very clever young man." His double meaning was clear.

Marc looked at him. Sykes silently dared him to go on. It was an impossible situation. If he lost his temper, Sykes could ruin him. Marc could feel that his face was red with rage. He picked up the transfer papers and walked out of the office without another word.

He would not even be able to say good-bye to Anna. She had told him that she would be spending the morning shopping.

He sat down at his desk and felt a great sinking feeling that almost made him dizzy. There was a humming in his ears. So this was the tomorrow they had talked about, he thought. This was tomorrow . . .

# 6

. . . and tomorrow and tomorrow. The war came to an end in convulsions of destruction and revelations of horror. Who could have foreseen the Holocaust, Dachau and Auschwitz? Who could have imagined Hiroshima and Nagasaki? A new plateau of human cruelty had been reached, a new dimension of evil. Man had tampered with the very structure of matter. He had violated nature. And the press turned it all into journalese: "Atom Bomb Ushers In New Era."

It was too much for ordinary people to comprehend. Ordinary people prefer the everyday problems of ordinary life. Making a living, getting married, having children. Working, shopping, eating, making love. There was more truth to be found in the streets and markets than in all the libraries of the world.

This was Marc's great revelation. And on the crowded troopship that carried him back to America he saw his future clearly in the dark waters of the Atlantic. He would go back to his people. He would be a lawyer in East Harlem. He would help the poor. He would lead them if he were chosen. And he would do what he could to rid the world of corruption and cruelty. It was not a decision made in the moonlight at the ship's rail. It was a decision made in the streets of East Harlem years ago, and on the beaches of Salerno, in the *bassi* of Naples, and in the monastery on the Isle of Capri. It was a decision made for him by all those who had ever suffered the humiliation of being poor. He would no longer retreat from his own past into splendid isolation. The ghost of his father approved.

By the late spring of 1948 he was deeply involved in the

neighborhood. He had a busy law practice on 116th Street. He had become an active member of the Italian-American Political Club, which his grandfather and Joe Malzone had started, and he devoted many hours to the community services provided by the club. In a second-floor office he listened to the problems of those who came for help. Word had long ago spread that if you were in trouble, you should "go to the club. Talk to the boss, Don Gaetano. And to the young Marco Adamo. He is very *simpatico*. He has the *pietà*. He understands."

On a typical mid-June day he left his law office at noon, stopped briefly for lunch at the Cafe Savarese, and went on to the club to be available until three o'clock. There was always someone waiting to see him, and sometimes several people. This time there were two—an old man, toothless and gray, with a cap and a cane and black di Nobile cigar; and a very stout woman in widow's weeds. "They are not related," said Angelo Rienzo, a retired bricklayer who spent much of his time at the club and had become a receptionist for Marc and the other volunteers. He had an enormous nose, and curiosity to go with it. They all made fun of him. It was not age but arthritis that had forced him into retirement, though he was past sixty. By the time Marc arrived, Rienzo seemed to know all about those who had come for help. "This man's name is Garibaldi Zullo, from 110th Street. They want to kick him out of his apartment because he don't always pay the rent. Poor man! His wife is dead. He wants to know how he can get a pension from the government and maybe some teeth."

Marc shook hands with the old man, who clutched his cap and looked scared. He kept nodding and bowing, as though to the authorities. The old-country humility had never left him. "Come in, come in," said Marc, who was always annoyed by that old habit. "Sit down and tell me a little bit about yourself. . . ."

Half an hour later Marc had the necessary relief applications filled out and he handed the old man a card on which was written the address of a free dental clinic near Lexington Avenue. The old man looked at him with watery eyes as though he were a saint and had just performed a miracle. The elaborate expressions of gratitude at the end of these sessions embarrassed Marc, and he tried his best to cut them short.

By midafternoon it was very warm. When Marc came

downstairs he had his jacket over his arm and his shirt was
open at the collar. He went into the back, where there was a
cooler for soda and beer, and helped himself to a bottle of
Coca-Cola. When he came out into the main room he saw his
grandfather at a table with several other men. It was clear
from the volume of their voices and the motions of their
hands that they were talking politics.

There were glasses and beer bottles on the table. Overhead
a lazy ceiling fan turned, stirring a warm breeze. There were
pictures along the wall, men shaking hands in small black
frames, and then some larger ones, among them a picture of
Harry S Truman and one of William O'Dwyer. The folding
chairs used for meetings were stacked neatly at one end of the
room, and Angelo Rienzo, the hanger-on, was pushing a
broom across the open floor.

Gaetano looked very distinguished in his gray suit and
striped tie. His hair was white and carefully barbered, and he
wore a neat mustache. With advancing age he had become
more and more meticulous about his clothes and appearance
and personal habits, as if orderliness could somehow control
the ravages of time. In spite of his fitness it was generally
assumed that he would soon have to retire from the leadership
of the club. It was also common knowledge that the man
being groomed as the next leader was the son-in-law of Joe
Malzone, Sal D'Angelo, one of the men now at the table. He
was, like Marc, one of the new breed, more American than
Italian. He was an insurance broker who spoke English without an accent. He had been to New York University for two
years before getting his license.

Another one of the men at the table was Vincent DeMarco.
He was broad-shouldered and younger than his baldness would
indicate. He was the grandson of Johnny DeMarco and the
son of Eddie DeMarco, who had been killed, gangland-style,
in 1938. Once a little dynasty in itself, the family had been
reduced to underlings within the new Mafia. The old "greasers"
were gone. The new bosses were "businessmen," almost
invisible behind the scenes.

Marc did not recognize two men at the table. Gaetano saw
him come down and cross the room. "Eh, Marc," he said,
"come here. I want you to meet these fellas. This is Rocco
Barone. And this is Tom O'Brien." He beamed at Marc.
"My grandson!"

"I've heard all about you," said Barone. "You're making

quite a name for yourself in the neighborhood.'' He was a man of about forty with hard lines in his lean face, and very clear eyes. It occurred to Marc immediately that he was imitating the quiet style of the new "businessmen," but that beyond the pinstriped, double-breasted suit and the gold cuff links he was crude and without class.

"I've heard of you too," said Marc. He hesitated at the extended hand with the little ring on the small finger. His tone and hesitation were ambiguous. He had indeed heard of Barone and would have preferred not to shake his hand. But he did, in a businesslike way, and then glanced at his watch. "I wish I could stay, but I've got a client at the office—"

"Never mind the client," said Gaetano. "Sit down for a minute. We were just talking about the fall elections. Very interesting."

Marc felt trapped. Gaetano had never gotten over the habit of ordering him around as though he were still a boy. It was so ingrained in him that he did not even know he was doing it. "Come on, sit down, sit down. You work too hard. And you shouldn't drink that Coca-Cola stuff. It will eat your stomach. Have a glass of wine, or at least a beer."

"All right," said Marc with a smile, giving in to the inevitable. "I'll have a beer. Then I really must go."

"Angelo," shouted Gaetano, "get us some beers." the arthritic bricklayer stopped pushing his broom and went into the back room.

"Very hot for June, isn't it?" said Tom O'Brien. There was a touch of the old country in his speech and red blossoms in his cheeks. He, too, was dressed as though he had connections.

"Tom here works for Bill Devlin," said Gaetano. "You know who Bill Devlin is?"

"Of course," said Marc. "Tammany Hall. He's on the executive committee."

"That's right," said Tom O'Brien, "and, with a little luck, maybe the next leader. But we need a good showing in the fall. You know what I mean?"

Marc wasn't sure that he knew *exactly* what he meant. His expression must have asked for an explanation.

"It's been tough since LaGuardia," said Gaetano.

"Yes," said O'Brien, "he fought us all the way. No patronage, no influence, no money. Our enrollments were way down. But now, of course, the Republicans are out.

Things are looking much better. And we have friends who are willing to finance our campaigns, so—''

"Yes, very good friends," said Barone.

Marc looked from O'Brien to Barone. Then he glanced at his grandfather and the other men and turned his head at the sound of Rienzo shuffling in with a tray of beers. There it was, he thought, the whole political scene in one room. The Irishman from Tammany, the Mafia connection, the local political club, and even the poor peasant on whose vote they traded. He knew all about it from a distance, but had never seen it up close. As Tammany influence and income declined, they became more receptive to the "businessmen." They traded political positions for political contributions. And illicit business needed protection in high places. Judges, councilmen, heads of departments, perhaps even the mayor himself. There had been a lot of talk. Marc did not know how much of it was true, but where there was that much smoke there had to be a little fire.

"Of course, I have always admired LaGuardia," said Gaetano. "And last year, when he died, I was very sorry. He was interested in East Harlem and the Italian-Americans. He was a man with principles, but I don't think he understood about certain things. About the clubs. The middleman. You know what I mean? We look after our own, and there are benefits to be had."

"There's nothing wrong with that," said O'Brien. He was looking at Marc. "We get very bad press. But we've done a lot of good over the years. Oh, we've had our scandals, God knows! Who hasn't? But we've put a lot of men to work."

Marc smiled. "Well, I have to admit—there are an awful lot of Irish cops."

They all laughed.

"So how does it look for the fall?" said Gaetano.

"Truman will head the Democratic ticket," said O'Brien. "No doubt about that. But Dewey will be tough if he gets the Republican spot. And then you have the new Progressive party and Wallace and that whole leftwing gang. And maybe the Dixiecrat defection in the South. They'll steal votes from Truman. But if he can hold farm and labor support, I think he's got a chance."

"Well, you always get a lot of single-line voters. Row A, Row B. Half the time they don't even know who they're voting for. The top of the ticket in a presidential year is very

important. Here in the twentieth congressional district we've
got a wide-open race. We're thinking of Dan Farrell. He's
been very loyal and hardworking.''

"Yeah," said Barone, "and with a name like Daniel Walker
Farrell, how can he miss?"

"Too bad it's not Italian," said Gaetano. "For an Italian
candidate we could turn out a better vote."

"Naturally, we're hoping for your support," said O'Brien.

"It's too early to talk about that. We have to see how
things fall out. Right now we don't owe nobody nothing, but
we're willing to listen."

"I think Farrell's going to be okay," said Barone. He was
playing with the ring on his little finger.

Suddenly, Marc felt a wave of disgust and anger rising in
him. There was something corrupt and unjust about this brute
in the businessman's suit. He was the enemy, and the mere
fact that he was there at the club at all disturbed him. Marc
took a final sip of his beer and stood up. "I really have to
go," he said.

"Too bad," said O'Brien. "There's still a lot to talk
about."

"Another time, maybe," said Marc.

"I tell you what. Mr. Devlin is having a few people over
tonight. Why don't you stop in?" As he talked he took a
small white card out of his wallet. "Here's the address.
Anytime after eight. He'd like to meet you."

"I'm afraid I—"

"Go on," said Gaetano. "What have you got to lose?"

"I'm going to my mother's for dinner."

"Come after dinner," said O'Brien. "Just have a drink.
Meet the man. I think you'll like him. He may be able to help
you."

"I don't need any help," said Marc.

"If you plan to go into politics you do."

Marc looked at the card being offered to him. He took
it and said: "I can't promise you anything. After my
mother's cooking it's pretty hard to do anything but sit still
and recover."

O'Brien's smile was friendly and considerably more benign
than Barone's. Marc was reluctant to get involved, but his
curiosity was aroused.

*     *     *

Felice's new apartment was large and sunny and only one block from the river. Marc and Larry both contributed generously to her support, and she was quite happy with her life and her sons. They wanted her to have the best of everything. There was a new refrigerator and a new stove in the kitchen. She often had the boys over to eat, as well as Larry's wife, Piera, who was six months pregnant. "Why should the poor girl cook?" she would say. "She already has something in the oven." And Stefano still came around, so familiar a fixture by now that no one even thought much about him. He and Felice no longer talked about marriage. They were fifty-four years old. What did it matter? And the scandal was such old news that not even the old women in the neighborhood bothered to talk about it anymore. Time had somehow fixed it all up. He was the uncle. And the older they got, the more he became the uncle instead of the lover. Marc had always liked him, but with a certain reservation, as if to love him as a father would have meant betraying his real father, who still lived, in some strange way, in the shadowy recesses of his mind. He lived like the ghost of Hamlet's father, asking to be remembered—and perhaps avenged. Someday, he promised himself, he would find out the whole story, the true story.

For dinner there was a little antipasto of mussels, followed by pasta and clam sauce. And then Felice's specialty, a *zuppa di pesce* so thick and fragrant with vegetables and fish and spices that they made a little chorus of *ooh*s and *aah*s when she brought it out. "Hey, Ma, what did you do? Buy out the fish market?" said Larry. "How we gonna eat all that?"

"Too much is better than too little," she said. "Besides, she's eating for two, and you're eating for three or four, the way you run around and sweat. I don't understand why they make you run when they pay you to fight."

"Because it's good for my wind, Ma. How many times do I have to tell you? So I don't get tired when I'm in the ring."

"Maybe you should run faster when you're in the ring. They wouldn't hit you so much in the face. Look at your nose. You had such a nice nose when you were a little baby."

"You should see the other guy's nose," said Larry. They all laughed at the old joke.

"I don't want to see no fights," she said. "If that's what you have to do, that's what you have to do, but I don't want to hear nothing about it. Come on, eat. Eat!"

After dinner the apartment was warm from all the cooking. Larry and Marc took a walk down to the river to cool off. They sat on a bench and watched the color of the water deepen as the light faded. Across the way was Randalls Island, and to the left the towers of the Tirboro Bridge still caught a touch of sunlight. "Remember when we were kids how we always talked about building a raft or a boat and crossing the river with it?" said Larry.

"Marty said it was impossible, because of the currents," said Marc. "He was probably right."

"It's funny how things seem so simple when you're a kid. I mean, you think you can do anything, even fly. Then later on you find out what it's all about and it ain't easy."

"It's called growing up," said Marc.

"It's too bad in a way," said Larry, looking dreamily at the river.

"Yeah," said Marc. "It *is* too bad. Kids have such wonderful imaginations. But speaking of dreams of glory, what did Tony say about the title match?"

"He says I got a shot at a match for September in the stadium with Sugar Ray Sanders, if I'm willing to settle for twenty-five percent."

"Why so little?"

"I guess Sanders is the draw."

"He's also a great fighter. Maybe, pound for pound, the best there is. He's liable to beat your brains out."

"Maybe, but before I hang 'em up I'd like at least one shot at the title. It's what every fighter dreams of. What am I supposed to do? Back off? If I can get into top shape, who knows? I have to shake a few pounds."

Marc turned more serious and put his hand on his brother's shoulder. "Look, Larry, you've been out of the service for two and a half years and you're still not as sharp as when you went in. You're married now, and your wife's going to have a baby. In a couple of years you'll be thirty."

"Yeah, but right now I'm only twenty-eight. Christ! What's wrong with twenty-eight? I'm in my prime."

"All right, then, it's not your age. Maybe you just don't have the discipline. You like to eat. You like to live a little. It's only natural. You have to be a madman to train the way some of these guys do. I'm not saying you don't have the talent. You've got a ton of talent. But we all have our limits. We can only go just so far."

"What the hell are you trying to say?"

Marc took a deep breath and then let it out, as though he were beginning a patient explanation. "Don't get mad. Let me put it to you straight. Mom doesn't want you to fight. Piera doesn't want you to fight—"

"She said whatever I decided was all right with her."

"Naturally, but she told Mom she was scared. And frankly, I'm scared too. First of all, Sugar Ray Sanders could hurt you."

"I can take care of myself."

"Second of all, he can make you look so bad that you'll wind up back in St. Nicholas Arena. But that's not the worst of it, Larry. *They* can hurt you."

"Who?"

"The promoters. Even your own people."

"What are you talking about?"

"They'll pump you up. The great white hope and all that. And when the odds are right, they'll put their money on Sanders."

"Nobody's talking about a dive."

"Larry, they don't have to. Don't you understand? The smart money has him figured."

"Yeah, but suppose I win. Just suppose—"

"Then I guess you get the belt and the smart money goes down the sink."

Larry frowned, as if he had just been dealt a low blow. "Well, shit, man, that ain't my fault, is it? I mean, I'm playing straight. I'm clean."

"Take it easy, Larry. I'm only telling you these things so that you know how the rest of us feel. I'm your big brother, remember? I'm supposed to look out for you."

"Rudy Wills says I can be ready in three months."

"Maybe you can. Maybe I'm wrong. I sure as hell would love to see you go out there and beat the shit out of Sanders. As long as you know what you're doing."

"You mean like trying to cross the East River on a raft?"

Marc smiled. "Yeah, like trying to cross the East River on a raft."

"I always thought it could be done. And you know what? I still think we could have done it."

Marc nudged his brother affectionately. "You crazy bastard!

You're probably right. If you get this match I'll be there, and I'll put my money on you too."

"Thanks, big brother. And thanks for looking out for me."

It was almost nine o'clock when Marc stepped off the bus at 73rd Street. But the summer days were long and there was still a hint of light in the darkening sky. Not that anyone would notice. There was too much artificial light along the avenue. Shops and streetlights and headlights in the traffic. Marc walked from Lexington to Madison. He paused to glance at the white card in his hand. A nice printing job, he thought. He had a fondness for the printed word and the craft he had never learned. He romanticized it. He thought in terms of fine, rare editions, not invitations to weddings.

When he looked up he was staring at a shop that looked vaguely familiar. It took several moments for him to realize what it was. A rising feeling of nostalgia almost brought tears to his eyes. It was the old pharmacy where he had worked as a kid. Mr. Schneider's pharmacy. Everything about it was exactly the same, down to the glass containers with colored liquids in them in the window display. He crossed the street as though it were fifteen years earlier and he was going to work. The shop was closed, but in the back there was a night light shedding a yellow glow through the interior. It was a ghostly light that brought back with a rush all the days he had spent there. He wondered whether or not Mr. Schneider was still alive. It was possible, though not likely. He had already been an old man in 1933 when they listened to President Roosevelt's inauguration on the radio. He shook his head as if to drive away tears and memories, and then referred once more to the white card. The apartment house he was looking for was right beside the old shop. It was massive and new and without character, like a monstrous future overshadowing a human past.

The lobby of the building was like a movie theater, complete with doorman in a pseudomilitary uniform. Marc showed him the card as though he were giving him the password. "Fifteenth floor," the man said. "Just press the button."

The machine went up. The silence hummed. He could not tell how fast he was rising. When the door opened his impulse was not to get out but to go back down and run as fast as he could. It smelled of wall-to-wall carpeting and wall-to-wall corruption. But he was in the grip of his own curiosity, and there was no turning back. He had to know who these people were, how they lived, how they operated.

He was greeted at the door by a colored maid right out of a Hollywood movie. She showed him into the immense living room of the immense apartment. There were perhaps forty people in the room, sitting, standing, drinking, smoking. They formed little circles and clusters from which clouds of smoke and laughter rose. There was a bar on one side of the room, and on the other side a large fireplace that may or may not have been real. He didn't know what to do.

Then he heard his name. "Ah, Marc Adamo. Glad you could make it." It was Tom O'Brien, a tall glass in his hand. "Come and meet Bill. I've been telling him about you."

Marc followed him through the crowd, wondering what there was to tell and why. Big Bill Devlin, as they called him, was presiding over a circle of men and women who seemed thoroughly amused by what he was saying. He had a full, rich voice with just a touch of Irish in it. His father had come from the old country, but Bill was born in New York. He was not only tall but broad, without being at all fleshy. Only in the flush of his face was there a touch of dissipation. But it was a good face, with sharp blue eyes, accented by a vacation tan and blond hair, graying gracefully. He wore his business suit well and looked as though he might be the head of some important corporation.

Tom O'Brien took his boss by the arm and whispered something in his ear. Devlin drew away diplomatically from his admirers. "So you're Marc Adamo," he said, extending his big hand. "I'm glad you could come. I've heard some good things about you. I've met your grandfather. A fine old gent. And not a bad politician, even at his age. Get yourself a drink and come into the library. We'll have a little talk where it's quiet."

The library was another stage set, full of matching book sets in tall walnut bookshelves, books whose pages were probably never turned by human hands. Marc was awed and offended all at once. There was a large desk and several black leather chairs.

They sat. Bill Devlin lit a new cigar. He offered one to Marc, who shook his head. Tom O'Brien smoked cigarettes. Marc noticed the stain on his middle finger.

"I'll get right to the point, Adamo," said Devlin. "We're looking over people who might be useful to us in the coming campaign. You're a smart young man. I'm sure you know what it's all about."

"Well, I do and I don't," said Marc. "Maybe you'd better tell me, so that we know what we're talking about."

"You're good-looking, you're educated, and you're a lawyer. And you're earning points in your district. What that means to me is that you're heading for a political career. Stop me if I'm wrong."

"I've given it some thought, but I haven't made up my mind."

Devlin smiled. "Any man who can say *yes* and *no* at the same time is a born politician. But let me go on. We've been getting support from the people in your neighborhood, a lot of support. Money and votes. But it's a two-way street. We have to make room on our ticket for people who suit them, one way or another. Some of them want people who will be sympathetic to their business pursuits. Some of them want ethnic leaders—Irish, Italian, Spanish, even Negro. Do you follow what I'm saying?"

"So far, yes."

"For years the Irish have dominated Tammany Hall. It's no secret. It's history. But times are changing. You Italians are beginning to flex your muscles. Maybe it's time for us to move over and make some room for you. There's a lot of in-fighting going on within the organization. I won't bore you with all the details. I happen to be a proponent of compromise. I think we can all work something out. I see no reason, for instance, why a promising young man like you can't get an endorsement from us for some sort of position. State Assembly maybe. Always a good place for a young man to start. Assistant D.A., general sessions judge. Who knows? If you're interested, I'll see what I can do. I don't make these decisions unilaterally. Everybody is pushing somebody."

"And right now you're pushing Farrell for Congress in the twentieth district."

Devlin recognized the observation with an appreciative nod. "They told me you had a quick mind."

"I'd have to be pretty slow to miss something that obvious."

"Well, don't be offended, Marc. There's nothing wrong with tradeoffs. There are a hell of a lot of Italians in East Harlem. They'd like to see one of their own get ahead. But you don't have to say anything right now. Just think about it." He stood up. "Give me a call in a week or two. Or get in touch with Tom here. He'll tell you what the next move is."

Marc didn't know what to say. He felt pushed and seduced all at once. "All right, I'll think about it. But don't you want to know where I stand politically on the issues?"

"What's the difference?" said Devlin. "As long as you're for motherhood and against Communism." He laughed at his own joke. "I've got to get back to my guests."

"Do you mind if I take a look at your collection?"

Devlin looked puzzled.

"Your books," said Marc, nodding toward the floor-to-ceiling shelves.

"Oh, yeah. Yeah, sure! Go ahead. Help yourself. But then come on in and talk to a few people. Circulate a little."

They went out and left him alone. He was relieved. He wandered around the room as though it were a real library. He shut out the noise of the party, recalling his days as a student, the stacks, the books, the long, quiet hours at night in which he had lost himself in the dreams of others—Shakespeare, Milton, Melville. How far from those good days he had come. And how harsh and real the world was compared to those more misty and meaningful realms. It was odd. As if reality got in the way of reality.

He glanced at the bindings, so gilded and handsome that they upstaged the books they bound. The library was all facade. It didn't matter what was behind it. It didn't matter that real people had written their hearts out to produce these great books and had, in some cases, died in poverty and despair. The complete works of Dickens, Scott, Balzac, Hardy. Even Smollett and Thackery, for Christ's sake! As if Big Bill Devlin even knew who they were. There they were like a bevy of prostitutes—concubines in the rich man's house. It was a kind of rape and it made Marc mad. He came across a copy of Machiavelli's *The Prince*. That was more like it, though Devlin had probably never read it. As he browsed through uncut pages he remembered Alyson and how he had helped her with her term paper. He had not thought about her for a long time, but she leapt into his mind as though she were actually in the room.

"Hello," said a female voice.

He was so startled he went pale for a moment. He turned to confront a young woman who was standing no more than three feet from him. "I'm sorry," she said. "I didn't mean to frighten you."

"I guess I didn't hear you come in," he said.

"It's a very thick carpet and a very noisy party."

"Too noisy for me, I'm afraid."

"What are you doing? Hiding from it?"

"I was about to leave."

"Why did you come in the first place if you don't like this sort of thing?" She was tall and slender and blond. At first glance not unlike Alyson, but there was something softer and more attractive about her. She was young, not more than twenty-one or -two, he thought, and not dressed like the other women at the gathering. She had a tweedy, collegiate look. A kind of suit with a full skirt. White blouse. A wisp of a red bow suggesting a tie. Her hair was parted in the middle and less than shoulder length. The more fashionable ladies in the living room were wearing Dior's "new look" and complicated hairdos, swept back or up.

"I was curious," he said.

"About what?"

"I wanted to see a political boss in action. A real pro. You know, this guy Devlin."

"You mean my father?"

He felt himself blush. "Your father?"

"I'm Catherine Devlin. Who are you?"

"Oh, nobody in particular. Just an idiot with a foot in his mouth. I'm sorry. I didn't mean to—"

She smiled. "Don't worry about it. Daddy *is* a political boss, I guess. At least that's what the papers call him. But I'm not interested in politics, and I don't really know anybody here."

"So I suppose *you* came in here to hide."

"I like books."

"Me too."

"You mean you're not in politics?"

"Not yet. Not exactly. I'm a lawyer."

"Oh! You don't look like a lawyer."

"And you don't look like a Devlin."

"I haven't been home all that much. Four years of boarding school. Four years of college. I just graduated last week."

"From where? Don't tell me. Let me guess. Bryn Mawr? Sarah Lawrence?"

"Boston University."

"How plebian!"

She shrugged. "I liked it. I didn't want to go to one of *those* schools. I wanted to be with ordinary people." It was clear the way she said this that she was serious about her convictions.

He responded with a warm smile. "I don't blame you. What did you major in?"

"Art."

"How useful!"

"I know what you mean. What do I do now? Hang out a shingle?"

"Why don't you just draw or paint?"

"It's not that simple. I don't particularly want to stay here. I'd like to be on my own. My father is always so busy, and my mother's not well. But my father doesn't want me living on my own. If I insist, he says I'll have to support myself."

"What's the point of having a rich family if you have to support yourself?"

"That's exactly how I feel, but you don't know Daddy. He likes to have his way. He's used to getting what he wants. At times he can be downright difficult."

"Ah, I can see it all now, the whole pattern of your life—tall, handsome, domineering father. Weak, submissive mother. Guilt, hostility, conflict."

She laughed. "We seem to have taken the same course in psychology. But I'm afraid you've got it all wrong. I'll just find a job and move out. I'm not afraid."

"Aren't you?"

She hesitated and frowned. She was leaning against the arm of one of the black leather chairs, her arms folded across her chest. "I don't know. Maybe I am. But why am I telling you all this? I don't even know you."

"I'm sorry." He pretended to reach into his inside pocket. "Would you like a copy of my résumé? Marc Adamo. Age thirty-two. Five feet ten. A hundred and fifty-four pounds. Graduate of Columbia College and Columbia Law School. Three years of military service—"

Her laughter mingled with his recital until he, too, broke down and laughed. "You're very funny," she said.

"I'm also single," he said.

"Is that good or bad?"

"When I walked in here this evening I thought it was bad,

because the place is full of couples. But now I think it's good.''

''Why?''

''Because now we can get the hell out of here and go to some civilized saloon for a cold beer. What do you say?''

Her smile was all the answer he needed. ''All right,'' she said. ''Why not?''

The place was called Corcoran's, a good old bar, a refuge from the storm since the turn of the century. Sawdust and old wood. Dim light from leaded chandeliers and tables rescued from a Bowery fire in 1898. ''Why do the Irish drink so much?'' said Marc.

''I don't know,'' said Catherine Devlin. ''Why do the Italians eat so much?''

''It's not the same. Good food puts you in touch with life. It's fundamental. Food-gathering and fertility.''

''What does fertility have to do with it?''

''I was talking about harvests, not sex, though, come to think of it, there is a connection.''

''A good old-fashioned Catholic girl like me wouldn't be knowing about such filthy matters.'' She affected the brogue with a twinkle in her eye.

''Is your family that way?''

''What way is that?''

''Catholic and strict.''

''My mother's very Catholic, and my father's very strict. It's a bad combination for an only child. And being a girl doesn't help. They're always on me about something. It was a pleasure to go away to school. My mother is odd. A bit hysterical, I think. I have a theory about the whole thing. She has never forgiven me for being born. You see, I'm the living evidence that she has, in fact, committed the awful deed. The Irish have an unhappy attitude toward sex.''

''Perhaps that's why they drink so much.''

They laughed. In the tinted light of the antique chandeliers the beer looked like snow-capped liquid gold, and there was a sudden magic in the moment that made them feel as though they had known each other for a long time. Their laughter faded into a quiet gaze.

She had a playful way of showing her shyness. A tilt of her head. A glance of her eye. There was something very lyrical and sweet about it. Very Irish. And it gave him a sudden sense of joy that made him smile.

They had another beer and lingered over it until eleven o'clock. It seemed as though they could go on forever, so easy was their talk. But she glanced at the graduation watch on her slender wrist and said: "I've got to get back. They don't know where I am. Daddy will be calling the commissioner of police and having the river dragged."

"With an old man like that, how will I ever be able to call you?"

"It's my mother you ought to worry about. She's always home and always on the phone."

"Well, suppose I give you my number? Will you call?"

"I didn't mean to suggest that I was being held prisoner. But my parents *are* difficult."

"Call me, then. I hear it's very fashionable these days for girls to go out with older men."

"You're not old enough to qualify."

Their hands touched across the table. In another moment she drew away and stood up. "It's really getting late. I have to go. If you're feeling heroic you can walk me home."

He did. And even kissed her gently on the cheek. She did not turn or stay for more. In fact, she seemed to be in a hurry to get away. He thought about it on his way home and decided that she was only afraid of displeasing her parents, and not eager to get away from him.

He was light and heavyhearted all at once. He could not sleep for more than an hour after going to bed. It was all starting again—the excitement. And, as before, the rose was beautiful but guarded by thorns.

Every spring for some years now Gaetano had proposed to Natalia. It was an old ritual and they both thoroughly enjoyed it. Natalia and Angela still shared an apartment and had a hand in the shop and factory. And Gaetano had his daughter, Laura, living with him again, a widow of fifty. These arrangements were fine. They gave Gaetano a place to go, and every day he visited the apartment of his sister and Natalia, which was only down the street. And every year in June he brought her a bouquet of flowers, which he had made up especially by the florist Martino. He would put on his best suit and fix his fedora at a rakish angle. He would be smelling of the barber and perhaps just a sip of cognac. It was always a Sunday, he would always stay for dinner, and wise old Angela would always pretend that she had been invited elsewhere so that the two lovers could be alone.

When they were alone and Natalia had admired the flowers, he would take her hands in his and say: "My darling, it's still not too late. We are old, but not *that* old. We could have a few years together, perhaps even a decade. Who knows?"

And she would look at him and smile. "My dear, it was never meant to be," she would say. "And the time has long since passed. From the very beginning we were destined to be lovers, not husband and wife. Even now, we like it better this way. Can't you see? If we lived together, we would be like all the others, just another old couple. We would sit around and talk about our diseases. As it is, we have our independence, and we have what we both always wanted, always needed— the eternal courtship. That is what romance is really all about, and we make each other feel young."

He nodded appreciatively at her female wisdom. "Nevertheless, my sweet, I want to go on record as having asked you again—and with all my heart. I know it is the right thing to do."

"You're very gallant and I love you dearly, but once again I must refuse."

"Absolutely?"

"Well, nothing is really absolute, is it?"

"Then there's still hope?"

"Of course, you fool."

"Good! Good!" And he would embrace her, and she would allow him a kiss. Then she would bring out the champagne and they would have dinner, as if all those years had never passed since the first time they made love in the little house in Caserta.

Renato was Gaetano's age but not nearly as fit. He was beginning to look very old. His hair was thin, his skin a bit yellow, his eyes sunken and sad, as if he were staring into the mouth of disappointment and knew that he did not have long to live. Whatever utopian dreams he still clung to had been crushed by the war. His final conclusion was that the human race was no damn good after all and that perhaps there was some merit in the concept of original sin. The old anarchist was even seen leaving the church early one morning, his hat shading his face as though he wanted to avoid recognition.

Fanny, on the other hand, was in her vigorous sixties and very much involved in the new Independent Labor Party, which had a large following in East Harlem and some support throughout the city. She had filled out over the years and was formidable-looking in suits that could not contain her bosom and in hats from which her reckless hair escaped. They still had their shop, and it was still a gathering place for left-wing malcontents, but it had been many years since they had published their newspaper.

Since his return to East Harlem, Marc had developed a closeness to these old friends of his father's, and he often stopped to see them. He liked the smell of the ink and paper and the cluttered atmosphere. The shop was something out of the past, and it had a nice old-world feeling about it. Besides, there was always somebody else there, and almost always a vigorous political discussion going on. Renato may have needed a cane to help him walk, but his mind was still as agile as ever.

A few days after his visit to Devlin's apartment, Marc stopped by to say hello. A man named Leonardo Caldieri was there, the head of the Independent Labor Party (ILP). He and Marc knew each other and shook hands. They were sitting on high stools around a work table. The table was stained with ink and littered with coffee cups and odd pieces of type. Fanny brought out the coffeepot. "We were just talking about you," said Renato.

"Now what have I done wrong?" said Marc.

"Nothing yet, but there is a rumor that they might put you on the Tammany ticket this fall for the assembly."

"Where did you hear that nonsense?"

"It's not true, then?"

"Of course it's not true. You know me better than that. I don't want anything from those people."

"Somebody said that Barone and O'Brien came around, and that you went to a meeting at Devlin's house."

"News sure travels fast."

"Well, you know, in this neighborhood—"

"I went to a social gathering there. And, yes, I had a talk with Devlin."

"He made you an offer?"

"More or less, but I'm not interested."

"You know why he's doing this?" said Fanny. "Because he thinks he can bribe your grandfather into supporting this awful man Farrell. He's in the pocket of the mob. You know that, don't you?"

"I thought he might be," said Marc.

"It's worse than that," said Caldieri. He was a slender, intense man of forty or so, with yellow stains on his fingers from chain-smoking cigarettes. "You see, they need respectability. People like you who are clean and well educated. They figure they can set you up while you are still young and innocent. Then they will own you, and you will have to return their favors."

"They are coming up to their summer convention," said Renato, "and there is a lot of bargaining going on, and a lot of money changing hands. You have no idea—"

"I'm learning fast."

"But we, too, have a summer convention, early in August. I mean, the ILP. And we, too, have been approached by Tammany. They want us to endorse Farrell. They're making all kinds of promises, but we don't want to do business with them. We have taken our stand against political corruption and organized crime. That means Tammany and the Mafia. So what do they do? They try to buy us out. We have to be very careful. We have the party. We have the votes. But on the right we are approached by the machine. And on the left we are approached by the Communists. We have to maintain our integrity."

"And how exactly are you going to do that?" said Marc.

"By running you for Congress in the twentieth district," said Caldieri.

"Me?"

"Yes," said Renato. "On the ILP ticket. Against Farrell and whoever the Republicans put up."

Marc started to shake his head. "I'll have to think about it. It's a big commitment."

"You mean the affiliation with the ILP?" said Caldieri.

"That's part of it. I'm sympathetic, but perhaps not quite as extreme as you people."

"We are the party of the working man. What more do you have to know?" said Caldieri. "You are for the poor and for a welfare state, in which basic human needs are provided for. Unemployment insurance, social security, national health, nationalization of certain industries. I've heard you talk. And years ago I heard your father talk."

"I'm not my father," said Marc. "I've got to make up my own mind about things. And times have changed. There is less exploitation. The unions have become very strong. I don't believe in revolution."

"Who's talking about revolution?" said Renato. "We are talking about electing people who will represent the working class. Is that unreasonable?"

Marc hesitated. "All I can say is that I am very flattered and that I'll think about it and talk to some people. I can't promise you anything."

That evening he talked to his grandfather at the Cafe Savarese, where he often had dinner. Marc did not tell him immediately about the ILP. They talked first about Devlin. "I knew he was going to approach you sooner or later," said Gaetano.

"How did you know?"

"They've been making a few inquiries here and there. I could tell. I didn't want to say anything to you or push you, because, naturally, I want you to make up your own mind. But you know how I feel. For fifteen years I have waited for the day that you would run for political office. It has been a dream of mine, something I would have wanted for my own sons."

"But *Nonno*, how can I get involved with those people? Isn't this guy Barone *màfioso*?"

Gaetano shrugged. "That's what they say, but what difference does that make to us? You don't have to get into his pocket. You can run straight."

"Devlin is not going to back me unless there are strings attached. You know that. And without his backing I'm not going to get very far. If I get into politics, I don't want to owe anybody anything, except my constituents, the people who vote for me."

"You are known in the neighborhood. Our name is known. You would be very popular. The machine would not own you. Once you are in you could be your own man."

"I don't trust them. And I don't know why you have anything to do with them."

"Eh, Marco, I've been around a long time. I know how to play the game. I make a few deals, but I never sell out. *They* know that. Why do you think they come around? Me and Joe Malzone, we keep the club independent. We are not Tammany. We are not *màfioso*. We look out for our own, that's all. Nobody owns East Harlem. Not Barone, not even his boss. They own the rackets, the protection, the numbers, but they don't own the people."

Marc looked at his grandfather as though he were admiring his little speech. "Do you think I could pull enough votes for the House of Representatives?"

Gaetano raised his eyebrows in surprise. "The Congress? They won't give you that. They have agreed on Farrell."

"I wasn't thinking of Tammany. I was thinking of the ILP."

"The ILP? What are you talking about?"

"They want to endorse me for the twentieth district."

Gaetano scratched his head. "*Dio santo!* I don't know, Marco. You would have to go against both the Democrats and the Republicans. How could you do that and expect to win?"

"I would take my message to the people. I would win on the issues."

"That's very idealistic, but there are certain political realities."

"Like what?"

"Like you can't win."

"Why not?"

"Because they have the machinery, the block captains, the campaign funds, the pressure of patronage."

"I could win if people like you supported me. The club, I mean."

Gaetano frowned. "Marco, you put me in a bind. I have people to deal with. Besides, we can get a lot of favors from them for our support. From the ILP we don't get nothing."

"But what if we win?"

"What if? What if? It's pie in the sky. You're a dreamer, just like your father. You go with the ILP and before you know it they'll call you a Communist."

"But they're not Communists."

"I know that and you know that, but now everybody is looking under the bed for Communists. The world is a little crazy right now."

"With the proper support and public relations the ILP could become like the British Labour Party—moderate, democratic, and socialist. We need a party like that in this country."

"But this is not England. In this country socialism is a dirty word. And people don't know the difference between socialism and communism."

"There are some very good people in the ILP, men of very good reputation. And don't tell me there isn't a need. The people are sick of the old guard, the old two-party system. They don't trust either party. They are cynical. And I don't blame them. I don't want any part of it. If I'm going to get into this, I will have to go with a new party. I would rather lose on my own than win with Devlin and Barone.''

"You are going to do it, then, eh?"

"Yes, I think I am."

"Marco, you are a fool," said Gaetano, but he was smiling with admiration. "If you do this, you know, of course, what I must do?"

"What?"

"I must support you. All the way. For blood. For honor. And we beat the shit out of them, eh?"

Marco's frown turned into a smile. He could not quite believe what he was hearing. He saw his grandfather's hand reach across the table. He met it with his own, and their handshake was like an embrace.

Catherine Devlin had been seeing Marc for several weeks without telling her parents. When she was out she was presumably job-hunting or visiting friends from college. The situation was ridiculous, but she was sure her mother would object, and Marc was sure that her father would object, because it was becoming increasingly clear that he was reluctant to join the "team."

They did ordinary things. They walked in Central Park. They went to the zoo. Several times they went to the movies. They saw *The Seventh Veil*, *Duel in the Sun*, and *The Postman Always Rings Twice*.

Finally, Catherine decided she was being childish and that she ought to have a talk with her parents. Marc agreed that it was the right thing to do. The next day they drove up to the Cloisters in Marc's new Ford convertible, a gift from Gaetano. It was a hot, hazy summer day that invited dreams. The top was down, and Marc was feeling good as they drove up Riverside Drive. "I love it," said Catherine. "It's beautiful."

"With all the money your old man has, I'm surprised that *you* don't have a car," said Marc.

"Are you kidding? They treat me like an infant. They're so damned old-fashioned."

"You should be a girl in an Italian family. It's not any better. Maybe worse. The father feels that he must protect his daughter's virtue until he delivers her to a husband."

"I guess my father feels the same way, but my mother is really obsessed."

"Did you talk to them last night?"

"Well, sort of. I didn't tell them that we've been seeing each other, but I told them that you called to invite me out today. If they knew that I was seeing you secretly, they would have made a big fuss about it. You know, lies and all that. Oh, God, what a miserable situation. I feel like an absolute idiot."

"What did they say?"

"Before my father told her to be quiet, my mother tried to tell me how dangerous Italian men are." She smiled and the breeze played in her blond hair.

"Only because they like women."

"Anyway, then my father was surprisingly nice about the whole thing. He said, 'Go out, have a good time, and try to talk some sense into that lad.' "

"What did he mean by that?"

"I don't know. I suppose it has something to do with politics."

"You mean he's allowing you to see me because he thinks you might be useful in bringing me into the fold."

"What difference does it make?"

"Damn it, it makes a difference to me. I think that's rotten."

"It's not my fault. And I'm not going to talk you into anything."

"I'm sorry," he said. They were driving past Columbia University. He caught a glimpse of some of the buildings and then of the Riverside Church and Grant's Tomb. Once again, for some reason, he thought of Alyson, another time, another car. Blond hair blown back. The drive across the George Washington Bridge.

"I told you it wouldn't be easy. God, I wish I had never come home. I should have gone to California or something."

"But don't you see, Cathy, the bind I'm in? Your father and I are about to become mortal enemies."

"But why? Just for politics? So you're on different sides, so what? Republicans talk to Democrats, don't they? It's all just a game."

"You don't understand, Cathy. If I run on another ticket, I'll be gunning for people like your father, for Tammany Hall and the Mafia connection. Organized crime and machine politics have to be broken in my district. They strangle democracy. They suck the blood of the poor. I have seen them at work here and in Europe and I hate them.''

She was silent and serious for a long moment. ''You really mean it, don't you?''

''Of course I mean it.''

''It's a little scary to see someone so dedicated. It sounds dangerous. Won't they try to stop you?''

''Sure!''

''They might kill you or something.''

He shrugged. ''They might.''

She moved closer to him and touched his arm. ''Do you think my father is mixed up with criminals?''

''I hate to say this, Cathy, but I know he is.''

''But only politically, right? I mean they make donations to campaign funds. There's nothing wrong with that. Other businessmen do it. Everybody wants a favor.''

''It's more than that. They are buying positions that will protect their illegal operations. There are millions of dollars at stake. There is bribery, extortion, and murder. It's a lousy scene, and I hate to see you touched by it, even this indirectly. I don't know what to tell you. I don't know what to do.''

They drove on for a while in silence. Then they arrived at the Cloisters, there among the cool stones in the hot July afternoon. The river drifted in the distance. A haze hung over the hills on the opposite shore. Among slender windows and gentle arches they looked at tapestries and paintings and artifacts from a world that was suddenly more real and infinitely more attractive than the modern world.

''It's only when you come to a place like this,'' she said, ''that you realize how noisy the world is. I wish I could go back to something as simple as this.''

He took her warmly by the hand. ''Come, let's sit here for a while.'' They sat down on a stone bench near a fountain that made a soothing sound. ''Let's just sit and let the world wash away.'' They sat side by side, hand in hand. A sparrow descended to the pebble walkway, then hopped to the fountain's rim. Catherine, in peasant blouse and long skirt, seemed to belong in such a setting. She watched the sparrow and Marc watched her. She was like a bird herself. A bit fragile, nervous, and quick, responsive to every sound. She had, too, that searching look that birds often have, as though they were on the track of invisible things. In that moment he felt, suddenly, as though he understood Catherine Devlin. She was sensitive and thoughtful and even a bit brooding under her Irish smile.

Though he had found himself on the brink of falling in love again, he had not actually tried to envision Catherine as his wife—not until now, that is. For some reason it was not very difficult. What was it about her, he wondered, that suddenly made it so easy for him to think of her that way? They did not have the same heritage. They were not the same age. And they had never made love. Still, it seemed to him, sitting there in that quiet place, that Catherine would suit him.

She smiled. He kissed her. Her lips were cool, like the cool arching stones of the cloister. There was something wonderfully delicate about her, something terribly feminine. He could feel her response to him, her need. And that need made him feel stronger. Not that she was weaker in any way. Quite the contrary. It was her soundness and depth as a woman that made him feel that way. And he loved her for being true to herself and honest with him.

He kissed her again, and she received him with her lips and a touch of her hand. The message between them was clear. In a few short weeks, without even talking about it, they had arrived at an understanding. She leaned away and sighed. "So where do we go from here?"

"I don't know," he said, "but we'll have to think of something, won't we?"

She nodded slowly, her eyes fixed dreamily on his. "It's *that* way, isn't it?"

"You know it is. Are you afraid to say it?"

"Yes."

"Well, I'm not. I love you, Catherine."

She kissed him so gently that their lips barely touched. "I love you too."

Two weeks later Big Bill Devlin came storming into his apartment, bellowing at the top of his voice. The news was out that Marc Adamo would be the ILP candidate for Congress. "Catherine!" he called out. "Catherine, where are you?"

His wife appeared from her bedroom, looking like a resurrected Egyptian mummy. She had cream on her face and a plastic hat over elaborate hair curlers. Martha, the colored maid, appeared from the kitchen, disapproving hands on hips.

"What in the world is the matter?" said Mary Devlin through her mask.

He sat down heavily in one of the large living room chairs and loosened his tie. He was shaking his head and muttering to himself. "Martha," he said aloud, "get me a scotch and soda."

"What is it, dear?" said the solicitous mummy.

He looked at her with a combination of distaste and contempt. She, who had once been so beautiful, was now only his wife. Their marriage had become a never-discussed formality. They even had separate bedrooms. "Where's Catherine?" he said.

"She went downtown to do some shopping with her friend Eileen. She's not back yet, but she ought to be any minute. What is it? What's happened?"

"That young man she's been seeing has just dropped a wrench in the machine."

"What do you mean?"

He raised his voice. "The sonofabitch is going to run for Congress against Farrell."

"You mean he's a Republican?"

"Worse than that. He's joined the damn Labor party. The ILP."

She put her hand to her mouth. "Oh! How awful. I was beginning to like him, in spite of the fact that he's Italian. You know, he doesn't really look Italian. I mean, he's so well educated, and he speaks English as well as we do. Catherine will be very disappointed."

"Catherine has probably known all along."

"Impossible, dear. She would have told us."

"Don't count on it. Don't count on anything."

"Please, Bill, don't lose your temper with her."

"She'll be lucky if that's all I do."

Two drinks later Catherine came in. She looked summery and happy, but the moment her father glanced at her she knew something was wrong. "Come here, Catherine," he said. "Sit down. I want to talk to you."

She obeyed, a bit pale at his tone.

"I want you to tell me the truth. Remember, I'm your father. Now, did Marc Adamo ever say anything to you about the Independent Labor Party?"

"Daddy, I don't know anything about politics. He may

have mentioned it, but it wouldn't have meant anything to me.''

"Come off it, Catherine. You're not that dumb.''

"Please, Bill," said Mary Devlin, who was fully dressed now and holding a drink.

"Don't interfere!" he shouted.

Mary retreated to the couch and sat down.

"You know as well as I do what the situation is," he said to his daughter. "I told you that we wanted him on our side. We had a spot all picked out for him on the ticket. It would have been the beginning of a solid political career for him. Now we understand that Marc is going to run against Farrell on a third-party ticket. Do you know what that means?''

She shook her head and kept her eyes fixed on her folded hands.

"It means that votes will be taken away from the Democrats. Our support will be split, and the damned Republicans are liable to walk off with that congressional seat. The irony of the whole thing is that he doesn't stand a chance in hell of winning. Furthermore, he'll be tossing away his whole career. The ILP is tainted with Reds. Once he gets in with them, nobody's going to touch him with a twelve-foot pole.''

"That's not true," she said in a quiet voice.

"What do you mean *not true*? Are you calling me a liar?''

"Marc says the ILP is a decent organization. Liberal Democrats, not Communists. Two years ago, he said, they endorsed the Democratic candidate for mayor.''

"That was two years ago. We offered them the same deal this time, and they turned us down.''

"Maybe they didn't like your candidate.''

"There's nothing wrong with our candidate. You don't understand, Catherine, and there's more to it than I care to explain. The point is that I am very disappointed in you.''

"Why, Daddy? What have I done?" She looked at him with a film of tears in her eyes, but also a certain defiance. "Just because I couldn't persuade him to do things your way—''

"You didn't even try.''

"Why should I?''

"Out of loyalty to me, that's why. And, what's more, if he was considering the ILP you should have told me. It might have given us more time to work things out. Now we've got a mess on our hands. If we lose this election, it's going to make a lot of important people unhappy.''

"What people?"

"Never mind. All you have to know is that it's going to be a mean election, and I want you to stay away from Adamo."

"But what difference does it make—"

"It makes a lot of difference. I know things about this guy that you don't. The election is going to get rough, and it's going to get dirty. There's going to be a lot of mud-slinging, and that nice, clean lad is going to come out of this looking like a bum. He's finished. Through! And I want you to have nothing to do with him. Is that clear?"

"What if I refuse?"

His face tightened. "If you refuse, Catherine, you'll be a young lady without a penny and without a family."

Mary Devlin gasped and started to cry. Bill Devlin stood up abruptly and marched out of the room.

The next day Catherine and Marc drove into the country north of the city. She did not tell him that she had to lie to get out of the house, nor did she immediately tell him about the scene with her father, but Marc could see that she was not very happy. It was not until they were on the Saw Mill River Parkway in Westchester County that he said; "Do you want to tell me about it?"

"Is it that obvious?" she said. "I thought I was doing a great cover-up job."

"It's all in your eyes, Cathy. What happened? Was it your father?"

She nodded, but for a few moments she didn't say anything. There was very little weekday traffic. The road stretched out before them, curving gracefully past wooded hills, rising to rocky crests through which a way for the road had been cut, leaving walls of stone on either side. It was deep summer, and the leaves of the trees were heavy and limp with the damp heat. Even the breeze created by the motion of the car was warm, but it felt good.

She told him about her father's outburst and his ultimatum. "I don't know what to do," she said. "It's not a question of moving out. I suppose I could manage that somehow. I could take any old job. I could double up with another girl or something. And it's not the money. I'm not worried about being disinherited or anything like that. It's . . . it's my family. They're all I've got. I have no brothers or sisters and hardly any other relatives. Do you know what I mean? They're my mother and father—for better or worse.''

''Then perhaps you ought to do what they say.''

''How can I? I mean even if it weren't a question of losing you. Even if it were something else important to me, I couldn't just give in. I have to live with myself. I can't be running scared all the time.''

''I'm glad you see it that way.''

''But what am I going to do?''

''Who knows? Maybe your father will change his mind,'' he said.

She shook her head. ''No, I don't think he will. It's not that he doesn't love me. It's just the way he is. He never makes idle threats or promises. He's a man of his word. In many ways I admire him.''

''He's not being very admirable right now.''

''They also gave me something else to think about.''

''Oh?''

''They said something about you. I mean my father did.''

''He's bound to be annoyed at what I'm doing. I told you he would be. I warned you from the very beginning.''

''He said that he knew things about you.''

Marc frowned suspiciously. ''What things?''

''He didn't say. He just suggested that there was something about you, something in your past perhaps, that could be used against you in the election. Do you know what he's talking about?''

''I'm not sure. Maybe.''

''You don't have to tell me if you don't want to.''

''I'll tell you when we get to wherever we're going.''

''Where *are* we going?''

''You said one day that you'd like to show me your summer cottage near Pawling. Why don't we go there?''

''All right,'' she said.

They didn't say much for the rest of the trip. He could feel that she was upset, and he himself was troubled by Devlin's threat. He could only assume that it had something to do with his father, and it was just possible that Devlin knew more about it than he did.

The cottage was a couple of miles beyond Pawling, on a dirt road that came off Route 22. It sat snugly on a rise overlooking a pond. It was made of fieldstone and slate and

blended peacefully into its surroundings. "It's very nice,"
said Marc.

"I love it here," she said. "When I was a kid we used to
come here a lot, sometimes for the whole summer. Now we
only use it on occasional weekends. Daddy's always so busy,
and Mom is sort of a hypochondriac. She doesn't like to be
too far away from her doctor. She's always calling him up."

A lawn sloped away from the cottage to the pond, and
there was an endless stretch of woods beyond it. They parked
the car and walked around. After a while they went in. It was
cool in the shaded interior. Catherine opened the shutters to
let the sun in.

Marc looked distracted. He sat down in a chair by the
empty fireplace. Catherine sat in another chair. She seemed to
be keeping her distance from him until the "dark secret" was
out. He had told her very little about his past, and even now
he wasn't quite sure how much to tell her or how exactly to
explain his father.

"You haven't done anything awful, have you?" she said
with an apologetic tilt of her head.

"Nothing that your old man can hold against me, as far as
I know. I think what your father is referring to is the fact that
my father was an anarchist and a draft dodger. He refused to
register during World War One. He was involved in demonstrations, and maybe some violence. I really don't know.
There were a lot of things attributed to anarchists in those
days. Assassinations. Bombings. I have no way of knowing
how far he went, but he was finally murdered in Providence,
Rhode Island."

"Murdered? My God!"

"We never found out why. Maybe your father knows more
than I do. Or maybe he's just going to capitalize on the latest
Red scare and call my father a Communist. Guilt by kinship."

"It's not fair. It's really not fair. How can you be responsi-
ble for what your father did?"

"Listen, don't get me wrong. I'm not ashamed of my
father. I'm proud of him. He had his convictions, and he
fought for them. Everybody has a right to do that. I have my
own convictions, and, damn it, I'll fight for them too. Even if
it means exposing your father."

"Would you do that?"

"I don't know, Cathy. If I had the evidence to prove that

he had done something wrong, you wouldn't want me to conceal it, would you?''

She did not answer for a moment. Then she looked down at her hands and said: ''He's my father, no matter what. I don't know. I hope it never comes to that.''

''I hope so too,'' he said. He got up and went to her. He lifted her face to his, then leaned over and kissed her. She stood up and was in his arms. He held her tight and felt her body against his.

''How did we get into such a mess?'' she said.

He kissed her hair and her cheek. He could feel that she was flushed.

''I don't know,'' he said. ''But don't worry. We'll find a way out. As long as we trust each other we'll be all right. And then, when the election is over—''

''What?''

''Why don't we do something ridiculously obvious.''

''Like what?''

''Like get married.'' He didn't even know he was going to say it until it was out.

''Do you mean it?''

''I guess I do. Unless you don't want to be married to a congressman and live in Washington, D.C.''

She laughed and threw her arms around him. ''You proposed to me. I didn't know you were going to do that.''

''Neither did I.''

''I don't know what to say.''

''Why don't you just shut up and say *yes*.''

''If I shut up, I won't be able to say anything.''

He suddenly looked serious. ''You don't have to answer right away. I know how you feel about your father.''

''My God! He asks me not to see you, and now I'm going to marry you. He'll have a stroke.''

''Does that mean *yes*?''

''Oh, yes, yes, yes, darling. That means *yes*.'' She kissed him several times in rapid succession. Then their kisses became longer and more passionate, and the stone fireplace, the sun streaking across the rug, the emptiness of the house, all conspired to heighten that passion. They wanted each other. Their bodies were aroused. It was summer. They were alone. They were in love. There seemed nothing now to prevent them, except perhaps Catherine's sense of guilt. Marc was afraid of it but had never really tested it. In another moment the problem was resolved. Catherine drew back from him and then took him by the hand. He could see in her eyes that she was not going to run away. "Let's go to my room," she said in a quiet voice.

They got undressed without saying anything. She was not even shy with him. For the first time he saw her completely nude. Her skin was white. Her body was graceful and tall, her breasts full but not large. He held her awhile before they got into bed and covered themselves with a sheet. Then slowly they drifted into a dream of passion. They explored each other. The act of love itself like a conversation in which they said the truest things and touched each other's souls.

In September Larry Adamo got his shot at the middle-weight crown. The closer the date came the more amazed he seemed. "Imagine that," he kept saying. "A title fight in Yankee Stadium. I thought it would never happen. After the war I thought I was washed up." To his brother he said: "I'm going to win this one for you, Marco, because it won't look good for you in your election to have a brother who's a loser—you know what I mean?"

"Don't do it for me," said Marc. "Do it for yourself. You deserve it. You worked hard for it."

"There ain't going to be no fight," said Rudy Wills, his trainer, "if you don't make the weight. Lay off the pasta. Stick to lean meat."

At the weighing-in Larry was less than a pound under the 160-pound limit. Everybody in his corner was relieved. There was a lot of money at stake. Big fights in ballparks meant larger crowds than you could get in any indoor arena, including the Garden. But there was something intimidating about the immensity of the place, and Larry was nervous.

In the dressing room, which still smelled of baseball, he paced up and down and listened to last-minute instructions from his manager and trainer. He kept flexing and unflexing his bandaged hands. Now and then he broke into a quick routine of punches. There was already a fine film of perspiration on his forehead. Sammy King followed him with a towel and fanned it at him every time he stood still long enough.

When Marc came in, Rudy Wills took him aside. "Your brother's as nervous as a cat," he said in a confidential tone. "Why don't you talk to him? Maybe you can get his mind off the fight for a few minutes. It might calm him down. He's going to wear himself out worrying before he even gets in the ring.''

Marc talked to the photographers and reporters. He gave them five more minutes to get their jobs done. Then he wanted them out of the dressing room. Manzella and Wills backed him up. There were some groans and protests, but one by one they left. Wills took Manzella aside and told him what was going on. ''Let his brother talk to him for a minute,'' he said.

''You're looking good,'' said Marc. He took the towel from Sammy King and wiped Larry's forehead and arms and chest. ''I was afraid you wouldn't make the weight. Imagine having to give up pasta. A hell of a situation. But wait until tonight. As soon as you get rid of this bum we'll eat up a storm. We're going to have *some* meal. And you can eat yourself right into the light heavyweight division.''

Larry smiled nervously. He sat down on the training table, but his body was still in motion. His shoulders and hands were moving. His adrenaline was up. Marc could see it in his eyes. It was that animal look, that survival look that he had seen sometimes in the war. It made men killers. But he knew that fear could also confuse a man, and he didn't want this to happen to Larry. He put his hands on Larry's shoulders and forced his brother to look him in the eye. ''Tell me the truth, kid. Are you all right? Do you feel okay?''

Larry kept nodding, perhaps a bit too rapidly. ''I'll be all right. As soon as I get out there, I'll be fine. It's just the waiting around. You know what I mean? The waiting around. Jesus Christ! It's a big fucking ballpark, ain't it?''

''Now, listen to me,'' said Marc. ''I want to tell you something. Three months ago I wanted you to hang it up. I didn't think you were up to a fight like this. But now it's different. Are you listening? Now you're in shape. Now you're good. Now you're better than Sanders, and you're going to beat him. It's your night. Don't worry about anything. Get in there and do your job, that's all. And later we'll eat like kings.''

The talk was helping. Larry's movements became less jerky. His eyes looked calmer. He reached out suddenly and put his arms around Marc. ''Thanks,'' he said. ''Thanks for coming down and being in my corner.''

Wills and Sammy King came over to put on the gloves and lace them up.

*     *     *

Marc had a ringside seat. Gaetano was there, and Joe
Malzone and Sal D'Angelo, and a dozen other people from
the club. Two rows back he even saw Rocco Barone and
Vince DeMarco. They nodded coldly in his direction and he
acknowledged the greeting. He still wasn't sure how things
would fall out with them, but his grandfather had assured him
there would be no violence. "A guy runs for Congress they
can't touch him. Otherwise the roof comes down on them,
and before you know it, there's another special grand jury or
a crime commission. Besides, we all know each other, and
we all got to live in the same neighborhood. So we live and
let live, right?"

Perhaps the look on Barone's face confirmed his grandfather's
conclusion, but he had no intention of cutting out references
to organized crime in his campaign speeches.

It was a mild September night with a harvest moon rising
over the stadium like something out of a Hollywood movie.
In that large setting the ring looked very small. The sky was a
dome over the arena, and the seats receded from the center
into the shadows of grandstands and bleachers. It was a noisy
crowd, much the same as one might find at a night baseball
game. It was almost World Series time, but there would be no
games at Yankee Stadium. The pennant winners this year
were the Boston Braves and Cleveland Indians. Still, there
were peanuts and hot dogs here, and ice cream peddlers. The
same guys in white who worked the ballgames.

The lights were hot and intense over the ring. There was a
section reserved for radio and television a few rows back. The
drama mounted. The sportswriters typed away in the press
booth, some of them with cigarettes dangling from their lips.
They wrote in superlatives about Sugar Ray Sanders, calling
him one of the all-time greats. They were generous with
Larry, but skeptical. "Adamo has a lot to prove. He's got a
record of twenty-two victories in twenty-four fights. He's
tough and gutsy, and he can still boast, at least until tonight,
that he has never been off his feet in any fight. His two losses
were by decisions. But he's never met anybody who could
last three rounds with Sanders."

The fight began. The crowd roared. Flashbulbs popped and
bells sounded. An airplane passed overhead in the darkness.
All the ritual of combat, thought Marc. Ceremonial conflict.
The beast in man asserts itself and the crowd calls for blood.

Under the glaring lights he saw his brother circling around the sleek black fighter. Sugar Ray danced back, came forward, jabbed with the quickness of a cat. He was impressive. He made Larry look plodding and heavy. It was the kind of fight the crowd liked, especially a New York crowd. The agile black man against the white slugger. Larry was shorter, broader, and stronger than Sugar Ray. He looked as though he could hurt him. But Sugar Ray was the champ. He had beaten the best, and his slender body was deceptive. His punches were deadly.

From where he sat Marc could hear the shuffling of their feet in the ring. He could hear the sounds they made when they took a punch. And he could see their sweating bodies and the absolute concentration in their faces. For the first five rounds Larry was the aggressor, but Sugar Ray was too fast for him. He slipped punches easily and sometimes even made Larry look inept. His left jab kept finding its mark and setting Larry up for that hard right hook that was beginning to take its toll. Larry's face looked red and puffy on one side. By the sixth round there was a cut over his left eye. After seven rounds the crowd began to boo Larry for his inability to keep up with Sugar Ray. He backed off and waited for the champ to come to him. The action slowed down. In his corner they said: "Let him come to you. Counterpunch. Nail him coming in."

By the end of the eighth round it was obvious to everyone that Larry was losing the fight on points. In fact, if it went the distance he didn't have a chance. His only hope was a knockout. Marc came to his brother's corner. They were working on Larry's eye. It was discolored and swollen. Larry winced when they dabbed at the cut with a swab. They broke an ammonia stick and gave him a whiff. He jerked back his head. Marc was not allowed in the ring, but he stood close behind Larry and said: "You can't box him. You've got to fight him. Get down in the street, Larry, and fight him!"

In the ninth round Larry went after Sugar Ray as though they were brawling in the schoolyard of P.S. 83. His punches were wild, but his attack was suddenly so ferocious that Sugar Ray was thrown off balance. There was a break in his rhythm and style. He made a mistake. Larry's hard right came crashing into his face. The black boxer stumbled back against the ropes with a dazed look in his eye. Larry went after him. He landed another right, then a left, then a hard right-and-left combination to the body. The crowd loved it. They were standing and stomping and screaming. But Sanders weathered the assault and went back to his corner to recover.

The next five rounds belonged to Larry. He was wearing Sugar Ray down. He had hurt him badly in the ninth and was taking advantage of it, but it wasn't easy to keep up such an undisciplined brawl. By the fifteenth and final round both fighters were exhausted and bleeding. Partisans for both men were chanting for a knockout. The whole stadium was on its feet. Sugar Ray had been told to stay away and take the decision. Larry went after him. Halfway through the round Larry cornered him, but his arms were heavy. He leaned into him, their heads butting. They were like dancers, almost like lovers, and one could see they respected each other, admired each other. Larry muscled him and mounted one last barrage of punches that made Sugar Ray's legs sag. But it was not enough to bring him down, and now his force was spent. A few more jabs, a final clinch, and it was all over. The bell sounded. The ovation from the crowd was deafening.

The fighters were back in their corners, spitting out their mouthpieces and being sponged down. They all waited for the decision. The emcee came out. A hush fell over the stadium. The mechanical, magnified voice made the announcement: "Judge Bradley scores it nine rounds for Sanders, five for Adamo, one even. Judge Peterson scores it eight rounds for Sanders, seven for Adamo. The referee scores it eight rounds for Sanders, six for Adamo, one even. The winner and still middleweight champion of the world: Sugar Ray Sanders."

The winner danced into the middle of the ring, his hands held high, his corner men around him. Larry came out to congratulate him. The two men embraced. The crowd applauded. And the police kept back the spectators who surged toward the ring. A way was cleared, and Larry climbed down to make his way to the dressing room. Marc was with him.

In the dressing room there was confusion. Reporters fired questions at Larry and his manager. "Are you going to ask for a rematch? Did he ever have you in trouble?" Larry didn't want to make a statement. He was exhausted and sore and kept shaking his head. Manzella and Wills protected him and, finally, cleared the dressing room.

They cut the laces on Larry's gloves and took them off. His hands were swollen. They unwrapped the bandages and brought out a bucket of ice. "You were great. Just great," said Marc. "You almost had him."

"Yeah, but he beat me. I had my shot, and he beat me. That's what counts. He outboxed me. He made me look like a clown for eight rounds. It's time to quit. Every part of me hurts."

"No, no, you were good, Larry. You did good. You went after him. You almost had him. Don't quit now. Get your rematch. Give it one more shot."

"You mean it? You don't want me to hang it up?"

"No, I don't want you to hang it up. I want you to go out a winner. Now, clean yourself up, and let's get the hell out of here. There's a big meal waiting for us. And all the pasta you can eat."

Marc fought his battle in another kind of arena. It did not happen all at once in a ring in fifteen rounds. It happened on streetcorners, sometimes in the rain. It happened in auditoriums and restaurants, and even in door-to-door stints that meant surprising people in their underwear or housewives in their curlers. But Marc did what had to be done. He did it all and learned a lot. He learned, first of all, that he could not be a professor on the streets of East Harlem. His first speeches were lectures, and those who knew better told him to roll up his sleeves and hit 'em between the eyes. He discovered that he had a gift for oratory, and he began to enjoy his performances. He would begin slowly and work his way up. He used his fist and stamped his foot on the wooden platform. He used the old trick of getting his audience to respond. "Are we going to allow the bosses to run our lives? Are we going to allow big business to run America?" And the crowd would answer: "Nooo!" He spoke in Italian to the Italians, in Spanish to the growing Hispanic population in the district, and in English to everybody. His message was clear, and he hammered away at it. He was for the poor. He was for the working man. He was for unions. He was for social welfare and free health services. And he was against discrimination, against those who thought they owned America because they were here first. "We are all Americans. All pioneers in a great adventure."

By the middle of October it was clear that he was not running as the spoiler who might upset the contest between the Republicans and the Democrats. He was running as a candidate who was confident he could win. The opposition took him very seriously. They attacked him more than they attacked each other. But neither Farrell nor Gardner was very good at public appearances. They were accustomed to working behind the scenes and making use of an organization that could put campaign workers in every ward and block. They did not respect the immigrants. They saw no point in even talking to them, and their contempt filtered through. They could not hide behind expensive posters, plastered billboards, or the thousands of leaflets that littered the streets after a rally.

Marc's work at the Italian-American Political Club stood him in good stead. His name was known in the neighborhood, as was his grandfather's name and his brother's name. He was one of their own, and this gave him a distinct edge in spite of the fact that he did not have a major party backing him. His enemies now knew that there was only one way to beat him. They had to destroy his image in the eyes of his own people.

The bombshell came two weeks before the election, in the form of a newspaper column by Peter Weston, a right-wing scandalmonger with low friends in high places. The whole thing was clearly a calculated attack, carefully planned. "LIKE FATHER LIKE SON," the item was entitled. It appeared in the *News*, and within two days almost everybody had seen it. "Who is this young man who wants to be our congressman?" wrote Weston. "He's a lawyer with only a few years of experience in a local practice in East Harlem among Italian-Americans who seem to have been taken in by his gift of gab. He has no political experience. He has never held a position in government. All he has done is find a legal way of putting his friends on welfare. No wonder neither of the major political parties would touch him. Who can blame them? He had to turn for support to a left-wing, Communist-infiltrated political party that ought to be outlawed before it becomes an instrument for overthrowing the government of the United States. Marc Adamo may not be a red-blooded American, but he sure has Red blood. We looked into the background of this arrogant young man and came up with some very startling information. His father, whose name was Sergio Adamo, was a certified anarchist, even more extreme than the Communists, a man who believed in destroying the government of our country, a man who owed his allegiance to no one. He had a criminal record. He served time in Leavenworth. He was a draft dodger, a pacifist. He was a suspect in a bombing, and he himself was finally murdered in a dingy roominghouse in Providence, Rhode Island. . . .''

Gaetano was very upset and Marc was furious. They sat in the kitchen of Gaetano's apartment and drank coffee only hours after the morning edition hit the streets. There would be repercussions, and they had to decide how to deal with them. "I knew they would pull something like this, the sons of bitches," said Gaetano. He was still unshaven and he was wearing suspenders over an undershirt. "It is like the opening of an old wound. I cannot tell you what grief I suffered because of your father. My own son! What a bitterness it has been all these years. But to bring it up now. This way! It is worse than anything your father ever did. I have learned to live with this hurt, maybe even to forgive. At least to forget. But now—now—I don't know what to do." He ran his hand through his white hair.

Marc felt sorry for him. He could see how complicated it was for the old man. His own rage was simpler. It made him fighting mad. He wanted to plan a retaliation. He wanted revenge. But what? And how? "I can't let them get away with it," he said. "I will have to defend myself."

"Defend yourself, yes. But why should you have to defend your father?" said Gaetano. "His sins are not your sins."

"I have to defend him because he has been attacked unjustly, and I am his son."

Gaetano rubbed his hands together and studied the aging skin and network of veins. "Perhaps it would be better to say nothing. Perhaps the dust will settle in time. The more you talk about it the more they will think that something is wrong."

"I would rather speak out. I am not afraid."

"But to deny a charge is almost to confess there is some truth in it. To ignore it is to treat it with contempt."

"I can't ignore it. I just can't. I have something to say, and I am going to say it whether it loses me the election or not."

Gaetano stared at him for a moment and then slowly began to nod in agreement. "Yes, I can see what you have to do. And that is the most important thing. I admire you, and I wish I could live my life again to be more true to myself. I have made mistakes and I have lived long enough to regret them. I wish my sons were alive again to know these things. . . ." There were tears in his eyes, but he would not let them fall.

Marc reached out to comfort him. "I remember the stories you used to tell me, *Nonno*, about *your* war, about the siege of Fort Macalle, about how you and your men were prepared to go down fighting. Well, that's how I feel. The other side may win, but they sure as hell are going to know they've been in a fight. And I learned that from you."

Gaetano's tears turned to a smile. "Good!" he said. "Good!".

It was election eve and there was the traditional bonfire at the final rally at the corner of 116th Street and Lexington Avenue. All day long there had been excitement in the air as the men and boys of the neighborhood gathered wood and heaped it up for the fire. There were orange crates and apple boxes from the market on Park Avenue. There was wood from the houses being torn down in the new slum-clearance project. There was broken furniture and even the limbs of a dead backyard tree recently cut down. It was a grand fire, and its light was reflected in the faces and eyes of the children who watched.

There were festival lights over the platform. And there was a huge sign with the names of the principal candidates on it. They were also the candidates of the Progressive party. And there was music. Songs of solidarity. Black spirituals. Italian songs. There was a singer with a guitar, and the noisy, brassy band that sometimes played in Jefferson Park on hot nights.

Several thousand people filled the street as though it were an Italian square. No traffic could go through. There were barriers and detour signs. There were policemen on horseback and many on foot. A crowd this size in East Harlem could easily get out of hand.

The crowd settled in for a series of speeches. The faces were not all familiar. Sometimes people asked: "Who's that guy?" And the answer might be a shrug or a name from the national scene that didn't mean much. It was the local election they were all interested in. It was Marc Adamo they were waiting for.

When Marc was finally introduced, a great cheering and hooting went up. The people in the crowd were obviously divided in their feelings. He held up his hands and pleaded for quiet so that he could speak, but the noise went on. After a while it began to subside, but there were still individual voices that called out: "We want Farrell," or "Adamo, go home." They were answered with a chant of "Mar-co, Mar-co!" A brief scuffle broke out. The mounted police moved in. It was broken up quickly. It was clear that the opposition had hired a few toughs to create a disturbance. "Hey, come on," someone shouted. "Let him talk." And he was echoed by other voices. "Yeah, let him talk."

Again Marc raised his arms. This time a hush fell over the crowd and he leaned toward the microphone. "I am standing here for the last time tonight to ask you to vote for me tomorrow, and I want to tell you why. . . ."

Gaetano was on the platform with the dignitaries. Other family members were visible in the lights in the front rows. Marc could see his mother with Stefano, and there was his brother, Larry, with a group of admirers and friends. Old Renato was leaning on his cane and holding Fanny's arm. Even Natalia and Angela were there, looking elegant and younger than their years. Aunt Laura was with her new boyfriend and her daughter, Lisa, who was now married. Earlier, Marc had caught a glimpse of Silvio and some members of his expanding clan. And off to one side, protected by one of Marc's friends, was Catherine Devlin, looking a bit too pretty for this kind of a street mob.

"Before I talk about the issues," said Marc, "I want to talk about something I read in the newspaper the other day. A columnist named Peter Weston had some unkind things to say about my father, and since my father is not here to defend himself, I want to say a few things on his behalf. He died over twenty years ago, and he was a good man. Mr. Weston never knew him. And Mr. Weston doesn't know anything about him. About where he came from and about how he lived. In fact, Mr. Weston doesn't know anything about any of us, because he lives in a big house in Westchester County and, for all I know, has never set foot in East Harlem. He is the kind of man who would not soil himself by coming into a working man's community, a community of immigrants." Marc's voice rose, and the crowd liked it. There was a round of applause.

"Let me tell you something about my father and the rest of my family. Right here on the platform is my grandfather Gaetano. You all know him." More applause. "It was *his* father who first came to this country. He came here in 1887,

over sixty years ago. And he came, as many of you did, as
your parents did, because there was no way to make a living
in the old country. The poverty there was so terrible that by
comparison we are all rich. He came here and worked for a
dollar a day at common labor. Does that sound familiar? And
in the Great Blizzard of 1888 he was offered the grand sum of
two dollars a day to shovel snow. He died in that storm. He
never went back to Italy. He never sent for his family. He had
a dream of America, and that dream died with him. But what
was that dream? It was a dream of freedom and opportunity.
It was a chance to live a decent life. In 1900 my grandfather
came and brought his family with him. And in time he made
America, as we say. In spite of the fact that he was called a
dago. In spite of the fact that we were all looked down on as
ragged, illiterate, and criminal. You all know the story. The
crowded tenements of Mulberry Street. For some it hasn't
changed much. The prejudice. The exploitation. Women and
children working in factories, and getting six dollars a week
for sixty hours of labor. The abuse from those who thought
we were stealing their jobs. That's a hell of a job to steal. No,
my friends, we were not stealing jobs; we were being taken
advantage of. And our only hope was to organize. We helped
build the unions, and the unions helped us make a decent life.
But the capitalists branded us all as radicals, as Reds. Sure,
some of us were! Why not? Poverty makes us bitter. You
know what I'm talking about. Poverty makes us angry. And
right here in East Harlem there are a lot of angry people.

"My father was one of those early radicals. Yes, Mr.
Weston is right. My father was an anarchist. It was his way
of attacking the problem of poverty. He envisioned a better
world. He worked hard to achieve it. And he died pursuing
his dream. I don't hold any of that against him. And I hope
you don't either. Mr. Weston was wrong to pick on my
father. He was wrong to call him a Communist. He was
wrong to imply that I am. And he was wrong because what he
did was a low, filthy political trick. I'm not going to let him
get away with it. And *you're* not going to let him get away
with it."

The crowd broke into wild cheering, whistling, and
applauding. Now their young hero was really getting warmed
up. This is what they had come to see, a fighter.

When the cheering subsided, Marc began again, in a quieter voice that inspired silence in the crowd. "I want to read

you something that was said over twenty years ago, by a man whose name you all know. He was Bartolemeo Vanzetti. He and his friend Nicola Sacco died for a crime they did not commit. They were convicted by prejudice. I want to read a part of Vanzetti's statement, because my father knew him, and if the ghost of my father were here today on this platform he might speak these same words." He paused and then began to read: " 'This is what I say: I would not wish to a dog or to a snake to the most low and misfortunate creature of the earth—I would not wish to any of them what I have had to suffer for things that I am not guilty of. But my conviction is that I have suffered for things that I am guilty of. I am suffering because I was a radical, and indeed I am a radical; I have suffered because I was an Italian, and indeed I am an Italian; I have suffered more for my family and for my beloved than for myself; but I am so convinced to be right that if you could execute me two times, and if I could be reborn two other times, I would live again to do what I have done already.' "

The silence in the crowd grew deeper, almost meditative. Marc went on: "There has been injustice in America, my friends. There has been prejudice and meanness. For some of you the American dream has become a nightmare. There is exploitation of labor. There is crime and political corruption. And you don't have to look very far to find these things. They are right here in East Harlem. And I say to you, get rid of them. Don't let yourselves be pushed around. Don't be afraid to speak out. America is our country, not theirs. We have come a long way from the hovels of Sicily and the *bassi* of Naples. We are all Americans now. We are free. Don't sell your freedom to the bosses. Don't vote the machine. Vote your conscience! Stand up and be counted! Thank you!"

The crowd roared, the fire blazed, the band struck up, and there was jubilation in the streets. Marc stood on the platform waving his arms in a victory salute. They would not let him go. Gaetano came and stood beside him. They looked out at the crowd and waved to familiar faces. Marc's brother, Larry, leapt up on the platform and embraced him. Over his shoulder Marc searched for Catherine. He had lost sight of her.

But she was there in the shoving, shouting crowd. And suddenly, behind her, was her father, Bill Devlin. She turned around and looked startled. He smiled. "It looks as though you found yourself a winner,'' he said. ''I hope you'll be very happy.'' She threw her arms around him and kissed him.

Marc saw this from the platform, and he knew exactly what it meant.

*About the Author*

Robert DeMaria was born in New York and grew up during the Depression, in East Harlem. In an era of street gangs, he considers himself lucky to have survived and escaped to Columbia College, where he earned his Ph.D. A Long Island resident for most of the last thirty years, he and his wife and their three children now spend winters in Port Jefferson and summers at the eastern tip of the island. Both Manhattan and Long Island figure prominently in his novels. Currently, Mr. DeMaria is Director of Creative Writing at Dowling College, as well as a professional writer with over a dozen books to his credit.

Ballantine presents another series from
the producers of *The Kent Family Chronicle*
and *Wagons West...*

THE

AMERICAN
PATRIOT

SERIES